Water
damage
noted
HS · 2-24

Dead Water

Also by Ann Cleeves

Dead Water

A Shetland Mystery

Ann Cleeves

Minotaur Books

A Thomas Dunne Book
New York

This is a work of fiction. All of the characters, organizations, and events portrayed in this novel are either products of the author's imagination or are used fictitiously.

A THOMAS DUNNE BOOK FOR MINOTAUR BOOKS.
An imprint of St. Martin's Publishing Group.

DEAD WATER. Copyright © 2013 by Ann Cleeves. All rights reserved. Printed in the United States of America. For information, address St. Martin's Press, 175 Fifth Avenue, New York, N.Y. 10010.

www.thomasdunnebooks.com
www.minotaurbooks.com

Library of Congress Cataloging-in-Publication Data

Cleeves, Ann.
    Dead water : a Shetland mystery / Ann Cleeves.—1st U.S. ed.
        p. cm.—(Shetland Island series ; 5)
    ISBN 978-1-250-03660-5 (hardcover)
    ISBN 978-1-250-03661-2 (e-book)
1. Shetland (Scotland)—Fiction. I. Title.
    PR6053.L45.S54 2014
    823'.914—dc23

                                            2013038928

Minotaur books may be purchased for educational, business, or promotional use. For information on bulk purchases, please contact Macmillan Corporate and Premium Sales Department at 1-800-221-7945, extension 5442, or write specialmarkets@macmillan.com.

First published in Great Britain by Macmillan, an imprint of Pan Macmillan, a division of Macmillan Publishers Limited

First U.S. Edition: February 2014

10 9 8 7 6 5 4 3 2 1

For Ben Clarke and Isla Raynor

Acknowledgements

Thanks as always to the magnificent team at Pan Macmillan, and to my agent Sara Menguc and all her associates. I'm delighted that Dr James Grieve was prepared to appear as himself. He knows that my grasp of his subject is weak and will make allowances. My friends in Shetland have been as helpful as always and I'd particularly like to thank Maurice Henderson of Shetland Islands Council, Jim Dickson and Ingirid Eunson. Ian Best and Lise Sinclair from Fair Isle gave invaluable help on building yoals. Any mistakes are mine.

Chapter One

Jimmy Perez stopped for breath and looked out to sea. A still, calm day, the light filtered through high cloud so that the water was shiny grey, like metal. On the horizon a bank of fog. In the deep pockets of the long oilskin coat that had once belonged to his grandfather were pebbles the size of eggs. They were round and smooth, and so heavy that he could feel the weight of them pulling on his shoulders. He'd collected the rocks from the beach at Ravenswick, selecting them carefully: only the roundest, the ones that were white as bone. In the distance, a little way out from the shore, there was a stack of rock shaped like a rough cross, tilted on its side. The calm water hardly broke around it.

Perez started walking again, counting out the paces in his head. Most days since Fran's death he performed the same ritual: collecting the pebbles from the shore close to her house and bringing them here, to her favourite place in the islands. Part penance and part pilgrimage. Part mad obsession. He rubbed the pebbles with his thumb and found a strange comfort in the touch.

On the hill there were ewes with young lambs, still unsteady on their feet. This far north lambing came late and they didn't arrive until April. New life. The bank of fog was rolling closer, but in the distance, on the highest point of the headland, he could see the cairn he'd built with his collection of Ravenswick stone. A memorial to the woman whom he'd loved and whose death still weighed on his conscience, pulling him down.

As he walked he recalled the stages of their relationship, the seasons of their passion. This too was a ritual performed on every visit. He'd met her in winter, with snow on the ground and hungry ravens tumbling in a frozen sky. He'd made love to her in midsummer, when the cliffs were raucous with seabirds and there was a carpet of wildflowers in the meadow below her house. In early spring she'd proposed marriage to him. He stopped for a moment, dizzy with the memory of it, and the sky seemed to tip and wheel around his head, and he couldn't tell where the sea ended and the sky began. Her challenging smile. 'Well, Jimmy? What do you think?' And she'd died in the autumn, in a storm that battered his Fair Isle home, sending spindrift high into the air and cutting them off from the outside world.

I'm mad, he thought. *I will never be sane again.*

From the cairn he could see the sweep of the North Mainland. Fran had loved it because she said this summed up Shetland in one view, the bleakness and the beauty, the wealth that came from the sea and the hard, barren land. The past and the future. In the distance, in a fold in the land, the oil terminal at Sullom Voe, in this strange silver light looking almost magic, a lost city. Everywhere land and water, and land reflected in water. To the south the line of giant wind turbines, still now. Below him the settlement of Hvidahus, three toy houses and a pier, and almost hidden by trees the crofting museum at Vatnagarth where he'd left his car.

It was six months to the day since Fran had died. He thought he wouldn't come back here until Fran's daughter Cassie was old enough to understand. Or he felt up to bringing her. He hoped the cairn would still be there then.

He walked down the hill into the fog. It lay like a pool over the lower ground, swallowing him up, so that he felt as if he were drowning. The museum car park, which had been empty when he arrived, was full now and there was music coming from one of the barns, and the windows were lit – square moons penetrating the gloom. The music drew him towards them and he was reminded of the folk tales of his youth, the trowes who seduced mortals with their fiddle-playing and stole a century of their lives. And he must look like something from a story himself, he thought, with his long black hair and his unshaven face, the long black coat. He peered through a window and saw a group of elderly people dancing. He recognized the tune and for a moment was tempted in himself, to take the hand of one of the old women sitting against the wall and spin her round the room, making her feel young again.

But he turned away. The old Jimmy Perez might have done that, especially if Fran was with him. But he was a changed man.

Chapter Two

Jerry Markham looked across at the voe that wound inland from the open sea. Behind him was the open hill, peat and heather, brown after a long winter. Ahead of him the oil terminal. Four tugs, big as trawlers, two alongside, one forward and one aft, nudged the *Lord Rannoch* backwards towards the jetty. The tankers were always moored to face the sea, ready for escape in case of incident. Beyond the still water he saw an industrial scene of oil tanks, office accommodation and the huge bulk of the power station that provided power for the terminal and fed into the Shetland grid. A flare burned off waste gas. The area was surrounded by a high fence topped by razor wire. Since 9/11, even in Shetland, more care had been taken to secure the place. At one time all that was needed to get into the terminal was a laminated pass. Now every contractor was vetted and put through a safety course, and every truck was inspected and badged. Even when the gates were opened, there was a further concrete barrier to block access.

Jerry took a photograph.

Overhead an Eastern Airways plane came in to land at Scatsta Airport. During the war the airstrip had been an RAF station. Now it carried more traffic than Sumburgh, but no scheduled flights landed here; no tourists or kids home from college would climb from the plane. These flights were all oil-related. Markham watched as a group of men climbed onto the runway. Fit men, they could have been members of a rugby team or an army platoon: there was the same sense of camaraderie. The male bonding thing that had some-how passed him by. Markham couldn't hear their voices from where he stood, but he could sense the banter. Soon helicopters would take them to start a new shift on the platforms or the rigs.

Once, more than 800 tankers a year had carried crude oil south from Sullom Voe; now just 200 arrived at the jetty, and the *Lord Rannoch* carried medium crude from Schiehallion, an Atlantic field to the west. The North Sea fields were almost empty. Markham knew the facts and figures. He'd done his research, but he was Shetland-born and -bred. He'd grown up with the benefits of the oil: the well-equipped schools and the sports centres, the music lessons and the smooth, wide roads. Oil was getting harder and more expensive to extract from under the seabed, but still the site looked busy; there was no sign today that the terminal was in decline. For a moment he wondered if Shetland would have been different – if *he* would have been different – and less spoiled, if the oil had never been discovered. And what the future would hold for the islands once the oil had all gone.

Markham shifted position so that he had a slightly different perspective and took another photograph. Beyond the perimeter fence a road was being built. Accommodation modules like steel cans were being set on concrete blocks. A new terminal was being constructed next to the old one, and a huge rectangular wall held the blocks of peat that had been dug from the hill to clear the site. As the oil was running out, gas had been discovered, and Shetland had welcomed the new energy source with enthusiasm. Gas meant jobs. Local trucks were already carrying rocks from Sullom quarry to form the foundations of the plant. Hotels, guest houses and B&Bs were packed with workers from the south. House prices were rising again. Gas meant money.

Markham walked down the hill, jumping over peat banks, to reach his car. He'd left it at the end of the track that led past the airstrip. There was construction here too: the metal ribs of a new control tower. The plane, having spilled its passengers, was already loading up with more. He was aware as he drove past that the men, queuing to climb the steps, were staring. There weren't many cars like his Alfa in Shetland. He sensed and enjoyed their surprise and their envy, and wondered what Annabel would make of that.

He took the road south along the voe towards Brae. Half a mile away from the terminal the only indication that oil came ashore here was a yellow buoy in the middle of the water. If there was a spill, a boom would be attached to the buoy to prevent oil contaminating the sensitive saltmarsh at the head of the narrow inlet. But already the tanks and the jetties, the harbour master's offices and the airport and the new gas terminal were hidden by a fold in the hill. Now there were only sheep and gulls, ravens and the sound of curlews.

At the end of Sullom Voe he came to the community of Brae and slowed slightly to join the main road. Brae showed more signs of the oil industry: a few streets of houses built by the council as homes for workers. Grey, utilitarian, hated by the tourists who came expecting picture-book pretty. Shetland didn't do pretty. It did wild and bleak and dramatic, but pretty would have been out of place.

Out of Brae he hit a bank of fog. It had been gloomy all day, no wind and that grey drizzle that seemed to seep through the skin to chill the bones, but suddenly he could hardly see to the bend in the road. Headlights came towards him very slowly and seemed to drift past through the mist on the other side of the road. He couldn't hear the oncoming vehicle's engine. There was a sense that nothing existed outside the bubble of the car. No sound. No sight. Then suddenly more headlights, this time coming from his left, very fast and directed almost straight towards him. He braked sharply and turned to avoid them. Even in the fog he'd been driving too fast, and he heard the screech of tyres on tarmac and felt the car spin out of control. But the fog still filtered out the impact of the noise. This was a dream skid. Or a nightmare. He sat shaking for a moment.

Then fury took over from shock. He tried to control it, to breathe deeply and stay calm, but failed. Some bastard had almost driven into him and could have killed him. Could have wrecked the car, which at the moment mattered more. The headlights of the vehicle that had run him off the road had been turned off, but he hadn't heard the maniac drive off. He got out of his vehicle and felt the aggression pulsing like a vein in his neck. He wanted to hit somebody. He hadn't felt like this for months and the anger was like a drug entering the system of an addict, providing a familiar comfort, the buzz of excitement. Since arriving in Shetland he'd been polite and understanding. He'd controlled his frustration. Now it had found a legitimate target and he let rip.

'What the shit were you playing at, you moron?'

No answer.

He couldn't see the car, except as a block of darker shadow, because the fog was so thick. He walked towards it, intending to pull open the door and force the offending driver out. Behind him there was a movement, sensed rather than heard, and he turned round.

Another movement. Air. A whistling sound of air moving. A sharp pain. Then nothing.

Chapter Three

Rhona Laing made tea. Earl Grey decaffeinated. The community shop in Aith had started stocking it specially for her. Her home had once been the Schoolhouse, solid and grey, and folk thought it was too big for her, a single woman. Folk thought all sorts of things about her, and occasionally she caught the tail-end of rumours that amused and irritated: that she flew to Edinburgh every six weeks to get her hair done, that she'd had a child out of wedlock and given him up for adoption, that she had a secret lover who sailed into Aith Marina after dark most nights and left again in the early morning. It was her policy neither to confirm nor deny the stories.

The house had been her project for her first six months after moving to Shetland and now it was finally arranged to her satisfaction. Furniture built to fit, so it looked like the interior of a grand ship. The captain's cabin. Everything with its place. The Procurator Fiscal's office in Lerwick was just as tidy. Clutter and mess made her physically ill.

She carried her tea to the living room and looked down the bank to the voe. There had been thick fog for most of the day, but it had lifted as she'd driven home from Lerwick and now the scene was washed with the clear light of spring. For as far as she could see, low green hills and water. Every evening after work there was the same ritual. The drive back from town, the tea, then a few minutes spent looking at the view. Even in the winter, when it had long been dark. A flat barge was making its way to the salmon cages further out towards the sea. The surface of the water was marked by mussel strings, the floats looking like jet beads on a thread. Everything as it should be. Then, closer to the marina, she saw that the yoal they would race at regattas during the forthcoming season was floating on the water. It should be hauled up onto the grassy bank, and there was no wind to have shifted it. They'd only brought it out from its winter storage the weekend before. She thought the local children, bored at the end of the Easter holidays, must have pushed it out, thinking it would be fun to cause mischief for the women of the place.

Rhona rowed with the Aith veteran women's team. Her only gesture towards becoming a part of her community. As Fiscal, she'd always thought she should set herself a little apart. It was hard in a place with such a small population to keep work and home separate, but she'd never felt the need for intimate friends. Yet she enjoyed being part of the vets' rowing team. The training nights followed by glasses of wine in one of the houses. The regattas when everyone turned out to cheer. She'd thought she'd be the fittest and most competitive in the group, but that hadn't turned out to be the case – a crofter from Bixter could beat her every time. Rhona liked the physical activity (she missed her Edinburgh gym sessions) and last year had felt stronger as the season progressed. So although she'd not long got in from work and was enjoying the tea, she felt responsible for the yoal drifting out on the tide. She changed out of her office clothes and went down to the marina.

The place was quiet. It was the time of evening meals, soap operas on the television and bathing children before bedtime. Wading birds were pecking at the seaweed on the beach. Her dinghy was tethered to her yacht at the mooring. The *Marie-Louise* was her pride and joy, big enough for speed and distance, but she could manage it single-handed without a problem. She pulled the dinghy in and rowed after the errant yoal, revelling even in this short time on the water at the end of the day. She'd moved to Shetland for the sailing. She was born to be on the water. An ex-lover had once told her that she had salt water, not blood, running through her veins.

She caught the yoal easily. She would loop a rope through the ring at its prow to drag it back to shore. She was thinking that she could make an evening of it. There would be enough light for an hour on the voe. No wind for sailing, but even when using the engine she never tired of the view. Shetland only made sense when it was seen from the sea. Then she glimpsed inside the open boat. Lying across the seats was a man. His hair was blond and his skin was white, so his dark eyes looked strangely as if he were wearing make-up. Rhona knew that he was no longer alive before seeing the gash in his head, the dried blood on his cheek; before realizing that this was no natural death.

Chapter Four

Sandy Wilson was still in the office when the call came through. He recognized the Fiscal's voice and his first thought was that he was in trouble: some procedure not properly followed. He knew she thought very little of him and wasn't surprised. He thought very little of himself. His boss, Jimmy Perez, was still on sick leave, inching his way back into work a couple of days a week, and it gave Sandy nightmares to think that in reality there were times when *he* was in charge.

'Sergeant Wilson.' Everyone in Shetland was on first-name terms. Except the Fiscal. Sandy knew he should listen carefully to what she was saying, but found his attention wandering. This was a nervous reaction to stress, which had got him into trouble since he was a peerie boy in the school in Whalsay. From his office window he looked down towards the harbour. The Bressay ferry had just left for the island across the Sound. The gulls were fighting over a scrap of rubbish on the pier.

'So I need you here. Immediately. You do understand?' Rhona Laing's voice was sharp. Obviously she had expected a swifter response from the detective.

Rhona had never thought very much of Sandy, as a man or as a police officer.

'Of course.'

'But before you leave you must tell Inverness. They'll need to send a team. The Serious Crime Squad and the CSIs.'

'They won't get here until the morning now,' Sandy said. He was on firmer ground here and could understand the practicalities. 'The last plane from Inverness will already have left.'

'But we need their advice, Sergeant. I've tied the yoal to my mooring in Aith. I assume I leave the body where it is. The forecast is good tomorrow, so it should be safe enough there, if it's properly covered. We should mark off the marina as a crime scene and keep people out. But we'll need screens too. You know how people gawk. And tomorrow's Saturday, so there'll be a lot of people about.'

'You'll not be popular keeping folk away from their boats on a weekend.' Sandy scratched his arm and thought there was nothing better than a bit of fishing at this time of the year. At last you could feel that the long, dark winter days were over.

'I don't aim to be popular!' the retort came, sharp as gunfire.

'Did you recognize him?' Sandy asked. 'The dead man, I mean.'

There was a pause at the other end of the line and he understood that she was considering the matter. He thought people always looked different when they were dead, and if you didn't know them well, it wasn't always easy to identify a body. But when the answer came it was unequivocal. 'I didn't, Sergeant. And that's another reason why I need you here. If he's a Shetlander, I assume you'll be able to tell us who he is.'

There was a pause. Sandy could hear the sound of water in the background. The Fiscal must still be at the marina, using her mobile. She was lucky to get any reception. That part of the island was a black hole when it came to phones. 'I'll send some people over to secure the site,' he said, 'and contact Inverness. I'll be there as soon as I can.'

'Good.'

He knew she was about to end the conversation and almost shouted, to hold her attention: 'Miss Laing!'

'Yes, Sergeant.'

'Should I tell Jimmy? Inspector Perez?' This had been troubling him since he first realized the implication of her call. Jimmy Perez wasn't himself, hadn't been since the death of his fiancée. He was given to black moods and bouts of rage that came from nowhere. His colleagues were sympathetic and had given him time. He'd come back to work too early, they said. He was depressed. But after six months their patience was wearing thin. Sandy had picked up mutterings in the canteen: maybe Perez should resign and devote himself to looking after Duncan Hunter's child. Promotion in the Shetland police service was about filling dead men's shoes. Perhaps Perez should do the decent thing: move on and give somebody else a chance to do the job properly.

At first there was no answer from Rhona Laing. Sandy wondered if her phone had cut out. Then she spoke. 'I don't know, Sandy. That's a judgement for you to make. You know Jimmy better than I do.' And her voice was almost human.

He put off the decision until he'd spoken to Inverness. There was a new man in charge there. He was English, and Sandy had to concentrate hard to understand the accent. 'I'll send up an inspector and a team,' the man said. 'You know Roy Taylor went back to Liverpool?'

'I'd heard.' Sandy thought it was all change now. Jimmy Perez was a quite different man, and Roy Taylor had moved south. Sandy had never enjoyed change. He'd grown up on the small island of Whalsay and it had been a huge adventure to go south to train for the police service.

'Taylor's replacement is a woman.' The superintendent came from London and his voice made Sandy think of gangster movies. 'Grew up in North Uist. Almost one of you.'

No, Sandy wanted to say. *The people of the Uists are quite different. They speak Gaelic, and the crofts are all sand and seaweed. A different landscape and a different culture. In the Hebrides you can't get a drink on a Sunday. Only an Englishman could think a Hebridean would have anything in common with a Shetlander.* He'd spent two days in Benbecula on a training course with the Highlands and Islands Police and thought he knew all about the place. But he said nothing. He wouldn't mind having a boss who was a woman.

'She's called Reeves,' the superintendent went on. 'Willow Reeves. You'll meet her and her team from the plane?' Sandy was thinking that didn't sound much like a Hebridean name. Weren't they all MacDonalds in the Western Isles? The superintendent had to repeat the question. 'You will meet them from the morning plane? Find them accommodation and show them the ropes? I take it Jimmy Perez is still out of action?'

'He's back part-time,' Sandy said. 'Still under the doctor.'

'Will he be up for this?' The superintendent's voice was uncertain.

'I think he'd want to know,' Sandy said. 'I think he'd hate something like this going on in his patch and not knowing.' This had only just come to him, but now he was sure it was true.

'So you'll do that, will you, Sandy? You'll tell him. I don't want Perez finding out on the grapevine and thinking we've excluded him on purpose. These days he can be a prickly sod.'

Sandy replaced the phone and felt overwhelmed by the choices he had to make. The Fiscal expected him in Aith, which was a good half-hour's drive to the north, and the superintendent wanted him to talk to Jimmy Perez, who lived in Ravenswick to the south of Lerwick. Sandy was happier when he was told what to do. More than anything in the world he longed for Jimmy Perez to be back and normal, clever and sharp. And telling him what to do.

He got back on the phone and organized a couple of uniformed officers to get to Aith and screen off the crime scene. 'We'll need someone on duty there until the team from Inverness gets in.' When he told his colleagues that the Fiscal had found the body, he sensed their hostility. She wasn't a popular woman.

He couldn't think of anyone in the islands who liked her or who would consider her a friend. When he went outside to pick up his car, the light was starting to fade. Perez would be at home because it would nearly be Cassie's bedtime. Cassie, the child of his lover, left to him in her unofficial will. The only reason, Sandy thought, that Perez hadn't run away from the islands and the memories of Fran's death.

The house was a converted chapel, very low and small, with a view over Raven's Head and down to the houses by the pier. Perez's car was parked outside. The door opened before Sandy reached it, and Jimmy Perez stood there, a mug of coffee in his hand. He looked as if he hadn't slept since Fran had died and was skinny and unshaven. Though he'd never been a tidy man, Sandy thought. He'd never much been one for caring about his appearance.

'Is Cassie in bed?' Sandy didn't want to start talking about bodies and murder if the girl was listening in.

'She's staying with her father,' Perez said.

Duncan Hunter, who'd been the wild boy of the islands, living in his huge inherited house on the voe at Brae. Duncan Hunter, ex-husband of Fran. Ex-best friend of Jimmy Perez.

Perez went on. 'It's the last weekend of the school holidays. She'll not have much chance to spend time with him for a few months. And you know what Duncan's like. He's always away south on some money-making scheme. I thought it best to catch him while he's here. Cassie should know her father.'

'And it'll give you a bit of time to yourself.' Sandy wondered if Perez would invite him in and offer him a dram or a beer. Jimmy had never been much of a drinker, but when Fran had been alive there'd always been beer in the fridge.

'I miss her,' Perez said. 'Desperately.' And Sandy wasn't sure if he was talking about Cassie or Fran now. He shuffled his feet and looked out at the sea. 'What do you want?' Perez said. 'I'm not really up for entertaining. I'm not the best sort of company these days.'

Sandy thought there was a hint of self-pity in his voice and perhaps work was the best thing for him at the moment. 'This isn't a social call,' he said and was surprised at how sharply the words came out.

Perez stared at him. Sandy had always been his most sympathetic colleague. Perez had always stood up for Sandy, and now it was Sandy's turn to defend him. 'You'd best come in then.'

The house was much as it had been in Fran's day. There were her paintings on the wall alongside Cassie's. A big photo of the three of them hung over the fire. The woman was laughing in it, her head thrown back, and Sandy felt tears come to his eyes. Fran Hunter had always been kind to him.

'Tea?' Perez asked. 'I don't keep alcohol in the house. I don't trust myself with it.'

'Tea's fine.' Sandy watched Perez reach for the mug and fetch milk from the fridge. 'There's been a murder,' he said. 'The Fiscal found a body in one of the racing yoals in Aith Marina. You know she rows with the older women.' He waited for a response. The old Jimmy would have raised his eyebrows at that and made a crack about the Fiscal and the time she spent on the water.

But today Perez set the mug of tea carefully on the table and turned to face Sandy.

'I'm on the sick,' he said. 'Not fit for that kind of work.'

'No point wasting your time then.' Sandy got out of his seat and made for the door. 'The Iron Maiden wants me in Aith, in the hope I can make an identification. You know what she's like if you make her wait. I thought you should know, that's all. I thought it would be . . .' he struggled to find the right word '. . . courteous to tell you.'

Again Perez seemed surprised, though not angry or annoyed. Sandy didn't usually stand up to him. Sandy didn't usually stand up to anyone. And these days anger seemed to be Jimmy's default emotion.

'I'm sorry.' Perez shook his head. An attempt to think more clearly? Or an expression of a kind of despair? Then, after a moment, 'It was good of you to come and let me know.'

Sandy hovered for a moment on the doorstep. The lighthouse at Raven's Head had been lit and the beam swung across his head. He wondered if at the last moment Perez would change his mind and be tempted to drive with him up to Aith. He'd be curious, surely. Curiosity had always driven Jimmy forward to see cases through. And for a moment Perez *did* seem tempted.

'Who are they sending from Inverness?' he asked.

'A woman.' Sandy felt lighter, more eager. 'Some woman with a strange name. But we've got the night to sort it out before she gets here.'

'Good luck with that then.' And Perez backed into the house and shut the door. He turned on the light inside, and through the window Sandy saw his shoulders hunched over the kitchen table, his head low over his mug of tea, so that he looked like an old man. It was as if Perez had briefly felt himself coming to life again and didn't like the feeling. It hurt him too much.

Chapter Five

By the time Sandy arrived at Aith it was fully dark. It had taken longer than he'd expected because there was a hennie bus on the narrow road between Bixter and Aith and it had gone slowly. Once it stopped to let out a lass to be sick on the verge. The girl had her leg tied to her friend's, as if they were competing in a three-legged race, and it had taken an age for the two of them to get down the steps. Any other time and Sandy would have been amused. Hen parties on the island were always good value. But tonight he was annoyed and leaned on his horn until the bus pulled in and let him past.

In Aith there was a constable at the entrance to the marina, who recognized his car and waved him through. Sandy had expected the Fiscal to be at home, but she was still at the scene, wearing blue jeans and a cagoule, a knitted hat over her immaculate hair. They'd switched on the lights in the marina and everything looked washed out and pale, except the water, which was black and oily. Rhona Laing came up to him as soon as he climbed out of his car.

'It was good of you to make it, Sergeant.' Her voice acid, all trace of the earlier compassion gone.

'I went to see Jimmy Perez,' he said. 'I thought it was a courtesy.' He was proud of the new-found word.

She hesitated. 'He didn't want to come along then?'

'He didn't feel up to it.' Sandy paused too. 'A pity. It could be just what he needs. Something to take his mind off things and get him out of the house.' The Fiscal didn't answer and he went on. 'I spoke to Inverness, and they're sending a team on the first flight tomorrow. I'll collect them from the airport and bring them straight here. Morag is sorting out accommodation. There's a new inspector.' He was going to add that it was a woman with a strange name, but thought better of it. He knew Rhona Laing wouldn't consider that relevant. He wondered what the women would make of each other and smiled in the gloom at the possibilities of a power-play. It would be good to have someone else as the target of the Fiscal's sharp tongue.

'This way.' The Fiscal led him along the jetty to one of the moorings. They'd put a screen at the end of the pier to stop prying eyes, and a piece of tarpaulin hid the body in the yoal. Davy Cooper, a uniformed sergeant, lifted one end and shone a torch so that Sandy could see.

'He's kind of familiar,' Davy said. 'But I can't put a name to him. I've opened the briefcase, but I couldn't find an ID. I didn't want to look in his pockets until the CSI gets here tomorrow morning.'

Sandy looked down at a man in his early thirties, who was dressed in jeans that would have cost him a couple of days' wages. 'It's Jerry Markham,' he said. There was shock to see him dead, though no sense of bereavement. They'd been distant cousins, but never had enough in common to be friends. 'His folk run the Ravenswick Hotel. He worked as a journalist on *The Shetland Times* until he went south to make his fortune. I didn't know he was home.'

'Of course it's Markham,' Cooper said. 'Now you say, I can see his mother in him.'

But Sandy wasn't listening. He was looking at the Fiscal, who seemed suddenly even whiter in the unforgiving lights. 'Did you know him, Ma'am?'

'No,' she said. 'I know his name of course, but we've never met.' She looked away from the body. 'It's getting cold, and I've not eaten. If you need me, you can find me at home.' She began to walk away, but just as she reached a patch of shadow she turned back to them. 'Will you inform the family?'

Sandy nodded.

'The press will be here as soon as the news gets out,' she said. 'They're always interested in one of their own. We'll keep the identity to ourselves for as long as we can, Sergeant, so I'd appreciate a bit of discretion when you arrive at the hotel.'

'Would you like to tell Peter and Maria yourself?' The last thing Sandy wanted was a drive back to Ravenswick, and the hotel was the smartest in the islands. He always felt out of place there. He imagined that the Fiscal would be a regular in the restaurant.

'That's hardly my role, Sergeant.' She was already moving away from him, and by the end of the sentence the darkness had swallowed her up.

On the drive back to Ravenswick, Sandy ran through the things he knew about Jerry Markham in his head.

Markham was a bit older than Sandy, though he'd still been at the Anderson High while Sandy was there. One of the fashionable boys. Editor of the school magazine. Star of the school play. He'd gone away to university and come back to write on the *Shetland Times*, got bored and miserable and moved south again. Now he wrote for one of those big London papers that had serious stories, and sport only on the back pages. Sandy's mother had been full of that when Jerry had got the job, and whenever his name was on an article she clipped it out to wave under Sandy's nose when he went home.

The parents were Peter and Maria Markham. Maria was a Shetland wife. She'd grown up in Northmavine. Peter was an incomer, what Shetlanders called a soothmoother.

What had Peter Markham worked at before they bought up the Ravenswick Hotel? Sandy couldn't bring it to mind, but thought it was something to do with oil. Then he remembered that there was a military connection: Markham had been stationed at the air-force base in Unst and that's when he'd met Maria. When he'd left the services he'd flown helicopters from Scatsta out to the rigs. The Ravenswick had been rundown before the Markhams took it over. It had been a laird's house, built in the eighteenth century, huge and solid and right on the water. Now it was completely refurbished and called itself Shetland's only country-house hotel. Fran and Jimmy had taken him for a meal there to celebrate their engagement. Only in the bar, but it still seemed awful expensive to Sandy. The food had been good, though, and if Sandy had a woman that he really wanted to impress, he'd take her there at lunchtime when there was a set menu and it didn't cost so much.

Sandy realized he'd reached Perez's house and was on the edge of the settlement of Ravenswick. There were still lights on in the old chapel, but the curtains were drawn. Perhaps Jimmy kept the light on now when he went to sleep. Perhaps, like a bairn, he got nightmares in the dark. Or perhaps he was sitting up awake, staring into the fire.

There was a fire lit in the entrance to the hotel. Peat that you could smell all the way from the car park. Stuart Brodie was on reception. Sandy had been at school with him too. The bar was full of residents drinking coffee or taking a dram after their dinners. The reception was all dark wood, with the smell of beeswax.

'Are Peter and Maria around?' Sandy leaned across the polished desk so that he was close to Brodie and didn't have to shout to make himself heard.

'They've just gone up to the flat.' Brodie was conscientious. A bit dull; he had no curiosity at all. 'Is it something I can help with? I wouldn't want to disturb them.'

'Point me in the right direction and I'll find my own way,' Sandy said. 'Don't ring them.' He took the grand staircase to the first floor and then a smaller staircase until he reached a door marked 'Private'. He knocked a couple of times, then at last he heard footsteps on the other side and it opened.

Peter Markham was still dressed for work in a suit, though he'd taken off the tie and there was a glass in his hand. His hair was turning grey, but he was still fit. He didn't come across to Sandy as an old man.

'Can I help you?' He seemed a little irritated by the interruption, but he wasn't rude. Perhaps guests often knocked on his door to complain or ask for help and, given the prices they were paying, Peter Markham couldn't afford to lose his temper.

Sandy introduced himself and the man stood aside. 'What is it, Sergeant? Has one of our guests been misbehaving?' He didn't recognize Sandy, but then his wife had dozens of distant relatives.

Sandy followed him through to a large sitting room. Once these might have been servants' quarters, but this end of the attic had been knocked into a large space and painted white. The polished wood floors of the hotel were here too, and there was a blue patterned rug near the wood-burning stove. Sandy thought it would be a bit chilly in the winter. He preferred a carpet. On a shelf near the stove was a sculpture of a gannet, almost life-size, made of driftwood. Sandy found himself staring at it. How had the artist made it look as if it was about to dive?

Maria Markham was slouched in a low armchair. She'd changed into a dressing gown, nothing glamorous, but the sort Sandy's mother might wear, fleecy and comfortable. She was staring at the television; Sandy suspected it had been switched on to help her relax, not because she was interested in the programme. There was a drink on the table beside her. Maria knew him at once. They were related in the way of the islands, remotely – she was a kind of aunt by marriage – and, growing up, he'd met her occasionally at weddings and funerals. She'd always been on her own; her husband and son had never accompanied her. And since she and Peter had taken on the

Ravenswick, Sandy hadn't seen her at family events at all.

She stood up, pulling her dressing gown around her, a little embarrassed to be caught like this, dressed so informally. 'Sandy! How lovely!' It didn't seem to occur to her that he might be here in a professional capacity. He thought she'd put on weight. Her chin was soft and fleshy. 'What would you like to drink? You'll take a dram with us? Were you downstairs earlier? We were so busy that I didn't see you. The place is full of folk here supervising the new gas terminal up the island. Good for business, but if it lasts, we'll need to get more staff. And the fog meant that the Edinburgh plane didn't go, so some of our guests were stranded for an extra night.'

'I'm here about Jerry,' he said.

'He's not back,' she replied. 'He's working. We're expecting him at any time. Why don't you wait? He'll love to catch up with you.'

Her husband, though, seemed to sense that this wasn't a social call. He stood behind his wife and put his hand on her shoulder. 'What is it?' he asked. 'Is something wrong?'

'Jerry's dead.' Sandy had broken tragic news a few times now and found that it didn't get any easier. Those words were so brutal that he felt as if he was killing the man again, but there was no gentle way to do it. Best that there was no doubt, no room for hope.

The couple stared at him. It was as if they were frozen. 'What do you mean?' Maria said at last. 'He's here in Shetland. He'll be back any minute.'

'No.' Sandy wished he was better with words. With people. 'His body was found in Aith. I saw it for myself.'

'Was it that bloody car?' Markham said. 'He drove it like a maniac.'

'No.' Sandy's brain scrambled to understand the implication of the words. Of course Jerry would have brought a car to the island. They'd have to trace it. He should already have started a search – Perez would have done that. 'No,' he said again. 'There wasn't a car accident.'

'What then?'

Sandy looked at Maria. Tears were running down her cheeks, but still she didn't move and she made no noise.

'We think he was murdered,' Sandy said. 'His body was found at Aith Marina and there was a head-wound. We'll know more tomorrow, when a team comes up from Inverness.'

There was an explosion of sound then. Maria was shouting and crying. Sandy wasn't given to fancies, but he thought there was the pain of labour in it. It was as if she were giving birth to her son again, screaming her way through the agony. Markham stood in front of her and held her tight until she was quiet.

'Jerry was our only one,' he said, looking over his wife's head at Sandy. 'After him Maria could have no more children.'

Sandy wanted to get out of there, to give them some time to grieve alone. He hated sitting in the big clean space, watching the woman he remembered as strong and full of laughter falling apart. But in the morning the new inspector from North Uist would fly in on the plane and she'd want to know what he'd found out. This was the only chance he'd have to ask his questions before she took over the investigation.

'What car did Jerry drive?' he asked.

'An Alfa Romeo.' Markham was still holding his wife to his chest, rocking slightly as if he were comforting a fretful baby. 'One of the small, sporty ones. Red, of course. A ridiculous thing. Old now. He bought it when he first moved to London.'

'Maria said Jerry was here to work.' Sandy couldn't imagine what a fancy reporter from a London paper was doing in Shetland. How could what was happening here be of interest there?

'Jerry said there was a story.' Markham spoke quietly. Maria was so still now that Sandy wondered if she'd passed out, if she'd worn herself out with her sobbing. Markham stroked her hair. 'He'd persuaded his boss it was worth following up and that he'd be the best person to do it, because of his local connections. So he'd get a few days home, all expenses paid, and the chance of a scoop too.'

'What was the story about?' Outside there was a sudden burst of laughter. Local diners were making their way to their cars and home.

Markham shrugged. 'He'd asked if I could get him into Sullom Voe. Did I still have any contacts there? I thought there'd be nothing at the terminal that would interest the paper. The oil's running out, after all. That place is old news. But I arranged for him to visit the press officer.'

'And that was where he was today?'

'Yes,' Markham said. 'That was where he was today. We were expecting him back for dinner; when he didn't turn up, we thought he'd bumped into old friends. You know how it is here, coming back. I tried to phone, but there was no answer. No reception, we thought. It never occurred to me that anything would have happened to him. We worried about him sometimes in London. But not here. Here we expect everyone to be safe.'

He was still talking when Sandy stood up. Sandy thought Markham was reluctant now to let the detective go. His face was tight with the effort of holding himself together. With just Maria for company, he'd not manage it.

Sandy drove north again. The windows were still lit in Jimmy's house. He wanted to stop and ask advice. *What should I do first? Tell me how I should run things.* But he drove past and went to the office, got onto the computer to check the registration number of Jerry Markham's car, phoned Davy Cooper, who was on watch at the marina, and asked him to wander round the car park and see if it was there. Sandy hadn't noticed it, and he thought he would have noticed such a flash car. Morag had left a note that she'd fixed accommodation for the Inverness team in Lerwick.

Sandy returned to his flat in the early hours of the morning. He switched on the television, with the sound very low – a young family lived underneath him and he didn't want to wake them. He drank a can of Tennent's without bothering to get a glass, then set his alarm clock and went to bed. He slept immediately. Even when he was worried, Sandy Wilson had no trouble sleeping. Jimmy Perez had always said that was a gift. Sandy thought it was one of the few he possessed.

Chapter Six

It was Willow Reeves's first murder investigation as SIO. The boss had called her into the office and said he'd like her to take it on. 'It takes a special sort of understanding to work in Shetland. They're on the edge of the known universe up there and they think the normal rules of life don't apply to them. They're mad buggers.' The implication was that she was a mad bugger too – though she came from the far west and not the far north – and that for her the case would be a piece of piss. No pressure then. If he'd known exactly where she'd come from, and how her family had been, he'd really have considered that she was crazy, but she never talked about that at work. What business was it of theirs?

They landed in Sumburgh on the first flight out of Inverness and her initial thought was how big and grand everything was. It was like a real airport, with the car-hire office and the lounge and the cafe. Everything shiny in the sunshine. Vicki Hewitt, the CSI, had worked in Shetland before and greeted the sergeant who met them like an old friend. 'Tell me,' she said. 'How's Jimmy Perez?'

The sergeant shrugged and muttered in an accent

Willow struggled to understand. 'Not so good. It's taking a long time.'

They all knew the story of Jimmy Perez and how his fiancée had got caught up in a murder investigation on Fair Isle, how she'd been stabbed by a psycho and how Jimmy blamed himself. It had been talked about in canteens throughout the Highland and Islands Police for months. There were people who blamed Jimmy too. What was he thinking, involving his woman in his work? Willow had never expressed an opinion. One thing she'd learned growing up in the commune in North Uist was that often it was best to keep your mouth shut. At least until you knew what you were talking about.

The sergeant drove them north up a fine, straight road, pointing out landmarks on the way as if he were a tour guide. She had hundreds of questions to ask him about the case. Overnight she'd read the preliminary report from Shetland and everything she could find about Jerry Markham. In her briefcase there was a file of cuttings of the stories he'd written. 'Tell me about Markham,' she said at last.

Sandy Wilson didn't seem offended by the interruption. 'His father was from the south,' he said. 'But his mother was a Shetland woman, and Jerry was born here and grew up here.'

'You knew him?'

'Oh aye, but I've not seen him since he moved to London.'

'So you wouldn't know why anyone would want to kill him? There were no rumours? No stories of enemies or grudges?' She understood that in small, tight communities grudges could be held for generations.

'He worked as a reporter on the *Shetland Times* for a while,' Sandy said. 'Before he got that chance to work on the London newspaper. It didn't always make him popular. Folk don't like their dirty washing done in public. And it's read by everyone. Maybe he thought he was practising for the big time while he was here, always on the lookout for the exciting story. But that was ten years ago. I don't think it could be the cause of him getting killed yesterday.'

Suddenly he crossed the road and pulled the car into a lay-by. He nodded down the bank towards a big house that stood right on the shore. It was built of grey stone and there was a high stone wall all round it.

'That's the Ravenswick Hotel,' Sandy said. 'Jerry's parents own it. Peter and Maria Markham.'

'What do local people make of them?' Willow thought it must be expensive, keeping a place like that going. None of the hotels on the Uists were that big or that smart.

'They like them fine. It's work for local people. The place is a bit pricey, but it always seems to be busy. It's for tourists and folk here on business, but the locals eat in the bar or in the restaurant if they have something special to celebrate.' And Sandy continued giving a history of the Markhams. Willow thought he'd go back a couple of generations, if she encouraged him. But she liked that. She liked to know that these people had roots. Her roots had very shallow soil to grow in. As Sandy talked she wished she'd thought to take a notebook from her rucksack to write it all down.

Lerwick seemed like a big town, with traffic lights

and supermarkets and factories on the edge of it. 'Do you want to drop your stuff at the hotel,' Sandy said, 'or should we go straight to Aith to look at the crime scene?'

'To Aith.' It was Vicki Hewitt, shouting from the back. 'The poor man has been there all night. That's long enough, don't you think? Has James seen him yet?'

James Grieve, the pathologist, was based in Aberdeen. Willow had never met him and felt a little excluded. It was like being the new girl at school and not quite fitting into the established gang, no matter how kind the other children were.

'He should be there by now,' Sandy said. 'The Aberdeen flight is the first one in, and we fixed a lift for him.' Already they were leaving the town behind and driving north past giant wind turbines spinning slowly on the hill. The land seemed bare and windblown. There were no trees, not even planted conifers. 'Morag met him.'

Aith was away from the main road. Willow had checked it out on the OS map at home the night before. This was a single-track with occasional passing places, and it ran across bare hillside and peat bog. There were views of water everywhere: of the sea, salt-water inlets and small lochs. When they did meet a car, the driver waved or nodded. *In a place like this strangers would be noticed, wouldn't they?* Though she supposed that the place attracted tourists and they might explore away from the main roads too.

Dropping down to the settlement, she saw evidence of the investigation even from a distance. More cars than you'd expect. The blue-and-white police tape twisting in the breeze. A group of people showing unnatural interest in one big rowing boat, which had now been winched up onto the jetty so that the pathologist could get a good look at the body *in situ*. As she watched, a white tent was erected around it. There were gawpers, of course. Even in a small community like this there'd be sightseers who thought it'd be interesting or exciting to see a dead body. Here, a couple of old men and a handful of children gathered on the edge of the action.

'We've taken over the school for the weekend,' Sandy said suddenly. 'It has Internet connection, phones and a kitchen so that we can feed the troops. Toilets.' He paused and she realized suddenly that he was waiting for her approval. It would never have occurred to her that he'd need it. This was his territory after all.

'Good!' she said. 'Great idea.' And she watched him relax and beam.

They parked in the school playground. Walking towards the jetty, they were approached not by the suited and booted police officers or the pathologist, but by a middle-aged woman who was standing just outside the cordon. When she saw Willow she held out her hand. 'Rhona Laing,' she said. 'I'm the Procurator Fiscal.' She had an Edinburgh accent. Classy Edinburgh, clipped and glacial. She wore a tweed jacket over a cashmere sweater and grey wool trousers. Sensible shoes that managed not to look dowdy. 'You must be Inspector Reeves. I understand that you're to be in charge of the investigation.' She allowed just enough surprise into her voice to annoy Willow. People were always thinking she didn't look the part. It wasn't her fault if she wasn't what they were expecting. 'You'll be reporting to me while you're here.'

'Of course.' Willow returned the handshake and wondered why women in power felt the need to play games. 'You found the body, I understand, in the racing yoal.'

'As I explained to Sergeant Wilson.' The Fiscal nodded. There was a breeze from the sea, but her hair didn't move. Either she'd had a fantastic haircut or used a serious amount of spray.

'And you live locally?'

'In the Old Schoolhouse.' Rhona Laing nodded to a square, solid house on the bank behind them. 'I thought some children had pushed the yoal into the water for a prank and I went to retrieve it.' She gave a little smile, but her eyes were wary.

'Thanks very much for coming to meet us.' Willow made her voice sincere. She'd been in the drama club for a while at uni. 'Perhaps we could take up a little more of your time when we've finished here. If you'll be in, that is. I don't want to eat into your weekend, and I don't know how long we'll be.' She glanced towards the white tent, making it clear that she was keen to move on.

There was a pause.

'Of course,' Rhona Laing said. 'I'll make myself available.'

It was only as they'd put on the paper scene-suits and pulled the boots over their shoes that it occurred to Willow that the Fiscal had expected to be invited to join them. The older woman hadn't realized that finding the body had put her in an ambiguous situation. Legally she was supervising the investigation, but she was a witness and might even become a suspect.

James Grieve, the pathologist, was walking away from the body. Well outside the cordon he stripped off the scene-suit. He was a small man, smart and dapper, with shiny black shoes. He greeted Vicki with a smile and a peck on the cheek. 'Miss Hewitt, we should stop meeting like this.'

Willow introduced herself. She felt awkward because she was taller than him. And a whole lot younger. She should be accustomed to both these things by now.

'Inspector.' He gave a gallant little bow. 'I'm away back to civilization. Or at least to Aberdeen. Everything, I suppose, is comparative. I'm assuming that you'll be too tied up here to be present at the post-mortem. You can give me a ring tomorrow. Early afternoon. I've arranged for the body to go south on this evening's ferry and I should have something for you then.'

'Cause of death?' she asked.

He raised his eyebrows as if she were an impertinent schoolgirl who was pushing her luck in class. Then he smiled. 'It looks as if he was hit very hard by the traditional blunt instrument. But after a quick glance at the body, you'd be able to tell that for yourself.' He bowed again and walked away.

Vicki Hewitt was already taking photographs inside the white tent. The yoal was bigger than Willow had expected, about twenty feet long, big enough for six people to sit in pairs to row. Jerry Markham was lying on his back across the wooden seats. It looked uncomfortable. His head and feet protruded beyond the bench into space at each end, so that his head was tilted backwards. His shoes were obviously expensive. To annoy her parents, Willow had once gone out with an army officer. He'd always worn good shoes too, and something about the stiff and awkward posture of the man in the boat reminded her of him. Though not enough for her to recall the soldier's name.

Markham's arms were folded across his chest and again there was something formal about the pose; certainly he hadn't fallen here after being struck. At his feet was a slim black briefcase, large enough to hold an electronic notebook perhaps, but not a conventional laptop. It occurred to Willow that, if it had contained anything useful, the killer would have taken it away. He or she was unconcerned about the remaining contents, and knew that they would provide no clue to their identity. It was even possible, given its prominence in the crime scene, that it was important to the murderer that the police should see whatever was inside. Willow stored that idea away for later.

The image of the man in the boat was sparking all sorts of references in her mind beside that of her former soldier lover. The form of a knight carved on the tomb in a medieval church: straight and stiff, arms crossed over his breast. A Viking, given a warrior's burial at sea, sent out in his longboat, which would then be set on fire. She suddenly became aware that Sandy Wilson was staring at her. Perhaps he'd been trying to catch her attention for some time.

'Ma'am?' The voice tentative.

'For God's sake, Sandy. "Willow" will do. It's a crap name, but it's the one I've been landed with.'

She was rewarded with a grin. 'Vicki says she'll be here all afternoon. I wondered what you'd like to do?'

Willow considered. 'You said that Markham's father arranged for him to visit the oil terminal yesterday afternoon?'

'At Sullom Voe. Yes. One of the security guys let him in, and he'd set up a meeting with the press officer.'

'Then we'll go there. First, though, we should have a word with your Procurator Fiscal.'

Sandy pulled a face, so Willow guessed that Rhona Laing wasn't the most popular woman on the islands.

'Come on, Sergeant. I'd guess she makes a decent cup of coffee. And after that we'll have a bar lunch, on my expenses.'

He gave a wide grin and Willow saw that she already had Sandy Wilson on her side.

Chapter Seven

Rhona Laing watched Sandy Wilson and the new detective inspector walk up the bank from the marina towards the house. She was standing in exactly the same position as when she'd first seen the yoal floating in the water.

I should have ignored it. The thought had been sniping away at her since she'd seen Markham's body. *I should have let the tide carry it out to sea. Done nothing. Said nothing.*

She composed herself. It was ridiculous to think in this way. She distracted herself by looking at the young woman at Sandy's side. She was tall and gangling, with long, untamed hair. No make-up. Trousers so long that they'd frayed at the hem, where her shoes had caught them at the back. A baggy cotton jumper in an indeterminate fawn colour, which could have been bought in a charity shop. Over it all a blue Berghaus jacket, unzipped and flapping loose. Rhona felt insulted by the lack of care that the woman had taken over her appearance. Hadn't she realized that, if women wanted to be successful in their chosen career, they should make some effort? She decided that Inspector Reeves had probably gained her promotion because the Highlands and Islands Police Service felt the need to fill some unwritten quota. The thought pleased her. Willow Reeves would be no competition. She and Sandy passed out of sight briefly to reach the front of the house. Rhona took a deep breath and waited for the doorbell to ring.

Inside the house, with its clean lines and lack of clutter, the detective looked even untidier and somehow clumsy. Rhona wanted to tell her not to move, in case she broke something. It was like having an unruly child in the place. Reeves wandered into the living room and stood there, seeming to take up more space than Rhona would have considered possible.

'Coffee?' After all, one did have to be polite.

'Oh yes, please.' The detective turned and smiled, and again Rhona thought she looked very young, hardly an adult at all.

In the kitchen, spooning grounds into the filter machine, Rhona wished she could see what they were doing in her living room. She wouldn't put it past that girl to snoop. To open drawers, lift the lid of her desk. There was nothing to see, of course. Nothing untoward. But still the notion made Rhona uncomfortable. This was her work coming far too close to home.

She carried in the tray and they sat on the chairs that were Rhona's pride and joy. They'd been imported from Sweden and she loved the pale curved wood and soft leather. The young woman was speaking.

'I'm wondering why the victim was placed in the yoal. That wasn't where he was killed. Obviously. But you'll have worked that out for yourself. We haven't found the crime scene yet. His car's still missing. When we find that, we might have more of an idea. So why go to all the trouble of laying him out in the boat? And why here? I just don't get it.'

Words and ideas were spilling from her in an incoherent stream. A mind that was as untidy as her body. Rhona waited for a moment before responding. Was Reeves an innocent, making a genuine request for the Fiscal's opinion, or was something more sinister going on here? Was she implying that Rhona knew more than she was letting on?

'I make it my business never to meddle in the work of the police,' she said at last. 'My function is purely supervisory. I'm sure you understand that.'

'But you live here in Aith.' Willow gave another of her wide, immature smiles. 'You know the other women in the rowing team. Would any of them have any connection with Jerry Markham, do you think?'

'There are six teams in Aith, of different ages and genders, and I couldn't speak for them all.'

'You share the boat?'

'Yes,' Rhona said. 'We share the boat.' She took a childish pleasure in thinking of the work that would make for the inspector – the phone calls and the interviews.

'But you can speak for your own team?'

The woman was persistent, Rhona thought. She had a dogged stubbornness. 'I wouldn't have thought they would have known Markham. I row with the veterans, and we're all over forty. Too old to have gone to school with him, surely? Of course I'll give you a list of their names and contact details. I have that stored on the computer in my office. I'll get it for you now. And I can give you the names of contacts for the other Aith teams.'

She was surprised when Reeves got to her feet too and followed her up the stairs to the small bedroom she had turned into a study. It felt as if she was being hounded by an untrained and very large puppy. The woman stood in the doorway and leaned against the frame as Rhona switched on the computer. The Fiscal couldn't prevent herself from thinking of the mark that the grubby jacket might make on the paintwork.

'Do you do much work from home?' The detective's question appeared guileless, but again Rhona considered before she answered.

'I have an office in Lerwick, of course, but I often catch up here in the evenings.'

'And what brought you to Shetland? It's very different from a successful practice in Edinburgh.'

Rhona checked that there was paper in the printer, then looked up. 'I love the sea,' she said. 'I always have. A successful legal practice in Edinburgh didn't allow much time for being on the water, and Shetland has magnificent sailing. Besides, in professional terms, it's always good to gain experience in a different field.' She wondered why she'd told the young detective these things. They were both true, but she seldom discussed her motives for moving to the islands. She thought that, like Jimmy Perez, the woman had the ability to persuade people to talk.

The printer chugged and spat out the list and contact details of the rowing team. 'You'll see that the squad is bigger than the six women needed to race,' Rhona said. 'We're busy people, and we can't all turn out for every regatta.'

Willow Reeves took the paper, looked at it briefly, then put it in her jacket pocket.

'When was the boat last in the water?'

'We had our first meeting of the season last week. Over the winter it was stored in a shed on the shore. We cleaned and varnished it, and last week the weather was good, so we took it out. A bit of light training to start us off.' Rhona thought how she'd enjoyed that evening. The clocks had just gone forward and it was light until eight o'clock. She'd realized how she'd missed the company of the women over the dark days of the winter.

'But it wasn't put back in the shed?' Willow broke into her thoughts.

'No. Too much fuss to get it out every time we're training. It sits on that grassy bank close to the water. We cover it in tarpaulin. It comes to no harm there.'

'And everyone in Aith would know that.' Willow was talking almost to herself.

'Almost everyone in Shetland would know that,' Rhona said. 'Anyone who came to Aith for the sailing, or who took a drive out this way on a pleasant summer's evening, or watched a regatta.'

'Of course.' Willow pushed herself away from the door frame to let the Fiscal past. 'I'm just puzzled by the placing of the body in the yoal. Why would the killer bother? Why risk being seen? It must have been put there in daylight. Yet Sandy's team has asked everyone who lives here, and nobody saw anything. Or claims not to have done. No strange car. Nobody mucking around near the boat. It's as if Jerry Markham arrived miraculously, conjured out of thin air.'

Rhona didn't know what to say to that, but she felt that a response was required. 'It was very foggy yesterday afternoon,' she said. 'Nobody *would* see.' She led the way down the stairs.

'You didn't notice anything odd when you came in from work?'

Again Rhona thought how persistent this woman was. She was beginning to find her presence in the house unbearable. She clenched her fists by her sides, felt her nails digging into the skin of her palm.

'I do think I might have mentioned it,' she said. 'A killer lifting a corpse into our racing yoal – yes, I do think I might have told you, without waiting to be asked.'

'I'm sorry.' Though Inspector Reeves didn't seem sorry at all. It was the routine apology of a sinner who intends to continue sinning. She smiled again. 'But it bugs me. Not understanding how it might have happened.'

'I'm sure there's a perfectly rational explanation.' Rhona remained where she was at the bottom of the stairs. She intended to make it clear that the detective's visit was over.

And at last the young woman seemed to get the message. She called to Sandy that they were ready to go. He got up from his chair to join them, and for a moment the three of them stood awkwardly in the hall of the house. Willow held out her hand. 'Thank you,' she said. 'You've been incredibly helpful. Really.' Then she had the door open, and she and Sandy were outside. Rhona stood watching to make sure they'd left the garden before closing it behind them.

She was shaking. *This is ridiculous. What have I possibly got to worry about?* She went into the living room and straightened the cushion on the chair where

Sandy had been sitting. She thought she should get out. She could go into Lerwick and use the gym at the Clickimin Sports Centre. Maybe have a swim, if the pool wasn't too full of screaming children. But she couldn't move. Usually she had no time for people without drive or energy, but she was overtaken by a lethargy that made her feel that she might sleep as soon as she sat down. The kitchen was at the back of the house and sheltered from the road by the straggling rowans that previous owners had planted as a windbreak. She felt safer here. The view of the marina that had prompted her to buy the Old Schoolhouse in the first place now left her with the idea that she was like a goldfish in a bowl. All the police officers and the sightseers could look inside. Better to stay here in the kitchen or in her office, until it was dark and she could reasonably close the curtains.

She opened a cupboard and took out a bottle of Highland Park and a tumbler. She poured herself a drink, sipped it and felt the warmth of the whisky. She carried the glass upstairs to the office and sat in front of the computer. She remained there for a moment. No more whisky until she'd made the call. She needed a clear head. She picked up the telephone and dialled a number she knew by heart. The voice at the other end of the line was curious and reassuring. If he was angry, he didn't show it.

'Yes?'

She would be the last person he'd be expecting.

'It's Rhona Laing.' She was quite calm now. This could have been a routine work matter. 'I'm afraid Jerry Markham has come back to haunt us.'

Chapter Eight

They had lunch in the bar in Voe. Another settlement close to the water. Another small marina. Sandy wondered where they'd all sprung from, these smart developments to cater for folk with sailing boats and motor cruisers. He couldn't remember there being so many when he was a child. Willow Reeves ordered soup and bannocks. She ate hungrily, and that pleased him. He didn't like women who were always worrying about how much food they put into their mouths. Two people he knew were in the pub, talking about the hen party that had happened the evening before. It had been the usual thing. They'd hired a mini-bus to take them round the bars in North Mainland and everyone had dressed up. This time, though, it had been a three-legged pub-crawl and the lassies had been collecting for charity.

'Did you see that Jen Belshaw? She doesn't have the figure for showing that much flesh.' More giggling like schoolboys.

Sandy almost joined in the conversation to describe the pair of women climbing out of the bus the night before, their legs still tied together, but decided just in time that it wouldn't be professional. He could have fancied a beer, but Willow was drinking water, so he stuck to the orange juice. They sat at the window, away from the chatting couple at the bar.

'Usually very tense, your Fiscal, is she?'

He felt for a moment that he should defend Rhona Laing. She might be a soothmoother, but she lived in Shetland now, and she'd been good to Jimmy Perez after the business on Fair Isle. Then he remembered her sarcasm, the cutting comments that had been directed towards him. 'She's not an easy woman,' he said. 'A stickler for procedure.'

'Honest, though?' Willow looked at him. Her hair was too long at the front and flopped over her eyes. 'Never any question of that?'

'Good God, no!' He was shocked that she could even imagine it. 'Not just honest, but efficient. You know, sometimes things go wrong, cases cocked up – not through any intention, not corruption, but because folk might be lazy. Not thorough. No question of that with the Iron Maiden.'

'That's what you call her?' Willow grinned. 'The Iron Maiden?'

'It's what Jimmy used to call her. Sometimes.'

'She just seemed very uncomfortable,' Willow said. 'If she were a witness, an ordinary witness, I'd bet ten pounds that she was hiding something.'

'She's a loner.' Again it seemed weird to be standing up for the Fiscal. 'No friends. Not here, at least. She seems confident enough at work. And when she's schmoozing with councillors and politicians. But perhaps she finds it hard to have people in her house.'

'Aye,' Willow said. 'Maybe that's all it is.' But she still sounded uncertain, and Sandy wondered what was going on in her mind.

There was no mobile reception in Voe, but once they joined the main road that led from Lerwick to the north he had a flurry of messages on his phone indicating missed calls. He was driving, so he pulled into the end of a track to listen. Where the track met the road there were two figures made of straw-filled pillowcases and clothes stuffed with rags. Where the face should be, life-size photos of the faces of the bride and groom-to-be had been stuck on. Sandy thought he'd seen the man around, but he didn't recognize the girl. This was a tradition before a wedding. They looked kind of spooky. If ever he got married, he wouldn't want a scarecrow figure of him at the gate of his parents' croft in Whalsay.

'They've found Markham's car,' he said. 'It was a call from Davy Cooper.'

'Where?'

'Near the museum at Vatnagarth.' He saw that she was none the wiser. 'It's a croft-house,' he said. 'Hasn't changed in years. Tourists go there to see what life was like in the old days. Volunteers dress up in old-fashioned clothes and pretend that they live there.' He paused. To him, it seemed an odd way to carry on. 'They have old farming tools. Peat-cutters and kishies for carrying the peats. We got taken there once from school and we got to try ploughing by hand.'

'And where exactly is this place?'

He could tell that Willow was impatient, not interested in tales of his schooldays. 'It's not so far from here.'

As they drove, Willow was looking around her, taking in all the details of the island. He turned off the main road and into a sheltered valley, with a copse of sycamores and beyond into open land and a view west towards the sea. Stacks of rock formed giant sculptures offshore and her attention was caught by those, so for a while she didn't notice the low croft with its roof thatched with peat and straw, the barn and the byre, and the kiln where the corn had been dried. Everything made of rough grey stone. Last time Sandy had been here it had been a bright summer's day and he'd been eleven. He'd lived in Shetland for most of the intervening years, but had thought of the museum as a place for tourists, not for him. He slowed down as he approached the museum and pulled into the car park behind the buildings.

Davy Cooper was there already. There'd been a piece on the Radio Shetland news that morning asking for information about the Alfa Romeo, he said, and a postie delivering to the museum had called in to say that she'd seen it. The car was in a space furthest away from the entrance of the museum and he'd taped it off, stringing the tape between fence posts.

Willow gave him a smile when she saw what he'd done. 'Quite right,' she said. 'It could be our murder scene after all. Is Ms Hewitt on her way?'

Davy nodded. 'And the key-holder of the museum. This time of year it's not open much.'

As they waited, another vehicle pulled up. Sandy recognized Reg Gilbert, the editor of the *Shetland Times*, and his old VW camper van. Rhona Laing had asked Sandy to be discreet, but it would be impossible to keep the identity of the murder victim secret now. Sandy wondered how Reg had got hold of the news – presumably the postie hadn't talked only to the police. There was nothing Reg liked better than a big story that he could pass on to former colleagues in the south. He'd taken early retirement from an English regional paper so that he could spend more time with his new young wife. But his woman had run off with her salsa teacher, and Reg had come to the islands to lick his wounds. He'd never been in Shetland before and had only taken the editor's job because it was the first one he'd seen advertised. None of this was a secret. Reg took up residence in the bar of the Grand Hotel every evening after work and told the story to anyone who would listen. He said that Shetland was about as far away as he could get from the cheating cow.

'Isn't that young Jerry Markham's car?' The journalist had a narrow face that made Sandy think of a rat. Thinning hair and enormous eyebrows. A long, red boozer's nose.

He put the question to Sandy, but Willow answered.

'You know Mr Markham?'

'I *knew* him, my dear. His body's in a bag and on its way to the ferry, so Jimmy Grieve can cut him open in the morning. I spoke to Annie Goudie, our funeral director, and she's just confirmed it. We must definitely speak of the Golden Boy of journalism in the past tense, wouldn't you say?'

'When did you last see him?' Willow obviously wasn't going to allow herself to be provoked.

'On Thursday evening. He offered to buy me dinner in the Ravenswick Hotel restaurant. Not as generous as that might sound, because his parents own the place and I'm sure he didn't intend to pick up the bill. All the same, I wasn't going to turn down an offer like that.' Reg leaned against the camper van. Rumour had it that he was so short of cash when he moved to the islands that it had been his home for the summer. He lived in it, in the harbour car park in town. The windows at the back had grubby net curtains, so Sandy couldn't see inside.

'And what was the subject of your discussion?' Willow's voice was still frosty.

'He was planning a big piece for his newspaper and he was a bit cagey. He knew I still had contacts in the London papers and was worried that I might follow it up on my own. Not that he said as much, but I could tell what he was thinking. And he thought right. I'd have been there like a shot, if I'd had the chance.'

Until now the day had been bright, with a gusty westerly blowing cloud shadows over the water. Suddenly everything was grey and Sandy felt the first drop of rain.

'But if Markham was buying you dinner – even at his parents' expense – he must have tried to get some information from you,' Willow said.

'Quite right.' Sandy saw that Reg had been going to add another 'my dear', but thought better of it just in time. 'No such thing as a free supper, in our business. That was my thought exactly.'

'So?' Willow showed that she was losing patience.

But Reg refused to be intimidated. 'I'm local,' he said. 'I have contacts. I can help you in all sorts of ways.'

'So?'

'So, if I help you, you make sure that I get the

story before the big sharks who, at this very moment, will be on the plane from Aberdeen.'

Sandy thought Willow would lose her temper at that. Even Jimmy Perez would have put Reg in his place and talked about obstructing the course of justice. But Willow just gave a little laugh. 'I don't play games, Mr Gilbert. And I don't do deals. Now, if that's all, I have work to do and I'll have to ask you to move on. This is a potential crime scene.'

'I didn't say I wouldn't tell you what we talked about.' Reg had a whining voice. He always spoke through his nose, as if he had a cold. 'I'm more than happy to help the police.' He was inquisitive, Sandy thought. He'd come into journalism because he liked to gossip. It would be torture for him to drive away at this point without talking about his meeting with Jerry Markham.

'Then sit with my sergeant in his car and tell him what you know.' Willow was disdainful. 'And if I ever need the support of the *Shetland Times*, I'll be in touch.' Sandy couldn't help smiling at that.

Reg and Sandy sat in the front of the car. It had started to rain properly now, but the inspector seemed unbothered by the weather. She just pulled her hood over the tangled hair and zipped up her jacket. Then, as it began to pour, she and Davy Cooper got into his vehicle. Sandy felt a twinge of jealousy. He wouldn't want her sharing her ideas with Davy instead of him.

'So what did Jerry Markham want from you?' he asked.

Reg Gilbert sniffed. 'Background,' he said. 'It had been a long time since he'd worked here, and his time with the paper was never more than work experience. He needed a local hack's feel for what was going on.'

'Be more specific! Or you can do what the inspector said, and piss off.'

'She's an inspector, is she?' Reg seemed impressed. 'She'd look all right if she tidied herself up. The bodywork's sound enough.'

'What did you talk about over dinner in the Ravenswick Hotel on Thursday night?' Sandy refused to be distracted and kept his voice firm.

'I'm not sure what he was after,' Reg said. 'He was playing things very close to his chest. At first it was all gossip, a chat about friends. I thought he'd lost his edge. Then he let on he was interested in the green industries – the big new wind farm and the tidal-energy project that's planned in the Sound. I said it wasn't like him to be saving the planet, and he just grinned. "That's where the future lies, Reggie and we'll all have to change." I told him I hadn't heard anything interesting about those developments. He asked about a couple of Nimbys who've been making a fuss about the tidal project, but I said there'd be no story for him there. The council's always been supportive in attracting new industry.'

'You'd have pushed for more information, though.' Through the rain-spattered windows Sandy saw a police car arrive and Vicki Hewitt get out of the passenger door. 'You'd have tried to find out what *he'd* heard. You wouldn't want a story like that on your doorstep and not be part of it.'

'Of course I wanted more.' Reg Gilbert sniffed. 'I wanted to know what he was doing here, snooping around on my patch.'

Sandy thought Willow Reeves would have liked to know that too. He felt as if he'd let her down by getting so little out of the interview.

Chapter Nine

Jimmy Perez was counting the hours to Sunday night and Cassie's return. Literally counting the chunks of time, aware of every minute. He hated the empty house and he couldn't settle to anything. When Cassie was around, there were distractions, obligations. Some days she irritated him so that he wanted to scream, but when she was here he couldn't give in to the self-pity that was always on the edge of his mind, waiting to take him over. He'd not fallen asleep until the early hours, but on Saturday morning he still woke at six. Radio Shetland news ran a piece about the dead man in the racing yoal at Aith. Still no identification, which was odd. There weren't many tourists in the islands this early in the season, and Sandy and the team would surely manage to put a name to a local within minutes. Maybe they hadn't passed on the news to the relatives yet, and that was the reason for the secrecy. Jimmy thought perhaps he'd made a mistake not going with Sandy to Aith the night before. That too would have been a distraction. But everything seemed to take so much effort these days. The doctor said it was depression; Perez saw it more as a kind of idleness.

Reg Gilbert phoned him at around midday. Jimmy had made the bed and washed up last night's pots, but he hadn't done much more. The ringing phone shocked him and he looked at it for a couple of seconds before answering.

'Yes.' This was progress of a sort. For the first months after Fran's death he'd just let it ring.

'What do you think of the Markham murder then, Jimmy?' No introduction. No need for one. Reg's nasal Midlands accent was immediately identifiable.

'I'm not at work this weekend. I can't help you.' The words came out as a growl and he was about to replace the phone when a stab of curiosity prevented him. Peter and Maria Markham were friends of a kind. He couldn't find an emotional response to the news. Nothing much moved him any more. But there was an intellectual interest that prompted a question. 'Which of them was killed?'

'It's not either of the parents,' Reg said. 'It's Jerry, the son. If you remember, he went to London, blagged a job on one of the broadsheets.' Reg sounded dismissive. In his often-stated opinion, regional reporters were the heroes of journalism, not the glory-boys from London. 'They've sent in a team from Inverness.'

'Of course,' Perez said sharply. 'They would. That always happens in a murder investigation.' He remembered the excitement of an inquiry, Sandy running around in circles, and the Fiscal watching at a distance for them to make a mistake. The conversations with witnesses and the slow unravelling of the mystery. For an instant he felt regret that he wasn't with the others at Aith, drinking tea from a flask and passing round the chocolate biscuits. But the moment soon passed. He couldn't find the energy, and he didn't want to get involved.

'They've put a woman in charge,' Reg went on.

'Then you're best talking to her.' Perez refused to give in to the nostalgia that made him think of murder as a kind of entertainment. After all that had happened on Fair Isle, that was sick. 'Like I said, I'm not working this weekend.'

'I wonder what the Fiscal will make of a woman heading up the inquiry,' Reg said. It was as if Perez hadn't spoken. 'Our Rhona's always considered herself Queen Bee.'

Perez was going to say that he didn't care what the Fiscal thought; instead he just replaced the receiver.

From his kitchen window he looked down towards the Ravenswick Hotel. A sharp squall came in from the south and rain blew slantwise across the glass. He realized that he felt hungry. The sensation was so unusual – he had to force himself to eat these days – that at first he didn't recognize it. He thought a bowl of home-made soup in the bar of the Ravenswick Hotel wouldn't go amiss. They always baked their own bread there and served it with Shetland butter. Imported butter never tasted as good. His mouth was watering. He decided that he'd walk down. The shower would pass through quite quickly and, who knows, he might fancy a pint or two while he was in the bar.

By the time he'd put on his shoes and his coat the rain had stopped. The sun had broken through the clouds and shone, like theatre spotlights, on the water. He pulled the door shut behind him and began the walk down the bank.

*

Stuart Brodie was on duty behind the desk at reception. 'Peter and Maria say they don't want to speak to anyone,' he said. 'But I'm sure it's okay for you to go up. You'll be here about their boy. Shall I ring through to them and tell them you're in the hotel?'

Perez shook his head.

'I've come for my lunch,' he said. 'I'd not mind a bit of a chat with you, if you have time. Do you get a break?'

'In half an hour.' Brodie glanced across to the grandfather clock in the hall. 'We've been busy. Lots of journalists from the south phoning to make reservations. Seems Jerry was a big man down there. And we were busy enough before.'

'Peter and Maria are keeping the place open during the investigation?' Perez couldn't imagine how that would be. They'd be living in the flat upstairs, knowing that beneath their feet people would be drinking and laughing and speculating about what had happened to their son.

Brodie shrugged. 'They've not told me otherwise, so I just do my job.'

The bar was quiet. The reporters from London hadn't made it here yet and the locals were being tactful and keeping their distance. They wouldn't want to be thought of as prying. The other residents were out at work, except for a couple of pilots still in uniform, drinking coffee. Perez ordered leek-and-tattie soup and a pint of White Wife, which was brewed on Unst. The beer tasted better than he'd imagined it would, and he sipped it as if it was expensive wine. Brodie himself brought the soup. As he came in, the pilots stood up and went out, so they were left with the room to themselves.

'Annie can take over from me now,' Brodie said. 'Or do you want to have your lunch in peace?'

Perez would have preferred that, but he didn't like to say so. He nodded for the man to sit down, buttered a piece of bread and dipped it into the soup. 'Can I buy you a pint?'

'Nah,' Brodie said. 'I'm working this afternoon.'

'When did Jerry Markham arrive?'

'Thursday morning straight from the ferry. He screeched up in that flash car of his and Peter and Maria came down to the dining room to have breakfast with him. The return of the prodigal son. Nothing was too much trouble for him. Chef had a full restaurant and he was none too pleased. Jerry didn't seem himself, though. Quieter somehow. I wondered if he might be ill.'

'Was he a prodigal son?' Perez dipped another bread roll into the soup. He found it strange that the questions came so easily to him.

Brodie shrugged again. He had a good line in expressive shrugs. 'He left under a bit of a cloud,' he said. 'Got one of the chambermaids here pregnant. Not a hanging offence these days, but she was quite an innocent soul. Grew up on Fetlar, to a religious family. She might not have expected him to marry her, but she looked for more support than she got. So did her parents.'

'What was the name of the lass?' Perez had never heard this story. But then he'd been living in his house in Lerwick when it had happened. Fran might have known about it, might even have told him. She'd come up with snippets of gossip when he visited, but he'd had his mind on other things then.

'Evie Watt. She worked here over the summer before she went off to university.'

'Francis's daughter?' Francis Watt was well known in the islands. He did a column in the *Shetland Times* every week about island traditions. He was probably the only man in Shetland to regret the coming of the oil.

'Aye.'

'Did she keep the baby?'

'I think she intended to, but then she had a miscarriage. Maybe it was for the best, eh?'

Perez thought that an outsider, and especially a man, couldn't really say what was for the best when a woman had lost a baby. His ex-wife Sarah had suffered a miscarriage and things had never been the same between them afterwards. She had a brood now with her second husband, a Lowland GP, and they lived in an old farmhouse in the Borders.

'Does Evie still work here?' Perez asked.

Brodie pulled a face. 'What do you think? This is the last place she'd want to spend her time. She'd never know when Jerry would appear from the south to catch up with his folks.'

'She's not still a student? Perez was thinking another pint would go down well, but decided immediately that he'd stick with coffee. He might go into Lerwick later and see if Sandy was back in the police station. He could pass on this information about the girlfriend. 'Her course must have finished years ago. What's she up to now?'

'I don't know.' Brodie seemed uncomfortable. He'd always suffered from acne and the spots seemed more red and livid as the conversation progressed. Perez wondered if the man had fancied Evie Watt himself. 'I saw her in one of the halls at Up Helly Aa, but she was with a gang of friends and we didn't chat. I think she might have moved back. Not to Fetlar, but to Shetland. That was the impression I had.'

'You haven't been in touch with her since?' Perez asked.

Brodie shook his head. 'She was way out of my league,' he said. 'Pretty and smart. No point setting yourself up to be disappointed, is there?'

'Sometimes it's worth taking a chance.' But Perez wasn't sure that was true. He would never take up with another woman.

On his way out of the hotel he decided that he'd call on Peter and Maria after all. Maybe it was the beer giving him a strange sort of confidence. He'd been in their flat a couple of times, invited in after dinner in the restaurant for coffee or a dram. He'd been with Fran on both occasions and had sensed that Peter Markham found her attractive. More than that, that the hotel owner had been obsessed by her. He'd been perfectly civilized and jovial, but he'd seemed almost breathless when he approached her and, even when his wife was talking, his eyes had strayed back to Fran. Perez had teased Fran about it: 'You've got an admirer.' And she'd laughed back. 'He's a very attractive man, Jimmy Perez. And he has much more money than you. You should take care!' The memory of that conversation brought his lover back to life for him for a moment and he was almost grateful.

He asked Brodie to let the Markhams know he was on his way up. 'I just want to give my condolences.'

And Brodie nodded as if he suspected Perez had planned the visit from the beginning.

The door at the top of the stairs was open ready for him, and Peter and Maria were in the room beyond. Because it was at the top of the house there were views all the way along the coast and across the Sound, beyond Raven's Head to Moussa. Briefly Perez's attention was caught by the view. He'd only been in the room in the dark before.

Peter Markham stood up. 'Do you have news for us, Jimmy?'

'I'm not involved in the investigation,' Perez said. 'Not officially. I wanted to say how sorry I am.' He saw that Maria hadn't moved. She'd glanced round when he came into the room, but remained quite still now, in her seat. He thought she'd aged overnight. Perhaps that was because she wasn't wearing make-up. Usually her eyes were lined with black. Fran had said once that she'd like to paint Maria. 'She reminds me of a Flamenco dancer. Experienced and soulful. Don't you think so?' And again they'd laughed together, joking that perhaps Jimmy and Maria's ancestors had come from the same part of Spain. Legend had it that Perez's forebear was a survivor from the Spanish Armada ship *El Gran Grifon*, which had been shipwrecked on Fair Isle. No reason why there couldn't have been other survivors, other relationships between the sailors and local girls.

'Sit down,' Peter said. He moved across the room so that he was blocking Perez's exit. He needed company and conversation and didn't want the visitor to escape too quickly. 'I'll make some coffee. You will have coffee with us, Jimmy?'

Perez nodded and said that he would. He sat with his back to the window so that he wouldn't be distracted by the view, by all that space.

'Would you mind if I asked some questions?' This was directed at Maria. Peter could still hear, but he was in the small kitchen that led off the living room, the door between them wide open.

She looked up. 'No,' she said. 'Ask away.' Showing that she couldn't care about anything now. Perez knew just how she felt.

'Is there anyone who might have wanted to hurt Jerry?'

'Of course not. Why would they?'

'No jilted girlfriends then?' Perez kept his voice light.

'He's talking about Evie.' Peter shouted from the kitchen before his wife could reply. 'That's what you're thinking, isn't it, Jimmy?'

'I heard she was pregnant and her family was none too happy.'

'They were barbarians.' Maria's voice sounded very loud suddenly. 'They came here and made a scene. The father foaming at the mouth like a rabid beast. As if it was solely Jerry's responsibility, as if the girl had nothing at all to do with it. But Evie was always the light of the man's life.'

'That was years ago.' Peter Markham came through with a tray of coffee. He set it on a low table. 'Evie went away to university and Jerry got his job in London. Her parents calmed down. I saw Francis Watt in Lerwick just last week and he was almost civil.'

'She lost the baby,' Perez said.

'Yes, we heard about that.' Peter stooped over the

table to pour coffee, and Perez couldn't tell what he thought about missing out on the chance to be a grandfather. 'Not directly from Evie, but through other people, as one does in Shetland. Word always gets out.'

'She didn't tell Jerry that she'd had a miscarriage?' Perez thought it was odd that the news hadn't come through their son.

'I don't think they were communicating much at that stage. She had been very much in love with him, you know. She was young and it hurt her when things didn't turn out as she'd hoped.'

'She was stupid,' Maria said. 'She should have realized that Jerry would want someone more interesting than her for a long-term relationship. She'd spent all her life on Fetlar. What would he see in her?'

'Oh.' Peter stroked the back of his wife's hand, an attempt perhaps to calm her, to prevent her speaking of the girl so unkindly. 'She was a pretty little thing. I could definitely see the attraction. But she could have had nothing to do with Jerry's death. She'd moved on. Francis told me that she's about to be married. Her husband-to-be is a seaman, older than her. He's a pilot at Sullom Voe. A good man, according to Francis.'

'Jerry had moved on too,' Maria said. 'He was doing brilliantly in London, Jimmy. His editor said he was the best reporter she'd ever worked with.'

Perez wondered if that was true. 'Where was Jerry yesterday?' he asked.

'I told your sergeant that. He was at the oil terminal, chasing some big story.'

'And did you know the name of Evie's fiancé?' Perez supposed it was a coincidence, Jerry Markham heading off to Sullom Voe, which was close to where the girl's new man worked, but it would have to be checked.

'He's called Henderson,' Markham said. 'John Henderson.'

Perez made his apologies for disturbing them and went, leaving his coffee untouched. The other questions could wait. It wasn't his case, after all. Halfway up the bank towards his house he paused and looked out to the sea. He had reasonable phone reception in this spot. A hundred yards on he'd lose it again. He called Sandy, his hands trembling a little as he hit the buttons. He asked what they'd planned for the afternoon, then wondered if he might join Sandy and the inspector from Inverness at the terminal, just to sit in on interviews. If he wouldn't be in the way.

Chapter Ten

When Sandy told her that Jimmy Perez would join them at the oil terminal at Sullom Voe, Willow wasn't sure what she made of it. She supposed she should be pleased that Perez was well enough to be part of the investigation. He'd been at this business for longer than she had and she could do with his local knowledge. Sandy was willing, but not sufficiently confident or skilled to make the intellectual leap that would bring a case to a conclusion. However, her experience was that male officers took over the decision-making and when that happened she became resentful, ending up sounding either shrill or defensive. A pre-menstrual harpy. And this was her first investigation as SIO. She didn't particularly want to share the glory.

The rain showers had blown away altogether now, though there was still a breeze. They took the road that ran north-east through the hills towards Sullom Voe.

'What's he like then, this Jimmy Perez?' she asked.

A sheep wandered onto the road and Sandy didn't answer for a moment. At last he said, 'He's a good man.' Another pause. 'A fine detective.'

That didn't seem much of an answer, but it was

clear it was the only one she was likely to get. They came upon the oil terminal quite suddenly. It was hidden by the peat bog until the road came round the hill, and the tanks and the power station looked alien there. It was like a set from an old science-fiction movie. She thought tourists could spend a fortnight in Shetland and have no sight or knowledge of the oil that had changed the islands so profoundly.

They stopped at the main gate. A security guard came to the car. 'You can't go in. You need clearance to get any further.'

'We have clearance.' Sandy had to explain who they were and what they were doing there. 'I spoke to your press officer this morning.'

The gate swung open and the concrete barrier beyond sank into the ground to allow the car through. 'Wait here. Andy will come for you.' The guard spoke through the car window. 'I heard about the murder on the radio.' He was a big man. Ex-services, Willow guessed. He seemed comfortable in the uniform.

'Were you on duty yesterday?'

He seemed surprised that she was the one asking the questions, speaking across Sandy through the open car window, but he answered anyway. 'I was on a late. Two till ten.'

'You'll have seen Jerry Markham here then? He visited the terminal in the afternoon.'

'I signed him in and then I signed him out again.' The man looked at her sharply. 'He was alive when he drove his fancy car out of that gate.'

'What time would that have been?'

'Four, four-thirty.'

'And who was he here to see?' Willow sensed the

man's antagonism, but couldn't work out why he was so hostile. He must realize that they'd have to ask questions about a suspicious death. She felt herself grow tense in response, but made an effort to keep her voice pleasant. No point losing it.

'Andy Belshaw, the press officer. I was expecting Markham. Andy had told me he was likely to turn up.' The guard shifted his feet. A raven croaked above their heads. 'I sent him along to the office. You can ask Andy what it was all about.' It was clear he wanted to get rid of them. Maybe he just didn't like the police. Willow was about to get out of the car so that they could continue the conversation properly when another vehicle came down the road behind them. It pulled into a space on the other side of the fence and a dark man got out and walked towards them.

'That's Jimmy Perez,' Sandy said. He shouted to the guard, 'You can let him in. He's with us.' Then he bounded out of the car. Willow followed more slowly. She thought Perez's appearance suited his name; he was dark-haired and dark-eyed and his skin was olive. She thought he'd pass unnoticed in southern Spain, but he stood out here. She wondered how he'd got on at school. She knew what it was like to be different in a small community. Sandy was bouncing around him, but Perez took no notice and walked towards her, his hand outstretched.

'You'll be the inspector from Inverness,' he said. 'You're very welcome.' And he smiled as if it took a great effort. 'You don't mind if I sit in? I'm supposed to be easing myself back gently. You'll have heard about that. Sandy will have told you.'

She nodded.

'Should we get on?' he said. She realized that she was staring at him and that they were all expecting her to speak.

She pulled herself together and nodded again. 'Of course.'

Everything about Belshaw was big: his hands, his head, his teeth, his voice. He was another incomer from England. Willow wondered how that worked. Did all these folk from the south lead an ex-pat existence, socializing only with each other? She had a brief image of colonial Africa, the white men with their exclusive clubs and their cocktail parties and their delicate wives. But surely, she thought, Shetland could be nothing like that.

Belshaw was welcoming. He offered them tea and sent his assistant off to make it. All the time there was that beam with the big white teeth, the jovial voice that sounded as if he was laughing, even when he was saying how sorry he was about Jerry Markham. 'He was a good journalist,' he said. 'One of the best of his generation.'

Belshaw's office was in a concrete block that looked as if it had been put up in a hurry and still had a temporary air. Out of the window a view of bare hillside and sheep. Perez had tucked himself into a corner and took no part in the conversation. He sat very still and Willow wondered if he'd always been like that or if he'd become half-frozen after the death of his lover. Had guilt and self-pity chilled him and made him sluggish? Was it a weird form of hibernation?

'You knew Jerry Markham?' Willow asked. 'Before he came here yesterday, I mean.'

'I've lived in Shetland for fifteen years,' Belshaw said. 'I came here on temporary contract straight out of university, an admin post in the press office. But I got hooked. Married a local girl. I knew Jerry when he worked at the *Shetland Times*.'

'You were friends?'

'He was younger than me, but we had a few beers together. You had to be careful, though. He was always after a story. No off-the-record with Jerry.'

'Did Jerry phone up to make an appointment?' Willow asked. 'Or turn up on the off-chance that you'd be free to see him?'

'Peter fixed it up,' Belshaw said. 'His father.'

'Why would he do that?' Willow asked. She saw that another squall had blown up and that the clouds had blocked out the view of the hill. Soon there'd be more rain. Weather moved through here as quickly as it did in the Uists. 'Why didn't Jerry phone you himself?'

Belshaw shrugged. 'Maybe he was on his way north. No phone reception on the ferry.'

Willow didn't push it, but stored the detail away. 'What did he want?' she asked. 'What had brought him all the way up to Shetland to talk to you?'

'Oh, it wasn't like that.' Belshaw smiled his toothy grin. 'He was coming up to visit his folks anyway and thought he might do a piece about the gas. A background article on the islands' contribution to energy needs. He was going to check out the wind farms too, and the plans to export electricity to the mainland. The new gas plant, just next door to us here. And he mentioned tidal power. There's talk about setting up a pilot project for that. All small-scale compared to us, of course. Perhaps his story was comparing renewables with traditional energy sources.'

'I see.' But Willow thought that wasn't the impression Jerry had given his parents. According to Sandy, he was in Shetland following up a lead on a big story. Of course Sandy might have got that wrong. He was a man who might get the wrong end of the stick. Perez shifted in his chair and she wondered if he had a question to ask. She looked over to him, but he gave an almost imperceptible shake of his head and another reluctant smile.

'I took him round the plant,' Belshaw said. 'Gave him the guided tour, showed him the safety measures in place for the oil. He was interested in the exercises – we practise for the possibility of a spill.'

'Did he speak to anyone else while he was here?' Willow asked. There was a sudden violent shower, rain whipping against the office window, the noise on the flat roof so loud that she had to raise her voice for Belshaw to hear.

'I don't think so. Maybe he had a quick word with someone he recognized from the old days.' Belshaw paused. 'He made a phone call. Apologized, but said it was important.'

'No idea who he was speaking to?'

Belshaw grinned again. 'None at all. He walked away, so I couldn't hear.'

Willow thought she needed to track down Markham's phone service provider and trace the calls.

Perez stirred again in his seat and this time he did ask a tentative question, looking to Willow for permission first. 'Do you know if Markham planned to go straight home? I wondered if he might talk to the harbour master or any of the pilots.'

Belshaw shook his head. 'I wouldn't know anything about that. They operate out of their own base next to Scatsta Airport.' He paused. 'I had the sense that there was something else he wanted from me. The tour I gave him was routine, after all, and he'd worked long enough in Shetland to know that stuff already. Perhaps he was hoping I'd know more about the gas and the renewables, but that's quite outside my area of expertise.'

Outside they ran through the rain to their cars. 'We'll meet back at the station, shall we?' She shouted the invitation to Jimmy Perez. He'd made no comment at all about what he'd intended to do next. He hesitated for a moment and then nodded.

'I'll follow you back,' he said. 'And I'll see you there.'

Chapter Eleven

Standing outside the police station, Perez felt a moment of panic. Across the road was the town hall, Scottish Baronial, with its impressive entrance and its turrets, and down the hill was the play park where they set fire to the Viking galley at the Up Helly Aa fire-festival. This place was as familiar as home to him. Usually he'd walk into the station without thinking about it. Only last week he'd been inside, chatted to the officer on duty at the desk, gone through to his old office with its view of the town. But now, with Sandy and the lanky woman with the wild hair staring at him, it seemed an impossible task to push open the door. He imagined the smell of the rooms inside, the colour of the gloss paint on the walls, and was overcome with an irrational terror. Fran's killer had sat inside that building and had justified his violence with a string of meaningless words. The memory of the encounter came back occasionally to disturb Perez and it was with him now, paralysing him and preventing him from moving, the anxiety and the rage making him feel physically ill. He could almost convince himself that he was having a heart attack.

'Why don't you come to my place?' he said quickly. 'Not the house in Ravenswick, but my old place down by the water. I was there only a few days ago to air it. There'll be coffee and tea. Beer, if you fancy it. We can talk there without interruption. You can come down in my car and I'll drop you back.' He knew he was talking too much, but felt he'd be better on his own territory.

'Why not?' Sandy said, as if it was the most natural offer in the world.

The woman said nothing, but she followed.

The house was tall and narrow and stood with its feet in the water. Once boats had moored outside to unload their goods. The rooms were filled with a reflected, liquid light.

'What a lovely place!' Willow walked ahead of him and looked around. She stopped just inside the door and he nearly knocked into her. The long hair brushed across his face and he smelled the shampoo she'd used that morning. Lemon. Perez stepped back, shocked because he wanted to reach out to touch her, to run a hand over the curve of her shoulder, and he'd thought he'd never want to touch a woman again. Furious again – this time at himself.

He sat them in the living room and went to the tiny kitchen to make coffee. There was a packet of biscuits at the back of the cupboard and he ripped it open and tipped them onto a plate. Chocolate digestives, Cassie's favourites. He pulled a can of lager from the fridge for Sandy. He heard the murmur of conversation, but made no attempt to listen. The flash of curiosity he'd felt earlier that day about the Jerry Markham murder had long gone. He wondered why he'd bothered to get involved, to walk down the hill to the Ravenswick Hotel to talk to Peter and Maria.

When he carried in the tray, Willow was still standing at the window, looking over the Sound to Bressay. She took the mug that he handed her and sat, straight-backed, on the floor. Sandy pulled open the beer and took a handful of biscuits.

'So what have we got?' Willow said. She looked at them, and Perez thought they were an odd team for her to be lumbered with. It didn't seem fair when it was her first major case. An emotional cripple who was likely to burst into tears or lash out at any opportunity, and a young Whalsayman who hadn't really had the chance to grow up. Suddenly he felt sorry for her and made an effort to become engaged.

'Did you hear that Markham left Shetland under a bit of a cloud?' Perez said. He described what he knew of Jerry's relationship with Evie Watt.

'I've seen her about,' Sandy said. 'She didn't go into bars much. You'd have her down as a quiet, studious sort of girl. Her father's always going on about the old ways in his column, and she seemed kind of old-fashioned to me too. Religious.'

'So she's not one for partying then?' Perez asked. Sandy liked girls who were up for a party.

'No,' Sandy said. 'Not at all.'

'But she fell for Jerry Markham.' Willow looked up. 'And was too naive to stop herself getting pregnant. Or perhaps that was her strategy. She thought it would be a way of holding on to him, the glamorous young journalist. Only he ran away.'

'She lost the baby soon after,' Perez said. 'It looks as if she's graduated and is working in Shetland. It might be worth tracking her down. She'd provide an insight into the man, even if she's an unlikely suspect.'

'Will you do that, Jimmy? She's more likely to talk to you than to an outsider.'

Perez thought this inspector from the Western Isles was pleased to find him something to do, something safe and easy to build his confidence. He didn't resent it. For once it was a relief to follow orders instead of give them. If he were heading up this team he'd do exactly the same thing. 'Sure,' he said. The next day was Sunday. He wondered if Evie was still religious, if she'd be at the kirk. Or had she lost that comfort while she was south at the university?

'We need to check Markham's phone.' Willow was talking again. She seemed quite comfortable on the floor, one leg stretched in front of her, the other bent. 'The Markhams will have the number and we can get the details from the service provider. The phone wasn't with the rest of his belongings.'

'Should I try Vicki Hewitt?' Sandy took another biscuit and held it carefully at the edge so that he didn't get melted chocolate on his fingers. 'She should be back from working the crime scene at the museum by now.'

'It can wait until tomorrow.'

Again Perez thought that was just the approach he'd take. No point rushing. It was more important to get a feel for a new place. They sat for a moment in silence. Outside the tide was falling and they could hear the water sucking at the shingle on the beach.

'This is delicate,' Willow said. 'I was wondering about the Fiscal . . .'

Perez looked up in surprise.

'What about her?'

'I think she's involved. Knows something. Not that

she's the killer – I can't see her carrying a bleeding body into a boat. Blood just wouldn't look good with cashmere. But there's something she's not telling us.' She looked across Sandy at Perez. They could have been parents discussing adult matters and ignoring the child in the room. 'Do you think I'm being stupid? Imagining things?'

Perez didn't answer directly. 'She's a very private woman,' he said carefully. 'And you can imagine how that goes down here. We love to stick our noses into other folk's business. I can see how she'd feel very awkward, an inquiry coming that close to home.'

'Was it really a coincidence?' Willow asked. 'The body being found in the yoal just outside her house. Why didn't the murderer leave Markham where he was killed? Rowing is the only activity Rhona Laing shares with the community. People would know she'd keep an eye on the boat, that she'd most likely be the person to find the corpse.'

'You think it was a kind of message?' Perez wasn't sure what he made of that. He'd never been one for conspiracy theories and weird signals. But if he'd considered weird theories and ideas last October in Fair Isle, Fran might still be alive. Now, maybe, he should be a bit more open-minded.

'Probably not!' Willow grinned at him. 'You think I'm being daft, don't you?'

'I think it wouldn't do any harm to check if there's ever been a connection between Markham and the Fiscal. We'd do the same thing for any other witness. She might have come across him when she was a lawyer in Edinburgh. She's only been here for a few years.'

'I'll get one of my team in Inverness to do the digging,' Willow said. 'There's a lad who's a wizard at that kind of thing. Sit him in front of a screen all day and he's happy.' She got to her feet. It took one supple movement, not a scramble. Perez thought if she weren't so tall, she could be a dancer or a gymnast. 'We should get back to the station and make some calls. I need to find out if anyone was in the museum yesterday afternoon. They might have seen the car being dropped off there. I mean it was daylight and it was an unusual vehicle. Maybe you could take that on, Sandy? Again it's more a job for a local.'

Sandy nodded. He seemed half-asleep in his chair. 'No problem. I'll get on to it first thing. I'm surprised we haven't heard more about the car already. Folk will know that we'd be interested.'

'From what you've told me, that's the odd thing about this case.' It came to Perez that this was astonishing. Different from any other investigation he'd ever known. 'Nobody saw anything. Not the car turning up at Vatnagarth or the body being put in the yoal. It's as if the killer was invisible.' He looked at them to make sure they understood. 'You know what it's like here. You think that Shetland's a big and empty place, but cut a peat bank five miles from the road and someone will have seen you do it. This murderer is clever. Or very lucky.'

'There was a thick fog in North Mainland,' Sandy said. 'The sort of fog you'd lose your way in. That's why nothing was seen.'

'Lucky then,' Perez said. But he wasn't sure he believed in that sort of luck after all.

Willow said they'd make their own way back to the

station. 'The exercise will do us good, and it'll help me get a feel for the place. I don't really understand a street map until I've walked it.'

When they'd gone the house seemed very quiet. Perez took the mugs into the kitchen and boiled a kettle so there was hot water to wash them up. He opened the window in the living room to let some air into the place. It soon smelled damp when it wasn't lived in. Then he ran over in his mind what Willow had said about the Fiscal. Rhona Laing wasn't an easy woman, he had to admit that. But surely she was honest. He'd have bet his last pound on her integrity. It was two strong women marking out their territory, he thought. That was what was going on there.

Driving back to Ravenswick, he realized that the wind had dropped. He stopped in the supermarket on the edge of town to buy food, and the surface of Clickimin Loch was still. His new hunger felt like a betrayal, but he found that he was ravenous again and stocked up on bread, fruit and eggs, plus a big vacuum packet of ground coffee. Then he remembered that Cassie would be home the next afternoon and he went round the shelves again for treats for her. Healthy treats of which Fran would have approved. Duncan, her father, always filled her with junk when she was staying at the Haa. He didn't want to care for her full-time, but bought her affection with sweets and presents when he did see her.

At home the light on his phone was flashing to show that he had a message. It was from Peter Markham, asking if there was any news on the investigation. 'Please get in touch if you hear anything.'

Perez played the message a couple of times, disturbed by the tone and the edge of desperation in the voice. Of course Peter would want to know what had happened to his son. But why did he sound quite so scared?

Chapter Twelve

Sandy walked Willow Reeves to her hotel before he went home to his flat. It was already dark and the public bar was noisy. They had to walk past the open door to get to reception and he felt he should apologize for the loud men, swearing and joking, out drinking on a Saturday night, but she seemed unbothered. The hotel Morag had picked was right on the water, not far from Perez's house. From the bedrooms it was sometimes possible to see killer whales in the Sound. Sandy told her that, aware again that he sounded like a tour leader.

'Sleep well,' he said. He'd waited until she'd checked in. He'd been brought up to be well mannered where women were concerned. Part of him still found it a little strange that a woman should head up the Serious Crime Squad or be Procurator Fiscal. He didn't think it was wrong, but it would take him a while to get used to it.

'No worries about that,' she said. 'I always sleep well.' And she disappeared up the dark staircase, her heavy holdall on her shoulder. He'd offered to carry it in to the hotel for her, but she'd stared at him as if he were mad.

*

The next morning she was in the police station before he was. She'd tied back her hair, but it still looked untidy and she was wearing the same shapeless jumper. She looked up from the desk they'd found for her in the small office that Perez had once used. A mug full of something that smelled herbal and looked like piss stood on her desk.

'I've tracked down Markham's mobile-phone provider,' she said. 'I got his number from his parents. There seems to be some problem – maybe he recently got a new number – but they're trying to find it for me. It's too early for news from Aberdeen on the post-mortem.'

'I'm going to head out to Vatnagarth,' Sandy said. 'I checked the council website and the museum's open this morning.' He always preferred to be out of the office. Here, he had the sense that people were looking over his shoulder, judging his work.

'Sure,' Willow said. 'Whatever you think.' Her attention had already been caught again by the screen in front of her.

In the copse of sycamores there seemed to be birds everywhere and the sun was bright as he approached the museum. A people-carrier was parked outside, but Markham's car had been removed. It would be taken south to Aberdeen on the ferry. The crime-scene tape had disappeared too and there was no sign that the police had ever been interested in the place.

There was smoke coming out of the chimney, so everything smelled of peat. The door was open and he walked into the tiny space that separated the but-end of the house from the ben. To his left another door led into a living room. The window was so small and the walls were so thick that there was very little light. He struggled to make out if anyone was there. Then he saw a large woman wearing a skirt that looked like sackcloth and a knitted jacket. The sort of clothes he'd seen in photos in his grandmother's house, so he wasn't sure for a moment if she was real or a kind of manikin. She was sitting on a Shetland chair close to the range. He felt that he was stepping back in time, into one of his grandmother's photos. Then the woman moved; she was feeding carded fleece into a spinning wheel.

'Welcome,' the woman said. 'Come in.' He had the sense that he'd seen her before, very recently, but he couldn't quite remember where. 'Look around at whatever you like and give me a shout if you have any questions. There's a booklet on the table.'

'I'm not a tourist.' He was offended. 'I'm investigating Jerry Markham's murder. His car was found parked outside the museum yesterday.'

She paused in her spinning and set down the fleece. 'I heard. What a dreadful thing!'

'And you are?'

'Jennifer Belshaw. Jen.'

Then he remembered where he'd seen her. She'd been one of the women in the hennie bus on Friday night. They'd been talking about her in the bar in Voe when he and Willow had stopped there for lunch the day before. The name rang another bell. 'Any relation of Andy Belshaw?'

'Aye,' she said. 'He's my husband. Why?'

Jerry Markham visited him at Sullom Voe just before he was killed.'

'Well, I've never met Mr Markham,' she said frostily. 'As far as I'm aware. I certainly had nothing to do with his death.'

'But his car was found outside the place where you work.'

She laughed. 'I don't work here. I'm a volunteer. I do this for fun. And I'm only in this morning because my friend was delayed. I'll be away to cook Sunday lunch for my family once she turns up.'

'Would anyone have been here on Friday evening?' He thought it was a long shot. He could think of more exciting places to be on a Friday night than a damp croft-house miles from anywhere.

'Yes,' she said. 'There were people here all day. We hire out the barn to community groups. In the morning a readers' group, in the late afternoon a tea dance for the over-60s' club.' She looked up at him. 'I play the fiddle, and I was here for that. Then in the evening a meeting to discuss the new tidal-energy scheme at Hvidahus.'

'You weren't here for the meeting?'

'No,' she said. 'Not my kind of thing. Besides, it was my friend's hennie. I couldn't miss that.'

'What about your husband?'

She laughed again. 'No way! He works in Sullom and sees renewable energy as a sort of witchcraft. He was in Brae at the sports centre. He runs a kids' football team.' She'd started spinning again and seemed completely relaxed.

'Can you give me contact details for the tidal-energy group?'

'Sure,' she said. 'Talk to Joe Sinclair and he'll tell you who was there.' She jotted down a number on a scrap of paper.

Returning to his car, he felt he'd conducted the interview poorly and that when she'd started laughing, she'd been laughing at him.

Everyone in Shetland knew Joe Sinclair. He was born and bred a Shetlander, but had gone to sea and worked his way up to being master of a giant container ship, sailing out of Singapore. Then he'd come home and for the last ten years he'd been harbour master at Sullom Voe. Sinclair had fingers in many pies and friends in high places. Sandy phoned him at home. One of his daughters answered, and when he came to the phone Sinclair sounded rested and relaxed. A man in late middle age enjoying a weekend with his family.

'I wasn't at Vatnagarth,' he said. 'I'm involved with Power of Water, on the steering group, but that would have been the opposition meeting last night and they'd certainly not have invited me along.' He gave a little chuckle.

'The opposition?' Sandy was already out of his depth.

'A small band of busybodies. They think we'll ruin the environment around Hvidahus by having a sub-station there to collect the power. Most of them are incomers, though Francis Watt stirs them up from time to time with his talk of corruption and conspiracies. You'll have seen his column in the *Shetland Times.*' In the background Sandy could hear Sinclair's teenage daughters laughing.

'Who would have been at the meeting on Friday?'

'A guy called Mark Walsh would have set it up. He worked as an accountant for some multinational in the south before taking early retirement and heading here for the good life. They bought the big house in Hvidahus and he sees the tidal-energy scheme as a threat to his investment. The wife's pleasant enough, but there's nothing Walsh likes better than causing mischief. I'm not sure that the good life suits him after all.'

Mark and Sue Walsh lived in a whitewashed house at the end of a track right by the pier at Hvidahus. It seemed to Sandy to be very grand. There were pictures on the walls and books everywhere and the garden was landscaped with flowers. The couple welcomed him into the kitchen, as if they didn't get many visitors and were pleased to see him. The woman chatted while the husband made coffee. They'd visited Shetland on holiday since they were students and had decided to move north when her husband took early retirement. They'd fallen in love with the house and its views as soon as they'd seen it. It was too big for them, but they'd decided it would make a classy B&B. This would be their first season as a business and already they were fully booked for July and August. She smiled. 'My husband doesn't really do retirement.'

Sandy drank the coffee, which was a bit strong for his taste.

'I understand that you were at Vatnagarth on Friday evening. A meeting?'

'The Save Hvidahus Action Group,' Mark Walsh

said. 'We moved to Shetland because it's so unspoilt. The last wilderness in the UK. Of course we believe in green energy, but not at the expense of the natural environment. Look at the dreadful new wind farm! It's time to call a halt to these major developments.'

Sandy didn't ask Walsh to explain further. He thought anything that would provide Shetland with cheaper fuel would be a good thing. 'Did either of you see a red Alfa Romeo in the car park when you left?'

'No, and we would certainly have noticed. There were only six of us and the place was empty when we left.'

'What time was that?' Sandy stirred more sugar into his coffee.

'Early. About eight o'clock. There didn't seem much point continuing, when Jerry Markham didn't turn up.' Walsh looked up. 'I was furious at the time, but of course I realize now that he was dead.'

'You were expecting Jerry Markham to be at your meeting?' Sandy tried not to sound too surprised.

'Of course. I thought that was why you were here this morning.' Walsh continued talking very slowly, as if to a small child or a foreigner. Sandy, who had already taken an intense dislike to the man, felt like hitting him. 'I wrote to Markham, suggesting that this was a story worth investigating. As he was a Shetlander. He said he was planning to visit his parents anyway, so he'd come along to the meeting. Of course he didn't show.'

'I saw Jerry Markham on Friday,' Sue Walsh interrupted. 'At about eleven in the morning.' She looked at her husband. 'You'd looked him up on the Internet, so I recognized him from his photo.'

'You didn't tell me you'd seen him.' Mark sounded affronted.

'No? It must have slipped my mind.'

'Where did you see Markham?' Sandy sensed the beginning of an argument.

'In the coffee shop of the Bonhoga Gallery. We'd like original Shetland art in the guest bedrooms and there was an exhibition of student work. I thought I might pick up one or two pieces cheaply.'

Sandy thought about that. The Bonhoga Gallery was in Weisdale on the west side of the island. What had Markham been doing there?

'He was with someone,' Sue went on. 'The place was quiet. The sun appeared briefly and I took my coffee to one of the tables outside, so I couldn't hear what they were saying. But it looked as if they were having an argument. Or if not an argument, then a disagreement.'

'Can you describe his companion?' Sandy asked.

'It was a woman. Slim. Well dressed. I'd guess she was middle-aged, but she had her back to me, so I couldn't see her face.'

'A local?'

'I didn't hear her speak.' Sue stood up and stared out of the window.

'Would you know her if I showed you a photo?'

'I don't think I would. As I said, I only saw her from behind.'

Sandy called into the Bonhoga Gallery on his way to Lerwick. It was a bit of a detour, but a pretty drive and he could get a bowl of soup and a sandwich there. The coffee shop was busier than the exhibition space above and he had to wait in a queue. A toddler in a high chair was screaming, so it was hard to think straight. Two lasses were serving. He thought he might have seen them about, but they were too young for them to be in his circle of friends. Then the family with the noisy child left and there was space for him to sit down. The soup was thick and good, and by the time he'd finished his meal and ordered a pot of tea the place was quieter.

He walked up to the counter. 'Were you here on Friday?'

But it turned out that the girls were still at school and only worked there at weekends. 'It's Brian here during the week,' one said. 'He runs the place and he does all the baking on Friday.'

Sandy nodded. He knew Brian and he'd catch up with him later.

Chapter Thirteen

The first regatta of the season was at St Ninian's Isle. They'd borrowed the yoal from the Weisdale team because their boat had been taken away for forensic examination. Rhona Laing wasn't sure where it would be now, or even if it was still in Shetland. She imagined scientists at the university at Aberdeen examining it, scraping tiny pieces of wood from the seats where Jerry Markham's body had lain. But she didn't like to ask too many questions about this investigation. She was already involved because she'd found the dead man. Now, she saw, it was best to keep a professional distance.

It was fine rowing weather, without too much of a breeze to cause a swell on the water. Later in the season they'd pick up a good speed, but today they wouldn't have the rhythm, the instinctive sense of pulling together that came after months of practice. It was mild for spring and there was no sign of rain. Down on the beach someone had already got a barbecue going and there was the smell of charcoal and charred meat. Cans of lager appeared from open car boots. Children were running along the tideline. St Ninian's was the view that appeared on all the tourist postcards. Not a real island at all, but a geological oddity, a tombolo, attached to Shetland mainland by a spit of sand. The sand was white and fine and the water very clear and blue. An image of paradise for the visitors.

A hoard of Pictish treasure had been found there and, though the originals were in Edinburgh, replicas were on show at the museum in Lerwick. Occasionally Rhona went to look at the brooches, the feasting bowls and the ornamental weapons, when she was in the museum for lunch and found herself lusting after the originals with an intensity that took her breath away. She longed to drink wine from the bowl and to feel the old silver against her lips, to pin a jewelled brooch onto a plain black dress and know that it had last been worn hundreds of years before.

Liz, the crofter from Bixter, had towed the yoal and the trailer behind her old Land Rover. It had been launched earlier and tied to a temporary pontoon. The team stood looking at it. A different boat. How would they cope with that? All around the talk was of the murder. 'Fancy you finding the body!' Liz said. 'What chance would there be of that? A strange kind of coincidence.'

The Fiscal was about to protest that of course it was a coincidence, what else could it be? She felt suddenly scared and flushed. But Liz continued before she could speak. 'I mean, you're the Procurator Fiscal. It's your job to supervise a murder investigation. It's like someone's saying, "Here's the body, get on with the job."'

And Rhona laughed at the idea with the others, and rolled up her jeans ready for the start. Theirs was the last race of the day. In the yoal she pulled on her gloves and started to row. She loved the sensation of skimming over the water, losing herself in the task of rowing and the strange clarity of the light. No space for thought. That smell of salt and tar and damp wood. They finished halfway down the field. If it had been any other race, Rhona would have been disappointed by that, but today it seemed unimportant. It had been enough to escape her anxieties for a while. The other competitors commiserated. It was hardly surprising, they said, when the team had to get used to a borrowed yoal. The Aith vets had been cheered across the finishing line by a sympathetic crowd.

Rhona had helped the others load the boat onto the trailer and was about to drive home when she saw the detective from Inverness among the crowd. The inspector had bought a veggie-burger from the barbecue and was drinking black tea from a paper cup. She could have been a tourist come to watch a local event, or a relative up from the south. Relaxed and informal, she fitted in.

She's dangerous, the Fiscal thought suddenly. *That woman could ruin my life here.* Rhona left the rest of the team and walked over the sand to Willow. Her feet were still bare and sandy from pulling the yoal out of the water, and her clothes were damp from the splashes from the oars. She felt at a disadvantage.

'Are you here to see me, Inspector?'

'I called at your house.' Willow threw a scrap of bannock to a herring gull. 'Your neighbour told me you'd be here. The first race of the season.'

'Would it not have waited until tomorrow in the office? Or is there some development in the investigation so urgent that you think I should know at once.'

Rhona was pleased that she kept her voice professional, but not hostile.

'This isn't a matter for you as Fiscal.' The detective tucked a loose strand of hair behind her ear. 'Could we talk somewhere more private?'

'Not here,' Rhona said sharply. 'Not like this. I'm cold and I need to shower and change. You can come back to my house later.'

'No need for that,' Willow said easily. 'Let me just walk up to the cars with you and we can chat there. I'm sure it's something that can be cleared up in a matter of minutes.'

It was impossible for Rhona to refuse, so she dusted the sand from her feet and put on her shoes, pulled on a sweater and followed Willow up to the car park. They sat in Willow's hire car. Rhona thought it would be unbearable to have the inspector in her own vehicle. It would be like spilling milk on the floor; you'd never get rid of the taint. Down on the beach people were clearing up, collecting stray bits of rubbish in black sacks. The sun was already low and they threw long shadows.

'This really isn't very convenient, Inspector. I have a busy day tomorrow and I'd like to get home.' The tone she was after was brisk and businesslike, but she suspected that there was an undernote of anxiety and that the detective would have picked up on it.

'We've discovered a little more about Jerry Markham's whereabouts on the day of his death.' Willow stretched suddenly and her body seemed to fill the small and tinny hire car.

'Yes?' The Fiscal's curiosity was genuine enough.

'He had a meeting with the press officer in Sullom

Voe in the afternoon. He claimed that he was researching a piece on new energies, on the gas that's being
brought ashore at the terminal. But also wave and
wind power. Shetland as the powerhouse of the UK.'

'I suppose that makes sense,' Rhona said. 'There's
been a lot of interest in the development of the technologies. The islands are full of the energy-company
people. It seems almost impossible to get a hotel room
at the moment.'

She might not have spoken. Willow continued.
'Markham was seen earlier that day at around eleven
a.m. in the art gallery at Weisdale.'

'The Bonhoga,' the Fiscal said.

Willow turned to her. 'You know it?'

'Of course I know it! Everyone in Shetland knows
it. They might not like the art, but they go for the
good coffee and the home baking.'

'Did you fancy coffee and cakes on Friday morning?'

The question was sudden and for a moment Rhona
was thrown. 'Of course not. I was working. Why would
I drive from Lerwick in the middle of a working day?'

'To meet Jerry Markham perhaps.'

There was a moment of silence. By now the car
park looking down at the beach was deserted. The
bonfire on the sand was still smoking, but nobody was
there.

'I'm sorry. What are you suggesting?' Occasionally,
when she was a practising lawyer in Edinburgh, her
reputation had been called into question in court.
She'd used the same tone of incredulous outrage then.

'We have a description of the woman Markham
met,' Willow said. 'Middle-aged, well groomed, slim.'

'That could apply to a thousand women in the islands.'

'Perhaps,' the inspector said, though it was clear from her voice that she doubted it. 'But not to a thousand women linked to our investigation.'

She leaned forward and Rhona could see the earnest face, the prematurely lined eyes. Even as she was considering her answer, the Fiscal thought that Willow Reeves clearly never used moisturizer.

'You do see why I had to ask you?' Willow went on. 'If I ignored that sort of connection I'd be failing in my duty as an investigating officer. I can't be seen to be giving you preferential treatment.'

For a moment Rhona was taken in by the gentle voice. Perhaps, after all, Willow Reeves was just going through the motions. But it came to her again that this woman was dangerous.

'I didn't leave my office on Friday morning,' she said.

'And other people will have been around. They'll confirm that. So now I've asked my questions and I can look elsewhere.' Willow nodded in approval. Rhona hesitated. The woman's words hadn't been phrased as a question, but clearly an answer was expected. 'My assistant took a day's leave on Friday,' she said. 'I had a meeting at lunchtime and I was in court in the afternoon, but before twelve-thirty I was on my own. I didn't drive to Weisdale or meet Jerry Markham in the coffee shop at the Bonhoga, but I can't prove it.'

Willow nodded and again there was a silence, broken only by the gulls calling outside. 'Do you have any enemies?'

'I wasn't killed by a blow to the head, Inspector. Shouldn't you be looking for the people who wanted Markham dead, rather than for those who dislike me?'

Willow threw back her head and laughed. The sound was surprisingly infectious and Rhona found herself smiling.

'I tend to make things complicated,' the detective said. 'Always have done. It's a failing – comes up at every appraisal I have – but humour me. This case is odd. Markham wasn't killed in Aith, but someone took the risk of sticking him in the yoal and floating him out to sea. It was a foggy day – everyone tells me that. All the same, it was a crazy thing to do. In the islands the fog can clear as suddenly as it arrives, and then everyone in the village, a crofter on the hill with his sheep, kids on the beach, a woman hanging out her washing would see the killer trying to lift a fully grown man into your boat. And, even with the fog, there was a chance that the killer would be disturbed. Dog-walkers, fishermen, they don't care about the weather. So why do it? And why there?'

'You think it was a message for me?' Rhona kept her voice impassive and wondered if she should encourage this line of enquiry or dismiss it immediately as ridiculous.

'I know – daft, isn't it? But like I said, humour me. Is there anyone who hates you that much? An offender who thought you'd treated him unfairly maybe?'

'This is Shetland, Inspector, not Glasgow. We don't much go in for revenge killings here. A man who's lost his licence for six months for drunk-driving is unlikely to go to the trouble of committing murder because he feels aggrieved.' Rhona found herself relaxing; she'd almost begun to enjoy this exchange.

'Anything more personal then?' Willow was staring ahead of her and it was hard for Rhona to tell if the question was to be taken seriously.

'A jilted lover, you mean? Something of that kind?' Best, she decided, to treat it as a joke.

Willow turned slowly to face her. 'Perhaps. Why not? You've had no stalkers? Odd phone calls?'

'No, Inspector, nothing of that sort. As I said before, this is Shetland. It would be extremely hard to get away with that sort of behaviour here and not be found out.'

Rhona thought Willow was forming an answer, but she didn't speak for a while and, when she did, it was to say that she wouldn't need to keep the Fiscal any longer. Rhona opened the car door and climbed out. Her shoulder muscles were already stiff after the day's activity. There was no longer any warmth in the sun and she felt chilled and achy, as if she might be coming down with a fever. Willow swung her long legs out of the car and stood up to say goodbye.

'Thank you for your time,' she said. 'Get off home.'

Rhona drove off, feeling as if she'd been dismissed and that the woman from Uist was very much in charge.

Chapter Fourteen

Jimmy Perez sat in his car outside the kirk and watched the people go in. Once there'd been a community here and you could still see where the houses had been, the crumbling walls and the outline of the fields, but now the church was all that was left and most of the congregation came by car. It was one of those still, sunny days that came occasionally in late spring. The light was reflected from the sea and from a small loch close to the road. He was sitting only a few miles from Sullom Voe terminal, but there was no sense of the oil industry here.

Perez had been dragged to services regularly when he was a boy. His father was a lay preacher and his mother's faith had always seemed strong enough to carry her through difficult times. More recently he'd wondered if the Sunday mornings of worship – the fine singing and the thoughtful sermons – had been more about continuing the tradition, a kind of comforting habit for her, than the reality of belief. Fran had dismissed faith as a trust in fairy tales. On impulse, at the last moment, he got out of the car, walked across the sheep-cropped grass and slipped into the back of the building. After the brightness of the sunshine the place seemed dark and he waited for his eyes to adjust to the gloom. The first hymn had already started and he helped himself to a hymn book and service sheet. The place was only half-full and most of the congregation were elderly. It seemed that the ritual of Sunday worship had loosened its hold on the younger generation.

After Fran's death he'd rejected his father's attempts to provide any sort of spiritual comfort, but now he found the familiarity of the words and the music relaxing. He couldn't be angry with a God who didn't exist. The sounds washed over him and allowed him space to think and remember.

During the notices the minister announced the forthcoming wedding of two members of the congregation. 'We're delighted that Evie and John will be married here on Saturday. Let's hope for fine weather and pray that they have a long and happy life together.'

There were fond smiles and even a smattering of applause. The happy couple were sitting at the front and gave a little wave to acknowledge their thanks. The minister continued, 'And I understand that Evie's hen party on Friday night raised £500 for our chosen charity of Water Aid. I wouldn't normally be one to encourage a pub-crawl, but on this occasion I'm sure we all thank those who took part. And we're pleased that Evie has a clear enough head to be with us this morning.' A little polite laughter, followed by the final hymn.

Perez left before the hymn had finished. He knew what it would be like if he stayed: folk would approach, wanting to welcome him into the fold. There'd be invitations back to houses for coffee or lunch. Questions. He'd never been sociable, but these days he found small talk impossible. Outside there was warmth in the sunshine and he stood for a moment and almost allowed himself to enjoy the sensation, before returning to his car. He wasn't sure now whether his coming to the kirk had been such a good idea. He'd found Evie's number in the Shetland phone directory, but when he'd called there'd been no response. This had been the nearest place of worship to her home and he'd thought he'd give it a go. Sandy had described Evie as religious, so it was worth a chance.

At home he'd felt restless; he'd agreed with Duncan that he wouldn't pick up Cassie until after she'd had her tea, and the empty day had stretched ahead of him. Now Perez thought it had been a mistake to come here to find Evie. He hadn't considered that she might be with her fiancé. He could hardly discuss the woman's dead lover in front of the new man.

But John Henderson drove off very quickly in a white car, as if he had an appointment to keep. Perez saw him briefly – a man in middle age, very smart in his Sunday suit. Evie waited until all the other people had left, then stood chatting just outside the door of the kirk to the minister, making the final preparations for her wedding day, Perez supposed. She had a round face and dark hair, and though he couldn't hear what she was saying, she seemed happy. Eventually the minister returned to the building and Evie walked across the grass to the road. There were no cars remaining and Perez assumed that she intended to make her way home on foot. He opened the door and climbed out.

'Can I give you a lift back to your house?'

Anywhere else such an invitation would be treated with suspicion, but Evie just smiled.

'No, thanks. It's such a lovely day and I was looking forward to the walk.'

'Could I walk with you then?' Perez had joined her now. She had her back to the sun and he had to squint against the light reflected from the loch. 'I'm an inspector with the police. We're investigating Jerry Markham's death.'

'I thought I recognized you.' Her voice was light and there was still a trace of the Fetlar accent. 'Your picture was in the *Shetland Times* when your wife died.'

'My girlfriend,' Perez said. 'Though we were engaged. We'd planned to marry.'

'Oh!' She was horrified. Her own impending marriage brought the tragedy close to home. 'I'm so sorry.'

They'd already started walking along the single-track road. A hire car with a couple of tourists came towards them and they climbed onto the verge to let it past.

Perez left his questions about Markham until they'd arrived at her house. It was tiny, a single-storey croft-house, freshly whitewashed. A kitchen with a small table, a sofa against one wall and a portable television; a bedroom and a shower room built onto the back. There was a view down to a pebble beach. She left the door open and the sound of sheep seemed to fill the room.

'You weren't tempted by life in the city then?' Perez knew she'd been to university in Edinburgh and achieved a good law degree, but hadn't taken the steps needed to become a barrister or solicitor.

'No,' she said. 'I missed the islands every minute I was away.' It was a dramatic statement, but Perez thought it was probably true. It was hard to imagine her in a busy street jostled by crowds, hemmed in by tall buildings, no view of the sky. Some Shetland kids thrived on the anonymity and the sense of freedom, when they escaped home for the first time. It seemed Evie hadn't been one of those. 'I bought this place as soon as I came back. It was dead cheap, hardly more than a wreck. My father helped me do it up.'

'Where do you work now?'

'For Shetland Islands Council, in the development unit. We encourage new business into the place. It's important as the oil reserves run out.' She switched on the kettle and spooned coffee into a jug. Perez sat on the sofa.

'You'll be busy now then,' he said. 'This business with the gas coming ashore at Sullom Voe.'

'That's not really my area of expertise.' She poured water onto the coffee and the smell reminded him of Fran, who'd been a coffee snob. 'I'm more interested in green industries. I think that's the way forward, especially in a place like Shetland. We could become almost self-sufficient and provide a model for the rest of the world.'

He thought she was an evangelist by temperament.

'Did Jerry Markham contact you when he was home this time?' There was a pause and he wondered if she was considering whether she might lie.

'He tried to contact me,' she said at last. 'He left messages on my answer machine here and on my mobile – he must have got that number from friends, because it's not the one I had when we were together.'

'Did he phone you at work?' Perez sipped his coffee. The mug had a bright-blue glaze and he recognized the work of a local potter, a friend of Fran's. *This is how it'll be,* he thought. *As long as I live in Shetland, there'll be no escaping her.*

Again there was a brief pause before she answered. 'No,' she said.

'Because he told people he was interested in a story on the oil and natural gas, and I thought he might have hoped you could introduce him to colleagues working on the project. He'd shown interest in the wind farm too, and in tidal power.'

'He would realize,' she said stiffly, 'that I'd have very little interest in helping him in any way at all.'

'Can you tell me about him?' Through the window he saw a pair of eider ducks on the water. Perez could hear them and thought they chuntered like a couple of old ladies gossiping.

'He hurt me,' she said. 'It's hard to be objective.'

'All the same, it'd be useful. Folk don't like to speak ill of the dead, but sometimes it's the failings that make them a target for violence. Can you understand why anyone would want to kill Jerry Markham, for instance?'

'Oh yes!' The response was immediate. 'I'd have killed him myself all those years ago if I'd had the chance. But he ran away south.'

'Would you mind telling me about it? It's not the facts I'm interested in as much as the man himself. The only sense I have of him at the moment is that he's a successful journalist. Was he always ambitious, even when he was working on the *Shetland Times*?'

'I suppose he was,' she said. 'And perhaps that was

what attracted me to him at first, the fact that he was so different from my family. He wanted much more out of life than they did. My parents spent their time trying to preserve the old traditions. My father builds yoals – beautiful boats using the old designs. It takes him months of work; he's a perfectionist. My mother's family have always been crofters. Now I'm proud of them both, but then it seemed as if they were living in the past and had no time at all for the future or the world away from Shetland.'

Perez said nothing. He could tell she was ready to talk to him. She just needed the time to get her thoughts in order.

'I was very young for my age,' she said. 'I'd been out at the High School and lived during the week at the hostel, but even while the other kids were going to parties, getting themselves invited to the town students' houses so that they could go into bars, that had never interested me. I was ambitious too, in my own way. I wanted a place at a good university, to make my parents proud.'

Perez nodded and that was all the prompting she needed to continue.

'I got a holiday job at the Ravenswick Hotel,' she said. 'I was thrilled to pieces. I'd looked at other waitressing jobs, but Peter and Maria paid well and I liked them. And I could live in.'

'You didn't want to spend your last summer in Shetland on Fetlar with your folks?'

'I knew it wouldn't be my last summer in Shetland,' she said. 'I always knew this would be my permanent home. I suppose I was ready for some independence. An adventure.'

It wasn't much of an adventure, Perez thought. Other kids might pick grapes in Europe or go back-packing across Africa, but Evie had settled for a job in a Shetland mainland hotel. Perhaps she guessed what he was thinking, because she grinned. 'I was a home bird,' she said. 'I hated living in the hostel at school, so really the Ravenswick job was a big deal. I felt very grown-up.'

'Was Jerry Markham living at home then?'

'He had a flat in Lerwick because he was working on the *Shetland Times*, but he spent two or three nights a week in the hotel. He was an only child. I thought he was being kind, coming home to spend time with his parents, but it was probably the free food and drink that brought him back to the hotel. He never paid for anything while he was there.' Evie poured more coffee into Perez's mug.

'How did the two of you get together?' Perez asked.

'I fancied him rotten from the first time I met him.' She smiled again. 'I was a late starter when it came to the lads. I didn't have a boyfriend at school. Jerry was older than me, a graduate, with a good job. He seemed to know everything – about films and books and music. I never thought that we might go out together. He was a fantasy. So sophisticated! I dreamed about him, blushed every time he came close to me. I suppose he realized and decided he'd have a bit of fun with me.'

'Perhaps he liked you,' Perez said. 'There'd be lots of girls in Shetland he could have fun with.'

She shot him a grateful glance. 'Aye, maybe.' She paused. 'There was a bit of a do for the staff at the hotel. The chef's birthday party. After hours, when the bar had closed to the visitors. The energy you have when you're young! I knew I'd have to be up at six to serve the breakfasts, but still I stayed up drinking most of the night.'

Perez smiled. Evie Watt still seemed very young to him. But he didn't want to interrupt the story.

'I don't remember much about it,' she went on. 'I wasn't used to the drink and I was on the spirits with the other lasses. Peter and Maria were there at the beginning, but they soon went off to bed and left the rest of us to it. At some point Jerry suggested a walk in the garden, just the two of us. Suddenly we'd left all the noise behind. It was a beautiful morning in late June and it was just getting light.' She turned to Perez. 'I do remember him kissing me and thinking I'd never be so happy again.'

'Did you get pregnant that night?'

She shook her head and gave a self-mocking laugh. 'I was a good girl, Inspector. I'd never sleep with a man on a first date. And Jerry didn't push it. Not then. For some reason he didn't want his parents to know we were going out, but he treated me like a real girlfriend. On my days off we'd meet in town and then we'd drive in his car, exploring the islands, heading off down small tracks just to see what was at the end of them. We first made love on one of those trips. In a tiny cove, with cliffs all around. You could only reach it at low water, and the tide came in and stranded us there. I hadn't planned to have sex with him and we didn't take precautions. Crazy! I can't even blame drink that time. It was the sun and the excitement. Romance, I suppose. And I was very naive. I didn't think I was likely to get pregnant the first time. Later we were more careful, but by then it was too late.'

They sat for a moment in silence. Perez was pleased that she still had happy memories of that summer.

'I was back home and packing for university when I took the pregnancy test. Already heartbroken because Jerry had made it clear that he didn't expect the relationship to last once I was at university: "You don't want to be tied down before you get there." My mother found me crying in my bedroom. My father was furious and phoned Peter Markham, demanding to know what sort of establishment he was running in Ravenswick, and how his son intended to fulfil his obligations to me.' She glanced up. 'All very Victorian, and hugely embarrassing to a seventeen-year-old, but I'd always been a Daddy's girl. I suppose my attitude was just as old-fashioned. I thought Jerry should stand by me. I didn't expect marriage, but he disappeared south as soon as the fuss blew up, leaving me to face everything on my own. That's when I could have killed him.'

She got to her feet and was rinsing the mugs at the sink when she next spoke, her back to Perez.

'I lost the baby. I'd decided to keep it and had geared up to face the world as a mother, and then it disappeared. There was real grief, of course, but I felt cheated too. No need for the dramatic gesture after all.' She paused. 'Jerry had never wanted to be tied down by a teenage girlfriend from the sticks. That was why he dumped me. It was nothing about me having freedom at uni, or even about the baby. He wanted to go south to make his fortune without any complications in his life.'

'Have you been in contact since?'

'I sent a couple of snivelling emails after I lost the baby. I thought perhaps he'd consider seeing me again. That he'd feel sorry for me. How pathetic was that! Using a dead baby to get him back! He didn't reply.'

Somewhere in the distance a dog barked. 'And now you're about to be married,' Perez said.

Her face lit up. 'Yes. To John Henderson. He's a pilot up at Sullom Voe. A widower. His wife died of cancer five years ago. I've known him since I was a peerie lass – he was a friend of my father's, and though he's not quite of the same generation, he seemed very old then. I'd have laughed out loud if you'd told me I'd be engaged to him.'

'How did the relationship start?' Thinking: *My love and I met over a dead body in a snowy field in the dark days of winter.*

'Through the kirk at first. Then John's interested in green energy and came to a couple of meetings that I organized at work. He's a kind man. Kindness can be very sexy, don't you think?'

Perez nodded.

'It was an old-fashioned courtship,' Evie said. 'My friends laughed at the way John treated me. They couldn't believe that we didn't move in together. But I loved it. Like I said, I'm an old-fashioned girl.'

'Did he know Jerry Markham was around and trying to get in touch with you?' Perez kept his voice light. Shetland was a small place, and it was probably a coincidence that Markham had visited the terminal just over the voe from Henderson's workplace just before he died. Probably.

'I thought I'd better warn him,' Evie said. 'I didn't want the two of them just bumping into each other. John is angry about the way Jerry treated me. He would never have treated a woman that way.' Suddenly she realized the implication of what she was saying. 'But he's a good man. Gentle. He wouldn't hurt a fly. John Henderson's not your killer, Inspector.'

Chapter Fifteen

Perez arrived to pick up Cassie from the Haa at six o'clock, just the time they'd agreed. Fran's ex-husband, Duncan, had her waiting for him and Perez sensed that the man was relieved the weekend was over. Duncan loved his daughter more in the abstract than in reality. He had too many other demands on his time to give her the attention she needed, and now that she had become a solemn and withdrawn child he didn't know quite what to do with her. He would have been more comfortable with a boy, robust and active. But Duncan's occasional lover Celia was much older than him and he would have no other children.

Once, Duncan and Perez had been close friends. Perez had spent weekends in the big house when he was a boarder at the Anderson High School, and the Hunter family had introduced him to a different, more relaxed way of living. They'd lost most of their money by then, but they had the confidence that went with generations of owning land and feeling superior. It occurred to Perez that this house was similar in age and size to the Ravenswick Hotel, though there the resemblance ended: the Haa was crumbling from the inside, and most of the rooms were boarded up and never used. Duncan preferred to spend his cash on playboy living rather than the family home. He held on to it through nostalgia and because it gave him a certain position within the islands – it still made him feel like a laird.

Now the men got on only for Cassie's sake. They had little else in common. It was an odd childcare arrangement – two men, both former partners of Fran, sharing custody of a little girl – and the welfare authorities had taken some persuading that it would work. It did work because Perez was determined that it should. This was what Fran had wanted and he had an obligation to her.

When Perez drove up, Cassie was sitting on the wall outside the house, reading a book. Her bag was on the gravel beside her feet. Duncan was looking at the engine of his jeep. Celia's car was there too, but there was no sign of her. Cassie was so engrossed in the story that she didn't hear Perez until he slammed the door shut. Then she smiled Fran's smile and jumped down to greet him, not making too much fuss in case she hurt Duncan's feelings. It seemed to Perez that a seven-year-old shouldn't care so much about hurting adults. It worried him that she was so anxious to please.

'Had a good weekend?' He put the bag into the back of his car, eager to get her home. There was school tomorrow, the start of the new term. And if he spent too long in Duncan Hunter's company he came close to losing his temper.

'Brilliant! We went fishing and cooked the piltock on a fire on the beach. Celia and I made brownies for pudding.' And he saw that she *had* had a good time, she wasn't just putting on a show for her father.

Duncan wiped his hands on a bit of rag. 'Everything OK, Jimmy?' He said the same thing every time they met. In his less generous moods, Perez thought Duncan was afraid that the detective would fall apart, leaving Duncan with sole care of his daughter. Then there would be no exotic business trips to Europe, none of the famous, wild parties at the Haa.

'Fine.' Perez opened the back door of the car and shifted the booster seat into its proper place so that he could strap Cassie inside. The last thing he wanted was a conversation with Fran's ex-husband.

'I heard there was some trouble at Aith on Friday.'

'Did you know Jerry Markham?' Perez straightened. Cassie had opened the book again and was lost in her story.

'I knew him when he worked on the *Shetland Times*. And he's been here to a party occasionally when he's been home. I haven't seen him recently.'

'You don't know anything about a story he was writing? Haven't heard any rumours about problems at Sullom Voe?'

'No.'

Perez thought Duncan probably would have heard rumours if there were any flying around.

Cassie was in bed and asleep early. Perez thought there'd been too many late nights at the Haa, too much sugar and too many treats. He was setting out her clothes for school the next morning when the phone rang.

'Sorry to disturb you on a Sunday evening, Jimmy. I've got Sandy with me and there have been developments. I wonder if we could meet?' It was Willow

Reeves. Perez pictured her and blushed at the memory of the stab of lust he'd felt when he'd followed her into his house in Lerwick.

'I'm sorry,' he said. 'My stepdaughter's in bed. I couldn't get a sitter at this sort of notice.' He always called Cassie his stepdaughter to outsiders. It would have seemed an impertinence to claim her as his own.

'Perhaps we could come to you then? It would be useful to have a chat this evening. Time's moving on.' And she made the arrangements, told him what time they would arrive. He would have liked to refuse, but she didn't give him a chance, and by the end of the conversation it was all fixed up.

She was about to end the call when he broke in. 'If you want a dram, you'll have to bring it yourself. I've nothing in the house.'

When they arrived Perez put cheese and oatcakes on the table. He found that he was nervous. He'd lost the habit of entertaining and wasn't quite sure what he should do. And he couldn't forget how he'd felt about the Uist woman in the Lerwick house. It hadn't been her fault, he supposed, but he found himself blaming her for what had felt almost like adultery. He realized he'd forgotten small plates for them and saw that his hand was trembling when he lifted the crockery from the cupboard.

Willow Reeves made herself quite at home. He'd lit a fire when he and Cassie had arrived back from her father's house, because it was still only April and the evenings were cold. Willow sat on a kitchen chair in front of it and stretched out her long legs across the sheepskin. He saw how tired she was, the skin around her eyes looking dark like bruises. Sandy set a bottle of whisky on the table – an obscure island malt that Perez had never tasted. 'A present from the boss,' he said.

So, Perez thought, *she's already the boss.*

Willow stirred and smiled. 'I brought it to Shetland with me,' she said, 'to remind me of home. And I'm taking it back at the end of the night.'

Perez fetched three small glasses and poured a dram for each of them, but he didn't speak. She was the boss; let her start the discussion.

The first sip of whisky seemed to revive her. She sat up and leaned forward. 'I'll sum up what we have so far, shall I?' And she continued without waiting for them to reply. 'Our victim: Jerry Markham, born-and-bred Shetlander, with an English father and ambitions beyond the islands. He went south to escape a shot-gun marriage to a local lass.'

'No,' Perez said. 'No, it wasn't quite like that. I spoke to Evie Watt this morning. Markham had got the place on the London newspaper before he found out she was pregnant. It was very embarrassing for all concerned, but he'd ended the relationship before the pregnancy was made public. He'd seen it as a summer fling, and she was in love for the first time. I'm not sure that provides a motive. She's getting married on Saturday to a local man.' He looked at Sandy. 'John Henderson? Do you know him?'

'Aye,' Sandy said. 'He's a pilot. Lives up north. Works out of Sullom Voe. Had a wife who died a while back. I don't know him well, but he's always seemed kind of boring. I can't see him committing murder.'

'But Sullom Voe's the last place Markham was seen.' Willow was tense now and Perez thought there was something of the hunting dog about her, her face all sharp angles and points.

'It is,' he said. He thought it was up to her to decide how important that fact might be.

'John Henderson hasn't had a woman since his wife died. Not as far as I know.' Sandy was sitting in the corner furthest away from the fire. He never seemed to feel the cold. 'I can't see him carrying on with all that nonsense with the yoal. Why would he do that? And what reason would he have for killing Markham anyway?' He paused for a moment. Perez thought he was rolling through the archives of his memory. Sandy held small details of Shetland gossip in his head better than an old wife with nothing else to do. Finally he spoke again. 'Henderson was always one for good works. He ran the Youth Club in North Mainland and still helps out with the lads' football team.'

'Markham had been trying to contact Evie since he came home,' Perez said. 'The first time he's made any effort to get in touch since he went away, apparently. Could be that Markham had heard about her marriage and decided that she was the one for him after all. A last romantic gesture.' The thought moved him almost to tears.

'And you reckon Henderson saw the man as a rival and killed him because of that?' Sandy made the idea sound like a fairy story.

'Or perhaps it was to do with work.' Perez looked up. 'Jerry's and Evie's work. Evie's involved in developing green energy in the islands, and Jerry's planned story included details of that. If Andy Belshaw is to be believed.'

'A small group of activists met at Vatnagarth on Friday night,' Sandy said. 'They're fighting the new tidal-energy scheme at Hvidahus. Worried about the impact on the environment apparently. They were expecting Jerry Markham to be there. They'd invited him, hoping that he'd cover the story.' Sandy looked around vaguely, and Perez hoped Willow had worked out that Sandy wasn't very good at detail, that he was easily bored.

There was a moment of silence, but Perez thought he could almost hear Willow Reeves's thoughts hissing and sparking in her brain.

'Could Markham have been killed to stop him going to that meeting?' She looked at them both, demanding a response.

'I can't see it was that important.' Sandy was dismissive. 'A group of soothmoothers, pissed off because their view might be spoiled.'

'Everything's connected,' Willow said. 'There are too many links to be coincidental. Andy Belshaw's wife volunteers in the place where Markham's car was found, and Markham was expected to attend a meeting there the night he died. Belshaw and Henderson both run a boys' footie club.'

'Evie Watt is probably involved in the tidal project,' Perez said. 'Sustainable energy comes within her remit.'

'Does it?' Willow looked up sharply. 'Where does Jen Belshaw work?'

'She's a school cook,' Sandy said. 'In Aith. Nothing

to do with the water scheme.'

'But where Markham's body was discovered. Another coincidence?'

'This is a small place.' Sandy shifted uneasily in his seat. 'People bump into each other.'

'So they do.' She flashed him a smile, but Perez could tell that she was unconvinced. She didn't believe in coincidences.

'And is it just chance that a woman looking very like the Fiscal had coffee with Markham the morning he died?' Willow reached out and took an oatcake from the table and ate it dry. No butter. No cheese. Was she concentrating so hard on the facts of the case that she didn't notice? 'Then the body was found on her doorstep when the fog cleared later in the day.'

'You have Rhona Laing down as a suspect?' Perez thought she was mad.

'Not that,' Willow said. 'No, maybe not that. But she's involved. She knows more than she's telling us.'

There was a moment of silence. Absolute silence. No wind outside. No traffic noise.

'Anything from James Grieve and the post-mortem?' Perez asked.

'Nothing helpful. Nothing that we didn't know already. Markham was killed by a violent blow to the head and placed in the boat post-mortem. The pathologist couldn't pin down time of death more accurately than we already had it – so between Markham leaving Sullom Voe in the afternoon and his body being found by the Fiscal at six-thirty. His last meal was fried fish and chips.' She paused. 'We don't know yet where he ate that.'

'Any more detail on the murder weapon?' Perez

was finding this discussion easier than he'd expected. After Fran's death he hadn't believed he'd be capable of talking about violent death in a dispassionate and professional way again. But this was like a habit, a learned script: the routine questions formed in his mind without too much thought. A performance.

'Grieve thought a spade or a shovel. Heavy, and wielded with considerable force. We need to find it. Something else for tomorrow.' She stretched and Perez thought again how tired she looked.

'Do we think the murder was planned?' Perez was talking almost to himself. 'That sort of weapon could be something you'd pick up on the spur of the moment, if there was a fight.'

'I suppose that's possible.' Willow frowned. 'But there were no other signs that there'd been a scrap. No grazes on Markham's knuckles and no other injuries. We'll organize a search for the weapon tomorrow.'

'I don't think you'll find it.' Perez stared at the fire. 'Anyone with a peat bank or a croft would have something like that in their house.' He felt he was being negative and unhelpful. 'You said there was a briefcase with him in the boat. What was inside?'

'A couple of postcards with paintings of local musicians. Shetland Arts give them away at the museum and the art gallery. He could have picked them up at the Bonhoga.'

'Anything written on the postcards?' Perez thought he'd seen the original of one of those paintings in Lerwick library, and the postcards – publicity for Shetland Arts – in the Bonhoga. The band was called Fiddlers' Bid.

Willow shook her head. 'Though he'd have had

time to post any he had written. There was nothing else in the case. Markham might have made notes if he was researching a story, but if so, the killer took everything with him or her. Too smart to take the briefcase – it'd be hard to get rid of that.'

Willow's phone rang. Perez thought it would be a personal call at this time of night. He wondered if she'd want to take it in a different room, but there was only his bedroom, and he was embarrassed to show her in there. He kept the rest of the house clean and tidy for Cassie's sake, but he never bothered much with his own space. It seemed, though, that the call was work-related and she stayed where she was. They sat watching her, listening, gathering only from her questions and occasional replies that this was someone with whom Markham had worked. When she switched off the phone she was frowning.

'That was a woman called Amelia Bartlett. Markham's boss. Seems she'd been away for the weekend. I'd left messages for her, but she's only just got them.' Willow looked at them. 'She doesn't have any idea what story Jerry was working on. If there was a story. As far as she was aware, Jerry was in Shetland on annual leave. She said he hadn't been himself lately. He'd been very quiet. She wondered if he'd been ill. Stress maybe. Burnout. And that was why he'd wanted the time out.'

Chapter Sixteen

Sandy caught John Henderson at work early on Monday morning in Sella Ness, just across the water from the oil terminal. This complex was run by Shetland Islands Council and there were no gates or barbed wire here. Sandy thought a terrorist wanting to attack the terminal could just drive down the road and row a small boat across the voe. Though maybe it wouldn't be that easy: the harbour master or the pilots would see what was going on, and there were probably closed-circuit cameras covering the water.

He found Henderson in Port Control, drinking a mug of tea and listening to Bobby Robertson, who worked for the vessel traffic service. There was a panoramic view over the water and the place looked just like the bridge of a ship, with radar screens and high-tech equipment that beeped and flashed. Sandy was intimidated by the instruments and the sense of efficient expertise, by the smartness of Henderson in his officer's uniform. The pilot was middle-aged, grey-haired.

'What's this about, Sandy? I don't have long.' The pilot looked at his watch. 'I'm just about to go out on a job.'

Sandy thought he was an intelligent man and he

shouldn't have needed to ask. He'd have heard about Markham's murder. 'Just a word,' he said. 'And maybe somewhere in private?' He could sense that Bobby Robertson was listening to every word, and he was a famous gossip.

'Just come along here then.' Henderson led him away from the control room and pushed open the door to a small bedroom. 'This is where I stay when I'm on night shift.'

'You'll have guessed what this is about,' Sandy said. 'Jerry Markham.'

'Aye, did you know him?'

Henderson nodded slowly. 'Not well, but I'd seen him around. Once or twice at the Ravenswick Hotel when he was still working for the *Shetland Times*.'

'You didn't like him?' Henderson had closed the bedroom door and Sandy felt trapped in the tiny space. He'd never liked being shut in. Was this what it felt like to be in a submarine? A prison cell? He was aware of his own breathing and wondered if Henderson could hear it too.

'I didn't like his column in the *Shetland Times*. It always seemed kind of unpleasant to me. Sneering and cynical. He made out he was better than anyone else. More cool. Those of us who loved living in the islands weren't worth bothering with.'

'And he'd been Evie's boyfriend,' Sandy said.

Henderson looked at him. His eyes were blue and sharp.

'What are you saying?'

'That there'd be no love lost between you. Nothing more than that.'

Henderson leaned towards Sandy. Not a threat, but

preparing for a declaration. 'Markham treated her badly,' he said, 'but if he'd done the decent thing and stood by Evie when he got her pregnant, she wouldn't be engaged to me. And she's the best thing that's ever happened in my life since my wife Agnes died. I still wake up in the morning and thank God for sending her to me. I have no reason to kill him.'

Sandy wasn't quite sure how to respond to that. 'How long have you been on your own?'

'Five years.' The man paused. 'I hadn't thought I'd miss the company. Agnes and I never had children, and I was used to being on my own. Then I got to know Evie and it was like coming alive all over again. A fresh start, you know.'

Sandy wondered if that might happen to Jimmy Perez one day: he might meet a bonny young woman and fall in love with her. He couldn't see it. Nobody would make Jimmy light up as Fran had done.

A thought occurred to him. 'You live in Hvidahus, don't you? Are you involved in this campaign to stop the tidal energy coming ashore there?'

'No, I don't see it as a problem. There'll be a bit of disruption when they widen the track and build the substation, but I can live with that.' He gave a little laugh. 'Besides, Power of Water is Evie's baby. She'd kill me if I objected.'

'The wedding's on Saturday?'

'Aye, in the kirk just up the road from Evie's house, and a party in the community hall in the evening.'

Sandy wondered how Henderson would get on at a party. It was hard to imagine him drinking too many drams and dancing with the pretty bridesmaids. 'Evie didn't fancy going home to Fetlar to be wed?'

'She has old college friends coming up from the south and it's easier for them to get to the mainland.' Henderson smiled. 'At least, that was what she said. But I think she knew how much it mattered to me to be married close to home. We're both members of the congregation there. Her family understands, and we'll go over to Fetlar on Sunday to visit the old folk who can't get out to the wedding. Evie will put on her wedding dress and we'll take them some cake. You know how it is.'

Sandy nodded. He knew just what was expected. 'Did you know that Markham was in Shetland this week?'

In the control room a phone rang. Henderson waited until it had been answered before he spoke again. 'Evie told me he was back,' he said. 'But I heard the news about the murder on the radio like everyone else.'

'Markham phoned Evie a few times when he was here. I wondered what that was about.'

'Evie didn't tell me about the calls until last night. She was worried I'd be upset that Markham was pestering her.' Henderson had one of those voices that didn't let on what he was feeling, so Sandy couldn't tell whether he was angry Evie hadn't told him about them before, or pleased that she'd let him know eventually. 'She didn't answer them.'

'Markham was over at the terminal on Friday afternoon,' Sandy said. 'Did you see him?'

There was a moment of silence. 'Why would I?' Henderson said. 'We bring the tankers in and then we take them out. Then we leave. We have no real contact with the terminal.' He looked at his watch again –

the only indication that the interview was starting to irritate him.

'Where were you on Friday night?'

'I was here,' Henderson said. 'Catching some sleep because I was on call.' He stood up. 'Now is there anything else, Sandy? I should be getting back to work.'

'Were you called out to work on Friday night?' Sandy asked.

'Not until the early hours of Saturday morning.' Henderson seemed almost amused by the question, but again Sandy had no real idea what he was thinking. 'But I have no proof for you. No witnesses. They don't lock us in.'

Outside a helicopter came in to land at Scatsta. The noise was very loud and the room seemed to shake. Sandy thanked Henderson for his help and left the building. As he walked to his car a group of men in identical blue overalls stared at him. He felt as if he was in one of those cowboy films he'd watched as a kid – the stranger riding into town.

In Lerwick the morning briefing was just breaking up. There was a whiteboard on the wall and Willow Reeves was staring at it, absorbed, as if the solution to the case was captured there in the scrawled names and photos. She didn't notice the rest of the team leaving or Sandy coming in. He coughed to get her attention and she turned, startled.

'We still don't know where the man was killed,' she said. 'There's no crime scene. If we had that, maybe we could move the investigation on. There'd be some forensic trace. It's driving me crazy. It's as if Markham drove out of Sullom Voe in the fog and then disappeared. How did his body get from there to a boat in the marina at Aith, and his car back to the museum? What did he do that triggered those events?'

'He gave somebody a lift?' Sandy said. 'Anybody walking along a road in the country, you'd stop and see if they needed a ride. Specially in that weather.'

'And would Markham do that too?' Willow demanded. 'Snooty Markham, who's used to city ways.'

'Maybe it would depend who it was.' Sandy was thinking, struggling to keep up. Willow seemed to jump from thought to thought, to build links and conclusions while he was still beginning the process. 'He always had a reputation for liking a pretty girl, even before he got Evie into trouble.'

'Could he have bumped into Evie on the road?' Willow asked. 'I still can't get my head round the geography of this place. Wherever I look there's water. It's disorientating.'

'Evie lives off the back road not far from Sullom. If he was going that way and she was out, he could have seen her.'

'But that's just about chance, and I don't see this as a random attack.' Willow grabbed her jacket from her desk. 'Come on. Let's go.'

'Where are we off to?'

She was already out of the door. 'I need to find where the man was murdered,' she said. 'We'll drive from Sullom Voe, on the route Markham would have taken towards his parents' hotel.'

Sandy was about to say that he'd just come back that way. But he saw that it would make no difference to Willow and, whatever he said to her, she'd make him do it again anyway.

A damp drizzle had blown in from the sea. It wasn't the thick fog that there'd been the day of Markham's death, but it blurred the outline of the hills and there was the sense of being closed in. Usually Shetland was about low horizons and long views, and today Sandy was reminded about his one trip to London and how trapped he'd felt by the buildings there. He was driving and he took the road slowly. Beside him, Willow was so tense that she made him feel anxious too.

'So what was it like where you grew up?' he said. He couldn't bear the silence. 'Did you look after your own there too?'

'I was one of the outsiders,' she said. 'I was born in North Uist, but we never really belonged.'

Sandy thought she'd stop there. She didn't seem the sort who would confide about her personal life. But perhaps she needed to fill the silence as much as he did, or perhaps she needed distracting. This was her first case, her big chance, and so far nothing was going to plan. So while he inched north along the smooth road that had been bought by the oil money, she started talking about her early life in the Western Isles, and by the time the giant tanks of Sullom Voe lurked out of the gloom he thought he knew all about her.

'My parents were hippies,' she said. 'After the good life. And they were good people. With some friends they bought a house in North Uist. A place big enough for a couple of families and outbuildings that could house more.'

'You grew up in a commune?' He sounded shocked, but he couldn't help himself. Communes were for dropouts and druggies, not kids who grew up to be cops.

'Do you find the idea amusing, Sergeant?' But she was joking too and not really angry. He liked that about her. You felt she wouldn't take herself too seriously, even now, when worry about the case was eating into her.

'I don't think many detective inspectors grew up in that sort of family,' he said. 'Didn't hippies believe they were outside the law?'

'Oh, we had our own rules,' she said. 'Everything discussed at length at interminable community meetings. No meat. No TV. All our income pooled, for the good of the commune. Children were to be cared for in common. And strangers were to be made welcome.' The last phrase came out in a hard and bitter voice.

'What happened?'

'One of the strangers betrayed us,' she said. 'Stole all our money.' Sandy waited for her to go on, but she stared out of the window into the grey rain and said nothing.

At last she turned back into the car. 'So you can imagine what it was like growing up there,' she said. 'We went to the local school and got teased for being the hippy kids. We wore weird home-made clothes. No leather shoes, naturally. We had no Gaelic of course, no real island culture. The adults tried to learn, but the islanders didn't make it easy for them to join in. In the end we were isolated and it felt like it was us against the world. I left for university, wanting to be like everyone else, but some of the old commune values stuck.' She laughed. 'I'm a veggie to this day. Do yoga. Meditate.'

'Are your folks still there?' Sandy asked.

'Oh yes, they'll be there forever now, milking their goats and saving the planet. How can they admit to themselves that they made a mistake? It would be as if they've wasted the last thirty years.'

He would have liked to ask how often she went to visit, but by now they were nearly at Sullom Voe, and anyway he sensed that she regretted having brought up her family for discussion.

The cloud was even lower. They passed the stuffed figures of the couple in their wedding outfits, and Sandy was driving so slowly that he could see that the photos covering the faces were those of John Henderson and Evie Watt. It seemed a strangely frivolous thing for Henderson to agree to. Even if Evie's mates had created the figures in the run-up to her hen night, he could have made her take them away now. Perhaps he had a sense of humour after all.

'What do you want to do?' He found that his attitude to Willow had changed since he'd found out that she'd grown up in a commune and that he regarded her with something like suspicion. Then he heard Jimmy Perez's voice in his head. *That's ridiculous, Sandy Wilson, and you know it.* He tried to make his voice warmer. 'Should I turn round and drive back more slowly? You can shout if you want me to stop.'

'Yeah,' she said. 'Do just that.' Then, with a smile: 'I suppose you think I'm daft.'

In the end he was the one to find it. Willow was

craning her neck and looking to the verges on either side, while he kept his eyes on the road. There was a junction with a small track leading off to the left. It would go to Swinning and branch again for Lunna. Near the junction the council had built a lay-by so that folk wanting to car-share could leave their vehicles and catch a lift up to the terminal or into town with someone driving from Brae. There were black skid marks on the main road swerving towards the lay-by. Sandy pulled to a stop, but avoided the tracks. They both got out to look.

'What do you think?' Willow was crouching, her nose almost on the tarmac. 'Was he forced into the lay-by? If it was him?'

'It looks that way. Or a car pulled out of the track in front of him. With the fog that thick, it could have been an accident. Could have been anyone.'

'Sure,' she said.

'Maybe we should wait. Tape it off and stick a bobby to keep watch until we can get Miss Hewitt back in.'

'How long will that take?' She was bouncing up and down on the spot, partly to keep warm because the low cloud was cold, but partly because she was so impatient that she was finding it hard to keep still.

Sandy looked around. None of the hills were visible. 'Could be a couple of days. The forecast says it's unlikely to clear until Wednesday. If we hurry, we could get her on this afternoon's ferry from Aberdeen.'

'We're the first people at the scene,' she said. 'Our decision.'

'Aye.' But he knew the decision had already been taken.

She took it slowly and didn't rush into it. Plastic overshoes. Gloves on her hands. She didn't have a full scene-suit, so she found a scarf in the car and wrapped it round her hair. Then she walked backwards and forwards across the empty lay-by.

'There might have been other vehicles parked there since Friday.' Usually Perez was the person to council caution while Sandy rushed in with daft ideas. He felt suddenly very grown-up.

'Over a weekend?' She looked up and waited for his opinion as if it mattered.

'Maybe not.'

'So they *could* have come from Markham's car.' She grinned. 'He'd have unusual tyres. We'll be able to check.'

Where the lay-by joined the hill there was a row of whitewashed stones, to stop vehicles running down the bank on foggy days like this. A couple of cars went north along the main road in the opposite direction. Too fast for the weather conditions, Sandy thought. The drivers didn't even see them because the fog was so thick.

Willow was bent double, looking at the crack between the stones. He thought she was more supple than anyone he'd known. Suddenly she straightened. 'There's a smear of blood on the underside of this rock. Washed down by rain maybe?' She grinned again at Sandy. 'The killer pulled Markham out of the car and hit him here. He fell and caught his forehead on the rock. You remember the wound. Not random. Planned. An ambush.'

'The blood could be anything!' Sandy being sensible again. 'A rabbit. A sheep hit by a car.'

'It could.' She nodded. 'But I'd bet my career that it wasn't. Let's get the whole lay-by taped and bring someone to keep an eye on it. And let's get Vicki Hewitt onto that ferry.'

Chapter Seventeen

Perez walked Cassie to school. There was a neighbour who had offered to take her as soon as they'd settled back in the Ravenswick house after Fran's death: 'Just drop her in, Jimmy, on your way to work and I'll take her down with my bairns. It would be no trouble.' But Perez had thanked her gravely and said he was working flexible hours at the moment. Later, maybe, he'd be very grateful for the help. He still took Cassie to school every day and couldn't imagine entrusting her to someone else.

Today she had a music lesson, so he carried her tiny fiddle in its case and her schoolbag.

'Are you going to work today, Jimmy?'

'I'm not sure,' he said, hedging his bets. Would Cassie worry about him being at work? Would she prefer him to wait for her at home?

'You should go,' she said. 'We need the money. There's a school trip to Edinburgh and I want to go. It's £150.'

'I'm still being paid!' He wasn't sure what he felt about her going to Edinburgh.

'But they won't give you money for doing nothing forever.' Her voice was matter-of-fact.

Before he could reply she saw a friend on the path ahead, took her violin and her bag and ran off.

He waited out of sight, watching her in the playground, until the bell rang and she went inside. As he walked up the bank from the school his phone had a signal and he phoned Willow Reeves, laughing to himself because he was taking orders from a seven-year-old. She answered quickly and he thought she sounded manic. Too much coffee and too little sleep.

'I wondered if I could help at all?' In the background Perez heard someone shout that they'd got the video conference up and running for the meeting with Inverness.

'We need all the help we can get, Jimmy!' He heard the laughter in her voice. He'd always liked women who laughed easily.

'I might just call into the Ravenswick and chat to the Markhams then,' he said. 'See if I can clear up the matter of Jerry's story, and why his editor knew nothing about it.'

'That'd be great.' She paused. There was more noise in the conference room and he could understand how it would be. Inverness ready to speak, waiting for her to shout the meeting to order. He thought she would end the phone call as quickly as she could, but she continued, her voice so low that he could hardly hear it above the background sound. 'Have you had any more thoughts about Rhona Laing?'

A vague idea floated into his head and then disappeared.

'Has your contact picked up anything between her and Markham?'

'Nothing.' Another pause. 'Not yet.'

'You want me to talk to her?'

There was another silence and for a moment he thought she'd switched off her phone, but it seemed she was answering a question in the room, because then she repeated, 'Not yet. First I'd like to know for sure who Markham met in the Bonhoga on Friday morning. The lasses Sandy spoke to only worked weekends. Could you check that out?'

Another easy job, Perez thought, to keep him out of mischief. Willow didn't trust him to talk to the Fiscal. Worried which side he was on? He wasn't certain himself. 'Sure,' he said. 'I'll go to the Ravenswick first and do the Bonhoga afterwards.'

Then she did end the call without saying goodbye.

It was the quiet time in the hotel. Breakfast over and the bosses of the contract firms working in Sullom had long left. The sound of vacuum cleaners in the distance, and in the kitchen someone was whistling tunelessly. Brodie was on reception again. Perez wondered if he ever slept or if he had any sort of private life at all.

'Is Peter in?' Perez asked. He wasn't sure if he could face Maria. Her grief was too raw and immediate. Peter's control made him an easier interviewee.

'He's out in the garden. Fresh air, he said.'

'How are they coping?'

Brodie shrugged. 'They're hiding out in the flat. No phone calls. No visitors. Maria hasn't been out at all, and this is the first time Peter's escaped.' Brodie paused. 'You wouldn't think it to look at him, but he's taking it harder than she is. The doctor's given her something and she's kind of doped. I don't think he's slept since Sandy came with the news about Jerry.'

'Were they close, Jerry and his father?'

It seemed an innocuous question, but Brodie hesitated. Perez waited and the silence stretched. At last Brodie said: 'Peter's old-fashioned. Honourable. Maria thought Jerry could do no wrong, but Peter dared to criticize. Occasionally.'

'And that caused some tension in the family?'

'Maria was always over the moon when Jerry turned up. I'd say that Peter was more relieved when he went away again.'

Perez nodded his thanks for the information and took the door outside. It had been designed as an informal English garden with shallow terraces leading down to the shore. The grey wall provided some shelter and there were trees and shrubs, the trees just coming into leaf, looking strangely out of place. Daffodils in the borders, and in a few weeks there'd be bluebells in the grass. Woodland flowers in a place where there were scarcely any trees. Despite the protection from the wind it was a chill morning. Peter Markham was huddled in an overcoat. He sat on a wooden bench in one corner, smoking a cigarette.

'Do you mind if I join you?' Perez remained standing. He'd have gone back to the hotel and waited there, if Markham had told him to.

'As long as you don't tell Maria I've started smoking again.' Markham didn't even raise his head to look at Perez.

Perez sat beside him. The bench was damp.

'Do you have news?' Now Markham did turn round.

'You know who killed my son?' The English accent was stronger than ever.

'No. Not yet.'

Markham stubbed out his cigarette, buried the end in the earth beside him. 'More questions then.'

'I was hoping for a conversation,' Perez said. 'I'm not sure I understand which questions I should be asking. And you knew your son. I don't think I ever met him.'

Markham didn't answer immediately. A blackbird was singing somewhere in the bushes.

'We spoilt him. He was our only son. I suppose it was natural.' He paused. 'I'd never have let on to Maria, but I was pleased when he got that job in London. I thought it would be good for him, standing on his own two feet. He was never financially independent, but I didn't mind that. It was never about money.'

'What *did* you mind?' Because Perez could tell that something was troubling the man.

'He was self-centred. Believed the world revolved around him. Our fault. Like I said, the way we brought him up. It'd have been different if he'd had brothers or sisters.' Another pause. 'Maria could deny him nothing. It didn't make him popular here. Perhaps he needed that ruthless streak, for the work he was doing, but I hated it. It wasn't the way a man should behave.' He stared over the garden. Perez wondered how it must be to feel that way about your son. It would be worse perhaps than grieving over the boy's death. 'I wondered if the way he acted had made him a victim.'

'He'd made enemies here in the islands then?'

Peter Markham shrugged. 'Nobody who cared enough about him to kill him.' He turned so that he was facing Perez. 'Sometimes I think we should have forced him to stay here and look after Evie. She could have made him accept some responsibility. But Maria wouldn't have it. An island girl wasn't good enough for her boy.'

'Jerry told you he was in Shetland this time for work.'

'That's right. I think he'd persuaded his editor that he needed to cover the gas coming ashore. The new energy.'

'Is that what he told you?'

'I'm not sure that he told me anything. I was busy. That day we were rushed off our feet. That was the impression he gave his mother.'

'His editor didn't know anything about a story,' Perez said. 'Jerry had arranged to go to a meeting about the tidal energy, but he'd told *her* he was taking leave.' He paused. 'She thought he might be ill. Suffering from stress. Burnout. She said he hadn't been himself since before Christmas. Not so sharp.'

'Jerry was fine,' Markham said. 'He would have told his boss he was unwell to get a few days away. He believed his own fiction sometimes. That was what made him such a good liar.'

'Did he often tell lies?' Again Perez was shocked that Markham could describe his son in such a clear-eyed way.

'He was a writer,' Markham said, as if that explained everything.

'Why would he come home,' Perez said, 'if he wasn't here for work?'

'He would have needed money. That was why he usually came back.' Markham took a crumpled cigarette packet from his coat pocket and struggled to light one, drawing deeply when he managed it.

'Had he asked you for a loan?'

'Oh, he wouldn't have asked me,' Markham said. 'As I said, his mother would refuse him nothing.'

'Is it OK if I talk to Maria?'

'Why not? She'll believe her son's a good man, whatever you say to her.'

Perez found the man's cynicism unbearable. He stood up. Markham spluttered on his cigarette. 'I loved him, you know,' he said. 'I just wish things could have been different.' Another cough. 'I wish *he* could have been different.'

Maria was in her nightclothes and dressing gown and in the living room the curtains were still drawn. Perez opened them and saw that Peter Markham was still on his bench in the garden below. The flat smelled stale, and Perez wondered if Maria had washed since Jerry's death. She had family in the islands. Why weren't they looking after her?

'Have you thought of moving out for a little while?' he asked. 'There are people who would put you up.'

She looked horrified at the prospect, and he thought briefly that she would never leave the flat at the top of the hotel. Like Miss Havisham in the Dickens book he'd read at school, she'd stay there mourning Jerry until she was covered in cobwebs and dust.

'I couldn't face it,' she said. 'Not yet. People want to visit, but I tell Peter to send them away.'

'Did you give Jerry some money when he came home this time?' Perez was sitting on a low easy chair and he was so close to her that he could keep his voice very quiet. Almost like a lover's whisper.

'I offered,' she said. And she turned to Perez, her eyes feverish and sparkling, glad of a reason to be proud of her boy. 'I offered him money, but he said he didn't need it. "I won't need your cash ever again." That was what he said.'

'What do you think he meant by that?'

'He was on the track of a story.' Maria was animated again. Manic. 'A story that would make his fortune.'

'Is that what Jerry told you?' Perez spoke again in his soft seducer's voice. 'That his story would make him a fortune?'

But she seemed caught up in her memories and didn't answer directly. 'That was what Jerry always wanted,' she said. 'Fame and fortune. From when he was a little boy. He thought he'd find it in London, but all the time it was here.'

'What did he tell you about his story?' Perez thought this was like groping in the dark for a shadow that kept slipping out of reach.

'Nothing!' Maria sat suddenly upright and he thought he caught the smell of spirit on her skin. She'd been drinking as well as taking prescribed medicine. Not this morning perhaps, but last night. Perez imagined her and Peter sitting in this room and drinking away the guilt in silence. 'It was secret.'

'Is that why Jerry's editor knew nothing about it?' Perez asked. 'Because he needed to keep it to himself?'

Maria nodded energetically. 'Anyone might betray

him.' Perez thought that sounded more like her son's statement than Maria's, and another scene came into his head. This time he pictured Maria and Jerry sitting in this room the night before the journalist died. Dinner was over and they were drinking. No Peter this time. He wouldn't be able to face it. He'd be downstairs playing the gracious host in the bar. But mother and son. Maria delighted to have her boy home, perhaps sitting literally at his feet. Good wine. The most expensive the hotel could provide. No expense spared for the prodigal son. And Jerry holding forth, talking about his plans, refusing her money with a grand gesture: 'Just you wait. I'll never need to borrow from you again.'

'But he'd have confided in you,' Perez said gently. 'He'd have told you what his story was about.'

Maria looked at him as if she suspected Perez of betraying Jerry too.

'It might help us find out who killed him,' Perez said. 'We have to know what brought him here, what he was planning to write about.'

She looked at him, seemed at last to be wavering, to be ready to tip over the edge and answer. Then there were footsteps on the stairs. Peter, chilled now and ready to come into the warm, appeared at the door.

'Jimmy!' he said, his voice so jolly that he must have been practising the tone all the way from the garden. 'Still here then? I was just going to make some coffee. You'll join us?'

Perez looked at Maria, hoping that she still might be persuaded to talk to him, but it seemed that whatever spell he'd put on her had been broken. She stood up. 'I'll take a bath,' she said. 'Leave you boys to it.' But at the door she paused. 'He was going to tell us,' she said. 'He was going to tell us his secret the night he died. We were waiting up for him.' She left the room before Perez could talk to her further.

'Do you know what that was about?' he asked Peter.

The man shrugged. 'I know nothing about any secret,' he said. 'You should take it with a pinch of salt. Jerry and Maria both enjoyed a drama.'

Perez declined the coffee and walked back to his house. He collected his car and set off for the Bonhoga.

Chapter Eighteen

Perez arrived at the gallery before the lunchtime rush. Once the Bonhoga had been a water mill and it was still a grand three-storeyed building. On the ground floor there was a shop and reception, and upstairs in the roof the exhibition space. Perez couldn't go up there. Whenever he'd come to the Bonhoga with Fran she'd drag him up to look at the paintings and drawings, and the memory was too raw. She'd exhibited there herself on a number of occasions. So he went straight downstairs to the coffee shop, where one wall was made up of huge windows looking over the burn.

Brian was a large man, hardly fitting into the narrow kitchen. If he was pulling a baking tray from the oven he had to twist his body sideways to reach inside. He'd been thinner when Perez had first met him. Then Brian had been cooking at the Sullom work camp, an English university dropout with a drug habit to fund, and Perez had charged him with possession of heroin. Now he was clean, but he was still in the islands, still cooking. Perez hoped he was settled and happy. It was hard to tell. Brian rarely smiled and carried around him an air of gloom. A habit as entrenched as the heroin.

The cafe was separated from the kitchen by a

counter. Brian was standing there, wrapped in a huge black apron, cutting slices of cake for two German tourists. Otherwise the place was empty. He nodded to Perez, but didn't speak until he'd carried the cake and coffee to his customers.

'What can I get for you, Jimmy?'

'Coffee,' Perez said. 'Black.' He paused. 'I'm here about Jerry Markham, the guy whose body was found in Aith last week. He was in here the morning that he died.'

Brian was pouring coffee and turned slowly to face Perez. 'I didn't even know the man.'

'I'm not accusing you of killing him.' Perez remembered that Brian had always had a streak of paranoia, was always frightened that he was being set up. 'But he was with a woman. Middle-aged. We're trying to trace her.' He sipped his coffee. 'You would recognize Markham? You'd know him when he worked on the *Shetland Times*?'

'Yes, I recognized him.'

'And the woman? Did you know her?'

Brian shook his head. 'I'd never seen her in here before.'

'Was she local?'

'I didn't hear her speak. They shut up when I took their drinks over.'

Perez thought about this. 'Did you have the impression that they were friendly?'

Brian seemed to have got the message that he wasn't a suspect and became more forthcoming. 'They weren't having a stand-up row, but I had the feeling there was an argument. No warmth. You know. One of them might leave at any time.'

'And the woman?' Perez said again. 'What *can* you tell me about her?'

'She was middle-aged. Smart. It looked as if it could be a work meeting. She was dressed for work, you know. Skirt and jacket. But that's not so unusual. People do arrange to meet here to discuss business. It's central. I thought she might have something to do with the gas. There are lots of strange faces around now.' Brian seemed to enjoy seeing himself on the side of law and order.

'Would you know Rhona Laing, if you saw her?'

'Who?'

'The Procurator Fiscal. She comes here for coffee, I'm told.'

Brian shook his head. 'Sorry, Jimmy. There are lots of people who come in for coffee. I don't know them all.'

Perez pulled a newspaper cutting from his pocket. A piece from the *Shetland Times*. He wasn't sure why he'd kept it. To show Cassie when she was old enough and had questions about her mother's death. It was the report on Fran's murder, and Rhona Laing had made a statement. There was a photo to go with it. 'This is her,' he said. 'Was this the woman who was with Jerry Markham the day he died?'

Brian put the paper on the counter and smoothed it. Perez hoped he wouldn't comment on the content of the story. He didn't need this man's sympathy, didn't think he could bear it. He would have to walk away or he might lash out. Pick up his coffee mug and hurl it against the wall. But Brian was focused on the task in hand. He narrowed his eyes and stared at the slightly grainy picture. 'I don't know,' he said. 'She looks familiar, but if she comes in anyway . . . Sorry, Jimmy. I can't be sure.'

'That's great,' Perez said. 'Really. You don't know how many people pretend or stretch the truth because they're so eager to help. Better to be straight.'

For almost the first time since he'd known the man Brian smiled. Perez pulled a couple of coins from his pocket to pay for the coffee, but Brian waved them away.

In the car Perez was tempted to reread the *Shetland Times* article about Fran. He knew it almost off by heart, but still he was tempted. Instead he put it back in his pocket. He took out his phone and looked at it for a long time before calling the neighbour who'd offered to look after Cassie for him.

'Sure,' she said when he asked if Cassie might go to her house to play after school.

'It might be late. I'm planning a trip to Fetlar and I haven't checked ferry times.'

'Look, it'll be fine.' A pause. 'She wanted to come before, you know, but she said you might be lonely. Why doesn't she come for a sleepover? Then you'll not have to rush back.'

He drove north very fast, thinking all the time about Cassie and what his neighbour, Maggie, had said. What a self-centred oaf he'd been! It wasn't Cassie's place to care for him. He thought he needed to lighten up when she was around, bring more laughter into the house. Put on more of a show.

Having made the decision to travel to Fetlar, he hated the idea that he might just miss a ferry. As he drove into Toft the Yell boat was in, and his was the last car on board. It seemed like a sign. In Yell he had time for a bacon sandwich in the Wind Dog cafe before the ferry to Fetlar arrived. He wondered what he was doing here. What was it all about, this hunger? This sudden need for action? He decided it was some sort of escape. He'd spent too long in that small house in Ravenswick. And he needed information to give to Willow Reeves. The desperation was the result of pride, or something like it. All he had yet was the fact that Markham had turned down his mother's loan. That seemed a big deal to Perez, but what did it mean? That Markham had suddenly become a more responsible man? Or that he'd discovered another form of income? And there was the secret that Markham had promised to share with his mother on the night of his death. Was that relevant or just one of Maria's fancies, a way of feeling closer to her dead son?

It was a couple of years since he'd been to Fetlar. The trip had been part of his courtship of Fran. She'd had a friend from the south to stay, and Perez had taken them both to see the breeding red-necked phalaropes on the loch there. Then it had been sunny and there'd been a promise of better times, a burning realization that this woman was special. *Why was I so cautious? She'd have married me sooner.* And he remembered what Evie had said about John Henderson. About him being a gentleman and not rushing her.

There was no sign from the road to show where Francis Watt had his boat-building business. Perez found it in a big shed beside a low white croft-house. The shed had windows at one end to let in the natural light and the view of a sweep of white sand, curving so that the bay formed the best part of a circle. It was a beautiful spot and he could see why Evie would be attracted to stay on the islands after growing up here. Perez had left his car on the road and walked up the track, buffeted by the wind and enjoying the exercise. In a small field beyond the house someone was working, bent double, planting tatties, but too far away to hear when Perez shouted, so he'd knocked at the door of the house and, when there was no reply, he'd wandered across the yard to the shed.

He heard the sound before he reached it. Metal on metal, regular and explosive. Through the open door Perez saw a yoal, almost finished, its keel held in a clamp, the curved sides regular and perfectly symmetrical. A work of art. A sculpture. The floor was scattered with wood shavings and sawdust and the smell of wood filled the place. At the far end of the shed stood a pile of planks, stacked so that the air could move through them. A middle-aged man, dressed in a fisherman's smock, was hammering grooved copper nails into the overlapping planks, the fit so tight that they'd be watertight. He was bending into the hull and it looked like awkward, back-breaking work. Perez waited until the man straightened. 'I'm sorry to disturb you.' He felt that Francis Watt was like an artist who needed to concentrate on his craft.

Watt squinted against the light. 'How can I help?'

'Jimmy Perez. I'm here about Jerry Markham.'

'Ah, Jimmy.' The voice serious. The man was remembering that Jimmy had been bereaved, and for the second time that day Perez hoped there would be no mention of Fran.

'Sorry about the noise,' Francis said. 'The clinking. Jessie hates it. She says she can hear the vibration even inside the house.'

'Worth it,' Perez said, 'to make a boat like that.'

Watt nodded to acknowledge the compliment and smiled. 'Come away into the kitchen. I'm ready for tea, and Jessie will be in soon too.'

The kitchen was cluttered and comfortable. A Rayburn with a basket of peat beside it, a scrubbed table under the window and a battered sofa against one wall. Francis cleared a pile of plans and drawings from the sofa so that his visitor could sit down.

'I've read your column in the *Shetland Times*,' Perez said. 'You have very strong views.'

'I think we've become too used to an easy life,' Francis said. 'It's made us greedy. Uncaring.' He gave a quick grin. 'I'm not popular for saying those things.'

He put a kettle on the range and took a cake tin from a shelf. Inside home-made date slices. No shop-bought biscuits here.

'Do you have strong views about tidal power?'

'It's one of the few things my daughter Evie and I argue about,' he said. 'It's fine to make Shetland self-sufficient in energy, but I have no interest in exporting it. I abhor that big new wind farm, hate driving past it on my way to Lerwick. There are too many people with vested interests here who hope to make their fortunes. There hasn't been a development in Shetland that hasn't had corruption at the heart of it. My Evie's honest as the day is long, but I'm worried that the taint of greed will stick to her too.'

'Jerry Markham was planning a story about the new energies,' Perez said. 'He'd arranged to go to a meeting of the Hvidahus action group the evening he died.'

Francis looked up, startled. 'I know nothing about that. I support the aims of the action group, but I don't get too involved. After all, Power of Water is Evie's big project, so I have divided loyalties.'

'Do you have other children?' Perez wondered where that question had come from. Sandy would see it as a waste of time. But not the new inspector. Perez thought she would work in the same way as him. She'd want to dig under the surface of a family too.

'A son,' Francis said. 'Magnus. He's away at university in Stirling. Computer science.' The man smiled. 'He'll not come back to the islands to stay. Evie's my last hope of keeping the family traditions alive.'

'Will she take on the boat-building?' Perez asked.

'Aye, she might at that, and bring John Henderson with her, once he's had enough of the oil work. That's what I'm hoping. Evie grew up with it and she has a feeling for working with wood.'

The door opened and a woman came in. Perez had seen her working in the field, planting potatoes. She was small and slender, round-faced, smiling. In twenty years Evie would look like her. She took off her boots at the door and went to the sink to wash her hands. Under her jacket she wore a smock just like her husband's, on top of faded cord trousers.

'This is Jimmy Perez,' Francis said. 'He's come to ask us questions about Jerry Markham.'

'Evie said you'd spoken to her.' The woman was polite, but prickly. 'You can't expect her to have anything to do with his death. All that happened years ago. She was hardly more than a child. Our fault maybe, for sheltering her too much. She's getting married on Saturday. You mustn't spoil this week for her.'

'Had you seen Markham since he was home this time?'

'No,' Watt said. 'We don't leave the isle much. It's a busy time of year and we have all that we need here.'

'When was the last time that you left Fetlar?'

The couple looked at each other, trying to work it out, to give an accurate answer. 'Maybe six weeks ago,' Francis said. 'Evie had a problem with the boiler in her house. John was on shift at Sullom and couldn't help. We went and stayed over, made a night of it.'

Perez thought it would be easy enough to check with the boys on the boat. They'd know if anyone on this small island had taken the ferry out.

'Why would anyone want to kill Markham?' he said. 'Why now?'

There was a pause. Jessie Watt poured herself tea.

'I knew him a bit when he worked on the *Shetland Times*,' Francis said. 'Before there was all that trouble with Evie. He was good at making enemies.'

Out of the window Perez saw a child running across the beach, chasing a dog. 'This story he was writing about the new energies. Might that have made him enemies too?'

'You're talking politicians taking backhanders? Playing fast and loose with the planning laws?'

Perez hadn't been thinking that way, but he could see that it might be a possibility.

'I wouldn't be surprised,' Francis went on. 'People get obsessed with money. But I've heard nothing of that sort. Nothing serious enough to kill a man for.'

'Anything at all?' Perez persisted.

Francis shook his head.

On the way out of the house, through an open door, Perez saw a small office. Clean and uncluttered, quite in contrast to the kitchen. A filing cabinet and a desk with a PC. It seemed the Watts were happy enough to use the new technologies when it came to promoting their business. Walking down the track to the car, he felt that he'd missed an opportunity and left the important questions unasked.

Chapter Nineteen

Rhona Laing woke early. It was still dark. Since the discovery of Markham's body her sleep had been fitful. Over the weekend she'd stayed up drinking late, but even the alcohol hadn't knocked her out properly. For the first time in her life she felt that things were running out of her control. And for the first time in years she longed for companionship, someone to talk to and someone she could trust. A body in her bed for the whole night.

Monday. A working week. She lay in the grey half-light, running through the events of the day. In the morning there was a trip to the north of Shetland mainland to see the proposed site of the new tidal-power project. The approval of the giant wind farm had made the development more viable. A cable would run from Shetland to the Scottish mainland to export electricity to the fuel-hungry UK. Once the cable was in place, Shetland could make a profit from the export of tidal power too. The islanders had become accustomed to the good life and wanted to maintain their standard of living. Local politicians had supported the wind farm, despite some objections from their electorate.

The trip wasn't official Fiscal business. Rhona was a member of many island committees that had little to do with her work. Her love of sailing had brought her north, but she didn't intend to be a Fiscal in the wilds forever. She'd always had political ambitions, could see herself in a position of power; in her wildest dreams she imagined a seat in the Lords. Baroness Laing of Aith had a ring to it. And that would only happen if she forged the right connections, made herself useful to the party. A senior politician had indicated that such a move wasn't impossible. Rhona had no strong feelings about green energy, but it had seemed to her that the topic would grow in importance, especially north of the border. So she'd read about it, represented the islands in discussions over the controversial wind farm. And now she'd made sure that she was a part of the tidal-power working group. Of course if the Jerry Markham connection came to light, there'd be no chance of any form of political preferment. She wouldn't even keep her post here in Shetland.

She put coffee into the filter machine and took a shower. Very hot, to clear her head. At least the Power of Water meeting meant she wouldn't have to go into the office this morning. She wouldn't have to answer questions about the investigation. Then it occurred to her that she still had leave to take before the end of April. Why not hand over responsibility for the Markham case to her assistant? She could say that she was compromised because she'd found the body. Ethically she shouldn't be involved. That would run well with the press. Drying herself, she felt slightly more optimistic. It would be a way to distance herself from the investigation and from Detective Inspector Willow Reeves.

She checked her emails and found a message from Evie Watt's BlackBerry, asking if they might meet at the proposed tidal-power site half an hour later than planned. Something unexpected had turned up and she was running a little late. That meant Rhona had time to call her line manager, say that she intended to take a few days' leave and explain her reasons. 'Just until the police have completed their investigation,' she said. 'We must be seen to be acting with complete transparency.' Then she called the office, checked her watch and saw that she could still fit in more coffee and a slice of toast.

They'd arranged to meet in the car park in Hvidahus, close to the coastal path and to the proposed site of the tidal generation. It had been years since Rhona had driven this way and she'd forgotten how attractive the valley was. Sheltered from the prevailing wind, it led to two small houses and then to the sea and a large white house looking out over a small pier. There were only three people on the working group: Rhona, Evie Watt and Joe Sinclair, who was the harbour master at Sullom Voe. He'd been co-opted because of his knowledge of the tides and because he was a local man who had influence in the islands. He could sway public opinion. There was already some opposition to the scheme, and Joe would be useful in smoothing troubled waters.

Rhona arrived before the other two and got out of her car. There was a squally breeze that took her breath away when she faced the sea. Here, a natural harbour looked out to the island of Samphrey, but further north the cliffs were enormous, great steps of rock leading down to the water. At the highest point was a small pile of stones that she hadn't noticed before. She watched a raven balance on the wind and then land on an untidy nest on one of the ledges. Glancing at her watch, she realized that Evie Watt and Joe Sinclair were even later than they'd agreed and experienced a stab of irritation. She felt poor punctuality as a personal insult.

She walked away from her car and towards the pier. Already tense and jittery, she found this waiting unbearable. She was tempted to drive away. An otter swam between the concrete pillars and onto the rocky beach, distracting her for a moment. It was eating a fish, delicate bites with very sharp teeth. Rhona had no sentimental attachment to the natural world. She thought nature was all about the survival of the fittest. The raven and the otter would kill to save themselves and their young. *And so would I.* The thought came without warning. She held it for a moment and then chased it away.

Sinclair and Evie arrived at the same time, though in different cars. Rhona saw the vehicles snake down the narrow road and walked back to join them. Evie seemed strangely distant and preoccupied. Rhona had never taken to the girl. She was efficient enough, but her childish enthusiasms were irritating. Principles were all very well, but sometimes they prevented real business from being done: compromise was essential. Rhona didn't want to be associated with a project that failed because of the young woman's reluctance to operate in the real world.

'Will you show us the proposed site then?' Rhona said. 'Now that you've arrived at last. So we'll know what we're talking about when we meet that professor from Robert Gordon University.'

She was pleased to see Evie blush. The young woman led them along the coastal path, which climbed steeply to the top of the cliffs. 'We'll get a better view of the whole site from here.' She pointed out the uninhabited islands of Samphrey and Bigga. Beyond, Yell was in the distance and the roll-on, roll-off ferry was crossing the Sound. 'The sea's very deep around Samphrey.' She looked back at Hvidahus. Already the cars and the houses looked tiny. 'We'd need to strengthen the existing pier, but we already have easy access to the water and there's a tremendous tidal stream at this point.'

'Won't there be problems with the planners? I thought this was a Site of Special Scientific Interest.' Rhona wanted to show that she'd done her homework too.

'There won't be any substantial development. There's already a building close to the site that could be adapted for the substation.' Joe Sinclair pointed in the distance to a low stone shed crumbling into disrepair, which squatted on short grass inland from a shingle bank beyond the pier. Rhona looked, but she was already losing interest. Evie was still talking, but Rhona found her list of kilowatts and depths and tide speeds boring. She was more interested in the strategic decisions.

'It used to be a salmon hatchery,' Evie said. 'So officially it already has an industrial use. And we're not talking a major development. Just an experimental project to check the feasibility at this stage. We'll walk down that way and I'll show you.'

'They'll need to put in a road to the substation. And improve that to the pier.' The Fiscal was arguing for its own sake now. Because it was expected of her. Really, she didn't care. 'I assume the turbines are substantial pieces of kit.'

But she saw that the scheme might work. Shetland had the confidence to see through grand designs.

'I'm already putting together funding bids,' Evie said. 'There are still grants available for renewable projects. And the Power of Water community programme has already raised a decent sum. We'll pull in more small investors, when folk start to see that it might become a reality.'

'I hear there's an action group, lobbying to prevent the scheme.'

Evie was dismissive. 'A couple of Nimbys who live in the White House, and a handful of their friends. No real opposition.'

Joe had started walking back down the path towards the hatchery. Perhaps he thought it was more tactful to leave the women together to sort out their differences.

The wind blew a hole in the cloud and a ray of sunshine caught the breaking waves and the pure white of the gannets below. Evie was standing in front of Rhona. All at once the Fiscal had an almost overwhelming impulse to push out, to shove the woman over the cliff. She could imagine herself doing it, had the sensation of movement in her muscles, the touch of Evie's waterproof jacket on the palms of her hands. Experienced the thrill and the exhilaration of watching the woman fall. Not for a reason that made any sense, but because she *could*. Because she was stronger, more ruthless. Because, as the woman's body twisted and bounced down the cliff, she would stop feeling helpless.

The sensation scared her. She stepped back, so that Evie was out of her reach even if she raised her arms. She found that she was shaking. *What's happening to me? What might I do next?* Turning, she saw that Joe had stopped and was staring at her. It was almost as if he'd guessed what she'd been thinking. She hurried to join him.

'Did you hear that the Walshes held a meeting of the action group on Friday night?' Joe said.

Evie had joined them. 'Like I said. They're a couple of Nimbys. No threat.'

'I did hear,' Joe said, 'that they'd invited Jerry Markham to the meeting.' He paused. 'Lucky for us that he died before he could write a story about the scheme. Who knows how he might spin it?' Rhona was surprised by the facetious tone of the comment; Joe walked on before the women could answer.

They'd arrived at the hatchery. It was built of stone, with a rusting corrugated-iron roof and a concrete floor. Evie pulled open the wooden door. Rhona saw that she was still troubled by Joe's information about Markham's link to the protest group.

'Will the police make a connection between Markham's death and the project?' Evie asked. She stood aside so that they could see in. The only light came through the open door. The place smelled of damp and mould and made Rhona nauseous. She stayed where she was.

Joe laughed. 'Markham had enemies enough. And we've done nothing wrong, have we? Why would we want to kill him?'

Chapter Twenty

Willow Reeves was back in the station. The lay-by with the skid marks was taped and guarded, and the mist had cleared enough for the planes to be running. Vicki Hewitt had arrived on the overnight ferry and Sandy had picked her up from the Holmsgarth terminal in Lerwick. They would be at the crime scene now. But Willow was restless and impatient. She got on the phone to Perez. No reception. Willow wanted to know if the manager of the Bonhoga coffee shop had recognized Rhona Laing as the strange woman who'd met Markham on the morning he was killed. Surely Perez should have news by now. Why hadn't he been in touch? She still wasn't sure what she made of the man. She brooded on the matter for a moment and then phoned her DC in Inverness.

'Have you found any link yet between Rhona Laing and Jerry Markham?'

'Nothing. And really, Boss, I don't think there's anything to find. No contacts in common. I don't think he ever even reported any of the cases she worked on before she moved to Shetland.'

So it's here. Willow stretched. Her muscles were tight and tense. She needed exercise. Yoga. A run. *Whatever was going on between Markham and the Fiscal happened here.* Or were the Shetlanders right, and there *was* no connection?

'Any news on Markham's phone?'

'Not yet. I'll chase it up again.'

She thought she needed to get more of a handle on the case, a better perspective. Maybe she should meet some of the people involved and not rely on the opinion of the local officers.

She found Evie Watt's work phone number and tried that. A woman said that Evie was out of the office that morning and passed on a mobile number. That connected, though the reception was poor. It sounded as if Evie was driving, using a hand-free device. Willow introduced herself and suggested that they might meet for lunch. 'If you haven't eaten already. That way I don't take up any work time. I'm a veggie. Verging on the vegan. Can you think of anywhere?' She sensed that the woman on the other end of the phone was surprised by the call, but after a moment's silence there was a response.

'I've been out onsite. I'm on my way back to town, but I'll be there in half an hour. What about the Olive Tree in the Tollclock Centre? Close to work for me, and you'll find something there to eat.' Then clear directions.

Willow was early and drove along to the ferry terminal to kill time. The NorthLink ferry was still in, but the place was quiet. A sudden squall blew up as she was crossing the car park to the Tollclock, and she knew she would look like a witch blown in by the gale, her hair wild. And Evie Watt did look astonished when Willow landed at her table.

'Brilliant place!' Willow said. She carried a plate

filled with salads, hummus and pitta bread. 'Just what I needed. Odd to find something like this in Lerwick. Not at all what I expected.'

'Oh, we're quite civilized really.' Evie smiled. Willow thought that already she had the woman hooked, that Evie was disarmed and ready to talk.

'Look, I'm sorry to trouble you,' Willow said. 'You must be frantic! A wedding on Saturday and so much to organize. I'm surprised you look so calm.'

'It's a very relaxed and informal do. And I've delegated most of the organization to other people. But I'm not sure how I can help you. I told Jimmy Perez everything I know.' Evie had chosen a seafood salad, but had eaten very little. Willow wondered if she was worried about putting on weight before the wedding.

The detective leaned forward. She could have been a friend, a bit older than Evie and not as pretty – no competition. They could be sharing gossip. 'I'm trying to follow Markham's movements on the day he died. He spent Thursday night in the Ravenswick Hotel. Friday morning he was drinking coffee in the Bonhoga with a middle-aged woman. Any idea who that might have been?'

Evie shook her head. 'Unless it was his mother. They were always very close. It was a sacrifice for Maria to let her son go south. She understood his ambitions, but she adored him. It always seemed a weird relationship to me – they were more like lovers than mother and son. I mean, I get on well with my dad, but our relationship isn't as intense as that. Peter must have felt left out at times.'

Willow nodded. She hadn't considered that Maria might have been Markham's companion. A mistake.

'We know he had lunch, on his own, in a chip shop in Brae.' Sandy had come up with that information. The owner had recognized Markham. 'Then he had a meeting with the press officer in Sullom Voe. Andy Belshaw. Why would he do that?'

'I suppose Andy would be the natural first place to start, if he was writing an article about the terminal.'

'Do you know him?'

'Sure. He runs the junior football team with John, my fiancé. He has sons of the right age, and John has always got on well with kids.' She paused. 'John's wife couldn't have children. An effect of the cancer treatment. She became ill in her thirties and was being treated for it most of their married life. John nursed her all that time.' Her voice was matter-of-fact and Willow couldn't tell what she made of all that, what it felt like to be engaged to some sort of saint.

'So he missed out on a normal family life,' Willow said. 'And now he's getting a second chance.'

'Aye, perhaps. We both want children, certainly.'

'Then Markham was supposed to meet an action group about a tidal-energy project. Was that anything to do with you?'

Evie looked uncomfortable. 'No,' she said. 'There are a handful of people in the islands who think the tidal project would spoil the environment around Hvidahus, where we're planning to bring the power ashore, but really it would have very little impact.'

'So they're like a lobby group?'

'Aye,' Evie said. 'Something like that.'

She turned her head slightly and Willow thought she couldn't push the point without alienating the woman. 'Tell me about Andy Belshaw,' she said. 'I only met the man briefly and I wasn't sure what to make of him.'

'I don't think he's that complicated! He loves his family, a few beers at the weekend with his pals, running the kids' football team. A bit competitive. He likes the team to win, and I have the sense that he's ambitious at work. He and John get on well, but they're quite different.'

'Your John is a bit more complicated then?' Willow kept her voice light. This was a strange conversation to be having with a suspect in a busy cafe. Her boss in Inverness would have forty fits if he knew.

Evie considered. Or perhaps she was thinking up a response that didn't give too much away. 'I don't know.' She laughed again. 'I hope I have years to find out!'

'And Andy Belshaw's wife? What's she like?' Now, Willow thought, this really did feel like gossip with a friend.

'Oh, Jen is lovely. She's the school cook at Aith. A bit older than Andy. Motherly, you know. Passionate about traditional crafts.'

Willow nodded.

'I should get back to work.' Evie tidied the plates into a pile. 'I'm having Friday off, and there's a lot to do this week.'

'Anything specific?' Willow realized she was enjoying the company of this woman and didn't want their encounter to end just yet, that she had a sudden and irrational dread of being left alone in a strange place.

'I'm trying to persuade a university research team to contribute to the project to develop Shetland as an experimental site for tidal energy. There's a place in North Mainland that would be perfect. The council could help with transport and accommodation costs, but the scientists seem to think Shetland is at the end of the known world. I've organized for the team leader to come and see the place for himself. I was onsite in Hvidahus this morning with a working party of inter-ested islanders, talking through our plans. So that's the rest of my week taken up. That and writing the place settings for the wedding, and doing a pile of baking for the party in the evening.' She got to her feet and Willow thanked her and let her go. At the door Evie stopped and turned back. 'You should come along to the party, if you're still around,' she said. 'You'd be very welcome. A traditional Shetland wedding is some-thing special.'

For the first time since she'd arrived, Willow found herself driving along the road north on her own. It was early afternoon and the road was quiet. Gusts of wind caught at the car and forced her to concentrate on the driving. But all the time she was running through the events and the people surrounding Jerry Markham's death in her head. Andy Belshaw, who worked at Sullom Voe, managing the news and spin-ning the image of the place. Evie Watt, who lived close to the terminal. John Henderson, who was based just across the water from there and piloted the huge tankers in and out of Sullom Voe terminal. Mark Walsh, who was Henderson's neighbour and opposed to tidal energy. Willow had marked them all on a map on the operations-room whiteboard in the police station in Lerwick. And the lay-by where Markham was killed, and the marina at Aith where his body had been found by Rhona Laing.

By now Willow had arrived at the lay-by. Vicki Hewitt, the CSI, and Sandy Wilson were both wearing scene-suits. The blue-and-white tape twisted and pulled at the fastenings in the wind. Willow stood outside the cordon and shouted in to them.

'So, Vicki, is this our crime scene, do you think?'

The woman looked up and grinned. 'Hey! Give me a chance. I don't work miracles in my spare time.'

Willow knew she should be patient, but in her head time passed, ticking like a metronome. Soon her boss would decide that she'd had long enough and would fly in himself to take on the case, like a lone sheriff to save the day. She yelled that she'd see them back in Lerwick for the evening briefing and got into her car. She tried Perez's phone again and this time it rang out. Perez answered, but the signal was weak and she could hardly hear him.

'I'll be on the ferry from Yell soon. If you can meet me at Toft in half an hour we can talk then.' In the background she heard engine noise and gulls. She wondered what he'd been up to and felt a small stab of anger. Did he think he had the right to play private detective and ignore her completely? But she was curious and knew she'd do exactly what he said. She looked at her map and headed north again.

On the road towards Sullom Voe terminal she saw the stuffed images of Evie Watt and John Henderson, the life-size photos still intact on the faces despite the weather, held around the heads with thin elastic. Evie's had slipped a bit and the straw was spilling out of the pillowcase. Willow remembered that there'd been a discussion of Evie's hen party in the bar at Voe and thought the same friends must have made the models for a laugh. Willow wondered briefly who she'd invite to *her* hen party, then decided the question was academic: she wasn't the marrying kind.

She'd slowed down to look at the dummies dressed up in the wedding finery and was about to continue when something made her change her mind. Instead she pulled her car onto the verge, got out and walked back to look at them more closely. She was interested to know what Evie's fiancé looked like and she still had twenty minutes before she'd arranged to meet Jimmy Perez. Walking through the long grass, she saw there were irises and marsh marigolds in the ditch. Not in flower yet, but in a few weeks they'd look magnificent. She wouldn't see them because she'd be long gone by then, the murderer in custody. She hoped. Getting closer, she thought the hen-party lasses had gone to a lot of trouble. Real shoes on the feet. A frilly white dress on the girl model. But on the other – not a suit as she'd expected, but navy-blue trousers and jacket. On the jacket a red-and-white lapel badge. The male dummy, which had previously been propped up on the bank, had slipped and was lying in longer grass. It was only as she looked down at it that she saw real hands and, behind the photographic mask, real skin, real hair.

A moment of panic. This was too close to a horror movie, to childhood fairy stories of a puppet coming to life. She couldn't move, couldn't think. Then she lifted the mask gently with the end of her pen, stretching the elastic that fixed it in place. The face beneath it coincided exactly with the glossy picture on the photograph. John Henderson was lying dead beside the figure of his bride-to-be.

Chapter Twenty-One

Willow stood by the side of the road and made phone calls. To Sandy Wilson, asking him to bring Vicki Hewitt along as soon as possible, keeping her voice even, betraying none of her earlier panic.

'And *what's* happened?' Sandy Wilson sounding out of his depth.

'John Henderson's dead. And someone stuck a photo over his face. So not an accident, and not suicide. Unless he put on the mask before stabbing himself in the chest.'

'Right.'

But Willow thought it wasn't right. This was planned and horrible and running out of control.

Next call was to Jimmy Perez, who was already at Toft where the roll-on, roll-off ferry from Yell had arrived at the Shetland mainland. Another explanation. This time the response wasn't a question, but a statement. 'I'll be there in ten minutes.' And the thought brought her comfort. Suddenly she wished she'd asked Perez to interview Henderson over the weekend. Even ill and depressed, Perez would have got more out of the man than Sandy had. And now it was too late. It was an error of judgement that she knew she'd come to regret over the coming days.

Perez arrived first. He stayed on the road with his shoulders hunched into his jacket and didn't even ask to look at the body. Following procedure to the letter, or because he couldn't face staring at a dead man? Willow couldn't decide. She couldn't tell how close to the edge he was. She wished they could get very drunk together; then she might find the nerve to ask all the questions that were bubbling into her mind.

'Somebody should tell Evie Watt,' he said. 'Before the news gets out. You know what this place is like. There are no secrets here.'

Except the identity of a murderer.

'Will you do it?' she asked. Only as the words came out did she realize how crass that was, but they'd been spoken and it was too late to take them back. And if Perez was working, he should be up to the job.

There was a silence. 'I'm not sure if I'm the right person.'

They stared at each other. Like dogs. Or lovers having their first row, neither wanting to set a precedent by backing down first.

'I was thinking I should take a look at Henderson's house,' he said at last. 'Hard to tell, but I wouldn't have thought the man was killed here by the road. It would be too great a risk. There's no fog this time.'

'Where did he live?' Willow asked. She'd seen the address written down, but again she felt hindered by her lack of knowledge of the geography of Shetland. And undermined by having a colleague who knew the place and its people better than she ever would.

'Hvidahus, on the east side, not far away. It's a newish bungalow. Henderson built it when his wife was first ill.' Perez looked up at her. 'And we should talk to the harbour master. Those are work clothes. Henderson was either getting ready for his shift at Sullom Voe or he'd just finished. It'd help fix the time of death to know when he was working.

They stared at each other again, and this time it was Willow who broke the silence. 'Wait till Sandy gets here and I'll come with you to Henderson's place. I want to see where he lived. In the meantime, see if you can get the harbour master on the phone.'

Perez nodded and walked away from her to make the call.

Willow made the final phone call on her mental list: to Rhona Laing. A polite and distant male voice said that the Fiscal wasn't available. When pressed, the man said that she had taken a couple of days' leave. He was her assistant. Perhaps he could help?

Sandy Wilson and Vicki Hewitt turned up and then it was like any murder investigation. The same routine and the same questions: questions Willow knew the CSI would refuse to answer with any certainty.

'Cause of death?'

'Looks like a stab wound, as you said on the phone. I'd guess he was killed elsewhere, though.'

'How long has he been dead?' Again Willow found it impossible to be still. All those days in the big barn in the commune – the daily meditation, lying on her back, staring at the beams in the ceiling, learning to relax her body and focus her mind. All that for nothing here, when she should be calm, and every nerve and muscle tensed and twanged and she hopped from foot to foot like a kid needing a wee.

Vicki looked up and grinned briefly, gave the old and practised response. 'Tell me when he was last seen and I'll let you know. Between then and when you found him. Otherwise, wait for the pathologist. He'll tell you what the man last had to eat.'

'Dozens of people drive along this road every day. Someone would have noticed a corpse on the verge.'

'Would they?' Vicki said. 'Of course, standing here we can tell it's a man, not a dummy, but driving past, glimpsing the figures from the corner of your eye, and being accustomed to them being here . . . Did you know?'

Willow thought that something about the dummies had made her slow down and pull over, but Vicki was probably right.

'It rained very heavily in the night,' Sandy said suddenly. 'Wouldn't his clothes be wetter than that, if he was out here since yesterday?'

The women looked at him. Willow nodded slowly. 'Of course. It would take them ages to dry out, there in the long grass.' She looked at Sandy. 'I need someone to tell Evie Watt that her fiancé's dead. Before news gets out. I met her at lunchtime and she'll still be at work. Will you do it?' Thinking that he'd better agree straight away, because she couldn't deal with another bolshie Shetland man at the moment. 'And make sure she has family or friends to stay with her, before you leave.' Sandy nodded gravely, turned to get into his car and she could have kissed him for not questioning her judgement.

Willow got Jimmy Perez to drive to Hvidahus, a community of just three houses at the end of a long track looking over a jetty and a sheltered bay. On the way he repeated the information gained from the harbour master.

'Henderson was supposed to start work at midday,' Perez said, 'but he didn't turn up. No phone call, either. It was completely out of character. He's never missed a day since his wife died. Not even through illness. Joe Sinclair, the harbour master, thought *he* must have made a mistake with the roster. Or that maybe John was caught up with his wedding preparations. But he was concerned enough to phone Hvidahus a few times, and Henderson's mobile. No reply. He was planning to drive out here himself once he finished work.'

'So we can put time of death at some time this morning.'

'Aye.' Perez drove across a cattle grid and pulled up outside the bungalow behind a small car. 'This is Henderson's vehicle,' he said. 'I saw him in it just last week.' The bungalow had been freshly painted white and windows looked out over the water. In the garden stood a small wind turbine and behind the house, in its shelter, a long polytunnel. The turbine hummed gently. Two hens pecked on the lawn.

'He was going for the good life,' Willow said.

'All this is quite recent.' Jimmy gave a small smile. 'Evie's influence maybe. He was wooing her with natural energy and the life of a crofter.'

They stood for a moment looking around them. The house close by was older, tiny, one storey made of grey stone.

'This would probably be empty,' Perez said. 'It's a holiday let, and I doubt there'd be people renting so early in the season. The big white house near the pier belongs to Mark and Sue Walsh, the incomers who've been making a fuss about the tidal power.'

Willow turned. From where they stood they looked down at a roof, tall chimneys, a sheltered garden of lawns and shrubs. 'We'll talk to them later.' She peered through the windows of the holiday let. Everything tidy. A pile of folded linen on the table, waiting for the first guests. No sign of occupation.

The side door of the Henderson bungalow was unlocked and led straight into a large kitchen. They stood on the step and stared inside. Everything looked new. More evidence that Henderson had been preparing his home for his new wife? Had he wanted to remove all trace of the first woman who'd lived here, who'd died here?

'Should we wait for Vicki Hewitt?' Perez asked.

'Probably.' But Willow went back to her car and pulled out a couple of scene-suits. 'I came prepared this time.' She kitted up, tucking her long hair into the back of her jersey. She put up the paper hood, adjusting the mask around her face, but lifted it for a moment to speak to him. 'Come on, Jimmy. Are you letting me go in there on my own?' She thought he seemed half-asleep.

Inside, she looked round. There was an integral dishwasher, but still Henderson had washed his breakfast plates by hand. A mug, bowl and plate stood on the draining board with a small pile of cutlery. The table had been wiped clean of crumbs. The tiled floor was spotless. On the workbench a kettle and microwave. A breadbin containing a loaf of sliced wholemeal from the Walls Bakery. No clutter. Nothing to indicate the personality of the man who'd lived there, except for a small cross, formed from a dried palm leaf, propped on the window ledge, evidence that he'd been at church on Palm Sunday.

Willow walked through to the living room. A leather sofa, a carpet the colour of oatmeal, plain brown curtains. All good-quality, all bland. A blank canvas. Willow thought Evie would have brought colour, art and books to the house. Pot plants. Hand-knitting and felting. Did Henderson not care about how things looked, or had he made a deliberate decision not to impose his taste on his new wife?

'No sign of a struggle,' she said. 'No blood.'

Perez remained silent.

She continued to the bedrooms. The largest looked like a hotel bedroom: large double bed, matching chest of drawers and wardrobe. It smelled of new carpet and fresh linen. Willow opened the wardrobe and wondered if Henderson had kept anything belonging to his wife – a special frock to remind him of their meeting, her wedding dress. She was sure Evie would have understood that and wouldn't have minded, but there was nothing belonging to the woman. Inside hung one man's suit, new, still in its polythene wrapper, and a couple of shirts. Bought for the wedding? She opened the top drawer. It was empty except for a small jewellery box, and at last there was some indication of Agnes Henderson: a plain gold wedding ring, a modest engagement ring with a small diamond, a string of pearls and a silver brooch shaped like a raven's head. Willow was aware of Perez, like a shadow, looking over her shoulder, but still he said nothing. She moved on.

The bathroom was spotless and functional. No candles, no perfume. Only one toothbrush. Evie Watt never slept here, Willow thought. She never stayed over. Then it came to her, almost as a revelation, that the two engaged people had never had sex. They were religious and had decided to wait until they were married. She felt tears in the corner of her eyes and wiped them away with her sleeve, hoping that Perez hadn't noticed.

It was clear that Henderson had slept in the smaller bedroom. It was at the back of the house. No view, except of a bare hillside. A single bed, made up the old-fashioned way with sheets, blankets and a quilt. On the bedside chest a Bible and a pamphlet of suggested religious readings and thoughts. A photograph on the wall of a group of men in uniform next to a sparkling new boat. One of the Sullom Voe tugs? Willow recognized John Henderson standing in the middle. Still there was no indication that anyone had broken into the house and stabbed him to death.

Willow turned back to Perez. 'What do you think?' His silence was beginning to irritate her.

He shrugged and moved back to the hall. Here the floor was laminate, and a steep wooden staircase, almost a ladder, led up into the loft. This time he went ahead of her. Perez clambered inside, then moved away from the top of the steps so that Willow could follow. The loft covered the whole house, and dormer windows let in light and gave a view right along the coast. There were no straight walls and Perez could only stand upright in the middle of the room. It was as if she'd walked into a different universe. The walls were painted red. A double mattress on the floor was covered with an Indian cotton cloth in patterned reds and gold. Posters advertising concerts, a festival called Wordplay and the Tall Ships Race were fixed to the slanting walls.

'What is this place?' Willow said. 'Evie's space, do you think? Is this like the polytunnel and the wind turbine? Henderson's attempt to woo her? To show that she wouldn't have to change for him?'

'Maybe.' At last Perez did speak. 'Or somewhere for Agnes to relax . . . '

'Would she have been able to climb the steps?'

'Not at the end,' he said. 'But when they first moved here she wasn't so ill. And she was a lively woman. Full of laughter. She was an art teacher. Taught me for a while at the Anderson High. My last year at school. She was very young then. Very bonny.'

'And Henderson kept the room like a kind of shrine.'

'I don't know,' Perez said. It was as if he found the question ridiculous. 'It was just an idea I had. I could be wrong.'

'No blood, in any event,' Willow said. 'This isn't our murder scene.' She thought the room told them more about John Henderson than it did about the killing.

Perez had fallen silent again. There was no answer. He went before her down the steps and, when she'd gone down herself, she found him in the kitchen, apparently lost in thought.

'That bread knife,' he said, nodding towards the draining board.

'What about it? Maybe Henderson had toast for his breakfast.' She was losing patience.

'But no need to cut the bread.' He pointed towards the open breadbin and the sliced loaf.

'So he used it last night!' But Willow knew that wouldn't do. Henderson had washed and dried up the night before. Everything had been put away. Only the breakfast dishes had been left on the draining board.

Perez shook his head and went outside. Quickly and directly, like a dog chasing a scent, he walked round the side of the bungalow to a small garage. Still wearing the latex gloves, he lifted the garage door. Again everything was neat and ordered. There were shelves with tins of paint, boxes of nails and screws. Hooks on the wall for garden tools. At one end a lawn mower. And, in the middle of the floor, a dark stain that must have been blood.

Chapter Twenty-Two

Sandy found Evie in her office in a smart new building on the water close to the museum in Lerwick. By the time he arrived there it was mid-afternoon. The bairns were on their way home from school in the streets outside and in the open-plan office the staff were drinking tea. Evie was sitting at her desk peering at a computer screen, a mug by her side. It took her a moment to place him and then she frowned. 'Is this about Markham again? I spoke to that woman from the Western Isles at lunchtime.'

He didn't answer. It occurred to him that he'd had to bring news of both violent deaths in this investigation, and he had the childish thought that someone else should have taken a turn.

'Is there somewhere quiet we can talk?'

Something about his voice must have alerted her. She stood up quickly and led him to a small interview room, flicked the sign on the door to *Engaged*. 'What is it, Sandy? An accident? Something at Sullom?'

'It's John.' Again he thought this was kinder done quickly. 'He's dead. I'm so sorry.'

'But not an accident?' Her voice flinty-sharp, and not what he'd been expecting. It had been easier to cope with Maria's tears.

'No,' he said. 'He was murdered.'

'Like Jerry Markham.' Not a question.

They sat for a moment in silence. She was rigid, her hands flat on the desk in front of her. Sandy didn't know what to say or do. *I'm crap at this job. Jimmy would have persuaded her to talk.* 'Morag's been in touch with your parents,' he said at last. 'They're on their way. They'll come here for you. I'll wait with you until they get here.'

'No!' The response immediate and bitter. 'I want to be on my own, Sandy. I want you to go.'

He saw that it was taking all her effort to hold herself together, that she couldn't bear to cry in front of him. John Henderson had been the only man with whom she'd shared her emotions. He thought she'd be silent and buttoned up for the rest of her life.

When he reached Hvidahus, Willow asked him about Evie and then sent him with Perez to the White House. 'You've met the couple, Sandy. They might be more comfortable talking to you.' But she directed her instructions to Perez. 'Find out what they made of Henderson. If he supported the tidal-energy scheme, they might have considered him an enemy. It would be useful to get an unbiased view. And they might have seen someone at his house this morning.'

Sandy and Perez walked down the track to the White House. Sandy would have liked to talk to Perez about Evie, about how she'd refused to cry, but then he thought that might be the most tactless thing in the world. He knocked at the door and, when there was no reply, pushed it open and walked inside. Perez followed. They stood in the wide hall that Sandy remembered, with its smell of furniture polish, a jug of daffodils on a polished chest. Beyond, in the kitchen, there were raised voices. Mark and Sue Walsh were arguing.

'Why can't you let it go?' the woman said. 'We have to live here. I want to fit in and make friends.'

'It's a matter of principle.' Walsh's voice was stubborn. 'You've read Francis Watt's column. There are Shetlanders who feel just as we do.'

Sandy felt awkward standing there, listening. 'Hello!' he shouted. 'Can we come through?' As soon as he'd spoken he realized it had been a mistake. He should have waited patiently to hear the row through to the end. That was what Perez would have done. He glanced apologetically over his shoulder and Perez shrugged an acknowledgement.

The couple hurried through then, all smiles and apologies for not having heard the door. 'Come in, Sergeant. How can we help you?' And the kettle was put on for tea.

'This is my boss, Jimmy Perez,' Sandy said. 'He'd like to speak to you.' And he felt a tremendous relief, because now he could hand the matter over to Jimmy. Perez was in charge again and things had returned to their proper order.

'Welcome to Shetland,' Perez said. 'I hope you're settling in here.' Sandy would never have thought of starting a conversation in that way. 'We have some very sad news about your neighbour.' And he went on to explain, very simply, that John Henderson had been killed. 'We think he was murdered in his own home. I know you'll want to help in any way you can. Were you here this morning?'

'How terrible!' Sue had fine hair, dyed a very pale orange, the colour of apricots. She ran her fingers through it. 'John was a lovely man.'

'You were close?' Perez was drinking his tea, leaning forward across the table.

'He came to see us the day we moved in and brought us eggs from his hens, and milk and bread. Such a kind gesture, we thought. He was very private, of course, but a man who would always help in a crisis.'

'You'll have known Evie then? His fiancée?'

'Of course.' But Sandy sensed a slight discomfort.

'It didn't cause any awkwardness between you? The fact that you were so opposed to the tidal-energy scheme that Evie was heading up.'

There was a silence. Sue threw a desperate look at her husband, who answered, 'We were all adults, Inspector. We were allowed a grown-up disagreement. We felt that the whole character of Hvidahus would be changed by the scheme and that the small experimental project could lead to energy generation on an industrial scale. Evie is an evangelist for green power. But we had perfectly amicable personal relationships. We were even invited to their wedding.'

Again Sue's hands flew to the fine, flyaway hair. 'Poor Evie!' she said. 'That such a thing should happen just a few days before her wedding!'

Sandy turned away so that he wouldn't have to look at Jimmy's face. But when Perez spoke, his voice was quite even. He returned to his original question. 'Were you here this morning?'

'Only until about eight o'clock,' Mark said. 'We went into Lerwick early for shopping and we haven't long been home. We treated ourselves to lunch in Monty's.'

'Did you see anything unusual? Any strange car on the track?'

Sandy thought Sue was about to answer, but Mark got in before her. 'No,' he said. 'Nothing like that.'

Chapter Twenty-Three

When they met up in the operations room it was already starting to get dark. At Hvidahus they'd have set bright lights shining into the garage to conduct a proper search. Vicki Hewitt and her colleagues would be there, and the place would be taped off. The organized buzz of a crime-scene investigation. James Grieve, the pathologist, had been called back from Aberdeen. He'd sounded relieved that he'd missed the last plane in and he'd have one night at home. Willow had the impression that Shetland wasn't his favourite place in the world.

'Do me a favour, Inspector,' he said. 'Find this killer quickly.'

At least now they were working there without an audience. By morning maybe sightseers would turn up. They'd be pretending to walk a dog, or to hike along the coast path, but they'd be there for a ghoulish glimpse of blood, to watch the police at work.

In the police station they'd set up a conference link with Inverness, but the boss listened to what was going on without saying much. How could he grasp what was happening in the most northerly place in his patch? He only visited a few times a year for meetings and official functions and seldom ventured far from Lerwick. Willow soon forgot about him and focused on the people in the room. On the whiteboard there were more photos and there was a new name at the centre.

'John Henderson,' she said. 'Widower, skipper of the oil-terminal tugs, voluntary youth worker and all-round saint. Apparently. And fiancé of Evie Watt, whose former lover just happens to be Jerry Markham. So what's going on here?' A pause. She turned to Sandy, who was sitting on a desk at the back of the room. 'You broke the news to Evie. How did she seem?'

'She was calm enough,' Sandy said. 'But so tense you have the feeling that she could snap at any time.'

'Could she have killed him?' Willow asked the whole gathering. 'I mean, I know it sounds mad, but she's the only link.'

'She doesn't have an alibi for early this morning.' Sandy spoke again. 'From eleven she was out on a site visit, checking out the place up north where she thought the tidal-energy plant might work. She was onsite with two witnesses, but she has no alibi before that.' He paused. 'The witnesses were Joe Sinclair and Ms Laing.'

'What the hell would the Fiscal know about water power?' Willow thought the woman was all over this case like a rash, but it seemed there was no way to pin her down.

'Apparently she was a member of the working party. Some sort of legal advisor?'

Perez had been quite still and quiet throughout the preparation to the meeting and sat a little apart. There was coffee on the desk in front of him. Now he raised his hand. Willow nodded across to him.

'But Evie's not the only link between the two men, is she?' His voice was very low, so they had to concentrate to hear the words.

'Tell us what you're thinking, Jimmy.' Willow leaned back against the desk and waited.

'Jerry Markham seems to have been planning a story around Shetland's energy. He asked his father to set up a meeting for him at Sullom, and he'd agreed to attend the action meeting called by the Walshes. He was sniffing around about the new gas terminal. And John Henderson worked as a pilot on the oil tankers. Another link. Not so personal. But more likely maybe than Evie Watt disposing of her men like a black-widow spider.' He paused. 'Maria Markham said he was working on something secret and he was planning to tell them the night that he died.'

'So we're back to Jerry Markham's story,' Willow said. 'The one that was going to make his fortune. Except, according to his editor, there was no story.'

'I've been thinking about that too.' Perez was still tentative. It was as if, after standing up to her earlier in the afternoon, he didn't want to come across as pushy or to undermine her further. She wanted to tell him to get over it – she wasn't the sort to feel threatened by a colleague. But part of her still resented the fact that he was the one coming up with the new ideas.

'Go on,' she said.

'What if the story wasn't for publication, if he was researching for quite a different reason?'

'Like?'

'I did wonder,' Perez said slowly, 'about blackmail.'

As soon as the word was spoken it seemed so obvious that Willow was astonished, horrified that it hadn't occurred to *her*. How had she ever thought she could do well at this business? Markham was a greedy man and he'd thought he could squeeze money from former contacts. But still she kept her voice even and didn't let on what she was thinking. Years of practice, when the Uist kids laughed at her hippy clothes and called her names. 'Well, yes, Jimmy. Of course that does make sense. So who was blackmailing whom here? And how does John Henderson fit in?'

Perez leaned forward now, joining in the circle, less of an outsider looking in. 'As I see it – ' his voice was hesitant and still so quiet that she struggled to make out the words – 'Markham was the blackmailer. His blackmail victim was the killer. And Henderson guessed what was going on. Or was in the wrong place at the wrong time. Was driving past, maybe, when Markham's car was forced off the road.'

'That holds together,' she said. 'It works as a theory, for the moment at least.' She looked at the group. 'But we won't get seduced by it, huh? We'll keep open minds until we get more evidence. That OK with you, Jimmy?'

He nodded and gave her that reluctant, out-of-practice smile. 'Of course,' he said. 'I would say just the same myself.'

On the whiteboard she wrote *Blackmail?* Then: *Who and why? What was the story?* 'So what was the blackmail about? Something to do with Sullom Voe, Jimmy? Is that the way your mind's working?'

'Maybe,' Perez said. 'Or maybe something to do with the tidal energy. Why else would he agree to go to the meeting at Vatnagarth? It might explain why Markham was so keen to talk to Evie when he was home this time.'

There was a moment of silence and then she turned to Sandy. 'Was Evie planning to go home tonight?'

'Her parents came to collect her,' Sandy said. 'They're taking her back to her house for tonight, then home with them on the first ferry tomorrow.'

'I talked to her parents earlier,' Perez said. 'Jessie and Francis. That's what I was doing in Fetlar. That's where they live.'

'And why did you feel the need to do that, Jimmy?' She heard the sharpness in her voice and didn't care.

'To get a handle on Evie Watt and Henderson,' he said. Answering the question, refusing to acknowledge her anger. 'To find out what they made of the marriage.'

'And what *did* they make of it?'

'They seemed happy enough. Henderson had been a friend. There was the age difference, but they thought he was a good man.'

'You can tell me all about it in the car,' she said suddenly, 'on the way to Evie Watt's house. I'd like to speak to her myself.' She didn't want this conversation in public. She sensed Perez's hesitation. 'That *is* all right with you, Jimmy? No childcare problems tonight?'

She thought she was being a bitch, but it was too late to take back the words. Jimmy picked up his jacket. 'No,' he said. 'Cassie's having a sleepover with a friend. No childcare problems tonight.'

Willow let Perez drive and still hadn't found the words to confront him when they were out of Lerwick and on the way north. In the end he was the one who broke the silence.

'I'm sorry,' he said. 'I shouldn't have headed out to Fetlar to speak to Evie's parents without talking to you first. It was wrong.' A pause. 'Rude.'

And that sucked away all her anger and made her feel deflated and flat.

'I need to know where you are,' she said. 'Where all the team are.' Which sounded pathetic and as if she was some sort of control freak.

'Of course.' He slowed down to let a boy racer overtake on the straight road close to Tingwall airstrip. 'Maybe I've been on my own too long. I've lost the knack of communication.' He hesitated. 'Like when you've had a stroke. You have to practise all over again.'

'Did you speak to the manager at the Bonhoga?' she said. Best to be crisp and professional.

'Aye. He didn't recognize the woman speaking to Jerry Markham.'

'Evie wondered if it might be Maria Markham,' Willow said. 'She said they were always very close. "More like lovers than mother and son." That was how she described them.'

'Maria didn't mention meeting Jerry for coffee.' Perez kept his voice flat. No indication whether he thought this might be a possibility or whether he thought Willow was talking rubbish.

'Could she be involved in the blackmail, do you think?' It was quite dark now. Willow had forgotten how black it was with no street lights, no car headlights. She was transported back to Uist, to the star map and the silence of her childhood.

'She could be protecting Jerry's memory,' Perez said. 'Oh yes, definitely that. But working with him to extort money? I'm not sure.' He paused. 'Maybe, if she'd convinced herself that it was due to him, that he had a right to it. But if that's the case, I'm not sure what the secret he was planning to share could have been.'

He slowed down to turn off the main road. There was still a white tent where the dummies of Evie and her fiancé had once lain in the grass. A police car with Davy Cooper inside.

'Do you want to stop?' Perez asked.

'No. I want to get to Evie's place while they're still up.'

On the walk from the car to the little house all they had to guide them was the light coming from one of the windows. At least the Watts weren't in bed and asleep. It hadn't rained again, but still there was the smell of damp grass and wet sheep's wool. At one point Willow stumbled and Perez caught her arm.

The family sat round a kitchen table. Willow looked in from outside and thought it could have been a stage set. The small table at the centre of the room. The sheepskins: two on the floor and a black one thrown over the back of the plain wooden chair. The brightly woven blanket covering the sofa. Photographs and drawings on the wall facing the window. A jam jar of meadow flowers, already fading on the table. And three characters.

The man was sitting stiff and upright. Willow thought he could have walked out of a play by Ibsen or Strindberg. In his mid-fifties, he had a brown face and a little moustache. His legs were hidden by the table, but he was wearing a hand-knitted sweater, Fair Isle-patterned in browns and greys. A sweater for special occasions, Willow thought. For church and parties, and for mourning the man who might have been a son-in-law. For comforting a daughter who'd lost the love of her life.

Each side of him a woman. The mother small, her hair still dark. One of those Celtic women, who keep their dark hair into middle age. Bright-blue eyes. Bright with a feverish concern for the daughter who sat across the table from her. She reached out in front of her husband to clasp the young woman's hand. And Evie Watt, as still and upright as her father, still wearing the clothes she'd been in when Willow had met her for lunch, allowed her mother to take it.

Willow remembered meeting Evie for their lunch in the Tollclock Centre, the conversation about the wedding, the impromptu invitation to the celebration party and thought: *This woman isn't a killer. She didn't stab her fiancé, dump his body by the road and make it look like a dummy, then talk to me about Jerry Markham. Nobody is that good an actor.*

Jimmy Perez approached the door and knocked. Willow continued to stare through the window. Jessie was startled by the noise and Francis got to his feet to answer. Evie didn't move. It was as if she hadn't heard it.

'Francis, I'm so sorry.' As Willow watched from the shadow, Perez put his hand on Watt's shoulder. The men stood very close for a moment, then pulled apart. 'This is Inspector Reeves,' Perez went on. 'She's in charge of the investigation. You don't mind if we come in?'

'Come away inside,' Francis said. The habit of good manners and hospitality meant he wouldn't refuse them entry, even tonight, even when his family was in crisis.

The women looked up when the visitors walked into the room, but didn't get to their feet. Willow saw that the mother had shifted chairs in the moment that her husband had left the kitchen; now she was sitting next to her daughter. Francis moved around the room, which was obviously familiar to him, switching on the kettle, putting teabags in a pot. Still Willow felt removed from the action: she had wandered onto the stage, but she wasn't part of the play. She needed to become engaged. She pulled out a chair so that it was facing Evie.

'I'm so sorry about John, Evie, and I know it's the last thing you need, but we have to talk. You do understand?'

Evie nodded.

'Can you think of any reason why anyone would have wanted to hurt him?'

'No! He was a good man. Everyone liked him.' She looked at her parents for confirmation.

'No one had anything but good to say about John Henderson,' Francis said. 'He didn't have an enemy in the world.'

'Yet someone stabbed him in the garage of his home at Hvidahus, drove him almost all the way here and set his body beside the dummy of you on the verge. Our crime-scene investigator found the original in the ditch further up the road. That would suggest to me that John had an enemy.' Willow kept her voice even, but looked to check that Evie had heard her and was taking in the words. She would have preferred to talk to the woman on her own, but could hardly send the parents away. 'I assume that you do want the murderer caught and punished.'

'That's not for me to worry about,' Evie said. 'That way lies madness.'

Willow saw that one of the photographs pinned to the board on the wall was of Evie at her hen party. She was in the bar in Voe, dressed up in some sort of animal costume. A fake-fur suit and furry ears. A glass of beer was on the table in front of her and she had her arm round a plump woman dressed liked a pirate. Both of them were pulling faces.

The silence that followed the words was broken by Francis Watt, who put the teapot on the table and handed round mugs. The ritual of tea, Willow thought, is like a liturgy itself, comforting because it's so familiar. She watched Jessie pour, waved her hand to show that she didn't take milk.

'But you will help us,' Perez said. 'You will answer our questions truthfully?'

'Of course! But I won't guess. I won't speculate.'

'When did you last speak to John?' he asked.

OK! Willow thought. *So now Perez is taking over my interview.* But she didn't interrupt. Perez seemed to have grasped Evie's attention. Demanded it and held it tight. Her eyes were fixed on his face. Two people who had lost the people they loved. They could have been alone in the world.

'On the phone this morning,' Evie said. 'We spoke to each other when we first woke up. Every day. Even if we planned to meet up later. He was an early riser and so am I. It was seven o'clock. I made tea, sat here and phoned John.'

'And what did you say?'

'The usual things.' For the first time Evie sounded close to tears. 'How much I loved him. How I couldn't wait to see him. How I was counting the minutes to Saturday when we could be together as man and wife.'

'He was going to work at lunchtime?' Perez asked.

'Yes.' Evie still directed her answers to Perez alone. 'I planned to meet him when he finished at eight. Just for a couple of hours.'

'Was the plan that you'd go to his house or would he come here?'

'He'd come here,' Evie replied. 'It was almost on his way home. We'd share a meal, talk over the final arrangements for Saturday.'

'Then he'd go back to Hvidahus?'

'Yes.' Her voice was firm. 'Then he'd go back to Hvidahus.'

'We're looking for a motive for his death,' Perez said. 'He was a good man. We understand that. Everyone says it. So perhaps he knew something about Jerry Markham's murder. Knew something or saw something. Did he mention anything of that kind to you?'

'No.'

But this time she hesitated, and Perez picked up on the pause.

'Maybe he didn't talk about it directly. Maybe he seemed concerned, tense, anxious.'

'The last couple of days he seemed a bit distracted,' Evie said at last. 'When we spoke today I asked what he would do for the rest of the morning. He was always a busy man. Not one for sitting around and reading the paper. I thought he might plan to be out in the garden. But he said there were some loose ends he had to tie up. It was as if he had come to a decision.'

Perez weighed the words. 'Did you ask what he meant? Weren't you curious?'

'A little curious,' she said. 'I should have asked him. But I thought it might be legal business. He'd talked about writing his will. And I was in a hurry. It was a big day for me. The meeting of the steering group. We talked about that too. Tidal energy and my grand project. John knew how much it meant to me.'

For the first time Willow moved her gaze from Perez and Evie, the stars of the piece, and looked at her parents. They sat side by side, the tea untouched on the table in front of them, their faces rigid, determined to be strong for their daughter.

'We'll come through this,' Jessie said. 'It seems desperate now, but you'll come through it.'

Evie turned her head to look at her mother with clear, dry eyes. She said nothing, the silence a sort of reproach.

Perez gave a little cough to pull Evie back to him. She returned her gaze to his face. 'One last question,' he said. 'The loft room in John's house – did you decorate that? Was it your space?'

Evie gave a little smile. 'No,' she said. 'That was none of my doing. I think he was almost embarrassed by it. The mess and the clutter. Not like John at all.'

'So it was all Agnes's stuff?'

'I suppose it was,' she said. 'And he could never bear to get rid of it. A kind of shrine. Though he never said. Perhaps he thought I'd be jealous.'

Chapter Twenty-Four

Perez drove Willow Reeves to her hotel before going home. He still sensed the awkwardness between them and felt an undefined guilt, the idea that somehow he had behaved badly towards her. It wasn't just disappearing off to Fetlar without letting her know what he was doing, or refusing to break the news of Henderson's death to Evie; it was insinuating himself into this case, where he had no right to meddle. Except that officially he was still on the team. And she had invited him to be a part of the investigation. And it was on his patch. There was a bubble of resentment along with the confusion.

At the hotel she didn't immediately leave the car. 'Do you fancy a nightcap? One drink before you go?'

It was the last thing he fancied, but how could he refuse when he still felt that he'd treated her in a way that wasn't quite honourable? So he walked with her past the noisy public bar to the residents' lounge. With its dark-panelled wood and leather armchairs, it had the air of a shabby gentlemen's club. Standard lamps with dusty parchment shades threw out small pools of light. In one corner two elderly American tourists talked about Shetland ponies and puffins. They shouted and weren't listening to each other, so would be unlikely to listen in to a conversation at the other end of the room. A middle-aged waitress came to take their order and Willow ordered two malt whiskies, then turned to Perez quickly. 'That is all right for you?'

'Sure.' Now he felt very tired and wanted to get to his bed. He'd had a text from his neighbour to say that Cassie was fine. *The girls had a high old time and now they're both fast asleep.* But still he'd have been happier back in Ravenswick, where he'd be closer to her.

'So, Jimmy,' Willow said. 'Where do we go from here?'

He thought for a while. *Was this a trick? Was he supposed to defer to her and offer no opinion of his own?* 'Maybe you'd like to talk to Maria Markham?' he said at last. After all, the woman had asked the question. 'You've not interviewed her yet, and if she was the person Jerry met in the Bonhoga, it'd be interesting to know what they were discussing. Why could they not have their chat at the Ravenswick Hotel?'

'Why not, indeed?' Willow was sipping the whisky. 'And you, Jimmy? Will you be up to working with us again tomorrow?'

That threw him. He'd assumed that he was part of the team now. It hadn't occurred to him that Willow would expect him to bow out after a couple of days on the investigation. 'Do you think I'm not up to it?' he asked.

'I think you're sharper than any other detective I've worked with,' she said. 'But don't expect me to like it. I don't enjoy the competition.'

He saw that it was a sort of joke, a compliment, but still it felt like a criticism. 'I'm sorry,' he said.

'I shouldn't wander off doing my own thing. And I shouldn't take over in interviews.'

She smiled. 'So, tomorrow? I'd like you to interview Andy Belshaw. Like you said before, he links the victims too. And Henderson might have talked to him, if they were mates. Will you head up to Sullom first thing? And I know you've phoned Henderson's boss, but you should see him too.'

'No problem.' He swilled the drink round his glass and swallowed the last mouthful. 'At least, I'd like to take Cassie to school first, if that's OK, but I could still be in Sullom for nine-thirty.' He stood up and paused, suddenly anxious, remembering her dig about childcare. 'That *is* OK?'

'Of course.' There was a silence and for a moment he thought she had more questions. But she stood too, leaned forward and kissed him lightly on the cheek. The touch was routine, two colleagues saying goodnight, but it shocked him and he felt himself blushing. The gesture felt almost like an apology, but why should *she* feel sorry? 'Take care, Jimmy. Let me know as soon as you have anything.' And she wandered off towards the stairs and her room. He stood, frozen for a minute, and then made his way outside.

When he got home it was past midnight. He went to bed and slept better than he had for months, and woke up suddenly to daylight and the sound of gulls fighting, worried that he'd miss getting Cassie to school. But it was only six o'clock. He made tea, listened to Radio 4 and then to Radio Orkney, showered and ate toast. Radio Shetland didn't broadcast in the morning, and Orkney carried the news of Henderson's death. No details. 'The police will make a statement later today.'

When he arrived at Maggie's house the children were still at breakfast and he drank coffee while he waited for them to finish. Cassie was chatty and giggly, the mischievous girl he remembered from the year before. He drove both girls down the bank to school, and for the first time since Fran had died he left before the children were called in from the playground.

He hadn't phoned Belshaw in advance. Better to catch him by surprise and, if he happened to be south on business, the trip to the oil terminal wouldn't be wasted. Perez needed to talk to Joe Sinclair, the harbour master, anyway.

The same security officer was on the gate at Sullom. Still unsmiling and officious.

'Mr Belshaw isn't onsite today.'

'Where is he?' The question mild and polite.

The man checked a clipboard. 'Working from home.' A sniff of disapproval.

If Perez had asked for an address, the guard would have refused to give it or made a fuss about it, and Perez didn't want to give him that pleasure, so he said nothing. He knew that Belshaw lived in Aith and that his wife was the school cook there. He could track down the Belshaw home in seconds. Driving past the Harbour Authority complex on the other side of the voe, Perez was tempted to call in there first, to talk to Sinclair and the pilots, but Willow had asked him to talk to Belshaw as a priority and she was the boss. He'd see Sinclair later. After feeding back the results of the Belshaw interview to Willow. No point making things hard for himself, or for her.

It was a fine day, mild and still. The Aith road was quiet and he just had to stop once to let a tractor pass in the opposite direction. He slowed down to come into the village and caught a brief glimpse of Rhona Laing, looking out of an upstairs window of the Old Schoolhouse. Willow had said the Fiscal was on leave, and Willow had notified Laing's assistant about the second murder. Perez couldn't understand why Rhona had taken time off. It wasn't like her to give up her role in a major inquiry. Perhaps she'd been told to back away because of her involvement, but he couldn't imagine she'd give way without a fight.

His first instinct was to pull in next to the Old Schoolhouse and talk to her. A courtesy, but also because he was curious to gauge her reaction to Henderson's murder. Then he remembered Willow's antipathy to the woman and thought again that he should check with the inspector first. In this investigation he wasn't free to make his own decisions. So he carried on through the village and pulled in next to the co-op. No phone signal in the car, but just enough to make a call when he got outside and walked towards the marina.

Willow too sounded rested, less stressed than she had the night before. 'Jimmy. What have you got for me?'

He explained about Belshaw working from home and that the Fiscal was in the Old Schoolhouse. 'I wondered if you'd like me to talk to her. About Henderson.'

There was a long pause, and Perez thought first

that Willow would insist on doing the interview herself, and then that the phone connection had broken.

'OK, Jimmy.' A small, hard chuckle. 'You'll be more tactful than me. But don't tell her more than you need to. And don't let her get away with anything.'

He was going to ask how she'd got on with Maria Markham, but this time the phone did go dead. Besides, there'd been background noise, which sounded as if she was still in the police station and hadn't yet made the trip south to Ravenswick.

In the co-op Perez bought a bar of chocolate and a bag of tatties for the evening's supper and found out where the Belshaws lived. The house was just out of the settlement on the way to Bixter, and he thought he'd walk up to the Old Schoolhouse first and talk to the Fiscal. He could do with stretching his legs and he enjoyed these mild spring days. He stood for a moment at the gate, looking in at her garden. He hadn't noticed it before and was surprised by its lack of order: overgrown shrubs and a patch of grass thick with clover. In one corner an old enamel bucket over a head of rhubarb. She obviously wasn't much of a gardener. His father had always divided people into those who loved the water and those who loved the land.

Rhona Laing took a long time to open the door. She was wearing blue jeans and a navy sweater. No make-up, which made her somehow look vulnerable. More attractive and softer. 'Jimmy,' she said. A touch of impatience in the voice. 'How can I help you? I was just about to spend a morning in the boat. I have a few days' leave owing.'

'Have you heard about John Henderson?'

'What about him?'

'He's dead,' Perez said. He wished she'd invite him in. It felt strange carrying on a conversation like this on the doorstep. Almost disrespectful. 'He was stabbed yesterday morning in his garage at Hvidahus, and his body was moved to the junction down towards Evie Watt's place. Made to look like a straw dummy. You'll have seen them there, kind of scarecrows, in the run-up to the wedding.'

The Fiscal stared at him. 'What is going on here, Jimmy? Two violent deaths in North Mainland in less than a week. And what is that strange young woman from the Hebrides doing to stop it?' Her voice was high-pitched and shrill.

Perez found it hard to believe that she didn't know about Henderson's murder. Surely her assistant would have been on the phone to her as soon as he'd been notified by Willow Reeves. 'Your office didn't let you know?'

'They've been told not to disturb me when I'm on holiday.' Still she was poised on the doorstep. Did she really expect him to go away and let her get to her boat? He couldn't understand her reaction.

'We should talk about this,' Perez said. 'It must be related to the Markham killing, and you're involved with that. You found the body.'

'And that was why I took leave.' Her voice was sharp. 'There was a conflict of interest. I do see that. Besides, Inspector Reeves made it very clear that she'd prefer me not to supervise the case.'

'We should talk,' Perez repeated. 'You're a witness of sorts.'

And only then did she move aside and let him in. She made coffee for him without asking if he wanted any. They sat in the kitchen. Perez had never been in the house before and it was rather grand, in a sleek, minimalist way. Clean lines, white walls, everything freshly plastered, the corners sharp as blades. No untidiness here. He wondered what Sandy Wilson had made of it.

'Did you know Henderson?' he asked.

She shrugged. 'I'd met him of course. Social occasions. Regattas. He was a great seaman. Instinctive.'

'What was your impression of him? As a man, not a sailor?'

She considered. 'He was quiet, thoughtful. Shy perhaps. Not one to put himself forward in a group. From what I've heard, he was quite different from Jerry Markham.'

'So you have no idea what connection there might be between them?'

She shrugged again. 'None at all.'

They sat in silence. Perez thought he liked her much better this way – quiet, a little unsure. 'I have to ask you where you were yesterday morning,' he said. 'Early. I know where you were later in the morning. You were at Hvidahus then with Evie Watt and Joe Sinclair to look at the tidal-energy site.'

Suddenly she was herself again, fierce and intimidating. 'Are you accusing me of murder, Inspector Perez?'

'No,' he said. 'Of course not. But you should tell me where you were. You know how these things work.'

'Oh yes.' Suddenly she seemed very tired. 'I know how these things work.'

'John Henderson lived at Hvidahus,' he said. 'That's where he was murdered. Did you see anything unusual? A car at his house?' But he thought it likely that the man was already dead when the tidal-power working group had been there.

'No,' she said. 'There was nothing unusual.'

'So where were you before you set out for your meeting?'

'I was here, Jimmy. I made some phone calls. From my work mobile, so I suppose I could have made them from anywhere. But my car was parked up on the road. Everyone in the village would have seen it.'

Perez nodded. Rhona Laing wasn't stupid. He'd check and find that everything was as she'd said. But a car wasn't the only way to travel round Shetland. The Fiscal had a fine boat, and most of Shetland's communities could be reached from the water. There'd been no roads in Shetland for centuries – all travel had been by sea. Perhaps this wasn't much of an alibi; he'd ask around and see if the boat had been there all morning too.

Chapter Twenty-Five

Rhona Laing closed the door gently behind Jimmy Perez and stood for a moment, leaning against it, as if blocking the way to other unwelcome intruders. Then she went upstairs and stood, hidden by the curtain like some nosy Shetland wife, to watch him walk back down the bank. Only when she saw his car drive up the hill towards Bixter did it feel as if she was breathing again.

Has it come to this? That I hide in my house like a common criminal?

Her plans for the day – to take out the boat with a picnic, to explore the voe and to moor up at a little beach for lunch – now seemed impossible. She had once represented a client with agoraphobia, and although she'd been professional throughout the court proceedings, her impulse had been to shake the woman. What was wrong with this person? Was it such a huge step to open the front door and walk out onto the pavement? Now, for the first time, Rhona Laing began to understand the irrational fear of the space outside one's home. The stranger's face. The unfriendly buildings. The threatening landscape. It would be easy to curl up in her chair with her back to the window. To drink tea or whisky. To shut out the world.

But to start down that path would be the worst possible mistake. Rhona could see that. And if she were in the house she'd be trapped, at the mercy of telephone calls and people knocking at her door. Perez might come back. Willow Reeves with her wild, untidy hair and her staring eyes might turn up with questions. Rhona thought she could mislead Perez, but the woman from the Hebrides would be harder to deceive. She couldn't face it.

So she went into the kitchen and finished preparing a packed lunch. She cut the sandwiches with a good, sharp knife so that the edges were neat and wrapped them in foil. She put fruit and biscuits into a bag and made a flask of coffee, poured milk into a little jar that she kept for the purpose. Pulled her oilskins from the cupboard under the stairs and went to her bedroom for a spare jersey, because in Shetland the weather could change in a second. And then she left the house, locking it behind her, and walked swiftly down to the marina, keeping her eyes on the path. She had a sense that only on the water could she come to terms with what had happened. The water was where she felt safe. It felt as if she was running away forever.

Chapter Twenty-Six

Perez found the Belshaws' home immediately. It had been built in the last ten years, one of the wooden Scandinavian kit-houses that had suddenly appeared all over Shetland. Theirs was painted pale blue, almost grey, two storeys and a wooden deck at the front facing towards Aith. It looked as if it should have a sauna at the bottom of the garden, but instead there was a swing and a climbing frame, a couple of plastic toy cars, a trampoline surrounded by a net. Behind, in the shelter of the house, he glimpsed a small vegetable patch, the rich soil newly dug.

Perez knocked at the door and Andy Belshaw answered immediately. He was wearing jogging trousers and a rugby shirt, carpet slippers on his feet. He looked pasty and tired.

'I thought you might turn up,' he said. 'I heard about John on Radio Orkney. A dreadful business. Come away in.' Perez thought he'd already picked up something of the Shetland accent.

'You didn't hear about it until this morning?'

'No,' Belshaw said. 'We switched the phone off last night because Lucy was ill. I checked for messages when I heard the radio piece. We'd had a couple of calls, people letting us know what had happened.'

He led Perez into the kitchen. It seemed that Belshaw had been in the middle of stacking the dishwasher. There was no indication, here at least, that he'd been working. No laptop. Everywhere signs that this was a family home. Drawings on the fridge door, a pile of children's clothes stacked on an ironing board in the corner. In a basket in the corner, knitting needles and some skeins of wool.

'Is that why you're at home today?' Perez asked. 'Because of John's murder? I know you were close friends. I could understand if you were too upset to go in.'

'We were very close. But no, my daughter's still not well. Tonsillitis. It's hard for the school to get a replacement for Jen at the last minute, and easy enough for me to work here. We'd fixed all that up last night. I'm glad, though. I wouldn't want to be onsite this morning. I couldn't concentrate.' He shut the door of the dishwasher and switched on the kettle.

'Have the press been onto you about it?'

'No, why would they?' A slight frown to suggest that he was puzzled by the question. Perez was unconvinced. Henderson might not have worked directly for the terminal, but he'd been employed by the Harbour Authority piloting within Sullom Voe. Belshaw must have realized that eventually the terminal would get a mention in the media and it was his role to manage that information. Surely he'd have prepared a statement. And surely, in this situation, a sick child wouldn't keep him away from the site.

'I was thinking it was quite a coincidence,' Perez said. 'Two murders, both in North Mainland. Jerry Markham was visiting the terminal the afternoon he died, and John Henderson was based with the Harbour Authority, just across the voe from you.'

There was a silence broken by the click of the kettle switching itself off. Belshaw stared out of the window.

'And you think the press will make the connection?' he said at last. 'What a nightmare! The environmental campaigners will have a field day. There's nothing they like better than a juicy conspiracy theory.'

'*I'm* making the connection.' Perez raised his voice. 'The fact that two men are dead is more important to me than the oil terminal getting a bit of bad publicity.'

There was another silence. Perez could just make out the faint hum of a children's song somewhere in the house. He thought the sick daughter must be watching television in her room and wondered how old she was. Absent-mindedly Belshaw spooned instant coffee into two mugs.

'Look,' Perez said, 'is there anything going on at the terminal that I should know about?' He felt his temper fraying, could feel the strands of control splitting like pieces of rope. His depression manifested itself in anger.

'What sort of thing?'

'You tell me! Dodgy investments, backhanders to contractors, people playing fast and loose with health and safety? Best to let me know, so we can clear this up quickly. The press will find out anyway. And if you don't cooperate now, you could find yourself charged with obstruction.'

'What are you saying, Inspector?' Belshaw seemed even paler, and as he set the mug on the table in front of Perez his hand was shaking.

'I'm saying that Markham was sniffing round Sullom Voe on the afternoon he died for a better reason than the details of the expansion of the site for gas. He could have got that from a press release and a quick phone call. So what was he doing there? Really?'

'Really? I don't know any more than you do.' Belshaw was almost shouting. Righteous indignation or panic? Perez couldn't tell. 'You know that I work for BP and have absolutely nothing to do with the gas terminal. Besides, renewables versus fossil fuels *has* been covered a few times before. Of course I asked him if there was anything else he might be interested in. But, honestly, he just seemed to be going through the motions. He asked all the right questions, but it seemed to me that he didn't really care. I thought he'd been sent there by his editor.'

Belshaw stood with his hands flat on the table, his face flushed.

A child called from upstairs. 'Daddy! Daddy!' She'd heard the shouting through the open door and was scared. Belshaw said nothing. He filled a tumbler with juice from the fridge and left the room. Perez heard murmured voices as Belshaw reassured the girl. Perez stood up and prowled around the kitchen, noticed that from the window there was a bird's-eye view of the marina. If the weather had been clear on the afternoon of Markham's death, there would have been a good view of the killer lifting the body into the yoal. Belshaw must have come back very quietly, because Perez was suddenly aware that the man was standing behind him.

'That's why we bought this site,' Belshaw said. 'For the view.'

'I don't suppose you saw the Fiscal's boat leave early yesterday morning?'

If Belshaw was surprised by the sudden change of subject, he didn't show it. 'I didn't see it,' he said. Then: 'I'm sorry that I overreacted. I was close to John Henderson. He made friends with me when I first arrived in the islands. It feels as though I've lost an older brother.' He turned and sat down again at the table. Perez joined him.

'How did you first meet him?' Perez asked.

'At the sports centre in Brae. I used the gym and so did he. He guessed I might be feeling a bit isolated and invited me to join the five-a-side team.' Belshaw looked up. 'He was godfather to our son.'

'Did you know his wife?'

'Yes, she loved company and we'd call to see her, even when she was very ill. It was never a *sad* house. John was great with her – natural. You could tell they had a special relationship.' Belshaw looked up over his coffee cup. 'I don't know how he could be so patient, so calm about her dying. I'd have been angry at the world.'

Oh yes, Perez thought. *I know how that feels.*

'Then you ran the children's football team together?'

'Neil, my son, is a sports fanatic. I set up the team at Brae and asked John to come along to help. At first it was a kindness. I thought it might distract him from Agnes's death. But he was great with the kids. Better than I'd ever be.' He looked up again. 'Oh God, the boys on the team will be devastated. I should phone their parents.' But he made no move to leave his seat.

'What did you make of John's marriage to Evie?'

'I was delighted, and so was Jen. Evie's a lovely girl and we thought he deserved to be happy, maybe start a family. He was a lot older than her of course, but there was no reason why that shouldn't work. It was a whirlwind romance. I think they only started dating six months ago, but John said he had no time to waste. Most people were never given a second chance of happiness. He said he didn't deserve her, but he was going to grab his chance with both hands.' Belshaw looked at Perez. 'How is Evie taking this?'

'She seems calm enough. I don't think it's sunk in yet.'

'Jen was going to visit her as soon as she left work. There's quite an age gap, but they're good friends.'

'I think Evie's parents were going to take her back to Fetlar,' Perez said. He was struck by a sudden thought. 'Did you talk to John about the Markham murder? Had you seen him since the body was discovered in the yoal?'

Belshaw gave a little nod. 'John wasn't at football practice on Friday night,' he said. 'He was working a late shift. Sometimes that happened and I worked with the boys on my own.'

'But you saw him after that? Once the news of Markham's murder was out?' Perez felt impatient and wanted to shift the conversation along.

'He came here for a late lunch on Sunday. Jen's idea. She thought Evie would be busy. "Your last lunch with us as a single man." That was what she said. It was mid-afternoon by the time we ate, because she had to take a shift at the crofting museum.'

Perez remembered Henderson's car speeding away from the kirk. He'd have been off home to change out of his formal clothes before the meal with his friends. 'Did you talk about Markham's death?'

'Of course! By then the news was all over the island. There was no escaping the gossip. Jen warned me that John might not want to discuss it, but he was like an old woman, wanting all the details.'

'How did he seem when he talked about Markham?' Perez asked.

Belshaw hesitated for a moment. 'It was always hard to tell what John was thinking. He'd seemed preoccupied all lunchtime, but that might have been work. He took his work very seriously. And of course there was the wedding. It occurred to me that he'd be remembering Agnes and wondering if he was doing the right thing. Not last-minute second thoughts, because he loved Evie, but just thinking about the last time he was married. Kind of honouring Agnes's memory, before moving on.' He paused. 'I did think it was odd that he wanted to talk about Markham and the murder. He was never one for gossip, for getting excited about another man's misfortune.'

'And that was how he seemed?' Perez leaned back in his chair. 'Excited?'

Belshaw seemed to consider. 'Maybe that's not the right word,' he said at last. 'But John kept coming back to the subject. He wouldn't let it go. Not while we were eating because the children were there then, but later, when we sent them out to play.'

'Did he have any theories about Markham's death? Did he speculate about the motive or the killer?'

'No.' Belshaw leaned forward across the table. 'Nothing like that. He seemed upset, disturbed. "Things like that shouldn't happen here." That was what he said.'

'You hadn't talked to John about Markham's murder before then? You don't know how he came to hear about it?'

'No. I was working on Saturday. I do the occasional day at the weekend. That was when you came to see me.' Belshaw drained his mug. 'I'm glad Jen invited John to lunch on Sunday. She rows in the Aith vets' rowing team and she should have been at the regatta at St Ninian's, but there were plenty of volunteers, so she was able to get out of it. It gave us a chance to spend some time together. That was the last time I saw him.'

Perez looked up. 'Is your wife friendly with Rhona Laing?'

Belshaw shrugged. 'They row in the same team. They both love being on the water. I don't think that makes them best mates.'

He got to his feet as his phone rang. It was obviously work-related. Perez couldn't think of a reason to prolong the interview and waved to indicate that he would see himself out. He pinned his card on the notice board in the kitchen before leaving, mouthing, 'Give me a ring if you think of anything.' Belshaw nodded and went back to his call.

Perez stood on the decking out of sight of Belshaw and looked down at Aith. A yacht was leaving the marina. It was white and rather grand and belonged, he guessed, to the Fiscal. So here was another connection. Jen Belshaw rowed with Rhona Laing and might have been the person to find Markham's body, if circumstances had been different. Perez wondered what Willow Reeves would make of that.

He looked at his watch. It was nearly eleven o'clock, probably the busiest time in a school kitchen. He imagined pots boiling on a hob, steam and chaos, assistants to overhear. There was no point in trying to chat to the woman now. But now would be a good time to visit Joe Sinclair, harbour master at Sullom Voe and John Henderson's boss. He'd be happy enough to make Perez coffee and to chat.

As soon as Perez climbed into his car his mobile rang. Willow Reeves.

'Jimmy.' The reception was bad and her voice crackled. 'How's it going?'

'I've spoken to the Fiscal,' he said. He thought that would be the interview that interested her most. 'And I've just finished talking to Andy Belshaw.'

'Good.' But she seemed distracted. 'Can you get back here, Jimmy? As soon as you can. There's been a development.'

Chapter Twenty-Seven

Sandy Wilson had taken the call. Willow Reeves had stuck him in the operations room, his job being to take referrals from the PC answering the emergency line that had been set up. Willow had given instructions that anything interesting or unusual should be put through to him – he had the local knowledge, after all, to weed out the usual weirdos and losers. So he'd sat trapped in the grey featureless room, with the sense that the investigation was continuing elsewhere without him. He'd wished he could be out with Perez.

Willow had stuck her head round the door. 'I'm just off to the Ravenswick Hotel to chat to Maria Markham. I want to see if she was the woman who met Markham in the Bonhoga.' And just at that moment the phone rang and the new PC, apologetic as if she hated to disturb Wilson, came on the line: 'There's a lass wants to talk to someone. She's from London. Says she was Markham's girlfriend. She wants to come up and see where he died.'

Sandy turned to wave at Willow, but she'd already sensed his interest and was back in the room, listening in. He offered her the phone, but she gestured for him to continue the call.

'Can I help you?' He made sure his voice was clear. Knapping for the woman on the end of the line.

'My name is Annabel Grey.' The woman was young, certainly younger than Markham, Sandy thought. But then Markham had taken a fancy to Evie Watt when she was only just out of school. Perhaps he liked his women that way. She seemed to take a breath before continuing. 'I'm a student. Final year in Oxford. St Hilda's. I've been away, out of contact, and I've only just seen the news. The Shetland murders.'

He wondered where she'd been. She made it sound as if she'd been travelling to far-flung and exotic places. Or to outer space. Cartoon images of space-ships and little green men floated into his mind.

'I was Jerry's girlfriend,' she said suddenly, dragging him back to the matter in hand. It sounded more like a statement from a politician – a mission state-ment – than a declaration of love. 'We were going to be married.' There was a sudden silence, as if she thought there was nothing else to say.

'When did you last hear from Jerry?' Sandy asked. He was always happier with facts: dates, times, places. And it must have been the right note to take, because Willow smiled and gave him the thumbs up. Anyone else might have felt patronized by the obvious gesture of support, but Sandy was just relieved that he wasn't messing up.

'I spoke to him on the telephone the day before he went north,' the woman said. There was a clarity in her voice that made Sandy wonder if she was a singer. It was hard to tell what she made of Jerry's death. It didn't sound as if she'd been crying, but perhaps she'd made the effort to put on a brave show. 'After that, as

I said, I was away for a few days and he couldn't get hold of me. But he sent me a postcard. It arrived this morning.'

'Could you describe the postcard?' Again Willow beamed at Sandy, like a nursery teacher encouraging a particularly stupid child.

'It was a reproduction of a painting,' Annabel said. 'Three musicians.' So, Sandy thought, the card was identical to the ones they'd found in Jerry's briefcase. He must have picked them all up from the Bonhoga at the same time.

'And what did it say?'

For the first time the woman seemed uneasy, less than confident. 'Look, this isn't really something I feel comfortable discussing on the telephone. I'm coming up anyway. I'll bring the postcard then. I need to see where Jerry died. I need to meet his family.'

'Do the Markhams know about you?'

Another pause. This time so long that Sandy thought he should repeat the question.

'I'm not sure,' she said at last. 'Jerry was going to tell them, I think, but he said he needed to wait for the right moment. Perhaps he hadn't had the chance.'

'Have you booked your travel?' Sandy asked. Back to the facts again. He felt happier already. 'We could help with that.'

'I'm speaking to you from Heathrow,' she said. 'I'm already checked in for the Aberdeen flight. I get into Sumburgh late afternoon.'

'OK.' Sandy was in awe of someone who could arrange travel so quickly, on a whim. 'We'll arrange for someone to meet you.'

'Will it be you?' Annabel asked, and for the first time she sounded anxious.

'I'm not sure.' Sandy was out of his depth again. 'Would you like it to be?'

'Yes.' The voice incisive. 'I would.'

He looked across at Willow, who nodded. 'Well then,' he said. 'Yes, I'll be there. And we'll organize accommodation for you.'

'Ah,' she said. 'Of course you will. I should have had more faith.'

Willow asked Sandy to go with her to interview Maria Markham. It was on the way to the airport, and she said Jimmy Perez could supervise the incident room as soon as he got back from Aith. He could keep tabs on the information coming in. Sandy wasn't sure what Perez would have made of that. Maybe he would have liked to meet Jerry Markham's girlfriend, but when he arrived back at the station Perez didn't say anything. He just nodded and took Sandy's place by the phone.

Maria Markham saw them in the hotel office on the ground floor, not in the flat. Sandy thought she wanted to keep them away from her personal space. She was wearing office clothes too – a grey, fitted suit, which looked a little too large, as if she'd already shrunk after hearing the news of her son's death. Her hair was clean and pinned back from her face and she'd put on lipstick.

'Peter's out,' she said. 'He has a friend who's a sailor and has offered him a day on the water. I encouraged him to go. He needed to get away from this place, just for a day. It was killing him. He didn't love Jerry as I loved him. Inevitably. A father doesn't have the same bond. But now he feels guilty, and thinks if he'd loved Jerry more, he'd have kept him safe. Quite ridiculous, but I can't help feeling that too. That somehow it was Peter's fault. We all need some-one to blame perhaps and, until the killer is found, I only have my husband.' She paused, embarrassed by the confessional stream of words. 'I'm sorry. All this must sound very silly.'

'We will find the killer, Mrs Markham.' Willow sounded so confident that Sandy almost believed her too. 'But we need your help. That's why we're intrud-ing on your grief again.'

Maria took her seat behind the desk, and Willow and Sandy sat opposite her like junior staff members, a waiter and a chambermaid, failing in their duties. 'So,' Maria said, 'what do you want this time?'

'You'll have heard of John Henderson's death?'

'Yes.' She shot a quick look at Willow. It was as if Sandy was invisible. 'Did Henderson kill Jerry and then commit suicide? A kind of remorse? I did wonder if that was what happened. I'd feel kind of cheated. It's not a real justice, to choose when you die.'

'No,' Willow said. 'It was nothing like that. Hender-son was murdered too.'

'Evie Watt's two men both dead.' Maria Markham gave a little laugh. Sandy thought there was some-thing quite mad about the woman. 'I wish I could believe that Evie was the killer, but I don't see it.'

'Jerry met a woman the morning before he was killed,' Willow said. 'In the Bonhoga cafe. She's been described as middle-aged, well groomed. Do you know who that might have been?'

'No,' Maria said. 'It was something to do with his story, maybe. A contact.'

'It wasn't you?'

'Of course not! If I wanted to chat with my son I'd do it here. I wouldn't drive twenty miles north to meet him.'

'But you didn't have much opportunity to talk here. Not really talk. You and Peter are so busy, and your son had just come in on the ferry the morning before. I'd understand that you might arrange to meet somewhere – ' Willow hesitated – 'neutral. Somewhere you wouldn't be interrupted. Everyone says how close the two of you were.' The women stared at each other. The background music in the bar was jazz piano and it seeped between them. Maria Markham spoke first.

'I've told you, Inspector, that I didn't meet my son in Weisdale the morning that he died. I wish I had. I wish I had another memory to add to my collection, but I didn't. I was here all day. Of course my staff will confirm it.'

'Of course.' Willow nodded gravely. There was a brief pause. 'Did your son know the Fiscal, Ms Laing?'

'No!' Maria gave that crazy laugh again, the one that made Sandy want to run from the room. 'Why would he? Unless he interviewed her when he was a reporter here. He might have met her then. But that was years ago.' She got to her feet. 'Are we finished here? I don't sleep well. I get tired easily.'

Willow remained where she was. 'Just one more question.'

Maria remained standing and looked down on them. 'What is it?' Sandy thought her voice *did* sound very tired.

'Did you know that your son has a new girlfriend?'

'No!' The retort was too loud and surprised them all.

'Her name is Annabel Grey and she lives in London.' She paused for a beat. 'Apparently.'

Maria recovered herself quickly. She straightened her jacket and sat down again. 'I'm sure,' she said, 'that Jerry would have told me in his own time if he'd found someone special. Perhaps that's why he'd made the effort to come home. He wanted to tell us personally, not by phone. He'd know that we'd be delighted.'

'Would you?'

'Of course. We only wanted him to be happy.'

They were early at Sumburgh airport and the plane was a little delayed, so they sat, drinking tea, waiting for Markham's girlfriend to arrive.

'What did you make of Maria?' Willow Reeves looked smarter today, Sandy thought. Maybe she'd had time to iron her skirt in the hotel bedroom, and she'd coiled her hair into a twist at the back of her head and fixed it with a comb.

'She seemed kind of crazy,' he said. 'But she's just lost her son.'

'Could she have killed Henderson, do you think?' Willow asked. 'In revenge for Jerry?'

'If she'd thought Henderson had killed her son? Yes, I do.' Sandy shivered slightly. A kind of disgust at the thought. Before Willow could answer, through the window beyond the baggage belt they saw that the plane had arrived. They stood up to cross the hall and meet Jerry Markham's new woman.

Chapter Twenty-Eight

Annabel Grey wasn't alone.

Standing beside Sandy, watching the passengers walk across the airstrip to the terminal, Willow tried to guess which of these women was Markham's girlfriend. Sandy had said she sounded very young. There was a small dark girl in a duffel coat and striped scarf, but she was waving to her waiting parents even before she came into the building. Not her then. Nor the smart lass in the trouser suit carrying a briefcase, who headed straight for the car-hire desk. Willow thought that she and Sandy should have prepared a card with Grey's name on it and should have stood there like the taxi drivers collecting the gas contractors.

In the end Markham's girlfriend approached them. She came straight towards them after coming down the narrow corridor from the tarmac – no bag to collect, just a small rucksack over her shoulder. And beside her walked a tall, distinguished man. Grey-haired, tanned from a winter holiday in the sun. Or skiing. Willow thought he might be a skier. He carried a leather holdall.

'You must be Sandy.' The woman spoke as if he was the only one that mattered, as if Willow was quite invisible.

And Sandy blushed and muttered that he was. He'd become a schoolboy again because this woman was startlingly beautiful, film-star lovely. Tall and blonde with a wide mouth and a slender body, and Sandy wasn't sure how to respond to her at all. Her eyes were red from crying.

'I'm Annabel Grey.' She held out her hand. Her voice wasn't loud, but it was clear, an actress's voice, and Willow expected everyone in the airport to turn and listen to her, was surprised to look round and see that there was no reaction. 'And this is my father.'

'Richard Grey.' He held out a hand. The voice defined him. *Public school*, Willow thought. *Then Oxbridge. He's a politician. Or an actor. No, a lawyer.* Because that was the impression he gave, walking beside his student daughter. That he was there as her advocate rather than as her father.

Annabel was wearing city clothes: a floral knee-length dress, black tights, black pumps and only a short grey jacket to keep out the Shetland cold. In London perhaps summer had already arrived.

Willow introduced herself. 'I'm the Senior Investigating Officer in the case.' Needing some recognition from this woman who seemed bent on ignoring her. Despite herself, the inspector resented the effect the visitor was having on Sandy Wilson.

'So you're in charge?' Annabel said. 'You'll find out who killed Jerry and the other man?'

There was, Willow thought, something childlike about her directness. No guile or pretence.

'Yes,' Willow said. 'I will.'

The woman stared at her for a moment before

giving a brief, approving nod. 'You see, Dad. I said it was right to come.'

They drove to the police station in silence. Willow switched up the heating in the car, worried that the girl would be cold, and found herself almost nodding off; she'd never been able to think clearly in the heat. Sandy, driving, was still tongue-tied and awe-struck. Willow sat beside him in the passenger seat, leaving father and daughter to take their places in the back. The woman, poised and apparently unemotional now, despite the sign of earlier tears, looked out of the window at the passing landscape. She spoke just once when they passed a brown tourist sign pointing to the Ravenswick Hotel.

'Isn't that where Jerry grew up, where his parents live?'

Sandy slowed the car so that she could see the grand house and the walled garden, but Annabel Grey made no further comment on the place. 'What a lovely setting!' the father said. He put his arm around his daughter's shoulders and pulled her to him.

Willow thought Jerry's women had this in common: a lack of hysteria, a dignity in grief. Evie Watt hadn't cried either, when she'd learned of John Henderson's death. Not in public at least.

She took Annabel and Richard Grey into her office, the office that had belonged to Jimmy Perez, not to the interview room. That was hard and impersonal. It didn't smell of offenders, but still the ghosts of the addicts and the drunks somehow lingered there. And perhaps because she was using his space, she asked

Jimmy, not Sandy, to sit in on the discussion. Sandy would find it hard to get beyond the woman's beauty. Perez was still so caught up in his own loss that he would scarcely notice it.

Annabel Grey was determined to tell her own story in her own way. She opened the conversation as soon as she took a seat.

'I want to see Jerry. Would that be possible, do you think?'

'His body's not here.' Perez answered before Willow could reply. 'It's gone to Aberdeen for the post-mortem.' He paused. 'The pathologist there is very good. Very respectful.'

It was clear that the woman was disappointed, shocked even. It wasn't what she'd been expecting.

'You see, sweetheart. I said that was how it would be.' Richard Grey patted his daughter's hand as it lay on the table. He looked up at Willow. 'I'm a barrister. Not in criminal practice, but I do have some understanding of the procedures.' The charming smile that was also a warning: *Don't mess with me.* Willow gave herself a mental pat on the back for guessing his profession, before thinking that this was an added complication she didn't need.

'I loved him.' For the first time Annabel's voice broke a little, but there was still the childish intonation. They sat in silence for a moment. Willow thought Perez might offer a word of sympathy, but when he spoke it was a question, blunt and matter-of-fact.

'Where did you meet Jerry Markham?'

That was all the encouragement Annabel needed to begin her story. Willow thought she had turned it into a legend, polished it by retelling, not just to her friends in her smart university, but to herself. 'It was in December, and I was home for the Christmas vacation. In the breaks I do some voluntary work – a regular commitment, started when I was still at school. I've been lucky in so many ways, and it's important to put something back. Don't you think so?'

Annabel looked up at them, but her father was the only person to respond, patting her hand again.

Left to herself, Willow would have urged the girl to continue more quickly, but Perez was content to wait. She hadn't seen him so still. Willow had heard about his legendary patience, but this was the first time she'd seen it in action. At last Annabel continued: 'This year there was an advent course in St Luke's, the church on the square close to where we live. Beside other things, I helped out with that.'

'Advent course?' Now Willow couldn't help interrupting. She felt a nerve in her ankle twitching. She'd been sitting still for too long.

'For people looking for answers,' Annabel said. 'An introduction to the spiritual life.'

'And Jerry was running a story about it?'

'No!' Annabel smiled. 'He was one of the participants. At first he couldn't take us seriously. I could tell. He was there for a joke or a bet. Or perhaps for a story. Yes, perhaps that's why he turned up that cold December day. Or because it was raining and at least there'd be some shelter and lunch and coffee. But in fact, of course, he was sent to us. He needed to be there.'

Oh, shit, she's a God-botherer! Another. As if there aren't enough already in this case. Willow's parents had been Buddhists in a vague, undemanding way, and she'd rejected all ideas of the supernatural before leaving school, had become an aggressive atheist. Another form of rebellion.

Annabel continued to speak. 'He fought it of course. People often do. But that made it even more wonderful when he finally let the Lord into his life. He'd been so certain, so antagonistic, and then all the barriers were down. It was a privilege to be a part of the process.'

'And now he's dead.' Willow couldn't help herself.

'And now he's dead,' Annabel agreed seriously. 'Faith isn't always an easy path.'

'You think he was killed because he was a Christian?' Willow made no attempt to keep the incredulity from her voice. In her head she had an image of Annabel at worship: a congregation of like-minded deluded souls, eyes half-closed, waving their arms in the air. Mad as snakes, but hardly a threat, hardly likely to provoke violence, just extreme irritation. She wondered if the girl's father was a church member too. Willow found it hard to imagine. Richard Grey seemed too sophisticated to be part of that scene.

'Jerry was committed to fighting evil.' The woman's voice was firm. 'And that takes courage.' She looked to her father for support and, although he nodded gravely, Willow thought the reaction was automatic. He didn't share his daughter's faith.

Perez broke in before Willow had a chance to speak again. 'Was there a specific example of evil? I mean, a specific reason for Jerry visiting Shetland so soon after his conversion?'

It occurred to Willow that Perez might well be a

God-botherer too. In these northern islands superstition would be rife.

Annabel didn't reply directly. 'We were planning to be married,' she said. 'Very soon. We saw no reason to wait. Jerry was going to be baptized, but once that was done, we'd decided to make plans.' She gave a wide, sad smile. 'Jerry spent Christmas with us. It was very busy for him at work and he didn't have time to get home. Dad always goes *completely* over the top at Christmas. The biggest tree in the universe. Carols round the fire. And this year it snowed. It was quite magical. Walking back from Midnight Mass on Christmas morning Jerry asked me to marry him. It was the best present ever.'

Willow was struck suddenly by the similarity between the two cases under investigation. Both Evie and Annabel were committed Christians marrying an older man. Henderson had been quite different in character from Markham, but the outlook of the women – so certain, so proud of their faith, even in their grief – had much in common. But she couldn't fathom how that could be a trigger to commit murder.

'But he hadn't told his parents about you, even though he missed spending Christmas with them and you'd become engaged?' The thought had occurred to her as soon as the girl had described the proposal.

'He didn't want to tell them on the telephone,' Annabel said. 'He thought he should talk to them in person.'

'Is that why Jerry came to Shetland?' Perez asked.

It was a simple question, but the girl hesitated. 'I think he might have told them while he was here,' she said. 'That was probably in his mind. But it wasn't the main reason for the visit.'

'What was that?' Perez gave a small and encouraging smile.

And Willow suddenly saw this moment as an epiphany, a revelation that this lay at the heart of the investigation. If they could answer that question, they would find their killer.

Again there was a silence. Outside gulls were screaming. The hoot of a cruise ship leaving the pier.

'He wouldn't tell me,' Annabel said at last, an admission she'd rather not have made. 'He said there were things he had to sort out before he could commit himself properly to our relationship.'

Willow was tempted to scream at the woman: *Didn't you ask him what he meant? Didn't you want to know if there was another woman in his life? Some sordid secret?* She felt her dislike of Annabel Grey as a fog in her head preventing her from thinking clearly. Why the antipathy? Because of Annabel's beauty? Her certainty? Her complacency? Her pampered childhood and her doting father?

'Didn't his secrecy make you doubt his affection for you?' Perez asked the question gently, but the answer was fierce and clear.

'No! He loved me and he wanted to spend his life with me. But his faith had made him question his past and his work. He needed time to get things straight in his head. I asked if I should come to Shetland with him, but he said this was something he had to do on his own.'

'And where did you go when he was away?' Perez asked.

'On retreat,' she said. 'In the Easter holidays the

University Chaplaincy organizes time out for anyone who wants to explore their faith more deeply. There's a house in Sussex, run by nuns. A place of silence and contemplation. No contact with the outside world. That was why I didn't find out about his death immediately.' She looked up at Perez, and Willow saw that her eyes glittered with tears. 'I had the sense that he needed my prayers.'

'You told my sergeant that Jerry had sent you a postcard,' Willow said. 'Do you have it with you?'

Annabel opened her bag and set the card on the table. The same picture. A painting of three men playing violins. Willow held it by the edges and turned it over. On the back, Annabel's home address in Hampstead. And two short sentences. *Nearly done. Home soon.*

'This is definitely Jerry's handwriting?'

'Oh yes,' Annabel said.

So Jerry had written the card and posted it before his death. But the message, Willow thought, was hardly any help at all.

Chapter Twenty-Nine

Later their colleague Morag took Annabel out for a short guided walk of Lerwick. Perez had suggested that she might like to see where Jerry had been at school, the office where he'd first worked as a journalist. While she was away, they interviewed her father. Willow had the sense that Grey was as keen as the detectives to have a discussion in Annabel's absence, and she felt throughout that he was in charge of the meeting. He set the agenda and told them what he wanted them to know. At one point, describing his work as a human-rights lawyer, he said, 'Ah sometimes, Inspector, I lose sight of the truth. I'm a weaver of stories. A persuader.'

She thought that was what he was doing here – conjuring a story of the Greys' perfect lives: the house on the edge of Hampstead Heath, the country retreat in Dorset, Annabel's academic brilliance. Not necessarily to deceive his audience in any way, but to convince them to treat his daughter gently. And because he wanted Willow and Perez to like him, to be swept along by the energy of his narrative. He was seductive. In her parents' world of the commune, he would be welcomed as a guru.

'So you'd met Jerry Markham on many occasions,' Perez said to start them off. 'You knew him well?'

But, like his daughter, Richard wanted to describe events in his own way. 'First,' he said, 'a little family history to set events in context. For the last ten years it's just been Annabel and me. My wife left me when our daughter was eleven. I adored Jane, but she was an impulsive woman, given to strange moods and depressions. She always resisted seeking psychiatric help, but I should have persisted. I see that now. She was obviously mentally ill.' He paused and looked wistfully into the distance. Willow felt like applauding his performance. She wondered if Grey believed that his wife's antipathy towards him could be considered a symptom of psychiatric disorder. If so, Willow was a sufferer too. Perez said nothing and waited for Grey to continue.

'Jane ran away with a younger man. She had some notion that she might take Annabel with her, but she soon realized that would be impractical. She could hardly look after herself, never mind a child.' Another dramatic pause. 'Besides, without Annabel to care for, I'd have fallen apart completely.'

It occurred to Willow that Perez might sympathize with Richard Grey. Without Cassie to look after, would he have survived Fran's murder? Perhaps that was why he was so tolerant of the man's posturing.

'Jane was a regular church-goer from before I met her,' Grey said. 'I think she liked the theatre of it – the dressing up and the ritual. And there was always someone around to offer her sympathy and give her attention. She used to take Annabel to Sunday School. I never understood the attraction, but Annabel still went, even after Jane disappeared. Perhaps she hoped that one day her mother would turn up in the congregation; of course that never happened. Jane lost all contact with us a couple of months after she ran away. Then, when Annabel was fifteen, St Luke's appointed a new vicar. He was young and evangelical and he appealed to the younger parishioners. I suppose faith became more real to Annabel then and she took a more active part in the worship. In the whole life of the church. It's influenced her deeply ever since.'

'I'm sorry,' Perez said, the famous patience finally wearing thin. 'I don't quite understand what this has to do with Jerry Markham.'

'It explains her infatuation,' Richard Grey said. 'When Jerry turned up at the advent course that day – challenging, screwed up, but very attractive – she thought she could save him. He was like a male version of her mother. Annabel is young and passionate, and Jerry Markham became the most important thing in her life. More important than her friends, or her academic study at St Hilda's.'

'And what did you make of him?' Willow asked. 'You must have realized that he had a reputation as a journalist. He was known to be ruthless and very ambitious. And he was a lot older than Annabel.'

Grey frowned. 'He wasn't the man I'd have chosen for her, but sometimes you have to let go. To allow the people you love to make their own mistakes.'

'So you thought Jerry Markham was a mistake?'

Grey hesitated. 'He seemed pleasant enough. Devoted to my daughter. Prepared to go along with the whole thing – baptism, confirmation – just to please her. He made her happy.'

'But you didn't feel you could trust him?'

'I didn't know,' Grey said. 'I suppose I wasn't sure she wouldn't get hurt. He reminded me too much of my ex-wife.'

There was a knock at the door and Morag was there, looking apologetic because they were back so soon. Annabel rushed ahead of her, flushed from the walk. 'I'm so glad that we came,' she said. 'I feel that I've met Jerry all over again. It's as if I've bumped into him in the street and followed in his footsteps along the waterfront.' She stood behind her father and kissed his head lightly. 'Thank you so much for bringing me.'

They continued the conversation standing by the marina in Aith, though now Annabel was with them, so it was difficult to revisit the subject of Jerry's suitability as a husband. A weak sun provided no heat and Willow had given Annabel a spare jersey, which covered her dress and looked on her like a designer outfit, something weird and boho seen on the catwalk. Richard had pulled a Berghaus jacket from the holdall and seemed perfectly at home. Out in the voe some kids were having sailing lessons at an after-school club, skittering over the water in tiny dinghies. Annabel had asked if she might see where Jerry had died. Perez had said immediately that they could take her to where the body was found. Willow admired his tact. This place, by the water, with the hills on all sides, would provide a better memory for the woman than a lay-by next to a busy road. *She* wouldn't have been so thoughtful. But then *she* wasn't taken in by long legs and innocence. To think that she'd believed Perez would be immune to that sort of charm!

Now Annabel sat on an upturned wooden crate looking out over the sea. 'It's lovely,' she said. 'More bleak than I was expecting, but bigger, more open. Jerry had shown me photos, but you can't really tell from those. You don't get an idea of the scale.'

'What did Jerry tell you about his life on the islands?'

Still Perez was leading the discussion. Willow had decided to let him get on with it – she'd worked out that Annabel was someone who would respond better to men.

'He talked about his parents, working so hard in the hotel,' Annabel said. 'He was very close to his mother. No siblings, so we had that in common, and with his dad so tied up with the business, I suppose that was natural. I know Maria phoned Jerry almost every day.'

'And Jerry didn't mind that?' Perez was standing beside Annabel's makeshift bench and, like her, he was staring over the water, so there was no eye contact. 'He didn't find it intrusive?'

'No. As I said, they were very close. I think he welcomed the way she kept in touch.'

'Who would Jerry have talked to if he had a problem?' Perez asked. 'His mother? You?'

Now Annabel turned so that she was looking directly at him. 'I didn't see it as a competition,' she said. 'Dad and I are very close, but Jerry didn't resent that, either.'

Willow looked at Richard Grey. No response at all.

'I'm not suggesting that you resented Maria.' Perez

gave an awkward little laugh. 'But in this case it's important to know if Jerry confided in anyone. We need to know what brought him to Shetland. Maybe he had a close male friend? Here or in London?'

'Jerry didn't find it easy admitting to problems,' Annabel said. 'And he certainly didn't like asking for help. A sort of macho thing. He thought he should be able to deal with stuff himself.'

'Did he ever talk to you about Evie Watt?' Perez asked. 'She's a young Shetlander. She and Jerry were lovers before he left the islands for London.'

'I'm sure Jerry had lots of girlfriends before he met me.' Annabel stared back at the sea. 'But this was going to be a fresh start for us both.'

Willow couldn't believe that the girl had never asked about Jerry Markham's past. That was what lovers did: shared their intimate secrets. It was part of the game.

'Evie's boyfriend was the second murder victim,' Perez said. 'So you do see how this is relevant.'

'You think Evie Watt killed them both?' The question came from Richard Grey. He'd been leaning against the harbour wall, apparently just enjoying the air, but Willow saw that he'd been following the conversation closely.

'No!' Perez said. 'There's no evidence for that at all. But it's a connection. A link that we have to explore.'

In the voe one of the dinghies tipped on its side and a young boy with bright-red hair climbed onto the hull, spluttering and laughing.

'Jerry talked about betrayal,' Annabel said. 'Late one night. We'd been out for a meal and he was walking me home. It was early January, before I went back to St Hilda's, a sharp frost, and he had his arm around me. We'd shared a bottle of wine. I asked about Shetland. Would he ever go back to live? He said it wasn't the paradise that people from outside believed it to be. When you trusted people and they let you down, that was the worst sort of betrayal.'

'Did he say who'd betrayed him?' Willow asked the question and felt that she was intruding into a private conversation. But this was *her* case, her chance to make a mark.

Annabel shook her head. 'That was all he said.'

Chapter Thirty

All evening Perez had the images of the women in his mind. He drove south to Ravenswick and collected Cassie from his neighbour's house. He ran her bath and listened to her chatting about her friends and her day at school, and still the images were with him. Two women, both attached to Jerry Markham. One a student, pale and fair, at home in the city. One small and dark, living in the islands. Opposites. Shadows of each other. Yet sharing a faith. A passion for God and for Markham. A belief that they could save him from himself.

When Cassie was asleep he made a fire with scraps of driftwood that he'd collected earlier from the beach. There was one dense piece of pitch pine that would last most of the night. Then he prepared for his visitors. This time he'd invited Willow and Sandy to come to his house to discuss the case; he hadn't waited for Willow to invite herself. A week ago he would never have imagined doing that. He would never have considered opening up his house, *Fran's* house, to visitors. He'd have slammed the door in their faces.

There'd still been soup in the freezer; it had been made by a neighbour at some time over the winter. And a home-made cake. All the women in Ravenswick had decided that he needed feeding in the months following Fran's death. He wiped down the patterned oilcloth on the table, laid it with cutlery and glasses and put the soup on to heat through. There were oatcakes from the Walls Bakery and he'd stopped in the community shop in Aith for bread and beer. He didn't see Willow as a woman who would drink wine. Not with veggie soup, at least. Then there was a sudden desire to run away, not sure after all that he could face the intrusion.

It was a still night and he heard their car stop at the bottom of the bank. He took a deep breath and had the door open to welcome them by the time they'd walked up the path. It was almost dark now and he could only see them as silhouettes, Willow taller than the Whalsay man. On the hill at the back of the house there were sheep like small white ghosts in the gloom. And in Perez's head more ghosts: of the woman who had allowed him to share this place with her, and of two dead men. Markham and Henderson. Like the women who had loved them, as different as it was possible to be.

The detectives followed Perez quietly into the house, not wanting to wake the child sleeping in the next room. They ate like old friends. No need for conversation at first. Perez hoped that meant the awkwardness between him and Willow was forgotten. Later, when he had made coffee and brought out the cake, they talked through the investigation.

'So do we really believe in Markham's conversion?' Willow said. 'Can people change like that? Suddenly. A clap of thunder. Saul on the road to Damascus.'

'I can kind of believe it.' Perez felt warm and easy

and wondered if that was some sort of betrayal, here in Fran's house. The idea of betrayal had become central to the investigation. Betrayal and transformation. But Fran had loved parties, people eating and drinking and talking, so he decided he could enjoy the conversation in tribute to her. 'In this case at least. Markham had a stressful job. Not many friends, from what we can gather. A small rented flat on his own in the big city. Homesick, maybe, though he'd never have admitted it. He was successful enough, but it must have been hard being a small fish in a big pool. Here in Shetland he was a star reporter, and everyone knows the Markhams of Ravenswick Hotel.' Perez paused for a moment and collected his thoughts. 'Jerry might have been quite low, don't you think, alone in London? That was the impression his editor gave. So he went into that church one lunchtime. Just to shelter from the rain, as Annabel said. Or in search of something. And he found friendship. A welcome. A way of belonging. To the church, but also to the Grey family. They even invited him home for Christmas'

'And he found a beautiful woman,' Willow said. 'Don't forget that. We know how Markham liked the ladies. Especially if they were young.'

'And money.' This was Sandy, joining in too. 'A flash house in London. He was always impressed by stuff like that. Class.'

'So perhaps he wanted to believe.' Perez hoped he was making sense. He felt he was groping towards some sort of answer. 'Perhaps he *wanted* the whole conversion experience. To please Annabel and the rest of them. To become the centre of attention again.'

'Then why did he come back to Shetland?' Willow

was sitting on the floor, though there were chairs enough for the three of them. She was stretched on a couple of sheepskins in front of the fire and her face was red with the heat. She'd taken off her sweater and was wearing a striped T-shirt, frayed at the neck. 'Why did he run away from his new girlfriend and all his new friends and bring himself back here?'

'To tell his parents that he was going to be married?' Perez remembered Maria's insistence that Jerry had something important to tell her. 'But not just that. He'd have told them straight away, if that was the sole reason for the visit.'

'Could it be that he was here to write a story, like he told everyone?' Sandy had been following the conversation, frowning with concentration. 'When he was working on the *Shetland Times* perhaps he'd come across something in the islands that wasn't right. I don't know – corruption. People on the fiddle. And this was his chance to prove to his new friends that he was a good man. A good Christian.'

'Or perhaps the conversion thing was all bollocks,' Willow said. 'He went along with it to get inside Annabel's knickers. And he was here to make a bit of money to impress his new woman. Perhaps the blackmail theory still holds.'

There was a silence. Perez got to his feet to pour more coffee. He had ideas about the case – he always believed more in the personal than the political – but it was Willow's place to move the investigation forward. In the end she threw the responsibility back to him.

'What do you think, Jimmy? Where do we go next?'

'I'd like to talk to Evie again,' he said. 'If Markham's change of heart was genuine, then Evie would be the person he'd feel the need to meet. He'd want her forgiveness, wouldn't he? He'd want to set things straight between them, before going back to start his new life with Annabel Grey.' Perez drained his mug and ran again in his head the conversations he'd had with Evie Watt. 'She told me Markham had tried to phone her, but she claims that she hadn't met him. Perhaps we need to check that. Evie looks young, right enough, but perhaps Sue Walsh was mistaken, and Evie was the woman Markham met at the Bonhoga.'

'So that's your plan for tomorrow, Jimmy?'

He wondered at Willow's change of tone. One day yelling at him for doing his own thing. Now giving him a free hand. 'Aye, if there's nothing else you want me to do. It'll mean a trip back to Fetlar, to her parents' place.'

'I'll come with you,' Willow said. 'A day-trip to an off-island. If that's OK with you, Jimmy, of course.' Her voice was mocking now, with some of its old edge. 'And we should fit in a visit to Captain Sinclair, the harbour master, too.'

Then Perez's anxiety returned, eating away at the new confidence. Maybe she didn't trust him to do his work on his own. Maybe she'd been told that he wasn't fit to be let out without a minder.

He was about to answer when there was a cry from the bedroom: 'Jimmy! Jimmy!' It was Cassie's voice, confused and panicky.

He was on his feet. 'I'm sorry,' he said. 'You'll have to go. Will you see yourselves out?' He didn't care that this might sound rude. He'd already forgotten all about the case. When he got to the girl's room she was sitting upright.

'I was having a dream,' she said. 'A terrible dream.'

He saw that she'd wet the bed, and he helped her out and cleaned her and changed the sheets. He sat by her, stroking her hair away from her face until she slept. He thought he would do anything in the world to make her happy.

The next day was still and clear, and the drive to Toft for the Yell ferry had the feel of a holiday day out. He'd picked Willow up at the police station after dropping Cassie at school, and she fed back to him the overnight news as he drove north.

'Vicki Hewitt thinks she'll wrap up her work at Hvidahus today.'

'Anything useful?'

'Henderson's killer was careful. No footwear prints in the garage. Loads of fingerprints of course. Mostly the ones you'd expect. Evie's naturally. Everything in the kitchen clean.'

'So nothing useful.' Perez turned and smiled at her and wondered why it mattered what she thought of him.

The lad taking their money on the ferry to Yell had been at school with Perez and chatted to him through the open car window all the way across. News of other school friends. Weddings and babies. He'd never been the most tactful of men. 'And who's this?' Nodding towards Willow, a great smirk on his face, as if she couldn't hear him.

'Ah,' Perez said. 'This is my boss.'

Then the drive across the length of Yell, bare hill-sides scarred with black peat banks. Yell had its bonny places, but you couldn't see them from the road north. On the crossing to Fetlar they got out of the car and watched the island approaching. The noise of the engine meant they wouldn't be overheard.

'So how will we play this, Jimmy?' The wind was catching her hair, blowing it across her face. 'I don't want to imply that I think Evie's been lying to us. Especially not in front of the parents. They'd never talk to us again.'

Perez thought of Francis and Jessie. They'd be protective of their daughter. And they'd been friends of Henderson and would be grieving in their own right. No doubt they'd have had hassle from the press too. 'Let's phone and let them know we're coming. Then, when we get there, we'll explain about Jerry Markham's girlfriend turning up from nowhere. That will seem courteous, as if we want to tell them before the media get hold of the news.' He considered. 'It's odd that the press hasn't mentioned Grey already. You'd think they'd have tracked her down by now, even if she'd been hiding away from the world until a couple of days ago. Do you think he was trying to keep his new relationship secret?'

'In my experience,' Willow said, 'most blokes would want to be seen out with a young woman as good-looking as Annabel. He'd be parading her in front of everyone who'd ever known him.'

'So why the secrecy?'

'The Christian thing? Maybe she has a tendency to evangelize in the pub? Might be a tad embarrassing in front of a bunch of hard-nosed journos?'

'Aye,' Perez said. 'Maybe.' The ferry was slowing as they approached Fetlar. He opened the door of the car. 'Do you want to see Evie on her own? You obviously got on well with her, and it might be easier for her to talk to a woman. An outsider. And there are things most of us would prefer not to say in front of our parents.'

'Sounds like a plan.' Willow got into the car beside him just as the ramp was lowered.

There was phone reception as soon as they drove ashore. Perez made the call, thinking that one of the parents would answer and they'd be more likely to respond to a Shetland accent.

'Yes?' It was Evie's mother. Aggressive, ready to attack.

'It's Jimmy Perez, Mrs Watt. One of the detectives investigating John's murder. How is Evie?'

A silence. 'Ah, Jimmy, I don't know. It's hard to tell. It's like she's frozen solid from the inside.'

'We're in Fetlar.' A ringed plover was running along the shingle behind the beach. 'I was hoping we might come to talk to her.'

'Oh, come along, Jimmy. Of course. Anything we can do to help.' He heard the relief in her voice and understood that she and Francis would be glad of company, someone else to distract Evie for a moment, to take the responsibility away from them.

By the time they got to the house there was the smell of baking in the oven. Jessie wouldn't think to ask them in without offering food. The parents stood in the yard as Perez parked the car, grave and silent, and so still that they reminded him of a grey photo of old crofters, the sort you might see in Vatnagarth museum. He couldn't decide what they expected from the detectives. Hope that there would be a resolution and that things would return to normal, that the traditions of boat-building and crofting would seem important to them again? He introduced the couple to Willow.

'Evie's in her room,' Jessie said. 'Would you mind waiting a while before talking to her? She's only just fallen asleep and she must be exhausted.'

'Of course.'

In the kitchen Jessie put on the kettle and lifted a tray of biscuits from the oven, slid them onto a cooling rack. The parents were waiting for them to speak, for an explanation of their arrival. Perez looked at Willow, but still there was an awkward silence. Perhaps, like him, she wasn't quite sure what to say.

'Have you found him?' Francis said at last. 'Have you found John's killer? Is that why you're here?'

'No,' Willow said. 'We have more questions. And some information. We wouldn't want Evie to read about it in the press.'

Then the door opened and Evie appeared. It seemed she hadn't been asleep at all, as if she would never sleep again.

Chapter Thirty-One

Willow took Evie for a walk along the crescent of sand that she'd seen from the Watts's kitchen window. With the flat land behind it, the beach reminded her of home on North Uist. There was a place very similar close to the commune, low ground just in from the sea, fertile strips of machair planted with crops. For the first time in months, she thought maybe she should take a trip back to the Hebrides and spend a week or so with her folks. The spring was always a busy period for them and she'd enjoy working on the land again.

Jessie had been pleased when Willow suggested the walk.

'What a good plan! It might bring some colour back into your cheeks, my love.' And Evie had been compliant. An obedient daughter doing as she was told. Not really caring, Willow saw. Nothing would matter to her now. Not the green tidal energy she'd been planning in the Sound off Hvidahus or her role in the church. The life had gone out of her. The parents watched from the doorway until the women had taken the path across the fields. Not waving, but looking as if this was a farewell, as if Evie was starting out on a long voyage.

They walked between the tide line and the water. There was that sense of free floating, of the air and the sea all around them. The tide was low, but there were no other footprints on the beach. Evie was wearing a long hand-knitted cardigan, the colour of heather, and though it wasn't a cold day she huddled inside it.

'Every day is worse than the one before,' she said. 'At first there was just shock, and I thought I could deal with it. With my faith, and the help of my friends and family, I thought I could cope with anything. But I can't. Not this.'

Willow had nothing to say.

'Everyone thought John was the lucky one,' Evie went on. 'Lucky to be marrying me, I mean. A widower. So much older. But it was quite the other way round. I couldn't believe my good fortune when he asked me to marry him. I'd dreamed of nothing else since our first date. Of that ring on my finger. Sharing the rest of our lives.'

Willow bent to pick up a shell. It was pink and perfect, a series of shining chambers inside, smooth to the touch.

'I don't think I believe in God any more,' Evie said. The confession was defiant. She sounded like a three-year-old shouting out forbidden smutty words: *bum, willy, poo*. Willow was sure she hadn't admitted any loss of faith to her parents. But this anger was surely healthier than the dumb compliance that she'd shown in the house.

'Have you any idea what Jerry Markham might have wanted to talk to you about?' Willow asked. 'You said he'd left a message on your voicemail.'

'No!' It was as if bereavement had given her the licence to be rude. Perhaps for the first time in her life. 'I don't care about Jerry. I don't give a shit about him.'

Willow wondered if Perez had behaved like this when his fiancée had died. Had he stamped his feet like a three-year-old and yelled at strangers. Perhaps in his own way he was still doing that. 'Would the message still be on your phone?' she asked.

Evie looked at her. 'I deleted it. Why?'

'Because if we find out why Jerry came to Shetland it might help us make an arrest, lock up John's killer.'

'I never believed in the death penalty,' Evie said. 'Not before this happened. I thought it was barbaric. Now I think I'd be prepared to kill the bastard myself. I'd stab him as he stabbed John.' She picked up a pebble and hurled it into the water.

'Jerry Markham had a new girlfriend,' Willow said. 'A young woman named Annabel Grey.'

'Is that relevant?' Evie's voice was flippant. 'I can't imagine Jerry going for very long *without* a girlfriend.'

'He met her in the winter, an advent course at a church in north London.'

There was a pause. 'You're telling me that Jerry got religion?' Now the woman sounded incredulous.

'According to Ms Grey.'

'Then she's lying!' Suddenly Evie took off her shoes and rolled up the legs of her jeans. She ran towards the sea. A tiny wave rolled over her feet. The water must have been freezing, but it was as if she hadn't felt its iciness. When Willow joined her she was still standing there, staring out to the horizon. 'Jerry was a committed atheist. He mocked me for my faith. There is absolutely no way he'd have changed his mind on that. He was too proud to admit anything beyond his own experience. Too arrogant. And even if he had been tempted to explore belief, he'd have kept it secret. Trust me, turning up at a church just wasn't his style.' She looked up at Willow. 'What's she like, this Annabel Grey?'

Willow thought for a moment. 'Young,' she said. 'Tall. Pretty.'

'Of course.' Evie's voice was bitter. 'Any girlfriend of Jerry's would have to be pretty.' She continued in a rush, an admission of hatred: 'I've been thinking that it was Jerry's fault. That John's dead, I mean. It was Jerry coming back that started this off. If he'd stayed away, I'd be married by now. I'd be happy.'

'We don't know yet what happened, what triggered these dreadful events.' But Willow thought that was probably true. Out at sea there was a huge tanker on the way south. Was that carrying crude oil from Sullom Voe? She turned back to Evie. 'Jerry hadn't mentioned in his voicemail message that he had a girlfriend?'

'He didn't tell me anything. The message was just: *Please call me back*. Something of that sort. A request. But I owed him nothing.' Evie walked on through the shallow water. Willow couldn't see her face and it was impossible to tell what she was thinking.

'Weren't you interested in knowing why he wanted to see you?' *Because surely we're all interested in ex-boyfriends. Especially the ones who have dumped us, the ones we really adored.*

'Perhaps I was a bit curious.' Evie stopped, watched

the tide suck at her toes, the tiny eddies in the sand. 'But I didn't see him.' She focused on a gull tugging at a bit of seaweed on the shore. 'I'd been besotted with him, you know. Part of me was afraid that all the old feelings would come back if we met, that some of the old attraction would still be there. I didn't need the complication. And I thought he'd want something. Jerry always did want something.'

'Might Jerry have contacted John?' Willow thought if the man had been desperate for Evie's forgiveness, he might have asked her fiancé for help in setting up the meeting. Jerry had been at Sullom Voe on the afternoon of his death. John Henderson had been working there, just across the water from the terminal. She imagined how that conversation might have gone: *I took advantage of your woman, got her pregnant and dumped her. Please help me to put things right.* You'd think that Jerry Markham would have realized that the right thing to do just before the marriage was to leave things alone. To stay away. But then Markham had always been self-absorbed and self-indulgent. He'd probably be selfish even in this.

'John didn't say anything about it,' Evie said at last. 'If Jerry met him or phoned him, John didn't tell me.'

'And things were just the same between you? Those last few days of John's life?'

There was a silence filled with gulls screeching.

'I don't know!' Evie screamed louder than the gulls. 'I was busy, about to be married, anxious about dresses and flowers and crazy stuff like that. And about work. If he was different, I didn't notice. Don't you think I wish I'd stopped? Dropped everything. Spent every last second with him.' She stopped abruptly. It was as if the needle had been lifted from a vinyl record mid-track. When she started again, the voice was almost a whisper. 'We never made love. Came close a few times. But we thought we had years ahead of us. Let's wait, we thought. Make the marriage night something special. And now? Now, I wish we'd never got out of bed.' She turned towards Willow and there were tears running down her cheeks. 'Then I might have been pregnant. Now I'll never have a child.' Willow put her arm round her shoulder and walked with Evie back up the beach.

As they approached the house, Willow saw that Evie's parents were looking out for them through the kitchen window. *Would my parents behave like that if someone close to me had died?* And she thought that they would. They'd be over-protective too. And they'd feel guilty, like Francis and Jessie, convinced that they should have been able to save their daughter from this pain. She thought again that it was time to take a trip to Uist to see them. Before it was too late.

Inside the house Evie reverted to the mode of obedient child. She'd left the anger on the beach. She sat at the table with her back to the window, sipped at her tea and crumbled a biscuit into the saucer. When Willow and Perez stood up to go, she hardly acknowledged their leaving.

Chapter Thirty-Two

Perez wished he were the person walking on the beach with Evie. Here, in the stuffy kitchen, surrounded by the clutter of the family's life, he could hardly breathe. Jessie chattered, a stream of pointless observations, as if words would somehow prevent her from thinking. She was washing up at the sink and turned occasionally for a response from him. He would nod or prompt her with a short phrase of agreement, and off she would go again. Francis said nothing unless he was asked a direct question.

'We told Evie's brother Magnus not to come back just yet,' Jessie said. 'He was planning to be here for the wedding of course, coming up on the ferry on Friday night, but we told him to stay put when we heard the news about John. Evie needs her space just now, don't you think so, Jimmy?' A look over her shoulder, a nod from him, and the words went on. 'We'll organize the funeral when John's body is released. He has no family of his own left now. There's a cousin, I think, somewhere in the south, but they've not met since they were bairns. Much better that we do it.'

She paused for breath and to carry the dripping baking tray to stand on the back of the range to dry.

'Was John already dead the last time you were here, Jimmy? I've been thinking about that.'

'I think he must have been.' Perez supposed this was information that was already generally known. Willow had released a press statement asking for people who might have seen Henderson early on the morning of his death.

'And we were here, carrying on as normal – me in the fields and Francis in his boatshed – and we knew nothing about it. That's such a strange thought. I'm glad we live in Fetlar. It means that Evie can escape from all the gossip about the murders. There'll be talk, because she knew both men. You know what folk are like, Jimmy. You know how cruel they can be.'

He nodded again. Then he spoke just to stop her. It would be easy enough to sit in the traditional Shetland chair with its high wooden back and listen, but he thought she must be exhausted with this need to fill the silence with all those words. He felt it was his responsibility to give her a rest.

'It seems that Jerry Markham had changed,' Perez said. It came to him that this was gossip of a kind too. Unsubstantiated gossip. They only had Annabel's and her father's word that it was true. Willow had asked Sandy to get details of the vicar, and other members of the congregation, so they could check it out. 'He'd joined a church in London and had found a girlfriend there.' Jessie and Francis stared at him.

Again it was Jessie who spoke first. 'That doesn't sound like the Jerry Markham we knew.' Her voice was unsympathetic. She needed to save all her concern for her daughter.

'I wondered if he'd been in touch with you. Perhaps he'd sent you a letter. An apology for the way he'd treated Evie.'

'No,' Jessie said. 'There was nothing of that kind. And it would take more than a letter to make me feel differently about him. You didn't see Evie at the time that he left her. You didn't see how thin and ill she looked.'

Perez turned to the man who was still standing, his back to the stove. 'Francis? Did you hear from Jerry Markham?'

'Markham would know better than to try to contact me.' Watt's mouth snapped shut like a trap.

'Peter Markham told me that you'd met him in the street a little while ago,' Perez said. 'He told me that you were on friendly terms then.'

'I had no quarrel with the father,' Watt said. 'No reason not to be polite to the man.'

And at that Jessie Watt started talking again about Francis's work. 'They're going to put one of his yoals in a museum in Bergen. Imagine that! He has a waiting list of folk wanting to buy boats from him.' And then even she lapsed into silence and stared out of the window at Willow and her daughter, walking along the beach. They all watched as Willow put her arm round Evie's shoulder and started back with her along the path across the field towards the house.

Willow and Perez had to wait a while for the ferry back to Yell and sat in the car at the pier, sharing notes.

'How was the girl?' Perez asked.

'Angry. And who can blame her.' The walk along the beach had given Willow some colour. She looked fitter, healthier. 'I don't think she had any idea that Markham had taken up with Annabel Grey, though. That was a complete surprise.'

'And she still says that she never met him after he arrived back?'

'Mmm. And that she deleted the message he'd left on her voicemail.' Willow turned to face him. There were freckles on the bridge of her nose. 'Where do we go from here, Jimmy? I still feel we're nowhere near finding out what went on.'

'Should we call in on Joe Sinclair on our way back to Lerwick?'

'Aye.' She seemed preoccupied. Was she dwelling on her failure to get a result? 'Let's do that.'

'It still seems a coincidence to me that Markham was at the terminal, so close to where Henderson was working, that afternoon. And Joe was out at Hvidahus with Evie and the Fiscal on the morning Henderson died. They were all there, within half a mile of where John was killed. He's on the edge of both of our investigations.'

'Sure, Jimmy. Whatever you think.' But he wasn't sure that she was really listening. She'd thought the conversation with Evie would bring a new energy to the inquiry. Now perhaps she believed that the long trip to Fetlar had been a waste of time.

Joe Sinclair was short and solid. Confident. Practical. Perez had served with him on a working party that had set out guidelines for a response to a possible major oil spill and had come to respect his straight-forward approach to problems. There was no bluster with Joe Sinclair. He might have his own agenda, but there was no obvious power-play.

On the wall of his office had been pinned a detailed large-scale map of Shetland and a photo of the last ship he'd skippered, a colour image of Shetland from space, a photo of his wife and grown-up daughters.

'You're here about John.' There was a coffee machine in the corner of the room. The jug was already filled with water and Sinclair tipped grounds from a jar into the filter and switched it on. 'I still can't believe he's dead.' And Perez saw that in this case the cliché was true. Joe looked at the door as if he was expecting Henderson to walk into his office for his next shift. 'He'd worked here longer than me and could have done my job with his eyes shut, but he preferred being out on the water. I'd come to depend on him.'

The coffee gurgled and Sinclair fetched mugs from a drawer, glad of an excuse to turn away.

Perez looked at Willow, offering her the opportunity to lead the interview. He'd already introduced her as the Senior Investigating Officer. But she shook her head briefly and throughout the discussion sat very quiet and still. Listening intently? Or still preoccupied by her encounter with Evie Watt, wishing that she'd taken a different tack, asked other questions?

'I'd like to talk about Jerry Markham first.' Perez took his coffee and set it carefully on the floor at his side. 'You knew him.' Not a question. Joe Sinclair knew everyone in Shetland. 'What did you make of him?'

There was a moment of silence. It wasn't the question Joe had been expecting. But he was accustomed to people asking for his opinion and he answered readily enough. 'He wasn't a bad lad. Spoilt rotten, and that wasn't his fault. Maria ruined him, and Peter would never stand up to her. It left Jerry with an unfortunate manner. Arrogant. He always managed to rub folk up the wrong way.'

'You came across him when he was working on the *Shetland Times*?'

'He turned up occasionally, sniffing out stories. Hoping for something from me when Andy Belshaw sent him away with a flea in his ear.' Joe paused. 'Andy was one of the people he managed to irritate.'

'Anything specific?'

Joe smiled sadly. 'There was a minor incident at the terminal. A bit of a spill. Not even big enough for us to put the boom across the voe. But Jerry turned it into a disaster and sold the story to one of the broadsheets in the south. That gave Andy a lot of hassle with his managers, who wanted to know why he'd let the thing blow out of proportion. Jerry was never his favourite person after that.'

'Yet Jerry was in the terminal the afternoon before he died. Andy met him and showed him round.' Perez wasn't sure how important this was, but wished he knew what Jerry had been doing at the terminal, wished there was a notebook, fragments of an article on a laptop, to point them in the right direction.

'Mr Markham was a hotshot reporter these days. Andy could hardly turn him away.'

'Did you know Jerry was back in Shetland?'

'No,' Joe said. 'I haven't been down at the Ravens-wick Hotel for months.' He gave a brief grin. 'I can't afford the prices in the bar these days.'

'John didn't mention him?' Perez finished his coffee, wondered if he needed more.

Joe shook his head. 'But then John wouldn't. He was the most private man I've ever met. If Markham was trying to get in touch, nobody else would know about it.'

'Markham didn't call in here the afternoon he died?'

'No,' Joe said. 'I was working that day and, like I said, I didn't even know he was back.' He paused and studied the photo of his family on his desk. 'Something odd did happen.'

'Yes?' Outside the office window, Perez saw that the weather was changing again. A front was coming in, bringing a westerly breeze and scraps of cloud.

'John was here in the office. He'd just come in from bringing in the *Lord Rannoch* and we were talking about the roster for the next couple of months. His mobile went. Usually he'd just ignore it, switch it off and say he'd deal with it later. But he apologized and went outside to take the call. Then he came back and asked if he could take an hour off.' Joe looked up from his desk. 'That was unprecedented. Even when his wife was ill, John organized things so that he never took time off work. So I said fine, of course.'

'Did you ask him what the call was about?'

'Not directly. I didn't want to pry. I probably said "Everything OK?" And he just nodded and went out.' Joe stood up and went to the window, looked at the sky with a sailor's eye. 'I thought it was something about the wedding. Evie panicking about details. You know women before the big day. And John was besotted with her. She was the only person he'd leave work for.'

'Did he go out in his car?' Perez was trying to eep his voice calm, but he thought this might be something new. If John Henderson had met Jerry Markham on the afternoon he died, they might be close to finding a motive for Henderson's death. If he'd seen or heard something, the killer might have been forced to stop him talking.

'I don't know. There was a thick fog. It came in very suddenly. It was quite clear when John came into the office for the meeting, but when he went I couldn't even see the tugs across the water. I don't think I heard his car, but then the fog muffles sound too. I assumed he'd driven away.'

'And he came back that afternoon?' Perez asked. He glanced across at Willow, who seemed sharper, more alert. She'd recognized the significance of this piece of news too.

'Yes, almost an hour after he'd left,' Sinclair said. 'He put his head round the door to let me know.'

'How did he seem?'

Sinclair gave a little laugh. 'How could I tell? John was never one for showing his emotions at the best of times. And I saw him for a second as he called in to let me know he was back.' He paused and became suddenly serious. 'But he didn't look like a man who'd just committed murder. Don't go down that route, Jimmy. John Henderson was a good man. I'll not have his memory sullied by rumours.'

They sat for a moment in silence. The wind blew

some scrap paper round the yard outside the office. Sinclair frowned at it as if it was an affront to his idea of order.

'John was working here after Jerry had died,' Perez said. 'Did he talk at all about what had happened?'

'Everyone was talking about it! Jerry Markham wasn't the most popular man in Shetland, as you'll have gathered. So it was almost as if folk were taking pleasure in the fact that he'd been killed. Enjoying the excitement anyway. The drama of the Fiscal finding him in the racing yoal.'

'And what was John's reaction?'

'He said it was wrong to treat another man's death as a subject of gossip. There was always something of the preacher in John, and sometimes the men didn't take to it. For example, he didn't like swearing. Get a bunch of seamen together and there's always going to be swearing. Usually he was mild enough and didn't make a fuss about it. Just a gentle comment that they should watch what they were saying. But the talk about Markham upset him. I thought he was going to lose his temper, but he walked away from them. Again I asked him if he was OK. He didn't really answer. That was the last time I talked to him.'

Andy Belshaw had said that Henderson had been excited about Markham's death and had wanted to talk about it. Was the discrepancy significant? Or was it the result of two witnesses with different perspectives? Perez wasn't sure.

'You worked with Evie on the tidal-power project?'

'Aye. And that was kind of a favour to John. She wanted some local folk to support her and reckoned

I'd know something about the tides. I asked John why he didn't do it himself, but he'd never been one for committees. The Fiscal was there too that morning.'

'And does she know about tides?'

Sinclair allowed himself a little smile. 'More than you'd think! She's a fine sailor. That Contessa of hers is a big yacht for one woman to manage, and she's a natural. She also has a sense of the next big thing politically. It's not the good of the planet that she has on her mind, but the good of Ms Rhona Laing.'

'How did they seem?' Willow asked. It appeared that she'd been following the conversation after all. 'The two women, I mean.'

Sinclair shrugged. 'They sniped at each other. Nothing rude. All very polite. But cats in a bag, you know. It was Evie's project, but the Fiscal's never been one to play a subordinate role. I let them get on with it.' He stood up. 'Look, I'm sorry – I've got to go. Yet another meeting. This one in Lerwick.' He walked with them from the office towards their car.

Willow suddenly asked, 'What do you make of her? Of the Fiscal?'

If the question surprised him, Sinclair didn't let it show. 'She's good at her job. A tad officious at times. Folk have taken a time to get used to her ways.'

'Has she ever visited you here?'

'No! What reason would she have to do that?'

The harbour master stood watching them get into the car. Driving away, Perez saw him stoop to pick up the piece of paper that had been flying around the yard and stuff it into a bin.

Chapter Thirty-Three

The Fiscal was back at work. She left her office, walked past the whitewashed police station and crossed the road to the Gothic town hall. Gusts of wind tugged at her skirt and made her eyes water. She hoped her mascara hadn't run, and in the lobby stopped for a moment to check her reflection in the glass door. She'd considered sending her apologies to this meeting, but had known all along that the only response to these murders was to behave as usual. That was the message she'd send to the forum. And pretending that she was perfectly in control was her way of holding things together personally too.

The Shetland Community Forum met once a month to consider matters of importance to the islands. It had been the brainwave of the police superintendent in Inverness as a response to increased drug abuse in the islands. Community engagement, he'd said, was the answer. Rhona Laing thought he must have recently attended a course on the subject. Something put together by sociologists. Naturally *he* never ventured north to attend these gatherings. A number of prominent Shetlanders, leaders of trusts and social organizations, councillors and politicians had been invited to join. Most months half a dozen people turned up, sat round a table and decided very little. Rhona was usually there, as a matter of principle: she'd agreed to join and so she should attend. After a particular long-winded meeting she'd agreed to act as chair. Today she expected a bigger turnout than usual and was regretting that decision. She wasn't sure she could go through with it, that she *could* hold herself together.

And at the top of the stairs she saw that there was a queue forming as people waited to filter into the meeting room. She saw Joe Sinclair waiting patiently in line and he gave her a little wave. Like her, he was a regular forum member. They served together on a number of island committees. She'd asked him once if he had ambitions to become a councillor – she couldn't imagine why else he might agree to all these time-consuming meetings – and he'd smiled knowingly. 'Not now,' he'd said. 'There's enough in my life at present. But I can't imagine retiring and having nothing to do.'

'You've got your boat,' she'd said. 'Your fishing.'

'Maybe, but I don't think that would be enough for me. I like to feel I have influence. So it's not bad practice turning out at this sort of event.'

It took longer than usual to provide everyone with tea and coffee. The urn ran out and a woman scurried away to boil a kettle. Outside it had started to rain steadily and water ran down the windowpane. Soon condensation made it impossible to see out. The main agenda item was the impact of the gas development at Sullom, but that was abandoned almost from the start. A tall, dark man stood up. He had an educated English accent.

'My name's Mark Walsh and I run a guest house in Hvidahus. I must say I'm surprised the police aren't present today to explain their lack of progress in the North Mainland killings. The murders have already had an effect on business. I had two cancellations yesterday.'

Without getting to his feet Joe Sinclair said, in an aside, but loud enough for the whole room to hear, 'I dare say the police have got better things to do with their time just now.'

The Fiscal was about to reply when the man continued. 'I hope these deaths will put an end to the proposed Power of Water scheme in our community. It seems rather more than a coincidence that Jerry Markham was killed on his way to attending a meeting objecting to the plans.'

There was a murmur of astonishment in the room. Rhona got to her feet. She saw Reg Gilbert, the editor of the *Shetland Times*, sitting in a corner at the back scribbling in a notebook. For a moment her mind went blank and she had a sudden and overwhelming impulse to run away. To walk out of the room, drive to Sumburgh and get on the first plane south. She imagined the sound of her heels clicking on the wooden floor and could picture her feet as she ran down the stone steps outside the building. After a couple of hours she would arrive in a city where nobody knew her. She would drink chilled white wine in a smart bar as the street lights were switched on, and the nightmare of the previous week would be over.

She became aware that they were staring at her. An awkward silence had fallen. She realized that of

course there could be no escape. Running away wasn't
an option.

'We all know your views on tidal energy, Mr Walsh,
and as far as I know, they have nothing to do with the
tragedy of two men losing their lives. Perhaps now we
can proceed to the items on the agenda.'

When the meeting finally ended it was still raining. Rhona looked at her watch and decided that there
was no point going back to the office. She'd already
handed over responsibility for the North Mainland
killings to her assistant and there was little else that
required her urgent attention. She waited until the
room was empty, gathering papers in an attempt to
look busy, before leaving, and was surprised to see
Joe Sinclair still in the corridor. Had he been waiting
for her? He fell into step beside her as they walked
down the stairs.

'I don't know about you,' he said, 'but I could really
use a drink after that. A few hours on the water is
what's really needed to clear my head, but a drink
would be the next best thing. What about you?' The
invitation surprised her, but she found herself agreeing to go along with him. Not because the idea of a
drink was so enticing, but because she couldn't face
returning immediately to an empty house, because
the evening stretched ahead of her. Because, left
alone, she would panic again and might even end up
crying.

He suggested the bar of the Mareel, the new arts
centre. She was surprised. She wouldn't have had him
down as a man who liked the theatre or art-house
cinema. Waiting at the table while he went to the bar,
she trawled her memory for what she knew of him.

He lived in Brae and was married, with two grown-up daughters. Happily married, she supposed. She'd never heard rumours to the contrary. The bar was empty. It was still early. Perhaps this was where he brought his other women, his secret lovers. The thought made her smile for the first time that day.

He returned with two glasses of red wine. 'I'd have got a bottle, but we're both driving.' So it was unlikely then that he was trying to proposition her. There was a small prick of disappointment. Had it come to this, that she couldn't even attract an overweight Shetlander in late middle age?

'What do you make of this place?' she asked. 'Will they make a go of it?' The arts centre had been controversial from its inception. Too expensive, some people had said. Too grandiose and flashy. Not needed in a place like Lerwick.

'I hope so.' He tasted the wine and seemed satisfied. 'It's here now. We need to support it.' He paused. 'The police were at my office this afternoon. Jimmy Perez and that woman.' And she thought that was why he'd brought her here. Not for sex or romance, but for information. Was he just an old gossip after all? Or was his motive more sinister?

'I suppose they were asking about John Henderson.' She kept her voice even. She couldn't let him know that she was as eager for information as he was. 'He worked for you, didn't he?'

Sinclair leaned forward across the table towards her. 'He was such a good man,' he said. 'I can't think why anyone would wish him harm.'

For a moment she thought she picked up a subtext to the words – another request for information? She shrugged her shoulders a little. 'You know I can't talk about the investigation. And, even if I wanted to, I know nothing about it. I'm too closely involved because I found Markham's body. I've handed the supervision over to somebody else.'

'That would be right,' he said. Outside, the light had almost gone. He looked up at her. 'What do you think Walsh is playing at?'

'That nonsense about Markham and the Power of Water? It's quite ridiculous to link the two.'

She'd expected him to agree with her immediately, but instead he came up with another question. 'When do you think it'll all be over? Did the police give you any idea at all?'

She shook her head. They talked about sailing until the wine was gone and then walked together out to their vehicles. He drove off very quickly and by the time Rhona reached the main road there was no sign of his car.

When Rhona arrived back in Aith it was completely dark. The council had put up a couple of street lights the year before and, while she'd complained at the time about light pollution, tonight she was glad of them as she parked her Volvo and opened her door. The rain had blown through and she paused for a moment, enjoying the smell of damp earth and salt from the voe. The drink with Joe Sinclair had lifted her spirits. Perhaps after all she would survive this. By the time the summer came, the drama would be finished and forgotten. She'd return to her old life of weekends on the water, trips south for shopping and civilization, rowing practice and regattas. Things would never be quite the same, but change was inevitable. A car, which had been parked further along the road, started its engine and drove away.

On the floor inside the house she found her mail. She carried it into the kitchen and set it on the table. Before checking it she opened a bottle of Rioja and poured herself a glass, then started wondering what she might eat for supper. The drink in the Mareel had given her a taste for strong, red wine and she realized she was hungry. It was a long time since she'd had a proper meal.

The letters were boring: bank statements, a renewal reminder for her house insurance. There was an invitation to speak at a conference in Copenhagen, which she set to one side. She'd check her diary later. Then, at the bottom of the pile, a postcard. A picture of three men playing fiddles. The back was blank. No writing and no stamp. She supposed it had been delivered by hand. Looking at the image again, she realized it was familiar. She'd seen it when Jerry Markham's body had been found. The first police officer to arrive at the marina had opened Markham's briefcase, looking for something to identify him. Glancing over his shoulder as he looked through the contents of the case, she'd seen an identical postcard.

She reached out for her wine and realized that her hand was shaking.

Chapter Thirty-Four

Waiting for Annabel Grey and her father at their hotel, Sandy Wilson felt jittery and nervous. Willow Reeves had given him a list of questions to ask the couple as they were driving south towards the airport. He was worried that he might forget something important. Or that he'd say something so stupid that the father and daughter would refuse to talk to him at all. And underlying the specific fears was a vague anxiety that he always experienced in the presence of people who were more confident and more educated than he was: a suspicion that he made a fool of himself every time he opened his mouth.

Annabel and Richard appeared in the lobby dead on time, the father carrying both the bags. Annabel looked as if she hadn't slept, and her face was gaunt and drawn. This morning she was wearing very skinny jeans, a long black top and the same grey jacket. But still she smiled at Sandy when she saw him, a smile that lit up her face and made his stomach flip. 'This is so kind,' she said. 'There was no need to give us a lift. We could have got a taxi, couldn't we, Dad?'

'Of course.' The man seemed rested, perfectly relaxed, his only concern being that for his daughter.

'There was no problem about you getting the time off work, Mr Grey, to come north at such short notice?' Sandy opened the boot and put the bags inside.

'I'm not needed in court today, and being a senior partner has certain benefits. Besides, Annabel will always come first for me. My colleagues all know that.' Grey climbed into the passenger seat. Sandy held open the back door for Annabel.

'There's been a change of plan,' she said. 'I hope it's not inconvenient, Sergeant. I spoke to Jerry's mother on the telephone last night and asked if we might meet. It seemed crazy to come all this way and not introduce myself to Peter and Maria. She invited us to call in to see them. I wasn't sure how long we'd be, so Dad phoned up to change our flights. That is all right? Of course we wouldn't expect you to wait for us. I'm sure one of them would give us a lift to the airport.'

Sandy remembered Jimmy Perez, the old Jimmy Perez, relaxed and patient, telling him that the most important skill a detective could possess was observation. Perez wouldn't drive away while that meeting was going on. 'No problem,' he said. 'The inspector told me to see you both safely onto the plane. I'm happy to wait until you're ready to go.'

It was mid-morning and the hotel was quiet. Business people were at work and the tourists were out enjoying the islands. A young woman, dusting the bannisters of the grand staircase, hummed a tune very quietly under her breath. Maria and Peter were in the lobby waiting, putting on a united front. Maria looked tense, like a cat when another animal has come into the house. Bristling – was that the word? Sandy stood back, pretending he wasn't even there, and let the four of them get on with it.

'Richard Grey.' The man stepped forward, his arm outstretched. 'Please accept our condolences. Such a terrible tragedy!'

Peter took his hand gratefully. He seemed pleased that Annabel's father was there.

'I've ordered coffee to be served in the library,' Maria said.

Sandy remembered the woman when he was a kid, at some of the wild Whalsay weddings. Laughing. Dancing like a demon with anyone who'd take her onto the floor. Drinking so much that she could hardly stand. And here she was behaving like the lady of the manor in some old English film. He supposed folk changed. Jimmy Perez had changed. And, if Annabel were to be believed, Jerry Markham had changed too.

The library was on the first floor, a long thin room with a window at the narrow end looking over the walled garden and then towards the water. Leather sofas and chairs. The walls lined with books that nobody ever read. In one corner a computer screen with free Wi-Fi so that guests could check their emails. There was a fire in the grate, which Sandy thought had been lit specially for the occasion, but still the room felt damp and unused. A woman brought in a tray with coffee pots, sugar and cream. A plate of home-made shortbread. Only four cups and saucers – they hadn't expected Sandy to be there. She wasn't a waitress, but was smartly dressed in a grey suit. One of the managers, Sandy thought. Wheeled in to impress.

'Thank you, Barbara. Could you bring another cup, please?' Maria again, imperious. Still Peter Markham hadn't spoken. But he couldn't take his eyes off Annabel Grey, Sandy saw that. What was it? Lust? Or was he envious? Of her youth and the life she still had ahead of her. Richard stood for a moment looking down at the water, before taking a seat in a big arm-chair. If he'd noticed Peter staring at his daughter he gave no indication.

They sat in silence until the fifth cup had been delivered. Maria poured coffee, handed round biscuits. They all waited for someone to speak. In the end Annabel Grey took the lead. That southern confidence, Sandy thought.

'Thank you for agreeing to see me. I know it must have been a shock. And coming on top of Jerry's death . . . '

'We knew nothing about you.' Maria setting down her marker. *I don't believe my boy loved you, lady.*

'He wanted to wait until he was ready to tell you. I think he planned to do it before he returned to London.'

'Jerry was here for a full day before he died! We had breakfast together the morning he arrived. We talked. Why wouldn't he say something? If your friendship was really as important as you make out.' Maria almost spat out the words towards the younger woman. Sandy expected Richard Grey to intervene, but he sat, watchful, his eyes moving between Maria and his daughter.

Annabel didn't react immediately and, when she

did speak, her voice was calm. 'It was more than friendship. We planned to marry.'

'He would have told us.' The words came out as a scream. Then: 'He would have told *me*. Why would he wait?'

'I think there were things he wanted to do first,' Annabel said. 'It's so sad that he never had the chance to tell you.'

At last Peter did speak. 'You must forgive my wife. She and Jerry were very close. She's upset.'

There was another silence.

'He was happy with me,' Annabel said. 'Peaceful. You should be pleased about that. I'm surprised you didn't recognize the change in him. You saw that, didn't you, Dad? You saw how Jerry was so much calmer when we were together.' She looked directly at Markham's parents, a challenge. 'Didn't he seem different when he arrived this time? Wasn't he more content?'

The couple looked at each other. Sandy couldn't tell what they made of that. Were they embarrassed because they hadn't noticed the transformation of their son?

'That was why he came home: to set things straight so that we could start a new life together. That was what he wanted. I think that's why he died.' Annabel looked directly at Sandy to check that he'd got the message.

'And what exactly do you think he wanted to set straight?' Peter Markham's voice was icily polite. Still he had Annabel fixed in his gaze.

'I don't know,' she said. 'I thought you might be able to tell us. Jerry said he had something to settle before he committed to me. He wouldn't tell me what it was and I didn't ask. Not my business, if he didn't want me to know. It was rooted in the past, I think. Something he felt guilty about.' Now she looked at both parents. 'You can't help me then? You don't know what killed the man I loved?'

Sandy watched Maria frown. He thought she might answer Annabel, make some suggestion, but Peter got in before his wife could speak. 'Really, I think you must have got hold of the wrong end of the stick, my dear. It's always tempting to look for explanations, don't you think, after a tragedy like this? Usually there are none. Nothing that makes sense, at least. Violence can be mindless and inexplicable. We all have to accept that.' He looked at Richard Grey, enlisting his support.

'Peter's right, sweetheart,' Grey said. 'Sometimes there's no explanation. Nothing that we can understand.'

Annabel looked at him. Perhaps she was disappointed that he'd agreed with Peter Markham, that he hadn't stood up for her. 'Could I spend a little time alone in the garden, Mr Markham? Jerry talked about it a lot when he described the hotel to me.'

'Of course.' Peter opened the door for her and seemed about to follow her out.

'I can find my own way,' she said.

'Shall I come with you?' Her father was already on his feet.

'No,' she said. 'Stay there.' It sounded like a command.

They watched her from the long window. She sat on a white wrought-iron bench by a small pond and seemed lost in contemplation, hardly moving at all.

'I don't believe her,' Maria said suddenly. 'She's not the type of girl Jerry would have gone for.' But Sandy thought that she was trying to persuade herself and not them. 'I'm sorry, Mr Grey, but she must have deluded herself that there was more to the relationship than there actually was.'

'My daughter's not deluded,' Grey said. 'And she doesn't lie. I saw the way your son looked at her. He adored her.'

The atmosphere in the room was so tense that Sandy felt like walking away. He would have preferred to wait for them in the car. But he stayed where he was.

In the garden Annabel stood up and shook out her hair. She didn't look up at the window, but she must have known that they'd be looking at her. Peter Markham watched her hungrily, but said nothing.

They arrived at the airport too early for their rescheduled flight. Sandy went in with them. He carried Annabel's bag again, sat the couple at a table and offered to buy them tea. He jotted down the names and contact details of the people in London who would have known Jerry – the vicar of the church where they'd met, other members of the congregation. The Greys seemed quite happy to pass on the information and didn't question why he needed to know.

'It must feel as if you had a wasted journey,' he said.

'Oh no, not at all.' Annabel looked straight at him. 'I expected Jerry's parents to find it hard to acknowledge me. This must be dreadful for them. He said they had no faith, no comfort in their lives.' She gave a little smile. 'Only alcohol, and the search for more money than they could ever need.'

'And I'm glad to be here to support my daughter during this terrible time.' Richard Grey smiled. His mobile phone was on the table beside him. The red light flashed to show that he had messages, but he made a point of ignoring it.

Sandy was thinking that alcohol and money would do well enough for him.

A group of men came in. Sandy recognized them as boys who worked for Shetland Catch, the fish factory. They piled up to the check-in desk, jostling and laughing, excited about a trip south. A stag do, by the look of it. Catching sight of the beautiful Annabel, there was more good-natured sniggering and pointing. They were behaving like six-year-olds. Sandy took no notice of them, but he felt himself flushing. He didn't want the Greys to think all Shetlanders were ignorant morons. Then the flight was announced and Sandy walked with them to security. He reached out his hand and Annabel took it into both of hers, held it for a moment.

'Thank you,' she said. 'For everything. We do appreciate it.'

She turned away, but Richard Grey paused for a moment before joining her.

'Tell me,' he said. 'Is Rhona Laing still the Fiscal here?'

'Aye.' Sandy tried not to look too surprised.

'Ah, a wonderful woman,' Grey said. 'She was a junior member of our chambers, you know, when she was younger. She didn't stay long. Too impatient and too ambitious. She soon moved on. Send her my best wishes, Sergeant. Tell her that Dickie Grey was asking after her.'

Then he too disappeared and Sandy was left with his mouth open, gawping like a fish on a hook.

Sandy arrived at the station before Willow and Perez got back from their trip north. He began phoning the contact details given to him by Annabel. His first call was to the vicar of the church that had hosted the advent course, the man who presumably had watched over Jerry Markham's spiritual journey. In the background Sandy could hear the sound of noisy children and occasionally the man seemed distracted by them. Once he shouted away from the phone in the middle of the conversation: 'Sal, will you tell the kids to shut up.' There was no anger in his voice, though. It was as if he thrived on the chaos of the family.

Sandy explained who he was and what he wanted.

'Ah, Jerry. A troubled man.'

'Was he?'

'He seemed that way to me.' A pause. 'He'd never been into a church in his adult life and I don't think he'd have ventured into one at all if he hadn't been at a low ebb.'

'Could you tell me about his relationship with Annabel Grey?'

'Annabel is a stalwart member of our church. Richard Grey doesn't attend himself, but he's been generous to us. He's a wealthy man. I suspect he'd inherited a private income. And of course he's had a successful career at the Bar. But those with money aren't always the most generous.'

Sandy wondered where this was leading.

The clergyman continued. 'Annabel took to Jerry immediately. There's something romantic perhaps about a dissolute man in need of rescue and reformation, and from the beginning Jerry was honest about his past failings.'

Another pause.

'And what did Annabel's father make of the . . .' Sandy struggled to find the right word '. . . attachment?' In his dealings with the Greys he hadn't been quite sure what Richard's opinion of Jerry had been.

'Ah . . .' The vicar hesitated once more. Sandy had the sense that he was choosing his words carefully. 'Richard was less impressed by Jerry's charms than Annabel was. I don't think he considered Jerry a suitable companion. You must understand, Sergeant, that father and daughter were very close. Annabel's mother left when she was very young, and she has no siblings.'

'Yet her father came with her to Shetland.'

On the other end of the line a door banged and the children's voices faded into the background. Sandy imagined that they'd been shooed into the garden so that their father might continue his conversation in peace. He pictured somewhere sunny and overgrown, with a swing hanging from a tree. 'Of course!' the vicar said at last. 'He'll do all that he can to help her come to terms with Jerry's death.' He paused. 'I'm not sure I should be telling you this, Sergeant. It's just my opinion, you understand. But I'm not sure that Richard trusted Jerry's reformation. His conversion. Richard asked me to persuade Annabel to take things more slowly and gave me the impression that he wasn't overjoyed at the prospect of the marriage. I said that Annabel was an intelligent young woman and that Richard should trust her judgement to do the right thing.'

'You thought it was a mistake then for Annabel to take up with Markham? You weren't convinced, either, that he was a changed man?'

This time the silence went on for so long that Sandy wondered if the line had been cut. Eventually the man answered, 'I don't know, Sergeant. Really, even now I'm not sure.'

Chapter Thirty-Five

Late afternoon and they were back in the briefing room in the police station. Outside the rain was coming down in sheets, bouncing from the pavements, spilling from the gutters. There was a meeting in the town hall and they watched people running up the steps, their hoods covering their faces. Willow, standing at the front of the room, seemed to Perez to have lost her confidence. She'd thought the murder of John Henderson, and then the arrival of Annabel Grey, would provide a breakthrough in the case and it hadn't. It only had left them with more questions.

'Sandy,' she said. Her voice was brittle with tiredness and a sort of desperation. Perez wanted suddenly to look after her, to give her small treats, in the way that he spoiled Cassie when she'd hurt herself or after she'd had a bad day at school. 'What have you got for me?'

Sandy had made notes in a book that looked like a school jotter. He stood up and read from them. Again Perez felt a rush of tenderness. Sandy tried so hard to get things right.

'Richard and Annabel Grey had arranged to meet the Markhams at Ravenswick on her way south to the airport,' he said. 'I went in with them and sat in on the meeting. I hope that was all right.' He looked up at his boss.

'Of course, Sandy. Good call.' Willow nodded at him and he seemed to relax. *Once he looked at me like that,* Perez thought. *Once he needed my approval.* 'How did it go?'

'Maria was a bit of a cow,' Sandy said. 'She didn't believe that there'd been any relationship between Jerry and Annabel. At least that was what she said.'

'And Peter?' Perez wasn't sure why, but he thought Peter's response to the Greys was even more important.

'He didn't say much at all.' Sandy frowned. 'He just stared at the lass.' He glanced down at his notes. 'Annabel went out into the garden. She said she wanted to be on her own to think about Jerry.' Another pause. 'I phoned the vicar of St Luke's, the church where the advent course was held, when I got back here. He was quite interesting on the relationship between Annabel and Jerry.'

'In what way?' Willow leaned forward.

'He wasn't convinced Jerry was genuine. The Christian thing. You know. He didn't *know* that Jerry was making the whole thing up, but he wasn't sure.' Sandy checked the notebook. Perez thought it had become a habit. Sandy knew quite well now what he wanted to say. 'And then there was Annabel's dad.' He paused for breath. And for effect.

'What about Richard Grey, Sandy?' Willow was sharp now.

'He didn't trust Jerry Markham, either. And Grey is wealthy. A private income, on top of what he makes as a barrister, according to the vicar.'

In his head Perez replayed one of the conversations he'd had with Maria Markham. Jerry had told his mother that he would never need to ask her for money again. Perhaps Markham had calculated that, if he married Annabel Grey, he'd be rich enough in his own right. Or at least in his wife's. Had he played the convert so that he could marry into a wealthy family? The idea seemed fanciful, but perhaps Jerry was desperate. He was a journalist and he understood about research. Had he turned up at the church that day because he knew Annabel would be there? Could anyone be that calculating?

'What do you make of all this, Jimmy?' Willow sounded suddenly cheerful.

'I think that if Jerry expected to marry into serious money, we have to reconsider his motivation in coming to Shetland.' Outside, the rain continued to batter on the windowpane and on the grey pavement. Perez imagined Cassie inside his neighbour's kitchen, sitting at the table with her best friend. Cosy. Safe. 'I mean he was hardly likely to risk blackmail if he was going to be rich soon anyway.'

'Would he have been rich, though? If Richard didn't like Jerry, and *he* was the one with the money.' Willow's thoughts were fizzing again. 'Richard seemed reasonable enough while he was here, but he's got his way now, hasn't he? There's no chance that Annabel will marry Jerry Markham. I don't know how these things work, but perhaps he threatened to disinherit Annabel if she went ahead with the marriage.'

Perez thought that sounded like something from the Jane Austen novels Fran had enjoyed so much. He'd tried to read them to please her, but they'd always sent him to sleep, so he'd never found out how they ended.

'Annabel's an idealist,' Willow went on. 'A romantic. She might have been happy to go ahead with the marriage anyway. Poverty might seem quite attractive to someone who's never had to live with it. But all we know about Jerry would suggest that he'd be quite keen on the money too.'

'Perhaps Jerry *had* changed.' Perez saw that there was a small river running down the street outside. 'Perhaps his trip north was his way of proving it. Some sort of test. Or quest.'

But even as he'd spoken the words he thought how ridiculous all this sounded. Like a legend, a story of gallant knights and fair ladies. Annabel had even taken herself off to a nunnery, for goodness' sake! And Jerry Markham had charged north. Not on a white stallion, but in a red racing car. Perez thought the solution to this investigation would turn out to be more squalid and prosaic than that.

'You think Richard Grey sent him back to Shetland to prove himself?' Now Willow sounded sceptical too.

'I don't know.' Perez thought the character of Jerry Markham was slipping away from him, growing vague and blurred. 'Really I don't know what to think any more about any of them.'

They sat for a moment looking at each other, the burst of excitement over, disheartened again.

'We could always ask the Fiscal about Richard Grey,' Sandy said.

'What would the Fiscal know about him?' Willow looked up sharply.

'According to Grey, they worked together in

London, when she was young. A junior member of chambers. Then she got ambitious and moved on.'

The room fell silent as they considered this information. Willow spoke first. 'That woman was born ambitious.' She looked at them. 'Is this significant? Another coincidence?'

'It's odd that Grey didn't try to make contact with Rhona Laing when he was here. If they were such old pals. If he wanted more information on the background to the killings, the Fiscal would be the person to help him.' Perez tried to tease out the strands of his thoughts, but reached no conclusion. As Willow had said, there were too many connections.

'I have remembered one thing.' It was Sandy – tentative, still eager to please. There was a silence while he gathered his thoughts. 'It's probably not important. The night Rhona Laing found Jerry's body in the yoal, the night we assume his car was taken to the car park in Vatnagarth.' He paused to catch his breath. 'Well, that was when Evie Watt had her hennie do. Her women friends in a minibus, all out on the lash. A three-legged pub-crawl raising money for charity. I saw them on the road to Voe. Maybe some of them saw something? The car?' When there was no response he added, 'I know it's a long shot.'

'It's hard to imagine Evie Watt getting bladdered,' Willow said.

'She was throwing up by the side of the road when I saw her.' Sandy frowned. 'I didn't recognize her at the time, but it came to me later that I knew her.' A pause. 'Maybe she wasn't used to it.'

'Or someone spiked her drink.' Perez remembered the photo of Evie in the animal suit in her house. She'd been pulling faces, looking rather odd.

'How would we get a list of the women on the bus?' Willow asked. 'I wouldn't want to trouble Evie or her family again.'

Perez thought she couldn't face the Watts again so soon. It was more about that than sparing their feelings.

'We could ask Jen Belshaw,' Sandy said. 'She was on the bus.' He turned to Willow. 'They were talking about her in the bar in Voe when we stopped there for lunch on Saturday. Don't you remember?'

She shook her head.

'Jen Belshaw,' Perez said. 'Married to Andy Belshaw, the press officer at Sullom Voe. Works as school cook at Aith, where the first body was found. Volunteers in Vatnagarth, where Markham's car was found. Rows in the same team as the Fiscal at the regattas. You didn't think to mention before that she was with Evie Watt on Friday night? Providing her maybe with an alibi for Markham's murder?' He'd raised his voice, but really he was angrier with himself than with Sandy. He'd intended to interview Jen, but then Annabel Grey had turned up and he'd forgotten to follow that thread of the inquiry.

'It's not just Jen Belshaw that's providing the alibi.' Sandy was fighting back. 'It's a minibus full of pissed women, in fancy dress and all tied to each other. Honestly, I don't see how Evie Watt could have moved that car on Friday night, even if she was sober.'

He sounded so self-righteous, and the picture he painted was so silly, that the mood in the room lightened again and Willow started to giggle.

'Jimmy, will you go and see Jen Belshaw first thing?' she said. 'She looked up at them. 'Let's call it a day now, shall we? Have an early night.'

They left the building together. The rain had stopped and the sky was lighter.

When Perez called into his neighbour's house to collect Cassie, the table was laid for supper and he was expected to stay for a meal.

'Really,' he said. 'There's no need. I have food in the house.'

But Cassie had helped to prepare the pudding and he could tell that she would be disappointed if they left immediately. And the casserole smelled very good, and Maggie and David were good company. They were careful not to talk about the case while the children were in the room, but later, when the girls were watching television and the adults were drinking coffee, Maggie mentioned it.

'It must be hard, Jimmy. Another murder investigation. So soon.'

He didn't answer directly. 'Did you know Jerry Markham when he was a boy?' he asked. 'You'd have been almost neighbours.' Maggie had grown up in Ravenswick. She'd have been older than Jerry, but not by so much.

'He was a classic only child,' Maggie said. 'Spoilt rotten. By his mother at least.' Then: 'Oh, I'm sorry Jimmy, I didn't mean that Cassie's spoilt because she's on her own. She's a lovely girl.'

He waved his hand to show that no offence had been taken. He wished folk would be less sensitive around him.

'Was he malicious, do you think?'

'No, just thoughtless. One of those kids who love

being the centre of attention, who try just a little bit too hard. I always thought that he was very young for his age. Maria had never really let him grow up. Even when he was in his twenties, he seemed to me like a little boy pretending to be an adult.'

Perez thought that helped him to bring Jerry Markham back into focus and to understand him better again.

By the time he had Cassie in bed, and her school clothes in the washing machine and her gym bag prepared for the next day, it was already late. Perez sat and watched the news on the television. Other tragedies. It was only when he was ready for bed himself that he checked his answer machine. One message. It was a surprise to hear the Fiscal's voice. She sounded calm. Calmer certainly than when he'd called to tell her that there'd been another murder. 'Something rather odd has happened, Jimmy, and I'd like to discuss it with you. I wonder if you'd give me a ring. When it's convenient. It's not urgent.'

He looked at his watch. It was too late to phone her tonight. He'd try her in the morning.

Chapter Thirty-Six

Sandy thought it was like old times, he and Jimmy Perez out on the island together heading up to Aith, and Jimmy almost back to his old self. Perez didn't say much in the car on the way north, but then he'd never been exactly chatty. And at least he didn't sit in the passenger seat, crouched and brooding, looking as if he might hit you every time you asked him a question. It had been a bit like that until recently.

When they got to the Fiscal's house, Perez told him to slow down.

But when Sandy asked if he should stop, Perez said to carry on. 'There's no sign of her,' he said. 'Her car's not there. She left a message on my answer phone at home last night. I tried to call her this morning, but there was no reply. She must have been on her way to work.'

Sandy couldn't see that it would be important. 'She has your work mobile number. She would contact you on that if it was urgent.'

'Aye, maybe.' Perez seemed about to say something else, but no words came out. Sandy thought Willow would want to talk to Rhona Laing about the Fiscal's connection to Richard Grey and she wouldn't be best pleased if Perez interfered.

When they got to the school the children were in assembly, singing a hymn that Sandy remembered from when he was a boy. It took him straight back to the school in Whalsay, he and his cousin Ronnie sitting at the back of the hall causing mischief. In the Aith kitchen two women, dressed in white overalls and white caps, were preparing lunch. One was peeling carrots by the sink and the other was rolling out pastry on a workbench. This was Jen Belshaw. She looked very different from when he'd interviewed her in Vatnagarth and she'd been dressed in old-fashioned clothes.

'You can't come in here,' she said. 'Health and safety.' She was a big woman, not fat, but soft and round. 'We don't know what germs you might be carrying.' Though she was telling them off, it sounded as if she was laughing at the notion too.

'Any chance we could have a few words?' Perez stood in the doorway to talk to her and Sandy couldn't really see past. 'It's about the murders.'

Jen Belshaw said something to her colleague and washed her hands in a little basin in the corner. 'We'll go through to the staffroom,' she said. 'There'll be nobody in there at the minute. I might even make you a coffee.' She led them into a pleasant room, easy chairs around the wall, a coffee table in the centre, and switched on a filter machine. 'So how can I help? Andy said you were round at the house asking about John.'

'Who was looking after your kids on Friday night?' Perez asked. Sandy thought that was a strange place to start.

'They stayed at my mother's. Except Neil, who was

playing football in Brae with Andy. Why?' She wasn't hostile, but she looked at Perez as if he were a bit mad.

'And you were out with Evie?'

'Aye, the hen party. A charity pub-crawl. Typical Evie. She couldn't just get pissed and make a fool of herself, like everyone else. She had to save the world at the same time.'

'Could you talk me through the evening?' Perez said. 'It's not that I'm accusing anyone, but you might have been witnesses.'

Jen poured coffee. She seemed in no rush to get back to the kitchen. Sandy thought she was one of those competent women who could knock up a good meal in about ten minutes, and who was never flustered.

'The bus picked us all up in our homes,' she said. 'Evie first, and then the rest of us. We started drinking in the Busta House hotel in Brae. We thought we'd better start there because it's kind of grand and, though Veronica had said it was OK, we didn't want to seem rowdy in front of their guests. So we just had the one drink, rattling the collecting bucket round the bar, and most of us were still quite sober.'

Perez nodded. 'And you were all dressed up in pairs?'

'Aye! Crazy!'

'How was Evie?'

And it seemed to Sandy that this was the important question and that the others had been to get Jen relaxed and ready to answer.

There was a pause.

'Was Evie quite herself?' Perez persisted. 'Only I

heard that she got very drunk, and I wouldn't have thought that was in character.'

'It was a pub-crawl,' the woman said. 'Of course she got drunk!'

'But she organized it.' Perez's voice was reasonable. 'I'd have thought she'd have paced it so that she didn't overdo things. Or had someone thought it would be funny to spike her drinks?'

And that was when Jen started talking, the words spilling out despite herself, as if they'd been building up for days and now some kind of dam had burst. A mixture of relief to be sharing the worry, and guilt that she was betraying her friend. 'I don't know what came over her. I think she'd been drinking in the afternoon. I asked if she'd been out with her mates at the office, but she said not. She was wild. I'd never seen her like that before, and I've known her for years. She was drinking vodka and she never usually touches spirits. The others thought it was funny. Evie's usually the one telling us to slow down. But I didn't like it. I stopped drinking after a bit, so that I could look after her.'

'Why do you think she was behaving so unusually?' Perez gave an encouraging smile. 'Last-minute nerves, do you think, before the wedding?'

Jen shook her head. 'She'd been besotted with that man from the first date. She's always wanted to marry him. No second thoughts there. And who could blame her? He was a lovely man.'

'Any idea then? You must have asked her.'

'Well, it wasn't exactly an ideal situation for a heart-to-heart. A bunch of lasses singing filthy songs in the back of the bus, and Evie threatening to throw up every five minutes.'

'But maybe you had some idea?'

'Jerry Markham was back,' Jen said. 'That was what had really freaked her out.' She looked at them. 'You know he got her pregnant when she was a kid?'

'Had she met him?' Perez asked. 'Is that why she was so upset? Had he tracked her down at work? Bumped into her by chance?'

The woman shook her head. 'I have no idea! By the time I'd got that much out of her she was so drunk that she was making no sense at all. I mean, slurring her words and hardly able to stand. You asked if anyone was spiking her drinks. It was the other way round. I was buying her tonic water and telling her there was vodka in it.'

'So what exactly did Evie say about Jerry,' Perez asked. 'If you could remember word-for-word, Mrs Belshaw, it would be brilliant.' That smile again, which made the recipient feel as if they were the most important person in the world.

'Oh, I can remember word-for-word.' Jen gave an embarrassed, little laugh. '"Fucking Jerry Markham!" That's what she said – over and over again. I'd never heard her swear before. It was shocking. Like hearing your grandma cursing. Or the minister.'

'But no more detail?' Perez said. 'Nothing more than that?'

Jen shook her head.

'Can I take you back to the events of that evening then,' he said, as if Evie's state of mind was of minor importance and he wanted to return to the main reason for their being there. 'Where did you head for after the Busta House? And it would be very helpful, please, if you could give us the timings for that.' Sandy thought he sounded like the person at headquarters who checked their expense sheets, a very boring little man called Eric, who only cared about the detail. Perez made Sandy write everything down and then read it back to Jen. He asked more than once about the red Alfa Romeo.

'I've already told you that I didn't see it,' she said. 'I know it ended up in the car park at Vatnagarth, but beyond that, I know nothing about it. We were in the bars for a lot of the time. It could have driven down the road while we were inside and we would never have noticed.'

An electronic bell rang then, and it was so loud that it made Sandy jump in his seat. They heard the children running out into the playground for their break.

'My God, is that the time?' Jen got to her feet. Sandy thought she was glad of an excuse to get away from them, and he couldn't blame her. 'I'll never get that pie cooked by dinnertime if I don't go now.' And she ran out of the room, leaving them to find their own way to the car park.

They sat in the car outside the school for what seemed like an age – Jimmy Perez staring ahead, although there was nothing to see except a brick wall. Sandy shuffled in his seat. Maybe he should just drive off back to Lerwick. He didn't like to disturb Perez when he was lost in thought. At last he couldn't bear the silence any longer and was forced to speak.

'Which way then, boss?'

And Perez turned slowly to look at him, kind of

surprised, like some sort of animal waking up after hibernation. A bear, Sandy thought. With all that shaggy black hair, he could be a bear.

'Let's head up towards Sullom Voe,' Perez said. 'I've had a bit of an idea and I want to get a feel for the lie of the land again. But we'll stop at the Old School-house on the way through, just in case the Fiscal's at home.'

Rhona Laing's car was still not parked outside her house, but Perez asked Sandy to pull in anyway. Sandy waited in the vehicle while Perez went up to the front door. He banged hard, but there was obviously no reply. Perez walked round the garden, looking through all the downstairs windows, and at last emerged from the other side of the house and came back to the car. 'It all looks tidy enough,' he said. 'I'll give her a ring at work when we get back to the station.'

Just as he was about to drive off Sandy looked back towards the house. For a moment he thought he saw a shadow at an upstairs window, a curtain moving. But the window was open, and it must have been the breeze blowing the fine cloth. He was imagining things. He didn't say anything. The inspector thought he was stupid enough as it was.

They drove through Brae and took the road that ran along the side of Sullom Voe and would eventually end up at Toft and the North Isles ferry. Before they reached the terminal Perez asked him to turn off towards Scatsta Airport. Sandy had never driven down here before; all the traffic at Scatsta was oil-related, so there was no reason to. A helicopter took off and hovered for a moment before heading out towards the

North Sea and the rigs. They seemed very close to the aircraft and surrounded by the noise. Sandy thought he could feel the power of the rotor blades rocking the car.

'Down there.'

It was a track and beside it an old sign, reading 'Authorized vehicles only'. There was no gate blocking the way, though, and it led to the end of a low headland that jutted out into the water. The area was covered with flat sheets of concrete, so it looked as if buildings had once been there and only the floors were left. Now the concrete was cracked, and weeds and even little bushes had pushed their way through. Sandy parked so that they were facing north.

'I think this was a military station during the war. Air-force, I suppose.' Still Perez sat, looking across the water to the oil terminal, the tanks and the flare, and to the lorries that carried rock over the newly constructed road to the gas plant. 'I suppose they flattened it when there was no further use for it.'

'Weren't they going to develop it as a business park at one time?' Sandy thought he had heard that or read it in the *Shetland Times*.

Perez didn't answer. He climbed out of the car and Sandy joined him. 'Imagine that you're Jerry Markham,' Perez said. 'You've just visited the oil terminal and had a meeting with Andy Belshaw. Routine stuff, if Andy is telling it how it was. Maybe the meeting was just to provide an excuse for Jerry to be at this end of the island. You decide that you want to meet John Henderson. We don't know why at this point. To apologize for the way you treated Evie? To wish him luck for his marriage? Or to warn him off, because you've decided that after all you want Evie for yourself? And all your life, you've had exactly what you wanted. Whatever the reason, you phone him while he's at work. We know from Sinclair that Henderson took a call. Where would you arrange to meet?'

'Here?' It seemed to Sandy that this was the answer that was expected. He thought with satisfaction that Perez was back to his old form, focused and sharp.

'That makes sense, doesn't it?' Perez stared out to sea, but continued talking. 'It's not overlooked. There are cars here occasionally – it's a place where kids come to practise driving before their parents let them out onto the roads. So a couple of vehicles wouldn't particularly attract notice.'

'*My* car might,' Sandy said. 'I mean, if I'm still pretending to be Jerry Markham.'

'The red Alfa Romeo. So it would.' And Perez smiled, so Sandy felt as if he'd passed some sort of test.

Perez strolled down the track towards the runway and the airport buildings. There was a new air-traffic control tower that looked like something from a science-fiction film. Long steel spider's legs and a glass body. In the lounge a group of men were drinking coffee in polystyrene beakers. They all looked rough, as if they'd been out drinking the night before, celebrating a last night of freedom before a new shift on the rigs. A dark man in uniform stood behind the check-in. The track from the main road was visible through plate-glass windows.

Perez introduced himself. The oil workers, all half-asleep, slumped over the chairs, took no notice.

'Last Friday,' Perez said. 'The day the body was found in Aith. Were you on duty?'

'It was a nightmare,' the man said. 'The fog came down late afternoon and there was no movement for hours.'

'Just before the fog,' Perez said. 'Did you notice any cars up at the old military site?'

'You mean the red Alfa, the one that was in the news?' The man looked up from his computer screen. 'I was talking about that to the wife, wondering if I should mention it to you. Then she said they'd found it in the crofting museum, so there didn't seem much point.'

Perez turned to Sandy and rolled his eyes in disbelief, and again Sandy thought this was just like old times.

'Was that the only car up there?'

'No.' The man was still preoccupied and fiddled about on his keyboard. 'John Henderson was up there too. You know him? The pilot? I waved at him as he drove past, but he didn't seem to notice.' He put his hands on the desk and looked up at Sandy and Perez, his face grey with shock, realizing for the first time the implication of his words. 'And now both men are dead!' A pause. 'Seems a weird coincidence, huh?'

Chapter Thirty-Seven

Willow found Rhona in her office. It didn't take her long to get there: the court and the police station were in the same building, though the Fiscal's office was grander than any of the rooms used by the police. Rhona Laing was sitting behind a large desk, reading a pile of papers. The room was brown. Brown wood, brown carpet and a brown leather armchair in one corner. On the wall a large painting of the sea in moonlight, an oil.

'Inspector. What are you doing here?' Laing sounded surprised to see Willow, although her receptionist must have warned her that the detective was on her way.

'I was wondering if you might help me.'

'Of course, if I can.' She took off her expensive designer spectacles and Willow thought how tired and strained she looked. The woman was controlling herself, but with such an effort that it was impossible for her to relax for a moment. Again Willow thought that Rhona must be involved in this case. She was too tense to be just a witness who had strayed upon a body by coincidence. Perez and Sandy had described the Fiscal as an honest and honourable woman, but Willow could sense her fear and her desperation, like a smell. She thought it wasn't time yet to put Rhona under too much pressure. The woman still had fight in her and Willow was worried that she might run away. She had money and it would be easy enough for her to hop on a plane and fly south. She'd have friends in high places to protect her, once she was away from the islands.

'I'd like to update you on the investigation, of course.' Willow made her voice polite, but not grovelling. That would only make Rhona suspicious.

'No need for that, Inspector. I have no official status in the case.'

Willow continued as if the Fiscal hadn't spoken. 'And it seems that someone you know has a peripheral link to the inquiry. I'd value your opinion.'

'Oh?' Rhona Laing was hooked now. She looked up from the papers and seemed to give Willow her full attention for the first time.

Willow smiled and looked around the room, making a pantomime of taking in its grandeur, the wood panelling, the heavy door. 'I wonder if I could buy you coffee? I'm not used to sitting at a desk for a whole day, and I imagine you find it tricky too. Everyone tells me what a great sailor you are.' She paused for a beat and glanced at the painting. 'This must seem like a prison.'

'Coffee? Why not?' Rhona making it clear that she wouldn't be so easily intimidated. She stood up, took a coat from the stand in the corner and followed Willow out of the building.

Willow had chosen her destination carefully. The Islesburgh Community Centre was in a building a short walk from the Fiscal's office. All these streets, named after Norwegian kings and princes, were rather grand. Grey, granite houses that wouldn't have looked out of place in a prosperous Aberdeen suburb, looking out over a well-tended park. But the Islesburgh was more democratic. It housed youth and community groups, meetings for young mothers, teenagers playing pool. Sandy had brought her here for lunch one day. 'It's fine,' he'd said, 'if you don't mind something cheap and cheerful.'

The cafe was self-service, there was a smell of chips, and toddlers were playing noisily in the small area reserved for them. Willow thought that here Rhona would be well outside her comfort zone. But it was anonymous too. Surrounded by steam from the coffee machine and with a background of chat, nobody would take any notice of two women sitting in a corner, away from everyone else. The other customers might have them down as social workers needing some privacy to discuss their clients.

Willow settled Rhona at a table and queued at the counter. She returned with coffee, to find the Fiscal clearing crumbs from the table with a paper napkin. Grinned to herself, but said nothing.

'So what is this about, Inspector?' Rhona's voice was shrill. 'I do have to work.'

'Two days ago we had an interesting phone call. From a young woman. A student at Oxford. She claimed to have been Jerry Markham's girlfriend. In fact, his fiancée.'

'Oh?' The Fiscal sipped her black coffee and pretended not to be interested. But Willow thought she would want to hear the rest of it. Everyone was taken in by a love story. If that's what this was.

'The girl's name was Annabel Grey.'

'Oh?' As if that was the only response she could give. As if anything else would have taken too much effort. Then Rhona frowned as if the name was familiar, but she couldn't quite place it.

'I think you know Annabel's father, Richard.'

A flash of surprise. Genuine? Willow thought so, but she wouldn't have sworn to it. It wouldn't do to underestimate Rhona Laing.

'Ah, Richard Grey. I haven't heard from him in years.' She pushed away the coffee mug, still half-full. A gesture of dismissal, Willow thought. And to show that this place wasn't good enough for her, though Willow had already decided there was nothing wrong with the coffee.

'He'd obviously been following your career,' she said. 'He knew you were working here and asked us to pass on his good wishes.'

Rhona sat in silence. Willow thought this last scrap of information had pleased her. She was glad to have been remembered. At the other side of the room a mother shouted at a child to give back another girl's toy.

'It would help us if you could fill in some of the background to Richard Grey,' Willow said at last.

'You can't think Dickie's a suspect.' Rhona Laing laughed. 'He's always managed to get exactly what he wants, without resorting to murder.'

'Just background,' Willow said. 'You know how important that can be.'

'Very well then, Inspector. The background to the Grey family.' And it seemed that this was a story the Fiscal would enjoy telling, that the memories were pleasant. That she was happy to revisit them. Perhaps, the inspector thought, they distracted her from other anxieties.

Willow nodded and waited.

'Richard Grey was very much a golden boy of his generation,' Rhona said. 'His family was reasonably well off. Not flash, you understand. Not *new* money. No horrible city traders or developers of green-field sites. But well connected. A family of writers and academics, liberal and interesting. Richard was bright. And charming. He had more charm than any man had a right to. It gave the impression that he was superficial, but that was a false impression, I think.'

Willow wasn't sure what she made of this, but she said nothing. It was better to let the woman talk. She was more likely to give away an important detail if she was allowed to ramble.

Rhona pulled back the coffee mug and drank from it. 'Then he married Jane. She was wild and beautiful, with an appetite for drugs and booze. The first woman to stand up to him. She refused to be taken in by his charm or his money. I genuinely think he adored her, worshipped the ground she walked on, but that didn't prevent him from treating her badly.'

'It sounds as if you knew him quite well,' Willow said.

'I worked with him. Or I suppose *for* him. My first real job as a barrister. And I fell for him. I was one of his serial affairs.' The woman looked bleakly across the table. 'I should have realized that nothing would come of it. There were so many stories of his adultery. But we all think that we're different, don't we? We all think we can change the man we love.'

Like Annabel, Willow thought. *She believed she could change Jerry Markham.*

It was almost as if Rhona were reading her thoughts, because she continued, 'Annabel was very young then. Five? Just starting school, I think. I remember Dickie showing me a photo of her looking very cute in her uniform. A blazer and a hat. I should have been conscious-stricken. How could I risk breaking up his family? But of course I wasn't. You're so selfish when you're in love. Entirely self-absorbed. And really there was no risk. Dickie was never going to leave Jane. The more badly she behaved, the more infatuated he became.'

Willow wished she'd recorded this conversation. Sandy and Perez would never believe the Fiscal could talk like this.

'I came to my senses eventually.' Rhona gave a sad little smile. 'Resigned myself that I wasn't a woman to play Happy Families anyway. So I moved back to Edinburgh. Retrained for the Bar in Scotland.'

'Were the Greys regular church-goers then?' Willow found it hard to reconcile Richard Grey's image of himself as a respectable family man with Rhona's story.

'I think Jane went to church.' The woman gave a tight little smile. 'Maybe she saw it as a sort of insurance policy? To compensate for the parties and the exhibitionism. *If I go to church, I'll be redeemed anyway.* Or perhaps she saw it as a kind of safety net.' Her voice was dismissive, implying that she didn't need such a crutch.

'Then she ran away.' Willow watched the Fiscal, wondering what her reaction would be.

'Yes,' Rhona said. 'It was the last thing anyone expected. Death by overdose we might have understood, but not that she would suddenly disappear. We thought she liked the lifestyle that Dickie had provided, and he'd never tried to restrict her. And by all accounts Dickie became a changed man when Jane ran off. He devoted himself to his daughter. No more one-night stands or flings with young and beautiful lawyers. So my London friends tell me. I'm not convinced. Perhaps he just became better at keeping secrets.'

'He didn't get in touch with you while he was here?' Willow wasn't sure this was getting her anywhere. She was gaining a fascinating glimpse into the Fiscal's past, but nothing relevant to the present investigation. Except, perhaps, the knowledge that Richard Grey wasn't to be trusted, and she'd already worked that out for herself.

'No.' But for the first time Rhona seemed less certain.

'Are you sure?' The Greys had had an evening to themselves. There had been nothing to prevent Richard hiring a taxi to Aith, turning up on the Fiscal's doorstep, looking for comfort or a rekindling of youthful excitement.

'We didn't meet, Inspector.' The Fiscal smiled sadly. 'I rather wish that we had.'

Chapter Thirty-Eight

Perez arranged to meet Willow for lunch. He wanted to tell her what they'd learned from Jen Belshaw and from the check-in guy at Scatsta, but not as a formal presentation with all the team listening in. He was feeling his way through this investigation and scraps of theory were blowing around his brain. Motes of dust in a sunbeam. He thought they'd disappear if he put them into words, but a gentle discussion might help him to organize his ideas.

They met at the Bonhoga and took a table in the conservatory, looking out over the burn. It was late, so the place was quiet.

'So, Jimmy,' she said. 'What do you have to tell me?' Willow was smiling and girlish and he thought she must have information for *him* too, but wanted to hang on to it for a while, to hug it to herself.

He was eating a bannock with smoked salmon and watercress and it was so good that he had to give it his full attention for a moment. Willow had her back to the light, so the wild hair looked almost red. She was completely absorbed in the task of drinking soup. Smelling it. Tasting it. Then she smiled again.

'Wow! This is something else. He's a brilliant cook.'

He loved the fact that something as simple as good

lentil soup could make her happy. Her arm was on the table, her sleeve rolled up a little, so that he could see fine hairs on her arm. In this light they looked red too. Today she was in a baggy sweatshirt and he caught himself wondering what shape she was underneath it, and then imagining her completely naked. Small breasts. Flat stomach. Larger hips, slightly out of proportion. The picture appeared from nowhere and shocked him, but gave him a thrill of excitement too. What would it feel like to run his hand over the body? Horrified, he banished the image from his mind. The power of the picture he'd conjured frightened him. This wasn't art – a nude that Fran might have created with a few charcoal sketches – but real flesh, muscle, hair. He felt that his imagination and his body were out of control.

She looked up at him, completely unaware that he was disturbed, and repeated her question.

'Well? What do you have to tell me?'

'Evie seems to have been disturbed on Friday night,' he said. 'I mean really disturbed. Jen Belshaw was her friend and said she'd never known her like it. Evie was drinking very heavily. It was her hen party, but nobody expected her to get drunk like that. She's not the kind.'

'I'm sorry, Jimmy.' Willow leaned across the table towards him. 'I just don't see Evie Watt as our killer. And even if I could be persuaded that she'd killed Jerry in some flash of temper, there's no way she'd have gone on to murder John Henderson. It's not possible. You saw what she was like when we visited her on Fetlar. Her world had fallen apart.'

Perez looked at Willow, allowing no thoughts but

those relating to the investigation. 'I'm not suggesting that Evie is a killer. Though I don't think we should rule out that possibility.' He was still convinced this was a domestic murder, despite the melodrama. 'I'm saying that she had contact with Jerry Markham. More contact than some unanswered phone messages.'

'I'm not sure. I think she would have told me if that was the case. We got on fine. Why wouldn't she?'

The question hung between them. Perez returned to his food without answering. He wondered if Willow's judgement was compromised.

'Evie Watt is not a liar.' Willow couldn't let it go. 'I just can't accept it. She's a decent woman who got pissed on her hen night. There's no more to it than that.'

'Maybe you're right.' Perez shrugged. 'But we should keep an open mind.'

'Anything else?' Willow was eyeing up the cakes through the open door. Making it clear that she didn't need telling how to do her job.

'I have definite evidence that Jerry Markham and John Henderson met on that Friday afternoon.'

'What sort of evidence?' He had her full attention now.

Perez described his meeting with the Scatsta employee.

'What time was that?'

'Around two-thirty. Just before the fog came down and stopped all the flights.'

'Might that explain why Evie was behaving so weirdly on Friday evening?' Willow asked. She wiped a piece of bread around her soup bowl, then ate it.

'If Henderson had told her he'd met Markham. She'd be angry, wouldn't she, that Markham was back, meddling with her life. Angry with both of them for getting together behind her back. It would seem almost as if they were ganging up on her. Or making decisions about her future without consulting her. As if she was a little girl.'

Perez thought about this.

'What decision could there be to make?' he said. 'John and Evie were going to be married. No question. Markham hadn't seen her for years. What could he want to tell Henderson? Something that might persuade him to break off the engagement at the last minute? Is that what you're suggesting? It would certainly explain Evie's weird behaviour at the hen do, if that was the case.'

'I don't know!' Willow put her head in her hands, a dramatic gesture. She had to push her hair away from her face. 'It's so frustrating. We're getting glimpses of a picture, but just not seeing enough to tell what really happened.' She paused, struggling to explain. 'Like a reflection in a broken mirror.'

'Phone records might help,' Perez said. 'It would be useful to know if Henderson spoke to Evie after he saw Markham, and before she went out for the hen night.'

'Of course they would! I'm still waiting for them, though. Some computer meltdown with the provider. I meant to chase them up again this morning.' She looked up at him. 'Do you think the meeting at Scatsta had a more obvious outcome? Did John Henderson kill Markham?'

Perez had been thinking about that. 'I can't see

how it might have happened. If we'd found the body out there, on the old RAF site, then I'd accept it. A row that blew into something more violent. But according to Sinclair, Henderson was only out of the office for an hour. I can't see that he'd have had time to drive south and set up the ambush, never mind stage the scene in the marina at Aith. And while he was the kind of man – calm, repressed even – who might have a flash of temper, I don't think that planning would have been in character at all. He had too much of a conscience.'

'Unlike the Fiscal.' Willow grinned. The schoolgirl about to reveal her secret.

'What do you mean?'

'I should have been in my office chasing up phone records this morning, but I ended up taking our Rhona out for coffee instead.'

'Did you now?' Perez found his response to the detective was becoming more natural.

'I took her to the Islesburgh Centre.' Willow grinned. 'No expense spared.'

'Not the Fiscal's natural habitat,' Perez said.

'She was all right,' Willow said. 'Expansive for her.'

'And?'

'She and Richard Grey – known to her as Dickie – were lovers in the dim and distant past. She was, and I quote, one of his serial affairs. It was before his wife ran off with her secret lover, but our Rhona had no conscience at all.'

Perez tried to take this in. 'Any bearing on the killings, do you think?'

'I've been trying to work out how, but I can't see it.' Willow gave in to temptation and went to the counter for lemon-drizzle cake, waved to Perez to ask if he wanted anything. He shook his head. On her return she continued as if there'd been no break. 'I wondered if Jerry Markham had found out about the affair, if Annabel or Richard had given away our Rhona's raunchy past. But why would they? Surely Annabel never knew about it. She was only five when it was all happening. And even if Markham had discovered that the Fiscal and Richard Grey had a fling fifteen years ago, what could he possibly do with the information? It hardly turns Rhona Laing into a potential blackmail victim.'

'No.' Perez considered how this might relate to the theories spinning around in his head. 'The only person who'd be hurt by the affair being made public would be Annabel. She obviously dotes on her father and believes in the public persona of respectable family man, given to charitable good work.'

'And Richard might be hurt too,' Willow said. 'Annabel obviously worships him. I imagine that relationship would take a bit of a nosedive if she found out about his sordid past.'

'We know Grey disliked Jerry and didn't want him as a son-in-law.' Willow stretched. The loose sleeves of her shirt fell back to her shoulders. Perez turned away briefly. 'I'd have him down as a ruthless kind of man, but I can't believe he'd come all the way to Shetland to commit murder. He'd have more subtle ways of warning Jerry off.'

'How did Rhona seem to you?' Perez remembered the message left on his answer machine.

'OK. A bit jumpy at first. But happy to talk about Richard Grey. Reliving the passions of her youth maybe.' Willow was getting to her feet. 'Why?'

'She wanted to talk to me, but I haven't been able to get hold of her. Obviously nothing urgent, or she'd have got back to me.'

Willow was fishing in her bag for her purse, but Perez told her he'd settle the bill. 'I want a chat with Brian anyway.'

She turned to him, on her way out. 'What's this, Jimmy? I hope you're not going freelance on me again.' A joke, but also a warning.

'If I have anything,' he said, 'you'll be the first to know.'

She nodded and ran up the stairs, her hair flying behind her.

Brian made them both tea and they sat outside so that he could have a cigarette. There was a gusty breeze and he cupped his hand around it to get it lit.

'What is it now, Jimmy? People will be talking if you keep coming in here. You know Shetland. They have long memories. There's no escaping the past, even if you want to.'

Perez looked along the valley towards Weisdale Voe.

'It's about Jerry Markham again. The meeting he had here the day he died. I wondered if you'd thought any more about it. Can you remember who paid, for instance?'

Brian glanced inside to check that there were no late customers. 'I wouldn't know who paid. I just give them the bill and they pay in the shop upstairs.'

'Who came to the counter for the bill? You'd get a better look then.'

'Do you know how many people I serve in here on a busy day?' He dragged on the cigarette.

'But this was Jerry Markham. A bit of a local celebrity. You'd have noticed, wouldn't you? Hoped for a tip?'

'Well, I always hope.' He pulled his jacket around his huge body, leaned back in his seat and shut his eyes. 'Markham came to get the bill,' he said.

'How did he seem?'

Brian looked at Perez. 'I don't know. A bit preoccupied. I had to tell him twice that the till was upstairs. When he was living in Shetland we took the money down here. And sad. He looked sad.'

Perez gave no response. He didn't want to break Brian's concentration. 'And the woman? Was she with him then?'

Brian seemed to sleep again. 'The woman walked off. She didn't wait for him. She must have had her own car. Unless she was going to the Ladies.' He opened his eyes. 'Look, Jimmy, this is all speculation. You wouldn't get a court to accept any of this as evidence.'

'And I wouldn't call you as a witness,' Perez said. 'Honestly.' He wondered if this had been worrying Brian all along, that he might have to go through the stress of a court case. Reliving unhappy memories. He felt stupid that it hadn't occurred to him before. 'So the woman,' he went on. 'Can you describe her to me again? One witness described her as middle-aged. Is that how you remember her?'

'I don't know, Jimmy! Maybe. Maybe she was younger. Some women could be any age from twenty to fifty, don't you think? And I wasn't really noticing. As I said before, it was busy in here.'

'And she was one of those women it's hard to age?'

Brian nodded. Perez slipped a photograph from a brown envelope and rested it on Brian's knee. He said nothing and waited for a reaction. Brian picked it up, holding it carefully by the edges.

'I'm not sure,' he said at last. 'But yes, this could be her.'

He handed the picture of Evie Watt back to Perez.

Chapter Thirty-Nine

Perez didn't want to go back to the station. Once he arrived there he'd have to report to Willow and tell her that Brian had thought Evie Watt might have been Markham's companion in the Bonhoga on the morning of his death. She'd think he was crazy. He knew what the team would be thinking if he passed on his suspicions. *Poor Jimmy Perez. Off work for months with stress-related illness. And now another murder inquiry, bringing that dreadful business on Fair Isle back to him. No wonder he's coming up with a bunch of strange ideas.*

So he drove north. Up to Bixter first, then cutting cross-country through the hills to Aith, following the route of the hennie bus. No real destination in mind. Enjoying the space and the empty road, the view over water. Curlews calling as a background to his thoughts. He wanted to be back to pick up Cassie from his neighbour before it got too late, before her bedtime, but there was no other objective than to let his mind wander around the possibilities. He'd always found driving through Shetland helped in that way. It was something about the space and the long horizons – though tell Sandy that and he'd look at you as if you were talking a foreign language.

In Aith Perez stopped at the marina, got out of the

car and looked up at the Belshaw house. From its position at the top of the bank there was a view over the whole settlement to the tops beyond. You'd see the Fiscal's house from there. He pondered the implication of that before walking back to his vehicle.

The school had closed for the day and Perez was tempted to drive back up the bank to talk to Jen Belshaw. But her children would be at home, it would be all noise and domestic chaos, and besides, he wasn't sure he was ready yet. He didn't have the right questions to ask. At Voe he passed the bar, another hennie bus stop and, at the junction to the main road, he looked south to where Markham's car had been ambushed. All the action surrounding the murders had taken place in such a small area, all in the North Mainland. The biggest proportion of Shetland's population lived in Lerwick and to the south, so he thought this was significant too, something that Willow, coming in from outside, hadn't considered. The only major players living outside this region were Peter and Maria Markham in the Ravenswick Hotel. It occurred to him that he'd never seen them away from their business, but of course that didn't mean they were stranded there, isolated from the rest of the islands. They could travel north too.

Instead of taking the road south towards home, he turned left. He drove on through Brae, where Joe Sinclair lived with his family. There was a kids' football match on the field, but no sign of Andy Belshaw. These looked like school teams and the woman referee, in a bright tracksuit, must be a teacher. Perez thought Andy would be in his office at the oil terminal, drafting his press releases and selling his stories, perhaps finding it hard to concentrate because he was still mourning his best friend.

There were no scarecrow figures now at the gate where the track led off to Evie Watt's croft, but in their place a mound of flowers. Some picked from gardens, daffodils and early tulips. Big bouquets, still in their clear plastic wrappers, bought from the supermarkets in Lerwick. Perez pulled his car into the side of the road and went to look. There were pictures and messages, many of them directed to Evie. *We're so sorry for your loss. We'll miss him, he was a lovely man.*

Perez felt relieved that Fran had died on Fair Isle. A small comfort. None of her acquaintances, her students or the other people, who would have enjoyed their own brief role in a life-and-death drama, could make it there. So there'd been no flowers to shrivel in the frost. No dying petals to scatter in the wind.

Perez saw, partly hidden by a bunch of imported roses, the corner of a card and recognized the image just from that. He felt in his pocket for gloves and lifted it out. The black-and-white reproduction of a painting of three fiddle players. The band Fiddlers' Bid. On the back, no message. He carried it carefully to the car, slipped it into an evidence bag. He knew he should immediately take it back to Lerwick and show it to Willow, but still he continued on his way.

Past Scatsta Airport and the Harbour Authority site: Joe Sinclair's empire and John Henderson's second home. Past the oil terminal, with its high security and, next to it, the major construction work to bring the gas ashore. Already the afternoon was drawing into early evening, the colour beginning to drain from the landscape. Cassie would be sitting with her friend at the kitchen table ready for her tea. Really he knew he should turn back, head south. But still he continued until he was driving down a small single-track road towards Hvidahus, realizing only then that this was where he'd been heading all along.

The tiny community was silent. He looked down at the small pier, boats moored ready for the summer. Mark Walsh's big house waiting for its first guests. The tiny holiday cottage was still empty. The only sound came from the gentle buzz of the wind turbine outside John Henderson's house. Now that he was here, Perez felt foolish. The house had been made secure and he didn't have a key. But still he stood there. This place had been built by Henderson and he'd lived here with his wife, nursing her. And this was where he had planned to bring his bonny young wife.

When he was a young DC in Aberdeen, Perez's boss had been unusual. A strange and thoughtful man, much mocked by his more macho colleagues. 'Sometimes detection is like acting,' he'd said once. 'You have to get inside the offender's skin, stand in his boots and see the world through his eyes. Understand what makes him tick.'

And this was what Perez did now. He imagined himself as Henderson, a cautious man, who valued routine and order. A man who was struck suddenly, in a thunderbolt from the blue, by a passion for a young woman called Evie Watt. A man who would have handed his love the world and denied her nothing. That thought helped Perez to shake and rearrange the facts as he knew them. Later he would remember nothing of his journey back to Ravenswick because his attention was focused on the characters in the drama.

As he drove up to his neighbour's house he saw Cassie looking out of the window towards the Ravenswick Hotel. He stopped the car and followed her gaze, and for a moment he saw how the murders might have happened – Willow's mirror made whole.

Chapter Forty

Willow slept deeply, without dreams, and woke to the sound of gulls and a foghorn – childhood noises, comforting. Outside the light was grey and she could see nothing from her window, not even the blurred outline of the island of Bressay. The mist hid everything.

When she got to the police station Perez was already there. She saw his black hair through the opaque glass pane in the incident-room door and recognized him from that. She opened the door and went in. He was using a corner of the long table as a desk. He'd never mentioned the fact that she'd taken over his office.

'Could you not sleep, Jimmy?'

He looked up, his face a series of planes and shadows. It could have been carved roughly from some hard wood.

'No,' he said. 'Not very well. And Cassie always wakes early, so I dropped her at her friend's house and came along here. She's staying at her father's tonight.'

Willow saw that Cassie was always at the front of his mind, his most important preoccupation.

'Anything come of your chat with Brian?'

He hesitated and she felt the return of the anger.

Why was he so determined to go it alone? If he'd obtained information from Brian in the Bonhoga, he should have been on the phone to her immediately. What right did he have to keep it to himself? Was he trying to protect someone here? One of his old cronies? The Fiscal? But then the thought of Perez as a corrupt officer was so ludicrous that she smiled.

'I'll make some coffee,' she said. 'You can tell me then.'

She set the coffee in front of him and felt suddenly like some sort of therapist or counsellor. *Go on, Jimmy, tell me all about it.* And when he did speak, it was as if he'd bought into that fantasy too.

'Ah, the ideas I'm carrying around in my head, you'd think I was mad,' he said. 'You'd think I was stark staring bonkers. You'd lock me up and throw away the key.'

She thought that was just another way of shutting her out, and she had too much pride to grovel to him.

'We'll stick to the facts then, shall we, Jimmy?' Her voice was frosty. 'The theories can come later.'

As soon as she'd spoken she realized her mistake. If she'd gone in gently and played the therapist, he'd have confided in her, but now she was just his boss again. He'd be worried about making a fool of himself.

He put a photograph of Evie Watt on the table in front of her. It wasn't the one they'd used on the board here in the incident room, and Willow wondered where Perez had found it. It had been taken at some Shetland Island Council function and Evie was smartly dressed in a skirt and a jacket, looking oddly grown-up. Willow had only ever seen Evie in jeans before.

'Brian thought this might have been the woman who met Markham the morning before he died.'

'Is he sure?' Willow remembered the young woman on the beach in Fetlar, her anger and her grief. Surely her judgement couldn't be that flawed. Evie Watt was no killer.

Perez shrugged. 'Brian's a reformed junkie. He's never been sure of anything.' He paused and was about to continue when Willow broke in.

'Hardly a star witness then. I'll need more than that, Jimmy.' She waited for him to continue, to defend his position, but Perez just shrugged again. He'd become moody, the man she'd first met when she arrived on the islands. She'd made this man coffee, bent over backwards to be pleasant to him and he behaved like a graceless and uncommunicative teenage boy.

'Anything else?'

'I went past the track to Evie Watt's croft yesterday afternoon. Where you found John Henderson's body. They've turned it into a kind of shrine. Flowers, candles, you know.'

She nodded.

'I found this there.'

It had been on the table all the time, but she'd been focused on Evie's photo and she hadn't noticed it. The postcard in the clear-plastic evidence bag. He slid it towards her. She turned it over. Nothing written on the back.

'It's the same as the one Jerry Markham sent to Annabel,' she said. 'There were others in his briefcase next to the body.'

'There'll be hundreds of them floating around

Shetland,' Perez said. 'They were handing them out free in the Bonhoga. It could mean nothing.'

But she could tell that he believed it was more important than that. 'If it had come loose from a bouquet or a gift, surely it would have a message on it,' she said.

'That was my thought.'

'So, Jimmy, what conclusion have you come to? What was this thing doing there?'

'The killer could have taken it from Markham's briefcase.' His voice was quiet, tentative. Was he worried that she would mock him for his ideas? Surely he must know her better than that.

'A trophy, you mean?' She frowned.

'Or a memento.'

'And then he left it at the place where John Henderson died. Why would he do that?' Willow was struggling to understand this.

'I don't know. To link the killings. As a sign? A message?'

'Who to?' Perhaps Perez *is* crazy, she thought. Perhaps he was right when he said he was mad.

'Ah.' He leaned forward across the table. 'That's the important question, isn't it?'

'To Evie Watt, do you think?' Willow found herself groping towards an explanation. 'Perhaps she did meet Markham in the Bonhoga, after all. Perhaps he passed on information. Something he'd discovered in his research.' Suddenly she was excited. She could feel the possibility that she might connect all these unrelated strands of the investigations. 'His story. The story that brought him to Shetland in the first place. Something to do with her work? The green energy? The Fiscal was on the working party for the tidal-power project. The Power of Water. Perhaps that's the reason Markham's body was left on the water at Aith. Another message. To a twisted mind. And Markham met Henderson too, perhaps looking for more information, or giving it. And the postcard is a message to Evie to keep her mouth shut. What do you think, Jimmy?'

She could tell he was considering the theory, running through the facts in his head. 'Yes,' he said. 'Yes, it could have worked that way.' She thought he seemed almost relieved. She wanted to ask him what weird and dreadful scenario he'd conjured up. *Why is my theory so much more attractive to you?* But she was a detective and not a shrink, and she was exhilarated because all these disparate facts were finally hanging together. So instead she concentrated on actions for the day.

'I'd like to see Joe Sinclair.' She looked at Perez. 'He was on the working party with Rhona Laing and Evie, but not a suspect in any way that I can see. An impartial witness. And I'd like to see the site for the tidal-energy project. He could talk me through it, couldn't he? All the technical stuff?'

Perez hesitated for a moment and then nodded.

'I was thinking I'd take Sandy with me,' she went on. 'Let him out of the office for a while.' *And there's no way I can put up with your moods today.*

Perez nodded again. She stood up, irritated by his silence.

'Would you mind if I spoke to Rhona?' he asked. She was on her way out and she had to turn to look at him. 'I know you saw her yesterday, but she left a message on the answer phone the evening before. Wanting to talk to me. You wouldn't mind?'

She froze, her hand on the door, revisited by the old suspicion that Rhona and Perez might be colluding over some part of the investigation. But if that was the case, Perez had no need to ask her permission before talking to the woman. He could just have picked up the phone. At least now he was keeping her informed.

'Of course, Jimmy. But don't give her any details. Nothing about the postcard or these recent ideas. I don't have to tell you that.'

He nodded again and she left the room.

They met Sinclair at the lighthouse at Hvidahus Point. Sandy was full of energy, like a dog that's been locked up overnight and is ready for a run. Sinclair had seemed unbothered by the request to leave his office and talk them through the project. The fog wasn't so thick here, but the day was still damp and grey and there was limited visibility, so the cliffs seemed to drop forever towards the sea, to disappear into the murk where the air met the water. There were few cliffs on North Uist, and Willow had always felt uncomfortable with height. She had the feeling that she might be sucked over the edge, or even that she might be pulled there by an irresistible temptation to jump. Just to experience the sensation of falling, of hurtling towards the water like a diving gannet.

Willow judged Sinclair to be in his sixties, but he walked without effort across the cropped grass. He was happy to tell them what he knew about the new energy project. He was a natural lecturer, concise and simple. 'There are two forms of potential green energy to be harnessed from the water,' he said. 'With wave power, the mechanisms float on the surface and it's the movement that generates the energy. Tidal power is quite different. For that there are turbines underneath the water. Imagine the wind turbines that we're all used to – like the ones in the wind farm on the hill just outside Lerwick. The only difference is that these are powered by the tide instead of the wind.' He paused, ignoring Sandy running after him, to check that Willow was taking in the information.

'And what's being planned for here?' she asked.

'Both eventually.' He led them down a steep bank so that they were almost at water level. 'This will be an experimental site, remember. But first we're concentrating on the tide. There's a tremendous race between here and the island of Samphrey. There are stories from local boys about the power of the water at this point. They say there's only twenty minutes of slack tide at low water. When they were laying the pipes to Sullom Voe, Delta Marine did a rescue exercise – they threw a dummy into the sea to practise pulling in a man who'd fallen overboard. The dummy disappeared in seconds, sucked under by the currents, and was never seen again.'

'What stage are you at?' Willow still wasn't sure how any of this was relevant.

'We're ready to set up a pilot project, using a local company to build most of the components and another to install the turbines. We need to strengthen the pier and rebuild the old hatchery close to it, widen the track a tad, but that won't take long.' Sinclair spoke with a breezy optimism.

'I thought there was some local opposition to the plans.'

'Incomers,' Sinclair said. 'They're more interested in the view than in providing a livelihood for our people. And Francis Watt, who'd have us all still cutting our crops with a scythe and milking our cows by hand, writing his nonsense in the *Shetland Times*.'

'This should mean jobs for Shetlanders then?'

'That's the plan. The scheme will be evaluated by a scientist from RGU in Aberdeen. He was up the other day.'

'And the Fiscal?' Willow asked. 'What's her role in the working group?'

'Ah,' he said. 'Rhona Laing is an ambitious woman. She gets on top of a subject quickly and easily. Shetland suits her fine at the moment, but I'd not be surprised if she moves on before long. We're too far from the centre of power for her. Let's say that she has a game plan for the future. Gaining knowledge and influence in an area that'll increase in importance is part of that plan. And from the working group's perspective, it's always useful to have a lawyer on board.'

The mist had turned into a fine drizzle.

'Can we see the hatchery?' This was Sandy, wanting to get inside and out of the wet.

'Sure.' Sinclair led them down the path, past the pier towards a low shed. A shingle bank protected it from the water.

'Who's providing the finance?' The question had come to Willow as they approached the building. The roof was missing stone tiles and the walls were crumbling in places. It would take considerable funds to get this weathertight.

'It's a partnership project,' Sinclair said, 'between the Islands Council and a number of private investors.' He answered immediately and the words were smooth and easy, but she sensed a slight discomfort. And he unbolted the door to the hatchery and pushed it open too quickly, as if he hoped to distract them.

'And who are the major investors?' Willow stood on the threshold and looked in. A smell of damp and something faintly chemical. There was mould on the stone flags and oily puddles where the roof had leaked.

Sinclair said nothing.

'You must know,' she persisted. 'You're part of the working group.'

'We put together a consortium,' he said. 'Local people. We see water power as the technology of the future and we want a part of it.'

'So you've put money into the project? You didn't see that as a conflict of interest, as a member of the working party?' Willow wished she knew how these things worked and what was normal.

'We'd all invested.' Now Sinclair was sounding defensive. 'Me, Evie Watt and Rhona Laing. Putting our money where our mouth was. That's how we saw it. But we're not talking big sums here. There are a lot of investors. It was all quite open and above board. There was an article in the *Shetland Times* and we made it clear that we'd welcome as many people as possible to join us.'

'Was the article written by Jerry Markham?' The question was sharper than she'd intended.

'No, no. He'd left long before we started planning this.'

Willow moved away from the door of the hatchery. 'I'll need a list of all the people involved,' she said. The rain was harder now. She headed back towards the car. The ground was boggy and her feet were already wet.

Sinclair walked quickly to catch her up. 'John Henderson had invested.' It sounded like a confession. 'That's how he and Evie first got together. At our first meeting. He said that if the project was happening on his doorstep, he wanted a say in how it developed.'

She stopped in her tracks and turned on Sinclair. Sandy, walking close behind her, almost bumped into her. 'Is there anything else I should know?'

'Peter and Maria Markham,' Sinclair said. 'They were members of the consortium too.'

Chapter Forty-One

Perez waited in the incident room until Willow and Sandy had left the building. They went out noisily, shouting their goodbyes to the officer on the desk. Then the building seemed unnaturally quiet. He went to the staffroom and made himself more coffee and prepared for his encounter with Rhona Laing. He'd already decided that he needed to talk to her in person, but that he should go through the proper channels and make an appointment.

His first call was to her office. It was nine o'clock now and she should be there. She was famous for being early. He got through to a local woman called Heather, who worked on reception and provided secretarial support for the Fiscal's office.

'I'm afraid Ms Laing isn't in yet. Would you like to call back later?'

'But you are expecting her at work today?'

A pause. Then some carefully chosen words. 'Ms Laing hasn't informed us that she won't be in.'

'But you'd normally have expected her in the office by now?'

'Yes,' Heather said. 'I would. Or a phone call saying she'd be late.'

Perez considered. On the other end of the line he

could sense Heather's concern. 'And she hasn't been herself lately?'

'No.' Heather hesitated again, then the words came out as a rush. 'Not since she found that body. But the Fiscal has seen dead bodies before. You wouldn't think it would be such a big problem for her.'

There was another silence.

'Would you normally buy Ms Laing's plane tickets for her and make her travel arrangements?' Perez asked.

'Only if it was work-related. Not her personal travel.'

'Has she mentioned a trip south to you?'

'No, but then she probably wouldn't.' Heather paused. 'She doesn't talk much about her life outside the office.'

'I'm sure she'll be in soon.' Perez replaced the receiver with a sudden and intense sense of anxiety. It was as if his world was shifting again. He had never liked Rhona Laing, had found her too shiny and slippery and certain. But he'd respected her. He wished he knew what was happening here, and that he'd tried harder to get hold of her the day before. He should have known that she'd never confide in Willow Reeves and that it must have been important for her to ask for his help.

He phoned Rhona's home number, suspecting there would be no response, even as he dialled. Then he sat at the table in the big room. It had filled up with people, but he hardly noticed them. The chat and movement provided a blurred background to his thoughts.

He should check the airport and the ferry terminal

to see if Rhona Laing had booked tickets south. But that would cause talk: it would get out that the police were investigating the Fiscal. Perez suspected that Reg Gilbert had spies in both airport and ferry company, and the last thing Perez needed was a spiteful, insinuating editorial in the *Shetland Times*.

So he stood up suddenly, picked up his coat and headed for the door. Only halfway down the corridor did he think that his behaviour might have seemed strange to his colleagues. He'd barged out of the room without a word. But now it was too late to go back.

On the pavement just outside the police station, on his way to his car, he bumped into Peter Markham. Perez was so preoccupied, so concentrated in his thoughts, that he didn't see the man and almost stumbled over the briefcase at his feet. And for a moment he didn't recognize Markham. Perez was accustomed to seeing him at the Ravenswick Hotel and here, out of context, he seemed slighter, rather shabby and nervous. Almost elderly. An old-fashioned commercial traveller, with his case of samples.

'Jimmy!' Markham seemed relieved to see him. 'I was just going to the police station.'

'Have you thought of anything that might help?' Perez felt awkward, confused still, disorientated, standing here in the grey mist that felt more like November than spring.

Markham lifted the briefcase. 'I've brought cuttings. All the articles Jerry wrote since he moved south. Maria kept them. I don't know how useful they'll be . . .' His voice tailed off. 'I wondered if you had any information, if Annabel and her father had thrown any light on the investigation. It was hard to tell when they came to visit us. It was all rather awk-ward.' The man pulled up the collar of his waxed jacket. 'Look, could we get a coffee? I can't face going back to Maria yet. Not without something to tell her.'

And Perez couldn't hurry away from him. He understood the man's desperation.

They sat upstairs in the Peerie Shop cafe. Downstairs there were two young women with toddlers in buggies. The weather had kept everyone else away.

'I have nothing to tell you,' Perez said. He wanted to be on the road to Aith and resented this interruption. His first wife had talked about his 'emotional incontinence' and his inability to turn away anybody requesting his help. He'd thought he'd become harder, but some habits were hard to give up.

'But you will find him, Jimmy, won't you? You will find the person who killed my son?'

'Yes,' Perez said. 'We will find him.' He paused before continuing. 'Have you received a postcard recently? A reproduction of a painting. Three fiddle players.'

Peter Markham looked at him as if he were mad. 'No. Barbara in the office opens all the mail, but if it was personal she'd pass it on to us.'

'This might not have a message on the back,' Perez said. 'Just the picture on one side and the address on the other. Will you check when you get back? Ask Barbara if she's seen anything like that?'

Markham went off then, pleased that he had something to do, feeling that his trip into town hadn't been entirely wasted. Perez left with the man's briefcase.

He'd tried to persuade Markham to drop the cuttings into the police station, but he'd refused. 'You take it, Jimmy. I won't need the case. And I trust you to make good use of them.'

Now Perez climbed up the narrow lane back to his car. The path was steep and he felt exhausted and unfit. *I'm not sure I can do this.* There had been talk when he was at his most depressed that he might take early retirement on health grounds, but he hadn't wanted Cassie to see him as an old and broken man. Now he wondered if he had rejected the idea too quickly.

By the time he reached Aith it was raining hard. He was tempted to phone Heather again, to check if the Fiscal had arrived at the office, but thought that might only cause panic. The visibility was so poor that he parked outside Laing's house without any concern that he might be seen. He couldn't make out the end of her garden, and the hillside where the Belshaws lived was invisible. Water dripped from the shrubs and small trees. The Fiscal's car was there, pulled into the drive. It was unlikely then, that she had gone into work. But why hadn't she answered her telephone? It occurred to him that she might be out on the voe in her boat. She'd have radar, surely. She was a long-distance sailor. The mist wouldn't bother her.

He knocked at her door. There was no reply. He turned the knob and pushed it open. Unlocked. That surprised him. He'd have thought Rhona would have the habit of locking her house when she left the place. He went inside and shouted her name.

There was mail on the doorstep. He stepped over it and shouted again. No response. He went into her living room and felt that perhaps he should take off his wet shoes. He imagined her wrath if he left marks on her pale carpet. Everything was tidy. No sign that she'd been entertaining visitors. He was reminded of John Henderson's place at Hvidahus. The clear surfaces and the clean lines. Everything functional. Except that John had his attic, the shrine to his first wife. In the kitchen there was order too. On the draining board a stained coffee mug was the only thing out of place.

Perez stood in the hall and yelled up the stairs. Going up, he wasn't sure what scared him most. That he'd find Rhona Laing's body or that he'd find her alive, wrapped in a towel perhaps just coming out of the shower, furious that her privacy had been invaded. But he came to the bathroom first and there was no steam and the shower tray was dry. He felt horribly tense, almost faint. Before Fran's death he'd never had these physical symptoms of stress. Now the pounding heart and the roaring sound in his ears made him want to flee. Still he continued. A guest bedroom, decorated in yellow and white, a white sheepskin rug on the floor. Did she entertain her smart Edinburgh friends here? Did she have friends? Real friends? He imagined there would just be acquaintances, people who might be useful to her one day. The room looked as if it had never been slept in.

Then Rhona Laing's bedroom, and for a moment curiosity overcame his anxiety. On the wall there was a huge painting of the sea. Everything in monotone, black and grey. A storm. Clouds and sea and spray. It wasn't like anything Fran had ever painted, but he knew that Fran would have loved it. He heard her speaking to him. *Look, Jimmy, isn't this a painting you could just jump into?*

Dragging his attention away from the picture he saw a double bed, either not slept in or made up as soon as Rhona had got out of it this morning. The duvet cover and pillowcases were white, made of heavy cotton. There were two large wardrobes and a chest of drawers. The wardrobes were full of clothes and it would have been impossible for him to tell if anything was missing. He moved on.

Now there was just one room left: the office. The door was ajar and he stood in the corridor for a moment and looked in. No body. He felt relief, immediately followed by irritation. Where was she then? Had she run away south, leaving her staff and colleagues to fret about her? Surely that wasn't Rhona's style. She might make a dignified retreat, but not a rushed escape on an overnight ferry. He walked into the office. It had a view over the garden. Still it was raining outside, soft and relentless.

He switched on her computer. It had been on standby, so there was no need for a password. Had she been surprised here then? By a visitor or a phone call that had made her hurry off, without coming back to her office. He thought in normal circumstances she would have switched off her computer if she were going out. Though she'd been troubled recently, and perhaps the open door and the live computer were just signs of her anxiety. The idea of prying into the Fiscal's emails was too much for him. He couldn't do that yet. Not until there was evidence that she was in real danger or that somehow she was involved in these murders.

He stood, unsure what his next move should be. A plane went overhead on its way to Scatsta and it seemed very low, the engine noise very loud. Visibility must be improving then. He decided to go to the marina and see if her boat was still there. He knew that the water was where she felt safe and happy.

Turning away from the desk he stopped for a moment. On the top of the in-tray was the familiar postcard. He flipped it over with a pencil. Nothing written there, not even an address. There were two possibilities: that the Fiscal had taken the card from Jerry Markham's briefcase when she'd found his body, or that the killer had delivered it to her. A message, just as the card left at the roadside shrine for John Henderson had been a message.

Chapter Forty-Two

When Willow returned to the police station Perez was back in position in the incident room, sitting at his place at the corner of the conference table. It was as if he'd never left. He was wading through a pile of newspaper cuttings.

'Did you track down the elusive Ms Laing?'

He shook his head.

'Anything wrong, do you think?' There were times, she thought, when she wanted to shake Inspector Jimmy Perez. She didn't care that the woman he'd loved had been murdered. She wanted him to communicate with her as if she were another human being.

'I'm not sure.' Now he looked up from the cuttings and frowned. 'And I'm not sure what I should do next. The door to her house was unlocked.'

Willow thought of her childhood in Uist. 'That's not unusual, is it? In a place like this.'

'Maybe not.' A pause. 'I think she might be out on the water. If she was troubled, that would be what she'd do. And I can't see her fancy boat in the marina.'

'So that's OK then, isn't it? She'll just come home when she's hungry or it gets dark. She's playing hookie from work, but we've all done that at one time or another.'

'Aye, perhaps. I'd be happier if I could speak to her, though.'

'You've tried her mobile?' Willow wondered how she'd come to be involved in this conversation. She needed the team to be checking out the consortium of investors in the water-power project. She felt as if Perez was sucking out all her energy.

'I got her personal number from Heather in the Fiscal's office. No reply.' Perez paused again. 'There was one of those postcards on her desk. Nothing written on the back.'

That caught her off-guard. 'What do you want to do, Jimmy?'

'Nothing,' he said. 'Not yet. Like you say, we'll wait until it gets dark. She should be home by then.'

Willow was struck by another thought. 'This boat of hers, could it travel long distances?'

He looked up at her. 'Aye. A Contessa 26 was sailed round the world in the Eighties. Single-handed, by a teenage lass.'

'Has she done a runner then, Jimmy? Should we be alerting the coastguard?'

'No need for that yet.'

But she thought he didn't sound very sure.

Willow stood by the whiteboard and led them through the visit to the tidal-energy site. 'I made Joe Sinclair take us back to his office so that we could get a list of investors from him.'

She'd already printed off enough copies for every-one in the room to have one, and she handed them round. 'More than 200 people in Shetland put money into the project. They bought shares and contributed anything from £200 to £2,000 each. Investors included Evie Watt, John Henderson and Rhona Laing. Peter and Maria Markham are also on the list, so I think we can assume that Jerry knew all about it. The philosophy was that this should be a community venture, and that everyone who believed in it and could afford to should have a stake in the scheme.'

She paused and looked round the room. 'Of course this might be coincidence. But I think we can put together a credible theory here. If Jerry discovered some financial malpractice, then we might finally have found the new and exciting story that brought him to Shetland. That would explain why he agreed to go to the Save Hvidahus meeting – he'd want the action group to give him more ammunition. You can imagine the possible headlines – *Green energy not so clean after all* – and the embarrassment that might cause to the people involved. They call the project Power of Water, and it's considered a flagship scheme for renewable energy. I've already got a team of forensic accountants on the case, but if we discover that a substantial percentage of the invested cash disappeared into one individual's pocket, I'd say we have a motive for murder.' She paused for breath. 'Markham's decision to attend the meeting of the opposition group fits in with the theory.'

Across the table Sandy raised his hand, frowning.

'Yes, Sandy?'

'So you think Markham was killed to stop the story getting out?'

'It's a possibility, isn't it? He was murdered on his

way to a meeting where he might have shared the information he'd gained.' She was starting to lose patience. She'd expected them all to be as excited as she was by the idea. Perez hardly seemed to be listening. His attention was still focused on the newspaper cuttings spread on the table in front of him. 'Jimmy, what do you think?'

He looked up slowly. 'You'll find Fran's name on the list,' he said. 'Fran Hunter. She invested £500 in Power of Water. Her contribution to saving the planet, she said.' He paused and seemed to choose his words carefully. 'Just because all our witnesses and suspects invested in the scheme, we can't assume that's what led to the killing. That many investors and a population this small, most households in the islands are probably linked to the project.'

Well, thanks very much for your contribution, Inspector Perez.

'All the same,' she said brightly. 'It's worth following up, don't you think?'

'Oh aye,' he said. 'It's worth following up.' But his attention had wandered back to the newspaper articles in front of him.

When the rest of the team had dispersed she stood behind him. 'What are all those things?' There was something strangely obsessive in the way he pored over the newsprint. She saw that his fingers were stained grey from the ink.

'Peter Markham brought them in this morning.' Perez didn't take his eyes off the table. 'Maria kept the cuttings. All Jerry's stories. Peter wondered if they might be helpful.'

'And are they?'

Before he could answer, his phone went. He looked at the number. 'It's Peter Markham,' he said.

'Then you should take it!' Again she felt impatient, with the desire to scream at him.

He nodded and pressed the button. She couldn't hear the other end of the conversation and had no idea from the inspector's expression whether Markham had anything useful to contribute.

'Well, thank you, Peter. It was good of you to get in touch.' Perez switched off the phone and sat for a moment in silence.

'Well?'

'I'd asked him to check if one of those postcards of the three fiddlers had been sent to the Ravenswick Hotel.' Perez frowned.

'And had it?'

'No.' He paused for a moment and turned to her with a sudden and brilliant smile. 'But still relevant maybe, eh? Like the curious incident of the dog in the night. The Sherlock Holmes story. The dog that didn't bark.'

'So because the Markhams didn't receive a postcard, one of the people at the Ravenswick Hotel could be sending them?' She wanted to yell at him not to speak in riddles, but was so relieved that he was talking to her again, and so seduced by the smile, that she held her tongue.

'Well,' he said. 'That would be one interpretation.'

'And the other?'

He seemed surprised that she hadn't grasped the logic of his thinking. 'That the Markhams aren't involved in this at all, except as grieving parents.'

'Is that what you believe?' She waited and realized how much she valued his opinion.

There was another long silence. 'I'm not sure,' he said at last. 'I need to speak to Rhona. I'll be glad when she sails back into the marina at Aith.'

If, Willow wanted to say. *If she sails back.* But there was no need. He was thinking the same thing too.

She nodded back to the newspaper clippings. 'You didn't say what's so interesting here.'

'As I see it, Jerry Markham wrote longer pieces.' Perez moved the pieces of paper round the table. 'This one is about life in a children's home – he did it after a child-abuse case. This is an investigation into river pollution. So you can see how a Power of Water story would appeal to him, especially as there's such interest in renewable energy. But why did he keep it secret? Why not at least pitch it to his editor to get a free trip north? I don't understand that.'

Willow picked up the pollution piece. It seemed well written and she read it all, just to find out how the case ended.

'Then there's this,' Perez said. 'Why would Maria keep this?' He slid a small cutting across the table to Willow.

It was obvious from the style and content that this wasn't from the broadsheet for which Jerry Markham had worked. It was from the personal column of a local paper.

'It doesn't say,' Perez said, 'but it's from the *Shetland Times*. The announcement of Evie Watt and John Henderson's engagement.'

Willow read it. It was very formal and old-fashioned. 'Francis and Jessica Watt are delighted to announce the engagement of their daughter Evelyn Jean to Mr John William Henderson of Hvidahus, North Mainland.' She looked at the date. 'This only went into the paper three months ago,' she said. 'I don't know much about these things, but isn't that a very short engagement? What was the rush?'

Perez didn't answer her question. 'Why would Maria go to the trouble of cutting this out of the *Shetland Times*? Why did it matter so much to her?'

'Perhaps it didn't,' Willow said. 'Perhaps she thought Jerry would be interested because of the Evie Watt connection. She cut it out so that she'd remember to tell him.'

He looked up, transfixed. 'Of course! Of course that was how it happened.' He got to his feet. 'I'm off to Aith,' he said. He was already struggling into his jacket, feeling in his pocket for his car keys.

'You're going to wait for the Fiscal?'

'Not just that. There's something I need to check.'

And before she could ask him what he meant, he'd already left the room.

Chapter Forty-Three

It was late afternoon in Aith, but still wet and grey, so it seemed much later, almost night. The houses had lights inside and on his way he'd glimpsed domestic scenes: children sitting at kitchen tables to do homework, a young man preparing an evening meal, an elderly woman knitting. But there were still no lights in the Old Schoolhouse, and when he drove down to the marina, Rhona Laing's boat was still absent from its mooring.

He was surprised when Andy Belshaw answered the door at the smart Scandinavian house on the hill and wondered why the man wasn't at work again today. It wasn't time for him to be home yet. The question was answered when Belshaw spoke. His voice was strained and scratchy, and when he waved Perez inside he said, 'Sorry. Throat infection. Must have caught it from my daughter. Welcome to the house of the plague.'

In the kitchen there was washing drying on a line hanging from the ceiling and Jen Belshaw was cooking, so condensation was running down the windows and there was no view outside. Perez smelled frying onions and realized that he hadn't eaten since breakfast. From a distant room came the beeps of a computer game and voices. In one corner of the kitchen a hand-knitted jersey was stretched on a wooden frame. Arms wide, it looked like a headless child.

'Inspector.' Jen turned from the stove. 'How can I help you now?' Polite enough, but he could tell she wasn't happy to see him.

'It's about John Henderson.' Perez took a seat at the table. 'It's time now for you to tell me the truth. For both of you to tell me the truth.'

'I don't know what you're talking about.' Jen added strips of lamb's liver to the pan. She'd dusted them first with flour, and her fingers were coated with blood and flour. Red and white, turning into a pink paste where they mixed. She rinsed her hands under the tap and turned down the heat.

'No?' Perez turned to her husband. 'But you knew, didn't you? You were Henderson's best friend.'

Belshaw shot a look to his wife, but she still had her back turned to him.

'Rhona Laing's missing,' Perez said. 'She went off either last night or today. Would you know anything about that? About why she might have left Aith in a hurry?'

'No!' It came out as a high-pitched squeak. Belshaw seemed flushed with fever and Perez saw that he really was too ill to have been at work. The inspector leaned forward across the table. 'I'm trying to prevent another murder here. You have to tell me everything you know. Both of you.'

'You can't blame John.' The woman moved away from the stove, drying her hands on a tea towel. 'He loved Agnes's very bones, but she was so ill. He knew she was dying and there was nothing he could do to give her peace. Imagine the stress he was under.'

For a moment Perez thought he had the whole thing wrong and that he was about to hear quite a different story from the one he'd conjured in his head. A story of assisted suicide perhaps, of Agnes helped to her rest. But Jen continued immediately. 'You can't blame him for taking his comfort where he could find it.'

'He had a lover?' Perez looked at them both for confirmation. 'While his wife was still alive?' He wondered what it might be like if the woman you loved died slowly and you had to watch. It had been bad enough on the hill on Fair Isle with Fran in his arms, and that had only been for minutes. A slash of a knife. A blade glinting in moonlight. Then it was all over. He didn't think he'd have had the strength to keep going for years, watching his lover grow weaker every day. At least he supposed he could do it – the practical stuff, the daily routine, pretending to be cheerful. But not on his own. He'd need an escape at the end of the day, someone warm and tender and soft. Someone to make him laugh occasionally.

'We don't know that he had an affair,' Belshaw said. 'We never knew for certain. And it wasn't something you'd ask someone like John Henderson. He was such a private man.'

'But there were rumours?'

'Oh!' Jen said dismissively. 'A place like this there are always rumours. Most of them mean nothing.'

'But you guessed, didn't you? Or you found out?'

The three of them sat, looking at each other. Perez's phone rang. He switched it off without looking at it. It would be Willow Reeves, on the warpath again, wondering what he was up to and why he hadn't asked permission to leave the police station without telling her where he was going, and demanding an explanation.

'Henderson's dead!' Perez said. 'You can't hurt him now.'

'You'd ruin his reputation.' Despite his sore throat, Belshaw was almost shouting. 'Bad enough that his body was all dressed up by the side of the road with that stupid mask on his head. I'll not have folk sitting in bars and laughing about what he got up to when his wife was ill. He would have hated that.'

'You cared about him,' Perez said.

'I told you, he was the nearest thing to a brother I'll ever have.'

I used to think that about Duncan Hunter, and he let me down.

'You should tell the inspector.' It was as if Jen had come to a sudden decision. 'He'll not make it public if he can help it.' She looked at Perez, a challenge. 'Will you, Jimmy? But this is horrible. Knowing there's a killer out there, having to keep the bairns indoors, and looking over my shoulder when I walk up from work on my own. That's a sort of cancer too.'

If he'd been feeling well, Belshaw might have continued to fight, but he was weak and feverish and he gave up immediately, collapsed in on himself, so that he looked smaller. He told his story in strange barks and whispers, and the voice itself increased the tension in the room, like fingernails on a blackboard. Jen fetched him a glass of water before he began.

'I don't know when it started,' he said. 'I don't know how long it went on. I think it stopped soon after Agnes died. Maybe John felt guilty, or maybe the woman finished it. If all she wanted was a bit of fun, the fact that he was single again could have frightened her off.' He sipped the water. 'We had football practice on Friday nights, just like now. We'd train the boys for an hour and then go for a beer, usually to the Mid-Brae Inn. It wasn't so much for the drink as the chance to wind down. The start of the weekend for me, and a break for John. It sounds daft, as if I was some kind of kid, but I looked forward to those Fridays. I loved the company, the chat.'

He paused. In the background the computer game was reaching a climax.

'Then he stopped coming. Not to the football training, but to the pub. He said he didn't like Agnes to be left on her own for so long. I was disappointed, but I understood.' He looked up at Perez. 'Then I called in to see Agnes. It was summertime and one of our neighbours had given us loads of raspberries. I thought she'd like them. John was at work. She was upstairs in that room John had made for her. Some days, if he knew he'd not be away too long, he'd help her up there in the morning. She loved the colour of it and the view from the window. I just let myself into the house. It was never locked. She was in fine form that day. It was almost the last time I saw her. We shared the raspberries and she teased me about John. "What are you doing to my man?" she said. "Are you turning him into a drinker? It was past midnight when he came in last Friday." And when I apologized – because what else could I do? – she patted my hand and said that she was only joking, and she was delighted we were friends and that John had one night out to relax.'

Belshaw had a fit of coughing then and wiped his mouth with a handkerchief.

'So you were suspicious?' Perez said.

'Curious,' Belshaw said. He paused. 'And a bit jealous, if I'm honest. I know it's stupid, but I didn't like the idea of John having other close friends. Even then it didn't occur to me that he might have a woman. I thought he was meeting up with mates from work and was too tactful to tell me that he preferred to be with them on his one night out.'

Perez looked towards the window. He wanted to reach out and wipe off the condensation so that he could see if Rhona's boat was back in the marina, but now this was more important and he turned his attention to the room.

'What did you do?'

'One Friday night I followed him.' Now Belshaw seemed embarrassed. 'It wasn't planned, but I'd decided to come home early, not to bother with the beer at all if I was going to be on my own. Usually I'd stay behind to clear up in the sports centre and John would be long gone by the time I left, but that night I was out early and he was just leaving the car park.'

'And where did he go?' Perez's voice was flat. He didn't want to give too much importance to the question, in case Belshaw reconsidered his decision to tell the story. And besides, he knew already what was coming.

'John came here,' Belshaw said. 'To Aith. He drove his car down to the school, so it couldn't be seen from the main road. He sat for a moment and then he walked back the way he'd come.'

'To the Fiscal's house.' It wasn't a question.

'Yes, to the Fiscal's house.' Belshaw paused for a moment before continuing. 'I thought they were having a meeting. Business. Something to do with that water-power scheme they've been rattling on about for years. They were still planning it then.'

'You don't believe in renewable energy?' For a moment Perez was distracted.

Belshaw shrugged impatiently. 'It'll not provide enough. Not for the whole country! For Shetland perhaps, but we can't live our lives here in isolation. In the real world we still need oil and gas.' He gave a rueful grin. 'Sorry – this is something John and I argued about too.'

'So you thought maybe John and Rhona were meeting to discuss the water-power project?'

Belshaw considered for a moment. 'No,' he said. 'I would have liked to believe that, but really I knew it wasn't true. Because if that was why John was there, he wouldn't have lied. And he'd have parked his car right outside the house.'

'When was this?' Perez asked. 'When did it happen?'

'Years ago. Neil was still a baby. Too young to play football, at least. And it's five years since Agnes died.'

Perez was doing calculations in his head. Jerry Markham would have still been living in Shetland then, and Evie Watt could have been a chambermaid at the Ravenswick Hotel. Or still at school. He was trying to work out what it could mean, how it could all hang together, when Jen Belshaw spoke.

'I saw him occasionally,' she said. 'Midsummer, you know, it's light all night and the youngest bairn could never get the hang of sleeping. So I'd be upstairs in the front bedroom, nursing her. And I'd see John slipping out of the house and running down the street to his car. Eager to be back with Agnes, I suppose. Guilty for having left her alone for so long.' She looked up at Perez. 'If I saw him, other folk might have done too. I didn't hear any rumours, but then people knew we were friends.'

'You're in the rowing team with the Fiscal,' Perez said. 'She never let anything slip?'

For the first time that evening Jen seemed to lighten up, to be her old self. 'Rhona? A brilliant woman to row with, but she'd not tell you what she had for breakfast without a court order. No, she gave nothing away.'

Perez left the house and stood for a moment on the wide decking looking down to the sea. The light had disappeared and it was impossible to make out the individual craft in the marina. He switched on the phone. A number of missed calls from Willow Reeves and a voicemail from Sandy, who sounded desperate. *Please get in touch, Jimmy. We think we've found the Fiscal.*

Chapter Forty-Four

Rhona's boat was called the *Marie-Louise*. On Willow Reeves's instructions, Sandy had called a few friends and asked them to keep an eye out for it. 'Nothing urgent, but we need the Fiscal's signature and we're not sure just where she might be,' he'd said, keeping his voice light. He thought he'd learned that from Jimmy Perez, the ability not to give away too easily what was in his mind. They didn't want the Shetland rumour mill labelling Rhona Laing as a murderer! In the end the *Marie-Louise* had been found at the Hvidahus pier by Joe Sinclair.

Joe had phoned the station and Sandy had taken the call. 'One of the boys from Delta Marine wanted to look at the Power of Water site and I met him there. I've never seen the *Marie-Louise* at Hvidahus before, and Rhona's not on board. It's probably nothing, but it seemed kind of strange that she'd leave the vessel there.' Sinclair said he'd called the Fiscal's phone number, wondering if there'd been a problem with the boat and she might need help with it, but there was no reply. Eventually, as the light started to go, he'd grown anxious and had called Sandy Wilson.

'With so many strange things going on recently,' he'd said, 'I thought you should know.' Then he'd paused. 'It's a big tide tonight. Rhona would know that. She wouldn't leave the *Marie-Louise* just tied up to the pier, where it might be damaged.'

Sandy's first impulse had been to call Jimmy Perez, but there was no reply and he'd spoken to Willow Reeves instead. He was no good at taking decisions for himself. Willow had thrown the question back to him. 'What do you think, Sandy? Will you go? I'm still waiting for the accountant to get back to me, with the information about the Power of Water co-op.'

He'd sensed from her tone that she wanted him to check it out. And Sandy remembered Perez slowing the car each time they passed the Old Schoolhouse in Aith, showing his concern about the woman. 'Aye,' he'd said at last. 'I think it's worth a look.' He'd thought that there was that good fish-and-chip shop in Brae and he could call in there on his way home. It felt as if he hadn't eaten proper hot food in weeks.

Perez must have picked up the voicemail, because he arrived at Hvidahus at the same time as Sandy. Sandy recognized his car, driving down the bank towards the water ahead of him, and felt a dizzying sense of relief. Jimmy Perez, not quite himself and a little bit mad, was better than no Jimmy Perez at all. In the big white house where the Walshes lived the curtains were drawn.

There was no natural light at all left now, and the grey drizzle formed a halo around the one street light at the pier. Perez opened his boot and brought out a torch, then walked over to meet Sandy. Joe Sinclair had disappeared. Sandy imagined the harbour master, warm and fed, watching television with his wife, with a can of beer in one hand.

'So what do you think has happened here, Sandy?' The inspector was already walking quickly along the stone pier towards the boat. Sandy had hoped that Perez would tell *him*, but now he was forced to consider the matter. He hurried after the inspector.

'Maybe she's done a runner? She thought we'd be watching out for her car and brought the boat here, arranged for a taxi to meet her perhaps, then went south to the airport. It's pure chance that Joe Sinclair came along.'

Perez had reached the mooring of the *Marie-Louise* and stopped suddenly. 'Is that what Willow Reeves thinks?'

'She thought right from the beginning that Rhona was involved in this case.' The pier was wet and Sandy walked slowly. The last thing he wanted was to slip and end up in the freezing water.

'So she did,' Perez said. 'And it looks as if she was right all along.'

It sounded as if he was talking to himself and Sandy didn't like to ask what he meant.

Perez shone his torch towards the vessel and then stepped aboard onto the narrow deck in the bow. Sandy stayed where he was. It might be a fancy yacht, but still there wasn't much room and, if the boat turned out to have been used in a crime, the last thing the CSIs would want would be his feet all over it. Perez stood for a moment. He seemed to be listening. His dark face was caught in the torchlight and looked all shadows. Then, without a word, he disappeared below. For a moment all Sandy could hear was the water against the jetty and the wind making the wires sing. Torchlight seeped through the hatch. He wanted to shout to Perez: *Well? What have you found?* But the inspector had never liked it when Sandy was impatient, so he stood feeling the damp on his skin and reaching through to his bones. And feeling tense, he had to admit. He'd never been good at waiting.

At last Perez emerged from below. He stood with only his head and shoulders visible.

'It's clean,' he said, 'as far as I can tell.'

'No sign of the Fiscal?' Sandy felt a bit ridiculous now. He realized he'd been scared that there might be a body. Rhona Laing stabbed, like John Henderson. Blood and guts spilled over a cabin. He'd never liked blood, even though he'd grown up on a croft and had helped his father to kill the beasts. He gave a little giggle to hide his relief.

'No.' It was hard to tell what Perez made of that.

'So we should tell Willow Reeves to check with Sumburgh and the NorthLink?' Sandy was wondering if Perez might fancy fish and chips too. Cassie was staying at her father's tonight, so he wouldn't have to rush home. It would be good – the two of them having a sit-down fish supper.

'That would be a start.' Perez climbed out of the hatch now and jumped out onto the pier. Sandy couldn't see his face clearly, but could tell from his voice that he was frowning. 'Willow Reeves was right about one thing,' Perez went on. 'Rhona Laing wasn't telling us the truth.' He strode away towards his car.

'Where are you going?'

Perez paused for a moment, the car door already open. 'To look for her.' As if Sandy had asked the daftest question in the world. 'In John Henderson's house.'

Sandy went to the passenger door. It was just a short ride up the bank. He could collect his car later.

'Not you,' Perez said.

Sandy felt as if he'd been slapped. 'What do you want me to do?'

'Tell Willow to check on Evie Watt. Where is she? Is she OK?' He paused. 'And then head off to the Ravenswick Hotel. I need you to talk to Maria. This is what I want you to ask.' Then he gave Sandy three questions and made him repeat them several times, until he was sure Sandy had got them exactly right.

Willow asked Sandy to call into the police station on his way south to Ravenswick. He knew that his phone call to her from Hvidahus had been garbled. He thought it was unfair of Jimmy Perez to rush off to John Henderson's place all on his own, leaving him to explain to Willow Reeves what was going on. He drove as fast as he could down the island, breaking the speed limit all the way.

He could tell she was furious as soon as he knocked at her office door, and her first words were a giveaway. 'So, what the fuck's going on, Sandy? Has Jimmy lost the plot altogether, do you think? Should we be calling for the men in white coats?'

'He said he was going to look for the Fiscal.' Here at least Sandy was on firm ground. That was just what Perez had said.

'And where did he hope to find her?'

Sandy shrugged. 'He was looking in the Henderson house.'

'Why there?'

Another shrug. 'Because we found her boat close by?'

'So you just let Perez go off alone?' Her face was flushed and her freckles seemed very dark, almost like scattered spots of ink. 'You didn't think it was a good idea to ask him to come in and explain his theories, the way his slightly deranged mind is working?'

'He gave me a message for you.' Sandy broke in before she could continue. He could tell she was all set for a good rant, and he still had to get to Ravenswick.

'And what was that, Sandy? What words of wisdom did he ask you to pass on?' Willow leaned back in her seat, her arms folded across her chest. Sandy decided she was probably being sarcastic, but he thought he would answer the question anyway. His best mate's parents had separated when he was a peerie boy and for the first time Sandy understood what it must have felt like to be caught in the crossfire between warring adults.

'Jimmy said you should get in touch with Evie Watt. He said you should check that she was OK.'

'He thinks Rhona Laing is going after Evie now?' Willow's voice had turned high-pitched, almost hysterical.

'I don't know,' Sandy said. 'I'm just passing on the message.'

'Evie's in Fetlar with her parents.' For the first time a touch of anxiety had moderated her fury. 'Isn't she?'

'I think so. But that was what Jimmy asked me to tell you.'

There was a moment's silence. Sandy could see that the inspector was thinking. She had one of those faces that were almost transparent. It was as if you could see the thoughts behind her eyes, passing like clouds across the sky on a windy day.

'What else did Jimmy Perez ask you to do?' Her voice was calmer now and quieter.

'He said I should go to the Ravenswick Hotel and talk to Maria. He said I should ask her three questions.'

He thought Willow would ask him what those questions were and had started to rehearse them in his head. But she only looked at him with those sharp blue eyes.

'You'd better get along then, Sandy. Let me know how you get on.'

The Ravenswick Hotel was busy. There was a big party in the restaurant, a birthday, and the guests were getting rowdy. Not unpleasant drunk, but noisy, lingering over coffee and drams. There were helium balloons, which had started to deflate, and a half-eaten cake with pink icing. The other diners had moved on to the lounge and the bar, and perhaps because there were so many people around, Maria was helping out. Sandy couldn't see Peter, but assumed that he was there too.

Maria was taking an order for coffee from a party of elderly tourists sitting in old leather chairs in a corner of the lounge. She looked very smart in a black dress and black tights, shiny shoes with pointy heels. Sandy thought she'd lost weight and that the dress looked better on her now than it would have done a couple of weeks ago.

He stood at the door and watched her until she'd

finished writing the order. She didn't see him until she was making her way back to the kitchen, then she stopped in her tracks.

'Sandy. You have some news for me?' He could see then that the dress and the efficient taking of orders, the smile for the tourists, were all a show. Her face was pale and drawn. She walked on without waiting for a reply. Suddenly, he thought, she found the laughter from the restaurant, the noise from the bar, even the muted classical music playing in the lounge unbearable. He followed her through the swing door into the kitchen. She handed the slip of paper on which she'd written the order to one of the staff and led Sandy on, past the sinks and the fridges to a small storeroom. She leaned against the wall, next to a huge drum of vegetable oil. 'Well?'

'No news,' Sandy said. 'Not tonight. But we're very close. Tomorrow we should have something for you.' Even as he spoke the words he wondered if he was being rash, if his faith in Jimmy Perez was misplaced.

'So why are you here, Sandy? What is this about?'

'I'm sorry to disturb you,' he said, 'but I have some questions. Important questions.'

'Go on then, Sandy.' Her voice was impatient. 'What is it this time?'

For an instant his mind went blank and he had a moment of panic when he thought he would never remember what Jimmy had told him. Then it came back. 'You cut a piece from the *Shetland Times* about Evie's engagement to John Henderson. Did you tell Jerry about that?'

'I sent him a cutting,' she said. 'We take a dozen copies of the paper here in the hotel for the guests. It was a kind of joke. I wrote in the margin. Something like: *Look who she's ended up with!*' Maria stared at him. 'What could that have to do with Jerry dying?'

'I don't know.' The truth. 'Inspector Perez thought it might be important.'

'Is there anything else, Sandy? You can see that we're busy.'

'Jerry's car,' Sandy said. 'The Alfa. Did you buy it for him? A present for getting that job in London?'

She was so tired now that she didn't even question why he wanted to know. 'No. We gave him money for his first six months' rent. He bought the car for himself.'

It took her longer to answer Sandy's last question. She grew animated and waved her arms around, and after a little while Sandy had to make an excuse and leave.

Chapter Forty-Five

In the end Perez left his car at the pier and walked up to Henderson's house. He went slowly, listening all the time for unusual sounds. Out on the water there was a boat. Boys after creels, perhaps. The first trip out of the season, caught out by the poor visibility and the change in the weather. In his head it felt like midnight, but here in Hvidahus it was seven o'clock. In the Haa, Duncan Hunter would be getting Cassie ready for bed. He would probably forget to read her a story. When he arrived at the Henderson house, Perez paused again and listened. Nothing unusual. He looked at his mobile and saw that he had reception. He made a phone call.

He replayed his search of the *Marie-Louise*. There'd been nothing on deck. No footwear prints to get Vicki Hewitt excited. Everything tidy. Ropes coiled and the moorings tight. Rhona Laing would be that sort of sailor. Even in a panic she'd follow procedure. Below deck it had been just the same. The cabin was immaculate. No bedding on the bunk, no sleeping bag, so Rhona hadn't planned to spend a night away. In the small galley Perez had found the same sense of order. Had that neatness first attracted John Henderson? Had he seen in the Fiscal's compulsive tidiness a sign that he'd found a kindred spirit? Someone quite different from Agnes, with her arty generosity and her exuberance. In the galley Perez had reached out and touched the kettle on the Calor gas hob. It was cold.

He'd flashed the torchlight around the cabin floor, but had seen nothing of interest. It was only as he was preparing to leave, to return to the deck and Sandy Wilson, that he'd glimpsed a scrap of litter, a piece of paper, wedged behind a clock in a wooden case. Not the sort of place it would get to by accident, but perhaps it had been put there to stop the clock rattling. Perez had pulled it out and shone the torch on it. A compliment slip from Jamieson's, the wool merchant in Lerwick. What had he been expecting? A postcard with a picture of three fiddlers?

Vicki Hewitt had finished her work in the Henderson house and it was locked. There was no light showing through the uncurtained windows. He opened the garage and found a door from the back of it that led into the kitchen. Everything was quiet. He fumbled to find a light switch and the sudden brightness made him blink. All quiet and all tidy. He'd hoped that the Fiscal might have come here. A last chance to mourn her former, secret lover. He'd imagined her brooding, a large whisky in one hand maybe. But it seemed he'd been wrong. Anxiety began to nibble at his brain. He felt his heart rate quicken. He opened doors into all the downstairs rooms. The place felt cold and dead. It was hard to believe that Henderson had been living here less than a week before.

He almost ran up the steep wooden stairs to the attic. He couldn't find a switch on the sloping wall and turned on a standard lamp. It threw odd shadows in the room, made the colours rich and exotic. Still no sign of the Fiscal. Against the wall were some of Agnes's canvases. Paintings she'd been working on in the last stage of her illness. On one wall there was a sketch that Perez hadn't noticed on his first visit, and he only saw it now because the lamp shone directly onto it. He recognized it immediately as a drawing of the painting that hung in Rhona's bedroom in the Old Schoolhouse. The large seascape. Had Henderson given it to Rhona after Agnes died? A parting gift? It seemed quite out of character for the man he thought he'd come to understand. Again, he thought this case was much more complicated than he'd realized. But there was no time to consider that now.

Outside, the drizzle had turned to rain. It flattened his hair and ran down his collar, but he hardly noticed. It was a weird thought that a few miles up the road the world was continuing as normal. People chatting about the weather and last night's television, sitting in living rooms and kitchens, getting bored and drinking coffee. Out here, and in Jimmy Perez's head, it was hard to believe that anything would be normal again. In his head there was a picture of Evie Watt, looking young and bonny, smiling. Then Evie Watt as a scarecrow in a make-believe wedding dress. His phone went. Reception was dreadful and he struggled to make out the words. He walked back up the hill until he found a spot where the call became clearer and spoke for a few minutes, then switched the phone off and almost ran down the road towards the pier.

His was still the only car there. No sound at all

except for water. The rain on the stone pier and the tide slapping against the harbour wall, so high that it almost washed over the top. It seemed that even the fishing boat had disappeared. Maybe the boys were at home now, sharing a beer. He walked on along the track towards the old salmon hatchery, to the building that would become an electricity substation when Evie's grand scheme was played out. It had turned to mud and he slithered and tripped in one place. Shining his torch towards his feet, he saw at least two sets of footprints. But no car tracks. Even in this weather it would be possible to get a four-wheel-drive vehicle down here, but there was no sign of that having happened.

As he approached the old hatchery he sensed he wasn't alone. There were voices. He supposed they were coming from inside the building. He'd reached it without realizing and switched off his torch immediately, hoping the light hadn't shone through a crack in the door, through the crumbling stones. He couldn't make out the words. The walls of the building were thick. Then there was silence, so he wondered if he'd imagined the sound, if his depression had created the voices and they were inside his head and not out there in the real world.

He stood where he was, incapable of moving or of coming to a decision. He must look ridiculous, standing here in the wet. Impotent. And suddenly he experienced the rage he'd felt when Fran had been killed, the desire to make someone – anyone – pay. A blind, confusing anger.

'What are you doing here, Jimmy?' The voice was like an echo of the voice in his head. There was the same bewilderment and the same madness. For an instant Jimmy didn't respond because he thought he was imagining the question, just as he'd thought he'd imagined the voices in the shed.

The boat, he thought. *Not boys out after creels. Of course the killer came by boat.* A stab of sanity.

The voice persisted. 'Why don't you just walk away, Jimmy? Back to your car and the real world. You know what it's like to need justice done.' Besides the weird feelings of disconnection, Perez experienced a sense of triumph, because he recognized the voice and realized he'd been right about the identity of the killer. He was still good at this business. His brain was working.

He found it impossible to pinpoint the direction from which the voice was coming. And for a moment he was tempted. What business was this of his, after all? He could get in his car and drive to Duncan Hunter's house, which was only a couple of miles away as the crow flew. He could sweep Cassie into his arms and take her home with him and first thing in the morning they could get a plane south. He even began planning where they should go. To see Fran's parents, of course. They were lovely people and always eager to see their granddaughter. He imagined the warm welcome there would be. Hot chocolate for Cassie and tea for him. Toast and honey.

Then he heard another sound, a moan stifled by the weather. He thought it must come from the hatchery, but it was impossible to tell. He shouted. 'Where are you?' and felt the sound of his voice vibrate around the place, washed away by the rain.

'This won't look like murder.' The killer's voice was

reasonable. 'This will be put down as an accident at sea. You know how many ships have been lost out here on the Rumble. You know what the tide would do to a body in this water.'

And suddenly Perez's mind cleared and thoughts were firing into his brain, fast and sharp. It was adrenaline perhaps. A need to survive. Not for himself, but because he had an obligation to Fran's child. The killer would have left the building and would be standing between him and his car; the invitation to walk away was a trap. Of course Perez wouldn't be allowed to leave here alive. Not now that he knew the identity of the murderer.

'Rhona Laing is a fine sailor,' Perez said. 'Nobody will believe in an accident. Not in calm weather like this.'

'Suicide then.' The killer was dismissive. 'Why not? Even better because folk will think she killed Markham and Henderson.'

Another silence. Perez strained to pick up the slightest noise. A footstep or a clearing of the throat that would mark the presence of the murderer. This was a horrifying version of Blind Man's Bluff. But the ground was so soft that boots would make no noise. Perez kept as still as he could. The tide must be on the turn, because the water washed against the pier now and not over it. The sound was quite different. It sucked on the shingle on the beach.

Then he heard the cry again, this time louder. A woman's voice, reminding him again of Fran by the edge of the pool in Fair Isle. And, very close to him, the faint rustle of a waterproof jacket. He held his breath. No rational thought now. The killer couldn't see him and had no idea that Perez was so near. Another sound. Wheezing. Perez launched himself towards the sound and pulled the killer to the ground, had his arm around the man's neck, could feel his hair against his own face and the man's skin, the hardness of bone and teeth through his own cheek. Perez tightened his grip and felt the man grow weaker.

Then suddenly everything was light. Blinding, so that Perez had to shut his eyes. Only two fierce torches, but still after the thick darkness the white light was shocking. And that was when he heard Willow's voice.

'That's enough, Jimmy. We'll take over now.' And, when he kept his grip around the man's neck, 'Let him go, Jimmy. That's enough.'

Chapter Forty-Six

'So,' Sandy said. 'How did you know that Evie's father killed Markham and Henderson?'

It was a full day later and they were in Perez's house in Ravenswick. A fire in the grate and another bottle of Willow Reeves's Hebridean whisky on the table.

'I didn't *know*,' Perez said. 'Not until I saw him there at the pier at Hvidahus.' *But I never trusted him. People who are certain have always scared me.* 'I thought he would do anything to make his daughter happy.' He paused. Confession wasn't his style, but he thought they deserved an explanation. 'It came to me when I drove into Ravenswick one evening and saw Cassie looking out of the window of our friends' house. She was looking out for me. I thought then that I'd kill to keep her safe.' He turned away, embarrassed, before continuing. 'Francis loved Evie. She was more important to him than his son, who wasn't interested in returning to the islands. She represented the future of Shetland to him. One day she would take over his business, live in his house in Fetlar. He'd become kind of obsessed with her. A danger when you're a parent. Sometimes you have to let your kids live their own lives. You have to risk them getting hurt. But I thought

Francis might be proud to think that he'd killed to save her pain.'

There was a silence in the room.

'And he had a terrible temper,' Perez went on. 'Maria confirmed that, didn't she, Sandy? I wanted you to ask her about Francis coming to the hotel when he found out that Evie was pregnant. She'd told me that he'd been foaming at the mouth with rage, but that's the sort of thing people say. I needed to know if it was true.'

'It was your third question for her,' Sandy said. 'Maria said Francis was wild, raving. He hit Peter and gave him a black eye. She'd wanted to make a formal complaint, but Peter wouldn't hear of it.'

'Francis couldn't stand the idea that Henderson's affair with the Fiscal might be made public,' Perez said. 'But he was much more bothered that Markham would tell Evie about it and spoil her wedding than with any notion of public shame. As Francis saw it, the man had already ruined his daughter's life once. And Markham threatened to tell Evie everything. He thought it would be the right thing to do, that Evie deserved to understand that John wasn't as perfect as she assumed him to be. The idea of it drove Francis mad. He was delighted that Evie was marrying the man everyone thought they knew: John Henderson, man of religion and the closest thing to a saint there is in the islands. John Henderson who'd nursed his dying wife. Imagine the scandal there'd be if folk found out that he'd been slipping off on Friday nights to have recreational sex with a stuck-up soothmoother. And how would Evie feel about it? Francis thought she'd be so devastated that she'd cancel the wedding.

And, without John's support, she'd never return to Fetlar and take over the family business. It would be the end of his world.'

The peats in the fire shifted and smoked.

'There had always been rumours that Rhona Laing had a secret lover,' Perez went on. 'A dark stranger who arrived by boat and disappeared again before first light. It wasn't quite like that, but the storytellers almost got it right. And we know that Ms Laing wasn't squeamish about adultery. She'd had a relationship with Richard Grey after all. Then Agnes died, and the affair with Henderson ended and Markham went off to London, and the Fiscal must have thought it was all over and forgotten.'

'I don't understand where Markham came into it in the first place.' Willow reached out and took a slug of whisky.

'Markham knew.' Perez thought Markham hadn't been the only one in the islands to guess about the affair. But he'd been the only person to exploit the knowledge. 'It must have been while he was still working at the *Shetland Times*. He blackmailed John and Rhona. He was a horrible man in those days. I'd guess it was the Fiscal who paid up. That's how Markham could afford that fancy red car. Everyone thought it was a gift from his parents.'

'But that was years ago.' Sandy was drinking beer, not whisky. He'd be the one to drive Willow Reeves back to her hotel at the end of the night. 'Why couldn't they all just let things be?'

'Because Markham was a changed man,' Willow said. 'Isn't that right, Jimmy? He fell in love and got religion all at the same time. A heady mix.'

Perez thought that Markham's conversion, his determination to be a good man, had led to two murders.

'I think he really had changed. Or he believed that he had. Maria sent him the cutting from the *Shetland Times*, which announced Evie's engagement to John Henderson.' Perez wondered what would have happened if Markham had never seen the announcement. Perhaps he'd have stood at the font in the smart Hampstead church while the holy water was dribbled over his head, then gone on to marry Annabel Grey and live happily ever after.

He lifted a peat from the bucket by the hearth and threw it onto the fire. 'Perhaps Markham still felt guilty about extorting money from the Fiscal and about the way he'd treated Evie. And he didn't want Evie to be hurt again by a man who had betrayed his dying wife. We know that Markham talked about betrayal to Annabel. In any event, Markham came north in an attempt to put things right. To be honest. He planned to tell his parents about Annabel too, I think. He would have done it the night he died. But mostly it was about coming to terms with his past, making himself feel better.'

They sat for a moment in silence. A car with a faulty exhaust was driving down the road towards the jetty. Perez knew the sound – it belonged to his neighbour. The fire smoked a little.

'That seems very self-centred,' Willow said. 'Didn't he think of the effect that would have on the people involved?'

Perez looked up at her. 'Probably not,' he said. 'Maybe Markham was still a selfish man. And aren't we all a little self-centred?'

There was another comfortable silence, before Perez continued speaking.

'On his first night at home, Markham told his mother that he wouldn't need her cash any more. That wasn't because he was planning blackmail, or because he was marrying into money. It was to show her that he was different. At last he was starting to grow up. Mark Walsh's invitation to the Hvidahus action group gave him the excuse he needed to be here, and I think he had decided that the friction over the new energies really might make a decent story. He asked Peter to set up an appointment at Sullom Voe and arranged to meet Reg Gilbert. Vicki Hewitt found Markham's camera in Francis Watt's office; it contained pictures of Sullom Voe with the new gas terminal.' Perez paused. 'Mark Walsh told Watt that the great Jerry Markham was coming to his meeting. Francis had always supported their opposition group, but that was the last thing he wanted. He'd disagreed with Evie over the scheme in private, but the last thing he wanted was Markham to rubbish it in public. It would have seemed like another assault on his daughter.'

'There was nothing to rubbish,' Willow said. 'The accountants have been over the Power of Water books and can't find a penny out of place.'

'But Francis was convinced that the scheme was rotten at its core,' Perez said. 'He told me when I visited him on Fetlar that there hadn't been a development in Shetland that didn't have corruption at the heart of it. He really believed the project must be based on council fraud, that there'd be a huge scandal and Evie would suffer. If he'd been less paranoid and trusted his daughter's judgement more, two men might still be alive. It's one of the saddest aspects to the case.'

'In the meantime Markham was trying to get in touch with Evie.' Willow was in her usual place on the sheepskin rug, as comfortable as a cat, long and sleepy.

'He phoned her and he left messages on her voice-mail,' Perez said. 'And perhaps he gave away enough of his concern for her to guess the gist of what he wanted to say. The night of her hen party something had certainly troubled her.'

'Who did Markham meet in the Bonhoga?' Sandy asked. He'd finished his beer. Perez could tell that he'd like another, but didn't want to ask.

'That was Jessie Watt. Brian, who runs the cafe, thought it might have been Evie, but they look very similar. It was Jessie, dressed up and smart. Markham had already phoned the Watts about Henderson's affair. The meeting was Jessie's attempt to persuade him to keep the matter quiet, but he refused. He said Evie should know the sort of man she was about to marry.'

'So Jessie knew that her husband was a murderer?'

Perez shrugged. 'She must have been a part of it – of Markham's murder, at least. The two of them left Fetlar together. The ferry boys said they hadn't seen the Watts leave the island that day, but Francis took his own boat out. He kept an old van in Vidlin for picking up tools and wood, to use on the mainland. Francis drove Jessie to the Bonhoga, where she had a last attempt to persuade Markham to go south and leave them all alone. Afterwards they followed Markham to Sullom Voe. That must have been a time of decision for them. They could have driven away and caught the ferry home, but Francis wasn't a man to let him go. By then he was furious and desperate to stop Markham telling Evie about Henderson's affair and to stop him writing about Power of Water.'

'Jessie says she tried to persuade him.' Willow said. She stretched. 'Stupid, weak woman. She can't have tried very hard.'

Perez thought that Jessie had spent her life believing that Francis was right. It would be hard to stand up to him about this.

'So they came back to the Lunna junction to wait for Markham, knowing he'd have to come that way to go home. They won't have known that he'd arranged to meet Henderson near Scatsta.'

Perez imagined the couple waiting in the tatty white van. There were always vehicles parked at that junction – it was a meeting place for car-shares into town. Nobody would take any notice of them. Perhaps Jessie had prepared a picnic. Something traditional of course: bannocks with reestit mutton, home-bakes. Had the plan just been to scare Markham? To send him on his way? *You've already broken our girl's heart once. Now you want to do it all over again. She has a chance for happiness, for a new life with a good man.* Or were the elaborate travel arrangements evidence that Francis Watt was already contemplating murder? Perez thought the couple would have spent the waiting time talking about Markham, winding each other up, persuading each other of his wickedness. The tension must have been unbearable as the light faded and the visibility grew poorer.

'How did they know it was Markham's car?' Sandy broke into Perez's thoughts. 'The fog would have been so thick by then that they wouldn't have seen it coming.'

'But they'd have heard it, wouldn't they?' Willow was lying on her side, propped up on one elbow. Her hair had changed colour in the firelight. 'That engine. There'd be nothing else like that in Shetland. Worth taking a chance on, anyway. Worth starting the van and driving out, causing the oncoming car to swerve into the lay-by. If they'd got the wrong car, they could pretend it was an accident.'

Perez nodded. And again he ran the scene in his head. Markham would have been shocked, and even the new, changed Markham would have been angry. He'd have climbed out of his car shouting and swearing. Anyone would. And Francis Watt, shut off from the real world by the fog, his nerves taut from the waiting and his wife's endless talking, had lashed out. He'd taken a spade from the back of the truck and hit out.

Perez hadn't taken part in the interview of Francis Watt. He hadn't trusted himself to stay calm and professional, but he would have liked to ask how Francis had felt at that point. Had he enjoyed the sensation of power? Was that why he'd decided to kill again?

'Then what happened?' It was Sandy again, wanting to move things on. Perhaps he had an appointment in town. A lass to meet, or there were friends waiting for him in a bar, ready to celebrate the end of the case. Perez got to his feet and fetched him a beer from the fridge.

'They didn't want to leave Markham there.' Willow

sounded cheerful now. The case was over and she hadn't screwed up. 'Soon traffic would be coming back from Lerwick and people would be collecting their cars after work. So they put him in the back of the van. Of course it was Francis's idea to take him to Aith. The Fiscal's home territory. An indirect message to the scarlet woman. In the interview Francis told me he thought it would be fitting to set Markham afloat on the water. So they loaded the body into the yoal. He looked in Markham's briefcase before they pushed the boat into the marina. Of course there was nothing much in there, because there wasn't much of a story at that point. Just a pile of postcards Markham had picked up from the Bonhoga that morning. Jerry must have posted one to Annabel Grey in Brae when he stopped there for his lunch. Francis took a few of them. Mementos.'

Another indication, Perez thought, that Francis had enjoyed the killing and wanted an object to trigger the memory of it.

'Late that night they drove Markham's car to Vatnagarth and then they steamed back to Fetlar,' Willow said. 'To make their boats and knit their jerseys and finalize plans for their daughter's wedding. As if nothing had happened.'

'But Markham had met John Henderson,' Perez said. 'And John suspected that Markham's murder was connected to the story. The old story of his affair with the Fiscal. I think he'd decided that he had to tell Evie all about it.'

'Even though she'd probably guessed some of it, guessed at least that Markham was in Shetland to pass on some gossip about Henderson. And she can't have cared, can she? She went out, got pissed and then decided it didn't matter. The next day she was behaving just as normal. She loved him and was going to marry him anyway.' Willow looked up at the men. 'Such a dreadful waste! What did Markham think he would achieve?'

'Henderson made the mistake of phoning Francis first,' Perez said. 'To warn him that Evie might be too upset to marry him. He'd have thought it was the honourable thing to do. The men were old friends. And perhaps something in Watt's response to the call made John suspect he was the killer.'

'So Henderson had to die too.'

'He did. And perhaps by then Francis saw himself as a kind of avenging angel. He must have convinced himself that this was for the best, that Evie didn't deserve an adulterer like Henderson after all. This time there was an even more elaborate crime scene. Henderson next to his wife-to-be, with the mask over his head.'

Willow took another drink. 'A forensic psychiatrist will have a fine time with that!' She looked into the fire. 'Jessie had nothing to do with that killing. Francis left home early and was just home by the time you visited them that afternoon, Jimmy. Jessie was working in the fields all day. She didn't ask where Francis was going in his boat. She didn't want to know.'

They sat for a moment in silence.

'In the end I think Watt blamed Rhona Laing for everything,' Perez went on. 'She seduced Henderson, not caring that his wife was dying. She began the whole business. In Francis's head, she'd even turned *him* into a killer.'

Perez sat back in his chair. 'I saw Evie this afternoon,' he said. 'She's staying with Jen and Andy Belshaw.' He thought of the young woman's fury, her blazing eyes and violent words. Hatred of her parents was helping her through her present grief, but that wouldn't last.

Perez wanted his visitors to go now. He was tired and needed to be left with his own thoughts and his own memories. The others must have realized that, because suddenly they were on their feet, and the door was open, and the chill night air was in the house.

Sandy went ahead of them, almost running down the bank to the car. Perez decided that he definitely had an appointment with a woman. Willow stood for a moment. 'I'm away south tomorrow,' she said. 'My father's birthday. I'm off on the first plane, so I'll not see you.'

'But you'll be back?' There was a moment of panic. He saw how much he would miss her.

'Oh, I'll probably be back. You know these cases. Always ends to tie up.'

He thought she would kiss him again as she had in the hotel that night. A dry kiss on his cheek. But she gave a little wave and followed Sandy down the hill. Perez stood in the open door and felt cheated.

Chapter Forty-Seven

The next day was fine and still and surprisingly warm. A week away from May, but it felt like summer. Rhona Laing served tea outside, on a round wooden table, sheltered by shrubs. Hidden from view, the space had the feeling of a child's den, a secret garden. Had she sat here with John, drinking wine or coffee, away from the prying eyes of her neighbours? Perez had been summoned by phone.

'Jimmy, I think you deserve an explanation.'

The tea was Earl Grey. Fran had enjoyed that too.

'I did care for John,' she said. 'It wasn't a thoughtless fling.'

Perez said that really it was none of his business.

'You saved my life, Jimmy. As I said, you deserve an explanation.'

'I should have made more effort to answer your phone call.' He poured more tea.

'And I should have been prepared to confide in you.' She looked at him coolly across the table. 'I've always struggled to place my trust in men.'

Perez thought she would find that even more difficult now.

Rhona continued. 'I'd allowed myself to be blackmailed by Markham,' she said. 'Ridiculous! That made it hard for me to tell anyone what had happened. It made me party to a criminal activity . . . If it had just been the affair . . .' Her voice tailed off. 'But I couldn't have people gossiping about John when Agnes was still alive. Markham was leaving for London. I assumed if I paid him off, that would be the end of it.'

'What happened the day you were abducted by Francis Watt?' Perez had read her statement, but that had been dry and factual. He couldn't imagine what it must have been like for her. She'd been imprisoned all day. And still had the marks of the encounter on her body.

'I was just about to leave for work, in the office checking my emails. I heard someone in the house. I think he'd been in there before. I'd had a sense, you know, of my space having been invaded, of my things having been moved, earlier in the week. I'd thought I was going mad, but he'd found some way in. Security isn't at the top of our list of priorities here. You know that, Jimmy.' Perez saw how grey she was and thought she'd been living in a nightmare since she'd found Markham's body.

'At first he was quite polite,' she said. 'He apologized for disturbing me so early. Then he changed. As if a switch had been tripped. He began to rant. About how I'd ruined his daughter's life. It wasn't the affair with John that he objected to, but that I'd let Markham find out about it. "Would it have hurt you to be discreet?" As if I'd been boasting about the relationship to everyone I met. Then he said I'd turned him into a killer. Until that point I hadn't believed that he was more than a strange middle-aged man.' She looked up at Perez. 'I reached for the phone, but he was too quick for me. And very strong. I suppose it's hard physical work, building the yoals.' She reached out towards her cup, but paused, her hand resting on the table. 'How could someone who creates such beautiful objects turn into a monster?'

'He wanted to protect his daughter,' Perez said. 'At least that was how it started. And he was convinced he was right, that in some sense the murder of Markham was justified. In his eyes, Markham was an evil man.'

'But he couldn't have thought that about John,' Rhona Laing said. 'Nobody could believe that John was anything other than kind and generous.'

Perez thought about that. It seemed to him that Watt's instinct for survival had taken over then. He hadn't been thinking about Evie when he killed John Henderson. He'd been protecting himself. At the same time hating himself for doing it. And that was why he'd attacked the Fiscal: he'd needed somebody else to blame.

Rhona was continuing her story. 'He wrapped me in a piece of tarpaulin and stuck me in a van, drove me down to the marina. Nobody was around. Besides, nobody notices a scruffy white van. I did struggle when he took me out, Jimmy, but he was too strong.' She sounded ashamed. 'He lifted me as if I was a baby, put me below in the *Marie-Louise* and sailed her round to Hvidahus. A long sail. I know that now, but I didn't at the time. I thought he intended to drown me then, out in the voe.'

She sat for a moment in silence. In the distance there was the sound of a curlew on the hill. 'He knocked me around a bit in the cabin and I must have fainted. I don't remember the trip to Hvidahus at all.'

Perez had been shocked by the marks on her arms, the bruised cheekbone, but hadn't mentioned them. Rhona Laing wouldn't be a woman to want sympathy. 'When I woke up we'd arrived at Hvidahus pier. He made me walk to the hatchery. He had a knife to my back.'

'You stuck the Jamieson's receipt behind the clock,' Perez said. He wanted her to know that she'd taken some control in the situation.

'It was in his jacket pocket. I thought maybe if the worst happened, it might help. Fingerprints. I don't know . . .' Her voice tailed off.

'It did help! I knew it wasn't yours. I didn't have you down as a knitter.'

She gave a sudden smile, winced because of the bruising on her cheek.

'But Jessie Watt . . . ' he said.

Rhona continued more strongly. 'Watt threw me into the hatchery. There was a padlock on the outside. Then he disappeared. To provide himself with some kind of alibi, I suppose. Jessie must have been around in Aith to collect the van and she'd picked him up. I heard the engine. The dutiful wife. Then I lost consciousness again. When I woke it was dark.' She shifted in her seat. 'And Watt was in the shed. I smelled him, heard him moving. And you turned up.' She looked directly at Perez. 'He was going to drown me. I love sailing and the water, but I've always had nightmares about drowning.'

There was a pause. A small bird was singing very

loudly in the bush behind them. Perez thought he should just walk away, but he was too curious.

'Agnes knew about you and John, didn't she?'

Another silence and Perez thought he'd over-stepped the mark and she'd refuse to answer.

'John told her,' Rhona Laing said. 'He was hopeless at lying. Just as he would have told Evie eventually.' She looked at him. 'Agnes gave me her blessing. She said John needed someone to help him through it. She said she was grateful to me for making him happy. I went to see her. She was a remarkable woman.'

'And the painting in your room?' Perez nodded towards the Old Schoolhouse.

'Yes,' the Fiscal said. 'Agnes gave that to me too.' Another pause. 'She thought John and I would stay together. But he couldn't do it, once Agnes died. Guilt, eating away at him every time he looked at me. If Watt had seen that, he'd have known that John had suffered enough.'

'What will you do now?' Perez asked. 'Will you stay in Shetland?'

'Oh, I don't think so, Jimmy. It's time to move on. To leave the past behind.' Rhona looked up at him, put a hand on his arm and said more urgently, 'Don't you think so, Jimmy? Isn't it time for you to move on too?'

He stood up and looked down to the sea and thought that, for him, it wasn't that easy.